UNDENIABLE

UNDENIABLE

ALISON KENT

HEAT | NEW YORK

THE BERKLEY PUBLISHING GROUP
Published by the Penguin Group
Penguin Group (USA) Inc.
375 Hudson Street, New York, New York 10014, USA
Penguin Group (Canada), 90 Eglinton Avenue East, Suite 700, Toronto, Ontario M4P 2Y3, Canada
(a division of Pearson Penguin Canada Inc.) • Penguin Books Ltd., 80 Strand, London WC2R 0RL,
England • Penguin Group Ireland, 25 St. Stephen's Green, Dublin 2, Ireland (a division of Penguin
Books Ltd.) • Penguin Group (Australia), 250 Camberwell Road, Camberwell, Victoria 3124, Australia
(a division of Pearson Australia Group Pty. Ltd.) • Penguin Books India Pvt. Ltd., 11 Community
Centre, Panchsheel Park, New Delhi—110 017, India • Penguin Group (NZ), 67 Apollo Drive,
Rosedale, Auckland 0632, New Zealand (a division of Pearson New Zealand Ltd.) • Penguin Books
(South Africa) (Pty.) Ltd., 24 Sturdee Avenue, Rosebank, Johannesburg 2196, South Africa

Penguin Books Ltd., Registered Offices: 80 Strand, London WC2R 0RL, England

This book is an original publication of The Berkley Publishing Group.

Copyright © 2012 by Alison Kent.
Excerpt from *Unbreakable* copyright © 2012 by Alison Kent.
Cover photograph by Claudio Marinesco.
Cover design by Sarah Oberrender.
Text design by Tiffany Estreicher.

PUBLISHING HISTORY
Heat trade paperback edition / October 2012

Library of Congress Cataloging-in-Publication Data

Kent, Alison.
Undeniable / Alison Kent.—Heat trade paperback ed.
p.   cm.
ISBN 978-0-425-25326-7
1. Ranching—Texas—Fiction.   2. Family secrets—Fiction.   3. Texas—Fiction.   I. Title.
PS3561.E5155U53   2012
813'.54—dc23
2011051848

PRINTED IN THE UNITED STATES OF AMERICA

10   9   8   7   6   5   4   3   2   1

To Walt.
I love you.

ACKNOWLEDGMENTS

Let me use this space for a few thank-yous.

To my agent, Laura Bradford, for believing in the Dalton Gang. To my editor, Wendy McCurdy, for loving Arwen and Dax. To fellow authors and good, good friends HelenKay Dimon and Loreth Anne White for the daily sanity checks, and to Anne Calhoun for saying the most beautiful words ever after reaching the end of the book. To May Khaw for reading early pages and asking for more. To my husband, Walt, for being willing to eat soup for dinner, and to my daughter, Megan, for loving a clean house.

I have taken some liberties with the timing of activities on a cow-calf operation in this part of the country, but only because doing so best served the story.

ONE

"DID YOU HEAR who's back in town?"

"Which who? Dax, Boone, or Casper?"

"Dax is the only one I care about."

"Good, because I've got my eye on the other two."

"Boone first? Casper second?"

"I'm thinking both. Maybe at the same time."

An unapologetic eavesdropper, Arwen Poole rolled her eyes at the bawdy speculation of her all-female crew. She'd heard the rumors, too. Everyone in Crow Hill had. The town was small, a south central Texas ranching community with a gossip mill strong enough to power the whole of the county's windmills.

The Dalton Gang—Dax Campbell, Boone Mitchell, and Casper Jayne—had come home to claim the ranch left to them by Tess and Dave Dalton, the elderly couple who'd died within weeks of each other after a marriage that lasted a lifetime.

The three boys had spent summers, holidays, and weekends

working the ranch, grudgingly at first, none loving the order to do so handed down by his parents to Boone, and to Casper and Dax by association. The Mitchells attended Crow Hill Baptist Church with the Daltons and knew the retired couple needed the help. Knew, too, their son and his friends needed the structure.

Where Boone went, Dax and Casper followed, and it wasn't long before the Daltons came to depend on the three to keep the place solvent. They also came to trust them when few others in Crow Hill did.

Because while the Dalton Gang gave their employers their best, they gave the rest of the population their fast-driving, hard-drinking worst, going through the daughters of the locals like fire through drought-ravaged grasslands.

Arwen had gone to school with the hell-raising trio, but as an observer, a fly on the wall. She hadn't run in their circles. She hadn't run in any circles at all—though she had spent more time than the three boys combined in what had been Crow Hill's only bar in the day. Of course she'd been sober, so they had her there.

The problem with Arwen's employees staking their claims to the three men now was availability. Dax wasn't, and wouldn't be until Arwen had her way with him. He knew nothing of her plans, but they'd been brewing since she'd first gotten wind of his return.

He'd been the only member of the Dalton Gang she'd had a crush on, and he'd looked right through her. He hadn't been alone in that, but she would always wonder about what might've been. She knew herself, so she knew she had to get him out of her system. One more piece of her past tossed out for good.

With the news of his return spreading, however, it looked like she was going to have to put her plan into motion sooner than she'd thought.

And stepping into the kitchen of her Hellcat Saloon, the lunch hour in full swing—grease popping on the grill, metal tongs clattering against big white platters, ice cream whirring in the milk-shake machine—she found a way to make it happen.

"Amy, is the order for Lasko's ready to go?"

Wisps of black hair escaping her hairnet, Amy peered into the brown paper bag printed with the saloon's clawing cat logo and counted the burgers inside. "Yep. A half dozen baskets, and all still hot enough to burn the tar off the roof. Give me ten seconds to lose the cafeteria lunch lady look and I'll hit the road."

"The road, and the Dalton Gang while you're at it?" This from Stacy, the afternoon bartender. She swung a bag of pretzels at Amy's head on her way from the supply room through the kitchen. "One of the three is usually there at lunch."

"No need," Arwen said, crossing her fingers Dax would be the one at the feed store today. From the pegboard beside the kitchen door, she snagged the keys to the saloon's delivery truck. "I'll make the run."

The activity in the bustling kitchen slammed to a stop. Amy froze, her hairnet in one hand. Black curls tumbled to her shoulders, the only part of her that moved.

Callie, one of the saloon's Kittens, famous for their bar-top dance routines, two-stepped to the side to avoid Amy and keep from dropping a crate of clean beer mugs. They rattled loudly, a gunshot in the quiet of the room that smelled of grilled onions and beef.

Luck Summerlin, the fourth member of Arwen's waitstaff on lunch duty, finally spoke. "Do you even know how to drive a stick?"

The company pickup was a big, bad, four-on-the-floor ex-tended cab dualie. Since Arwen's cottage sat on the block behind the saloon, she walked back and forth to work, and since she spent most afternoons in her office, and most evenings hustling to make nice with the customers bellied up to the bar, she couldn't remember the last time she'd been behind the wheel. It was very possible Luck had never seen her drive.

But, yeah. She knew exactly what to do. She palmed the keys in one hand, hefted up the lunch delivery in her other arm. Then she headed out of the kitchen with a wink, saying, "It's a stiff rod with a knob on top. I think I can handle it."

WHATEVER ELSE MIGHT have changed in Crow Hill during his absence, Dax Campbell knew he could count on Lasko Ranch Supply for more than his need for feed. Landowners, ranch hands, old-timers, and those aiming to fuel the gossip mill gathered in the parking lot before breakfast to shoot the shit of the day, or at lunch to share the food that flowed as freely as the news.

Like all communities of folks making their living off the land, Crow Hill knew about getting the word out. Trucks passed on a country road and occupants traded the latest. A driver dropping hay bales at one ranch carried stories from the last. Drifters looking for work brought with them the grim truth of what they'd learned at the place they'd tried before.

Dax wasn't after the grim truth or stories or the latest. His reason for hanging out at the feed store was all about getting laid. It had been way too long since he'd taken the time, even *had* the time for that particular pleasure. And being out of touch all these years meant scoping out the lay of the land.

Word of the inheritance he'd be sharing with Boone Mitchell and Casper Jayne had reached him in a bar outside of Bozeman. He'd been drunk, he'd been cold, and for the first time in years, he'd been homesick. Not for the place he hadn't seen since the summer after high school, but for his boys.

Learning of the passing of Tess and Dave Dalton on top of that ache had almost done him in. He'd loved the Daltons, considered them family. They'd been there when his mother had taken up the causes of less privileged children instead of seeing to her own. They'd encouraged him to live his life his way when his father insisted he follow the path of all Campbell men.

Dax had wanted to cowboy—not go to college, and definitely not to law school to add *Esquire* to the end of his name. Tess got that. Dave got that. Casper and Boone got it, too. They'd sent him packing with promises to keep in touch. He hadn't, and had nothing but his vagabond life to blame.

But that night in Montana, finding out he'd lost the Daltons had him missing his boys with an unimaginable hurt. Every good memory of his teenage years was connected to Boone and Casper. The summers they'd spent working the Dalton ranch were the best times of his life.

In fact, outside of honoring the Daltons' wish that he help keep the place they'd poured their hearts and souls into from being sucked up by Crow Hill's First National Bank, the only thing that would've brought him back to Texas was raising some Dalton Gang hell. But he needed a woman—or two or three—to do it up right.

"Campbell! Was wondering if you were planning on showing your beat-up old face around here. Not that I couldn't have gone the rest of my life without seeing it."

Dax let the screen door slam behind him before he turned toward Bubba Taylor, who was just as gap-toothed and curly headed as he'd been in high school, though now carrying a gut that appeared over the years to have never met a beer it didn't like. "Now, Bubs. I don't think my face is any more beat-up than your wife's."

A chorus of sharp snickers and a couple of guffaws punctuated Dax's words. Bubba, proud of getting in the first shot, seemed at a loss for another, which pretty much reflected the IQ Dax remembered him displaying most of the time.

Josh Lasko, another classmate who, word had it, had taken over running the store from his dad, made his way out from the register, his boots clomping on the worn plank floor. He offered Dax his hand for a hearty shake. "Good to see you, Dax. Damn good, but c'mon. Cut Bubba some slack. It's a wonder he's got a wife at all when you look at the face God gave him."

Dax pretended to consider the ugly mug of the man in question, asking Josh, "You sure it was God?"

That loosened Bubba's tongue. "Hey now. What's with all the ganging up on Bubba here?" Hands out, he looked to his posse for help. Getting nothing but murmurs and shrugs, he dug for a comeback, snickering. "I ain't the one who screwed myself out of a hilltop mansion and into a ranch so rundown it ain't worth a salt lick."

Dax had done plenty of screwing, true, and the fallout hadn't done a damn thing to help his situation at home. But neither his history with women nor that with his folks had squat to do with his partnership in the Dalton place. "That's the difference between you and me, Bubs. I know the value of a salt lick. You want to insult my property, you'll have to do better than that."

"It wasn't your property I was aiming for," Bubba tossed back, turning to his cronies with a smirk at having gotten in the last laugh.

Dax let him have it. The hours he was working these days, catching up with friends he might want to see already took time he didn't have. Wasting it on the likes of Bubba Taylor wasn't a luxury he cared to indulge in.

"Gentlemen." He nudged his hat brim up a notch, gave Bubba his back, and walked to the register with Josh. "Wondered how long the woodwork could hold them back."

Josh gave a single shake of his head. "Might've been a bit longer if you'd picked up any manners out wherever the hell you've been."

It had been five years since he'd last counted the places he'd worked. Before that . . . He didn't even want to think about the miles he'd driven, the horses he'd rode to ground, the cattle he'd herded. "I've been everywhere, man. I've been everywhere."

The corner of Josh's smile dimpled. "Yeah, that's what I'm talking about."

Dax shrugged. He was who he was. "I left in a hurry. Didn't have time to head back to the hilltop mansion for etiquette lessons."

The other man leaned forward on both elbows, his head low as he spoke for Dax's ears alone. "Bubba and his bunch? You gotta expect some of that, leaving like you did, then coming back to take over a property a lot of folks could've been putting to good use. Rain's been in short supply. Makes grass hard to come by. Too many animals being sold at a loss because of it."

Nothing Dax didn't know or hadn't seen employers face over the years. Ranching ran in the blood of a lot of families, but that didn't keep hearts from breaking when troubles bit deep. "I came back for Tess and Dave. And for my boys. Not because I had some grand dream of ranching in Crow Hill."

"And not because of your family?"

He'd been back a week, Boone and Casper a couple weeks longer. He hadn't seen his folks or his sister yet; he hadn't seen much of anything but the back end of cows and the bottom of bank accounts, but the inevitable was on its way. "Found an attorney in Dallas to take care of my third of the partnership papers. His legal advice didn't cost me an arm and a leg *and* a soul."

"I hear that," Josh said, giving Dax cause to wonder if his old man billed clients a price similar to what he'd demanded from his only son.

But Josh didn't give him time to ask. "So what brings you to town today? That lawyer of yours get you up to speed on your payables? 'Cuz I was thinking of taking a 'round-the-world cruise, and if you pony up, I can do it."

At least Josh's reminder of the state of Tess and Dave's affairs didn't grate in the way of so many others. Josh's grandfather had wrangled cattle on the King Ranch with Dave Dalton, years before the two made their way to south central Texas. That had Josh counting the Daltons as family, too, the Dalton Gang an extension.

But it didn't mean Dax and the boys weren't still on the hook for the debt. They did, however, have a secret weapon in Boone's sister, a loan officer at the First National Bank. "With the budget Faith's got us on, you should be able to afford the drive to the port in Galveston real soon. Maybe even the gas to get back."

Josh straightened, laughing, but the sound was cut off by a loud round of catcalls rising from the corner. Dax looked over his shoulder in time to see Bubba and his bubbas nearly topple the barrel holding their card game as they jockeyed for position at the window.

Elbows gouged and shoved. Bootheels landed on boot toes. Hats were jerked from heads to clear lines of sight. Reminded Dax of a bunch of bawling calves jammed into a chute. "Looks like someone needs to put a lock on the beer cooler."

"Nope," Josh said. "Looks like lunch." He circled the counter and headed for his own window, this one tucked on the far side of an old wardrobe now stocked with square cans of unguent and dark brown bottles of antiseptics and thick leather gloves.

Curious, Dax followed, leaning a raised arm along the window casing and squinting into the glare of the sun. The view that finally came into focus looked like way more than lunch to Dax.

The woman bent across the front seat of the pickup, dragging a big, brown, grease-spotted grocery bag into her arms, had the most gorgeous ass Dax had seen in weeks. Course, the only asses he'd seen during those weeks belonged to the calves he'd been working, but still.

All he needed now was for the front side to be as outstanding as the back. She straightened, wrapped one arm around the bag, and turned. Her dark jeans rode low on her hips and bunched around her boot vamps. The shoulder-hugging sleeves of her T-shirt showed off some mighty fine guns. But it was the way the same shirt lay flat against her belly and scooped low on her C-cup chest that made his mouth water.

He blew out the breath straining his lungs to bursting, not exactly proud of the groan that came out on its tail.

Hallelujah, and come to Papa.

Josh chuckled. "You know who that is, don't you?"

Dax lifted his gaze to her face. Dark wavy hair, shoulder length, shining like strong coffee in the sun. A wide mouth with sweet peachy lips, and big bright eyes. Green, he'd bet. To go with the freckles on her nose.

And no. If he'd seen this woman before, the two of them would be acquainted in the most intimate of ways. "Not a freakin' clue."

"Then let me be the one to fill you in on some of the better things that have happened since you've been gone." Josh slapped Dax on the shoulder before walking away. "That, my man, is Arwen Poole."

NATURALLY THE ONE day Arwen decided to make the feed store run, it was Bubba Taylor and his goon squad who'd placed the order. If she'd thought to check the ticket before her spur of the moment decision, she would've gone after Dax another time.

The problem with working the Wild Wild West were the predators that hovered at watering holes. And Arwen hated feeling like prey.

A quick scan of the parking lot failed to turn up a truck door sporting a D hooked over a T that was the Dalton Ranch brand. What she did see—and sense crawling all over her—were a half dozen pair of shifty eyes, Bubba Taylor's being the beadiest.

She hefted the bag higher, holding it directly in front of her as she climbed the wooden steps to the porch. Both creaked beneath her weight, but neither was as loud as the hinges groaning when Bubba pushed open the screen door.

"Hey, Arwen." He winked, taking up space she needed to get by. He kept his hand on the wooden frame, the torn-away sleeves of his plaid shirt revealing a thick tuft of hair and his disregard of deodorant. "Long time no see. Thought Amy might be delivering today."

Arwen shoved the bag into his hands, causing him to step back and out of her way. Only then did she take another breath. "Sorry, Bubba. You're stuck with me."

"I don't mind." He looked her up and down, settling his gaze in her cleavage, and then he actually licked his lips. "As long as you don't mind getting what's coming to you."

Because, of course, that's why she was here. To be sexually harassed by Bubba Taylor. "Money, Bubba. Cash. Preferably before you eat."

Bubba sneered. "Ah, well. If that's all you want, then lemme pass the hat for donations."

Rolling her eyes with a muttered, "Lord save me," Arwen headed for the register, fresh air, and the safety of Josh Lasko. He was leaning into his forearms where they were crossed on the counter, and he smiled as she got close.

"How're things, Josh? Your daddy doing okay?"

"He's getting there. Doc's put him on enough meds to choke a bull. Cut him back to one rib eye a month."

A cowman facing a beef-restricted diet was not a pretty thing. Arwen sympathized. "Sorry to hear that. We've got a mean veggie burger on the menu if he wants to stop in and give it a try."

But Josh wasn't having it. "I'm afraid he's made his last trip to the saloon. At least for a while. Dad's not a heathen like Bubba Taylor, but he's still got an eye for the gals, and that ticker of his might not stand the strain of your Kittens."

She laughed at Josh's sidestepping effort not to call his father a dirty old man. "Tell you what. Next time he's in town, let me know and I'll bring a veggie burger over." When Josh briefly eyed the fit of her shirt, she added, "I'll even find something less heart-stopping to wear."

"Well, it's not that I really want to see that happen, but for his sake, I appreciate it." His face coloring, he looked quickly away, nodding over her shoulder. "Looks like Bubba's collected enough to pay you, though I hope you weren't counting on anything like a tip."

"It's Bubba Taylor," she said, resigned to this trip being more hassle than mission accomplished. "I'm not even counting on getting out of here with my virtue intact."

"I'm happy to help you run that gauntlet."

The voice came from the shadows. It was a voice Arwen knew well, though it was seasoned now, deeper and richer, as if hung up to age. She tried to swallow, found her throat had swelled. Tried to breathe, found her lungs fighting her heart for the room.

Was he leaner? Rougher? Hard-edged and worth all the years she'd waited?

He'd never been soft, but his body had matured, his build less a cocky teen learning the fit of things and more the cowboy he was now. His was a long, rangy strength defined by lean hips and a purposeful swagger, by a narrow waist and wide shoulders and the sharp relief of tendons and veins. He needed every bit of the weight he carried, and she wondered if he'd outgrown his love of excess.

But then she met his gaze, and she was taken back to eighteen when she'd lusted after the things he'd made her feel as much as she'd lusted after him. And, oh, *oh*, but the lust was grand, her pulse ticking wildly, her skin tingling, her sex anticipating and growing damp. There were so many things she wanted him to do.

Beneath his hat, his hair was shaggy, a darker blond than she remembered, and as careless as was the scruff of whiskers he hadn't bothered to shave. His jaw was square, bold, his mouth wide and wicked as he smiled. His eyes were the intense blue of high summer skies, and hot. Texas sun hot.

"Dax." It was all she could say. Her mouth was bone dry.

"Arwen." His voice rolled over her, the one word, her name.

She didn't know if she'd ever heard him say it. She didn't know if getting him out of her system was going to be as easy as she'd thought. She did know if she let him walk her to her truck, she wouldn't be driving away alone.

Sounded like a hell of a plan. "I'd better get Bubba's money before he finds something else to spend it on."

Dax came closer. He didn't speak. He just smiled, his dimples cutting crescents in the stubble covering his cheeks. He didn't ask when he took hold of her upper arm and turned her toward the door, or say anything as Bubba silently paid her.

On the way out, he moved his hand to the small of her back. He kept it there as they crossed the porch and walked down the steps. Once in the parking lot, they turned toward the long row of pickups along the side of the store, and that's when his hand drifted lower, his thumb inching under the hem of her shirt, his fingers slipping beneath the waistband of her jeans.

She glanced up, wondered if his eyes would give away what he was thinking, if hers would tell him that he was why she was here. This was what she wanted, but he didn't have to know that, and she didn't have to make it so easy on either of them. Yet she didn't dislodge his hand. And she didn't pretend his presumption put her off.

All she did was cut her gaze over his shoulder toward the window, asking as she looked back, "Are you invading my personal space for the benefit of Bubba and his boys, or for your own?"

He paid no attention to their audience, his gaze holding hers, a rope pulling tight, choking. "You left out the third option."

He'd lassoed her. If not for the onlookers fogging up the store's window, she would've stripped to her skin then and there. But he didn't have to know that either. "Which is?"

"I'm doing it for you."

"That so."

He nodded, his gaze sliding from her eyes to her mouth before moving lower, lingering along her scooped neckline as if he had all the time in the world. As if he would *take* all the time in the world. She couldn't wait to find out if he would, but he didn't have to know that most of all.

He reached for his hat brim, pulled it low. "I figure . . . sixteen years? It's about time."

Oh, who was she kidding? He knew. He knew everything. And he'd known it all along. That left her with only one thing to say.

"My truck or yours?"

TWO

Darcy Campbell yanked off her sunglasses that were little help against the white hot June sky and blinked to adjust to the interior of the Hellcat Saloon. She scanned the room, breathing deeply of flame-seared beef and fresh-baked bread and the fire-roasted *chiles* that went into Arwen Poole's famous salsa.

Finding her favorite corner table empty, she didn't wait for the hostess but headed that way, the heels of her navy pumps striking the glossy concrete in a rhythmic and angry click. She dropped into the chair that put her back to the wall and tossed her satchel into the seat at her right.

Screw it being noon. She needed a pitcher of margaritas. Extra salt, double tequila. Unfortunately, Campbell propriety—and Mrs. Kyle's three o'clock deposition—determined the only liquid she'd be imbibing at lunch was iced tea. And that with artificial sweetener—another bit of Campbell propriety.

Not that she was bitter.

Much.

Getting out of the Campbell and Associates law office for lunch should've helped her mood, but didn't. She was eating alone while the firm's two men dined on grass-fed Angus and drank Prairie Rotie from the family's favorite hill country vintner. Because only potential *associates* dined with The Campbell at the Crow Hill Country Club.

And Darcy, a daughter, a girl, a disappointment, would never make partner. Especially with Greg Barrett and his penis working the same partner-track hours and now landing the Trinity Springs Oil account for the firm.

"Hey, sweetie." Luck Summerlin set a tumbler full of ice and Darcy's lunchtime drink on a Hellcat logo coaster. "I heard the news. How're you doing?"

Wow. Crow Hill was small, but Greg had only announced the Trinity Springs news this morning. She reached for a packet of sweetener, tore it open, and poured. "Who told you?"

Luck propped a knee in the empty chair on Darcy's left, her long legs bare between her boots and her denim shorts, and shrugged. "The Kittens were all over it earlier. Lots of ribald chatter."

The chatter part Darcy got. But ribald? Greg? "Then their imagination's way better than mine. Ribald's not exactly the word I'd use."

Luck looked aghast. "Considering he's your brother, I hope not."

Her brother? "Wait." She stopped stirring her tea, glanced up. "Who are you talking about?"

"Dax? The only brother you have? Unless you're keeping family secrets about an even badder bad sheep." Luck narrowed her eyes, braced her hip against the chair back. "Who are *you* talking about?"

Darcy waved off answering, the acid in the pit of her stomach simmering. "Why are you talking about Dax?"

"You don't know?"

"Know what?"

"He's here."

"Here where?"

"Jeez, Darcy. Here. In town. Well, at the Dalton Ranch, anyhow. Boone and Casper, too."

She knew about the others, but not her brother. The Dalton Gang. Together again. Their inheritance made it inevitable, but still . . . She really needed to stop working under a rock and pay attention. And then it hit her. Dax. He was back. After all these years, he was back. And she felt . . . nothing more than a simmer of emotion.

And then a scalding rush of resentment sent her temperature soaring.

Probably not the reaction Campbell propriety called for. "Dax is here? Are you sure?"

"Oh, yeah. I'm sure. And you didn't have a clue, did you?"

When Darcy shook her head, Luck let out whooping, hollering Hellcat roar, and across the dining room, the Kittens working the lunch shift responded in kind. Customers joined in, slamming bootheels on the floor, banging beer bottles on the bar, drumming hands on any surface until the racket rattled the walls.

It was a Hellcat Saloon tradition Darcy's headache could've done without. Flipping the bird at propriety, she braced her elbows on the table and buried her face in her hands. First Greg. Now Dax. The son her father had never had and wanted, and the one he'd had and disowned. She might as well get a rope.

Chair legs scraped across the floor as Luck pulled out the one she'd been leaning on and sat. "Seriously? He hasn't let y'all know?"

Darcy left her pity party and reached for her tea, thinking she should be anxious to see him, curious how deep her anger at his abandonment ran. "He hasn't let *me* know. I can't speak for Mom, and The Campbell wouldn't tell me if he had. I knew about the will so I assumed he'd show his ass sooner or later."

"Lotta girls out there hoping to see it."

"Ew. Luck. He's my brother."

"Then you'll just have to trust me. Dax does wicked things to a pair of jeans."

"Can we change the subject? Please?" Though at Luck's words, the image of Josh Lasko wearing Wranglers came to mind. As did the image of Josh Lasko wearing nothing at all.

Funny about chemistry and attraction. She'd never pictured Greg in anything but the suits he wore to the office each day— Italian, designer, Manhattan appropriate. She still hadn't figured out what he was doing in Crow Hill, though she knew The Campbell's reputation had tempted many a young lad.

But Josh Lasko . . . He was kind and strong, silent and shy, and wholesome in ways that made her want to ignore their twain never meeting disparity. Not that her spending her days in her family's law office while he spent his in his family's feed store meant anything to her. Her parents on the other hand . . .

"How 'bout we change the subject to lunch?" Luck pulled her pad and a pen from her apron. "Do you know what you want to eat?"

"Grilled chicken salad. Fat-free ranch on the side." She thought of returning to the office without having dined on grass-fed Angus or drinking Prairie Rotie. "Garlic toast. With extra garlic."

"Got an afternoon appointment with a vampire?"

Ugh. Mrs. Kyle's deposition. "Just the salad, I guess. The garlic would've been of more use warding off the morning's bad news."

"What happened this morning?"

"Nothing." Darcy sighed. "Greg."

"Daddy's little protégé still looking to become partner?"

"Something like that."

"You know . . ." Luck tapped the end of her pen to her chin, head cocked, ponytail swinging. "The best way to get your mind *off* your troubles with one man is to get *into* trouble with another."

Josh Lasko again. In his Wranglers. Out of his Wranglers. In her bed. Darcy squeezed the muscles of her sex until the tingles there had her aching.

Luck went on. "Or, considering how hot Greg is, you could keep it all in house, if you know what I mean."

She knew, but no. She was not going to dip her nib in the company ink. Or . . . whatever. "Really? You think he's hot?"

Eyes rolling, Luck returned her pad and pen to her apron. "I swear, Darcy. It's like you live in a cave. He's tall and he's built and he's all kinds of rich. Not to mention being totally *GQ*."

"Then what was all that about Dax and his jeans?"

"Jeans are every day, every man, and everywhere. Greg Barrett is an exotic. And a yummy one at that." Luck popped up to turn in Darcy's order, leaving her with a quick wink.

Leaving her wondering, too, if Greg was so yummy, why she'd never seen it. Why it was Josh Lasko, not the exotic, who tumbled through her fantasies. And how soon her brother's return was going to turn her pretty nice life upside down.

Because it would.

THREE

I N THE END, Dax took his truck and Arwen hers. It wasn't that he didn't like the idea of her sitting up against him, his arm around her shoulders, his fingers in her hair. Finding a back road, an empty barn, pulling into a pasture to warm up for the main event.

But since a truck bed quickie wouldn't be enough to hold him, and since he hated the idea of rousing her after exhausting her to drive him back for his wheels, and since he'd *have* to rouse her because he had a hell of a long second half of the work day ahead, two trucks it was.

Then there was the fact that they were driving into town, not out of it, and that left them with few off-the-beaten path places to get naked and party. It also meant that when they got to where they were going he'd be ready to blow.

Arwen Poole. Who'd've guessed it?

The girl who'd been raised in the back of a bar had turned into an amazing example of Mother Nature's best work. He remembered her from school, but that was more about her name and her widowed father than her appearance sticking with him all this time.

He'd listened for years to his mother bemoan the sorry conditions the girl lived in. Because instead of devoting her time to her family, Patricia Campbell had served on all sorts of boards of all manner of charities sworn to protect those who couldn't protect themselves.

But the courts had never deemed Hoyt Poole an unfit parent. And Wallace Campbell had finally put his foot down. No more talk of the Pooles. If his wife was so gung-ho to be charitable, she could damn well begin her charity at home and get him another drink.

Dax had never understood why his father guzzling Glenlivet from the La-Z-Boy in his library was any different than Hoyt Poole downing Bud at the Buck Off Bar. Both men were drunks, making Dax and Arwen adult children of alcoholics.

And wouldn't Oprah have a field day with that?

He shook off the memories and trailed Arwen through town, past the First National Bank, Nathan's Food and Drug, the Municipal Plaza. The long squat building housed the city manager, the water district, the volunteer fire department, and the county sheriff's substation—just as it always had.

To be fair, he hadn't done much looking around, being tied up with work since setting foot back on the ranch. This was his first time to cruise the main strip. He'd yet to take a trip out to the mansion on the hill, the one where he'd spent his first eighteen years, the one where Patricia Campbell worked to save the world, where Wallace Campbell drank himself into a nightly stupor.

The one where Dax was no longer welcome.

He ditched his thoughts of the past as quickly as he could,

preferring to think of the immediate future as he followed Arwen onto a quiet side street and into a small, private, shell-and-gravel lot. They parked side by side in front of a six-foot cedar privacy fence that had him frowning.

Huh. What was she doing, bringing him to the Buck Off Bar's rear entrance? He knew he hadn't misread her intentions. Was she thinking he needed a few drinks to loosen him up? And, if so, was she kidding? He pocketed his keys, tugged his hat down low, leaned against the truck's cab, and waited for her to join him.

But she didn't join him. She circled his truck and kept on walking, her ass in those jeans making it really hard for him to wait for an answer as to why they were here. Then she tossed him an over-the-shoulder look full of good times, and he forgot the question. He pushed off his truck, headed for the gate she'd unlocked, and walked through.

The bar's covered back patio, now scattered with picnic tables instead of rusty junk, sat on his left. Huge commercial ceiling fans stirred the heavy noonday air, but still the place was empty—a curiosity satisfied when he saw the evening hours for the outdoor service printed on the chalkboard listing the labels of imported beer.

Wondering when the Buck Off Bar had started selling more than Budweiser, he glanced to the right. A small frame house, its postcard-green yard ringed by beds of yellow flowers, sat on the other end of the lot. Baskets of ivy and fern hung from the front porch where a big orange tabby took him in from the pillows on the swing.

He gave the place another once-over. Cozy. Homey. Seriously out of place. Someone thought a whole lot more of Crow Hill than he ever had, planting flowers in a place where he'd never seen them grow.

"Mind telling me what we're doing here?" The sun beating

down on the top of his head, he looked from the house on one end of the block, to the vacant patio on the other, back to Arwen where she stood in between.

She sighed the sigh of patient saints, shook her head, and turned for the bar. "If by *here* you mean why did I bring you home with me, then we must've crossed signals somewhere."

Like the dog he was, he shadowed her steps. "Wait. I'm confused. You still live in the bar?"

"I never lived in the bar, Dax. And if you'll look at the sign, you'll see it's now called the Hellcat Saloon." She hopped up onto the patio and made a beeline for the covered ice chest in the corner. "I own it. And across the yard, that's my house."

The burgers she'd brought to the feed store. The sign on the side of her truck. The logo he'd noticed on her T-shirt when not looking at her tits. Seemed Arwen Poole was full of surprises.

"Want a beer?" she called to him, one hand holding open the top of the ice chest as she rummaged for two longnecks with the other.

"Sure." Though first he had to regain the upper hand he'd held when they'd left Lasko's because something about her had him seriously off his hell-raising game. He wanted to get into her pants and she wanted him there.

Yet here he was, thinking about her father bringing her with him to the bar so often the news reached Dax's mother in the mansion on the hill.

"A beer would be great," he said, coming up behind her as she closed the chest. He took the bottles from her hand and set them on the lid, trapping her against it with his body when she turned. "I could use a burger, too. It *is* lunchtime. And I *am* hungry."

"You're in luck then because burgers are our specialty." Eyes downcast, she toyed with his denim shirt's mother-of-pearl snaps. "We use local beef, and offer the standard pickles, lettuce, onions, and tomatoes, along with your choice of cheese. Or you can go with grilled onions and mushrooms, fried onions and jalapenos, avocado slices and sprouts, or bacon and a fried egg. We also have a veggie burger that's as good as it gets."

He stared at her hand, watched her move from snap to snap, rubbing, circling, yet never popping a one. Her movements seemed almost involuntary, as if her mind was elsewhere, and not on the food she'd described.

But his thoughts were giving him trouble enough, so rather than wonder about hers he enjoyed her touch, her fingers slender, nimble, her nails short and polished clear. He pictured them on his bare chest, thought they'd look damn good ringed beneath the head of his cock.

A burn caught fire at the base of his spine, and like he'd just eaten the dirt floor of a corral, his voice scraped its way up his throat. "What've you got in the way of dessert?"

"Every sweet thing you could want," she told him, her lips flirting as she worked her way to his belt.

His breathing hitched. His cock followed suit. His balls tightened, and his heartbeat brought up the rear. "Then I say we skip the stuff that's good for us and go straight for the bad."

"I like the way you think," she said, grabbing his belt buckle and tugging him close.

Oh, yeah. This girl was going to be fun.

He reached for her hands, shackled them in the small of her back. Her breasts were full and firm where she pressed against him, the tips pierced with dangling rings. He wanted to taste the salt of them, to flick them with his tongue, tug them with his teeth. He wanted to feel the metal warm from her body's heat. He wanted her above him, dragging them down his chest.

Pretty damn close to strangling, he let her go and lifted her to sit on the ice chest. With his hands on her knees, he spread her legs and stepped between them. She did that thing with her mouth again, half smile, half *gotcha*, and when she looped her heels around his hips, he ground himself on her fly.

She made a sound, a sigh or a muttered sort of curse. He couldn't tell, but he didn't need to. Even with two layers of fabric between them, he could feel she was ready. It drove him beneath the hem of her shirt to her skin. Shivering, she pressed her mouth to his neck, kissing him, licking, nipping as he reached the rear clasp of her bra and released it.

That sound again, rising from her chest, and lower, from her belly, as if he'd stirred something there to life. The thought primed his cock further. He was full and aching. Later, he'd play with her mind. Later, once they'd extinguished this fire.

It was consuming him, devouring, burning his skin to cinders, and Arwen was just as hot. He palmed her ribs, sliding his hands up her sides until his thumbs felt the weight of her breasts. She let go of his shirt and leaned back, her fingers spread on the ice chest, her eyes closed, and she wet her lips, waiting.

God, but she was gorgeous. Lush and ripe, her mouth, her tits, her ass that he couldn't wait to get his hands on. He hooked an arm behind her and she arched further, nearly begging. He bent, lifted her T-shirt, and buried his face.

She smelled like citrus and clean air, sweet and fresh and female. The skin between her breasts was damp with perspiration, her arousal salty, musky, warm. He wanted her naked. He wanted to taste her, to push his tongue inside her. He wanted to wrap his hand around his cock and watch her take it to the back of her throat.

This time the guttural sound was all his, his spine tingling, his balls heavy. Her chest rose and fell with her short, rapid breaths. He caught the ring dangling from her nipple, tugging her into his mouth. She cried out, threaded her fingers into his hair and cupped his skull to hold him. Then she began to rock, her hips moving back and forth, the rhythm timed to the beat of the music rattling the saloon walls.

Dax tongued and sucked, her nipple, her pebbled areola, the plump flesh that filled his hands. It wasn't enough. He knew it. She knew it. And he was already retreating when she pushed him away. She held his gaze while she fastened her bra, adjusting herself inside the lace cups. He shifted his stance to relieve the strain behind his buttoned fly then stepped back to give her room to hop down.

She did, hooking two fingers around the necks of the beer bottles and offering them like bait. Her hair was mussed, her T-shirt wrinkled and bunched at her waist, her pupils as black as a wide-eyed calf's.

"We can go in for a burger," she told him, her voice labored and low. "Or we can cross the yard and finish this inside my house."

ARWEN HADN'T TAKEN but five steps into her kitchen when Dax grabbed her wrist and tugged her to the door. He'd closed it, locked it, and now he pushed her against it, reaching for her jeans once he had her restrained. He popped the button, lowered the zipper, slid his hand into her panties and his tongue into her mouth.

She thought she just might die. A gorgeous death. A beautiful death. The lust of her life doing her in. And that's what got to her the most. This was Dax Campbell. His hands, his mouth, his fingers sliding through her folds, teasing, tormenting. Dax Campbell.

The man she'd swore to work out of her system was taking her apart.

She'd had sex. She'd had orgasms. When without a partner, she had no trouble taking care of herself. But oh, what a fool she'd been to think she could file Dax away in the same box of toys. This was *so* far beyond her experience with physical pleasure; this was bliss, and it crawled inside of her, and her heart raced to escape the emotions clutching and scrabbling with greedy fingers.

She had no idea what he'd done with the longnecks, only that her wrists were crossed and pinned over her head. The hand not shackling hers urged her to spread her legs, and then a finger was inside her, two fingers, stroking her pussy while his tongue slid over hers like a cock, possessing. Claiming, and oh *God*, she was in trouble. So much trouble.

She had to shut down, close the door on everything but what he was doing to her body. She couldn't think about who he'd been and who she'd been. She couldn't think at all.

She struggled. She wanted to touch him, to get rid of her clothes and his clothes, to make them equal, but his thumb was on her clit, pressing down, pulling up, playing her side to side and robbing her of control. This wasn't what she wanted, yet it was everything she wanted; Dax Campbell in her house, owning her.

His mouth bruised hers, and she let him. His fingers stretched her channel as if checking the fit. She wanted his cock there, filling her, banging bottom, impaling her and lifting her from her feet. She'd dreamed of this so long, and it was happening, but it wasn't enough. She bit down and caught his lip to tell him.

He laughed, the sound deep and earthy, a hungry sound, as if she had no idea what she was asking for, or what she just might get. He pulled his fingers from her pussy, slid further between her legs and toyed with the bud of her ass.

"You bite me, I'm going to bite back," he said, pushing the tip of a finger into her tight rear hole.

She squirmed, wanting less, wanting more. "You call that biting?"

He let her go, his eyes dark, dangerous, his gaze smoldering as he dropped it to the skin of her belly bared by her open fly. "Get rid of 'em. I'll wait."

She was wet and swollen, but no matter how desperately she wanted him, she wasn't going to make it that easy. She had to control this or she wouldn't survive.

She stood on one foot to tug off a boot, stood in her sock while she pulled off the other. She knew he was waiting for her take off her pants, so she took off her T-shirt instead, stretching her arms slowly as she lifted the hem, shaking her head as her hair freed the fabric.

Dax's hands were at his hips, his erection thick behind the denim of his jeans. He still wore his hat, the brim pulled low, his pulse beating in the hollow of his throat. She wondered about the veins on his shaft, how blue they would be, how distended, and she reached for the rings he'd tongued earlier, lifting her nipples from the cups of her bra.

The words he bit off were raw and dirty, words polite people didn't know, didn't speak if they did. She was glad he knew them, that she inspired them, that he said them with no apologies. That he was driven to jerk at the snaps of his shirt, the buttons of his jeans, because this is what she'd wanted.

Sex. Bodies. Skin on skin.

Covered by white cotton, his cock filled the V between the denim gap, the capped head set off by its thick ridge. She thought he would reach for her then, would lift out his cock and fist it, but he reached for one of the longnecks on top of her refrigerator instead. His gaze held hers and he pulled a long swallow, backhanding his mouth when done.

"I'm still waiting."

The hat shadowing his face. The shirt hanging open. The fly of his jeans open, too. He was her fantasy, and he was here, and she would deal with the repercussions later. She skinned down her jeans and kicked them away, wanting to do the same with her panties, but wanting more to be stripped by him. This was her dream, her indulgence. She held her lower lip with her teeth, standing her ground, having her way.

The corner of Dax's mouth turned up and he shook his head, lifting the beer. He swallowed again, his throat working, a powerful mix of emotions simmering in his eyes. And then he was there, one arm behind her, his hand manacling her wrists in the small of her back, the empty bottle hitting the floor and rolling across the black and white tiles.

He nudged her legs apart with one knee, and she let him, surrendering, closing her eyes as his lips found the base of her neck. He breathed her in, nuzzling her, kissing her, his tongue swirling against her skin. Between her legs, he breached the elastic of her panties, used the long side of his index finger to open her outer lips. His hips pressed forward, and the head of his cock swept against the inner . . . and stopped.

"Arwen." He whispered her name, the single word torn free, a caress, a curse. "I don't have a condom."

Her eyes slammed shut. God, where was her brain? She knew better. She *knew* better, yet she'd almost gone forward without this much-needed conversation because she'd wanted him for so long.

He drew his tongue along her collarbone to her shoulder, then back to the hollow of her throat, wetting her, branding her, *was that what he was doing, making her his?* He soughed his next words against the corner of her mouth. "It's been a while since

I've done this, and I've tested safe. But we can wait, or we can improvise. I'm good with whatever."

She wasn't good, and she knew he was lying about putting this off. "No waiting. No improv. I'm clean and on the pill."

She held her breath, waiting, anticipating, her clit extending in response to the butterfly strokes of his tip. The plum-full cap was delicious and ripe, moisture seeping from his slit as he prodded, tested, in and out, in and out, *sweet* sweet *lord*, in and out. And still he held her immobile. And still she couldn't touch him, and she wanted more than anything to touch him, and *why wouldn't he let her touch him?*

He tucked his cheek to her chin, his quick shallow thrusts giving way to full penetration, opening her, filling her. And that's when he finally bit her back, sucking on the skin above her collarbone and catching it between his teeth. He'd warned her. But, oh, she'd never expected this, the slide of his shaft in her pussy, the slide of his tongue healing the bruises he'd left on her flesh. Bruises she'd see in the mirror later.

Bruises reminding her to be careful what she wished for.

The pressure built, and she gripped and released his unyielding cock, her muscles pulling him deeper, her moisture creating a hot, slippery lube. She tugged free of his hold, digging her fingertips into the balls of his shoulders and moaning, aching, coming up on her tiptoes to pull him with her, squatting to hold on when he eased away.

He laughed at her desperation, and he fucked her, and he was a dangerous man, and she couldn't get enough. The hand behind her slid down to her ass, spreading her cheeks, his thumb finding her hole, pushing in. She clenched around him, drawing another wicked laugh, the sound cocky and victorious and in need of a check.

Letting go of one muscled shoulder, she slid her hand between their bodies, beneath his shirt, circling a nipple, then his navel, then the base of his shaft, where she squeezed and released as he thrust.

The groan that rolled from his gut shattered her, the hunger, the need, the toll of the years spent away. She wasn't sure she had what he was looking for, or if she wanted that sort of involvement when it went against her reasons for bringing him home. But it way too risky to ask, and it was too late for her anyway, and then it was too late for him.

She came apart, shuddered, his semen pulsing, hot, coating her walls. The vibrations rocked through her, through him, through her. His shaft was still hard when he finally slipped free, his cock sticky and dripping cum down her thigh. She sank against the door, aching, sore, tender and used, wrapping one hand around the knob to keep from falling.

Dax collapsed against her, his breath hot on her neck, and a sound she swore was a purr rattling with it. They stood there, breathing, calming, Arwen waiting for the room to quit spinning so she could find something in the familiar that made sense. Wondering if she ever would, or wanted to.

Putting a name to what had passed between them was beyond her, but she was pretty sure what she *hadn't* done was work Dax Campbell out of her system for good.

FOUR

THROWING ROOSTER TAILS of gravel as he braked in front of the bunkhouse, Dax steeled for the ass chewing he knew he'd be walking into—and knew he deserved. It was a weekday. It was a workday. He'd gone to town to pick up an order at Lasko's, and come back to the ranch sex drunk and needing a five-hour nap.

The burgers and six-pack he'd brought with him were as much an apology as lunch, but judging by the scowl on Boone's face and the shake of Casper's head, buying his way off their shit list was going to take more than Angus beef and imported beer.

His friends had spent the morning pulling his share of the workload along with their own, having only a couple of part-time hands for help. That after ironing out a legal three-way split just last week that included the division of duties around the ranch as well as the ownership. The ass chewing would only begin to cover his sins. He had every bit of whatever hell they threw at him coming.

Squinting into the heat waves shimmering off the hood of his truck, he held up the longnecks and booted his door closed. "I come bearing gifts."

Making his careful way down the building's rickety stairs, Boone shoved back his hat, wiped his forehead with his sleeve, then rolled a bottle of ice water over his skin before tugging down the brim to shade his eyes. "Those bite marks on your neck? I'd say that's not all the coming you've been doing."

"What can I tell you—" It was all Dax got out before Casper grabbed the grocery bag out of his arm and headed toward the rear of his truck.

Peering inside, he said, "You can tell me you got the spool of wire else you're gonna be the one chasing down the next runaway calf."

"I did," Dax said, though Casper had to have seen it as he lowered the tailgate to use as a lunch counter. The kitchen in the bunkhouse had two chairs and no table, yet none of the three felt right moving into the main house. It still belonged to the Daltons. Thinking otherwise hadn't settled in and might never.

Figuring it best not to press his luck, Dax ran a thumb over the bruise Arwen had given him, leaving off the part about having to stop by Lasko's a second time for the wire, since he'd kind of lost his way on the first trip. "And I would've gone after this morning's calf. You just got there first, being an early bird and all."

"Not an early bird." Casper tossed him a burger wrapped in yellow waxed paper. "An insomniac. Wondering if we'll be able to make this thing work."

Boone caught the second package. "Insomnia comes with the territory. Hard to think about letting down Tess and Dave. Still getting used to their trusting we wouldn't."

They were here, they were doing all they could to keep the ranch afloat. If they failed, Dax would move on. He'd done it before. "Tess and Dave knew this wasn't going to be easy for who-ever took over. And Dave in particular knew how far an extra hour spent catching up on sleep could go toward making a success of a long day."

Thoughts of the Daltons settled between them as they ate. The responsibility they'd been given. The belief the older couple had shown in three troubled teens. The very real possibility they'd fuck this up like they had so many other things in their lives.

It wasn't easy being weighted with a reputation that had an entire town wagering how long they'd last.

Wouldn't surprise Dax a bit to learn his father had bet his forfeited share of the Campbell estate that he wouldn't make it to summer's end.

"Is that what that bite mark is?" Casper asked between chews. "Catching up?"

Dax bit into the burger that was as good as Arwen had prom-ised, and tried to block out the picture of her tits. "Either of you ever know Arwen Poole? From high school?"

Boone held his beer in front of his mouth. "She the one whose dad lost it after her mom was killed in that rollover on 10? Out near Luling?"

"Yeah." Dax nodded. "He went on disability or something because of the accident. Had to raise Arwen himself."

"He did a lot of it in the Buck Off Bar, if I'm remembering things right," Boone added before guzzling down a long swallow.

Dax remembered things the same way. Hard not to with it being beat into his head by his mother. "She owns it now. Though she calls it a saloon. That's where the burgers came from."

"Must be the place Faith was talking about. Where the girls dance on the bar." At the glaring look from Boone, Casper stopped. "What? The other day at the bank. You were there. Unless you giving me the evil eye kept you from hearing anything she said."

Dax was leaving this one alone. Like Arwen, Boone's little sister had grown up while they'd been away, and though Casper had toed Boone's hands-off line in high school, Faith no longer needed her big brother's protection.

Boone wasn't of a mind to agree. Faith being their loan officer at the First National Bank would be putting her in Casper's path too often for Boone's liking. But at least the other two butting heads over Faith took the heat off of Dax.

He finished his burger, tossed the ball of waxed paper into the grocery bag, and thumbed the top from a second beer. Closing his eyes against the sun's blinding light, he brought it to his mouth. The heat returned before he'd managed even a sip.

"Is Arwen Poole the one who bit you?" The tailgate rattled as Casper boosted up to sit, a dust cloud rising from the seat of his jeans.

"I ran into her at Lasko's." A noncommittal answer. "She was delivering lunch to Bubba Taylor."

Boone snorted. "He smell any better than he did in high school?"

"Nope. Doesn't look any better either."

"Fuck Bubba Taylor," Casper said, using his shoulder as a napkin to wipe the grease and the drought's sandy grit from his mouth. "I want to hear more about Arwen. You two play vampire in the kitchen while she cooked?"

"She doesn't do the cooking. She's got a couple of girls flipping burgers." Girls who probably earned more than the part-time hands here on the ranch. Dax frowned, staring at his longneck and deciding how much more to spill. "She lives behind the saloon. Little house used to belong to Buck Akers when he owned the bar."

Another snort from Boone. "That piece-of-shit shack?"

Dax thought of the flowers, of the cat. Of the black-and-white kitchen floor that brought to mind old movies. "It's not a shack anymore. Surprised her water bill hasn't bankrupted her. The grass is so green it looks like she doused it with a bucket of paint."

That brought silence as all three looked around the place they'd inherited. They were living piecemeal per Faith's budget, buying supplies as they needed them and *only* the supplies they couldn't do without. The spool of galvanized steel barbed wire in the bed of his truck was an example. As far as anything on the spread being green . . . South Central Texas had been so long without rain that nothing held color for miles.

Brown was everywhere. Dirt, dead grass. Paint chipped from the bunkhouse to expose the wood beneath. The hay they were having to pay for and truck in since the end of Dave Dalton's days hadn't left him with the health or the money to bale his own. The cows and the horses, though they were born that way and Dax couldn't hold it against them. Still, they added to the dull and lifeless landscape.

If he was going to stay in this place for the extended length of time he'd signed on for, he needed more reason than the view from here. What he needed was green grass and yellow flowers. An orange tabby. Sweet creamsicle tits and hair that shone like campfire coffee lit by the light of the moon. Yep, those would do nicely. Nicely enough he thought he could put off sampling more of the local wares awhile longer.

What he couldn't put off another minute was work. He screwed up again, he wouldn't get off this lightly. He downed the rest of his beer, backhanded the moisture from his mouth, and dropped the bottle in the bag. He might've fucked things up with his family, but he wasn't going to do the same with the people in his life who mattered. The people who accepted—and respected— the choices he'd made.

Hopping into the truck bed for the spool of wire, he made a *Gimme* motion in Casper's direction. "Toss me your gloves."

Head shaking, Casper tugged them from his belt and pulled them on. "Uh-uh. You and your damn bite marks got the only break you're gonna get today."

Or not so lightly. "Hope that doesn't mean I have to restring the south pasture fence on my own."

"Nope, but we gotta wait for Diego to get back with the flat-bed since he's got the stretcher and staple driver."

And because we can't afford more than one of either, Dax mused with an irritation he directed at the spool, shoving it with his boot to where Casper waited.

Boone got the lunch trash out of the way, crimping the top of the bag and tossing it to the bunkhouse porch where it landed with a breaking glass clatter. "Wonder what possessed Arwen Poole to hang out her shingle in Crow Hill. Figured she would've left not long after we did, what with her situation being as crap-tastic as it was."

Dax couldn't say but was curious about the same. "We didn't spend a lot of time talking, but I'll find out what I can."

"That mean you're seeing her again?" Casper asked, hefting the wire to the ground and giving Dax the side eye from beneath the brim of his beat-up straw hat.

Laughing, Dax held up both hands. "From here on, after-hours only. I swear on every almighty dollar I left behind at the mansion on the hill."

"You know those dollars would come in handy right about now," Boone said. "I don't think Faith was kidding when she said we could do with picking up pennies and collecting aluminum cans."

"Then sign me up for the picking and collecting. I'm too old and worn out for law school. Even if I had any interest in going.

Which I don't." He jumped to the ground, slammed the tailgate shut. "The family firm will just have to grind to an end without me."

"I don't know. Hear tell Darcy's doing all she can to stake her claim to the throne," said Boone.

Except Boone knew as well as Dax that Dax's father would never crown a female successor. A pang of guilt punched the center of Dax's chest and he struggled to draw breath. If nothing else, he needed to see Darcy. And soon. His sister didn't deserve to be left to fight the good Campbell fights as well as the bad ones alone.

Yeah. This had to be done. "Why don't I ride out and find Diego, get him to help me with the fence? You two can get back to whatever else needs doing."

"And why would you volunteer to do that?" Boone asked from where he was leaning both forearms on the bed of Dax's truck.

"I was thinking of heading into town early in the morning. Having breakfast with Darcy." When his partners both started in with the loud and colorful words, he cut them off. "Hey. I've been back a week. I need to see her."

Casper nodded, though still had to ask, "You gotta do it on company time?"

"It's Darcy, man. And I won't be long." But wanting to be all aboveboard and honest since he needed his friends at his back, he added, "Arwen, I'll see on my own."

FIVE

ARWEN'S FAVORITE ROOM in her house was the bath. The pink and aqua retro tiles made her happy, as did the pedestal sink. Taking out a back porch storage closet she knew she'd never use had allowed her to enlarge the room by half. She'd added a skylight, French doors into a dressing area, and turned the room into an oasis with flowers and candles, with music, with all the mirrors a girl could possibly need.

But nothing matched her love for her vintage claw-foot tub. Knowing exactly the size and shape she wanted, she'd searched for months before finding one to fit her needs. And every night when she stretched out her legs and sank chin deep into water that smelled of herbs and a hint of citrus, she forgot the hassle of haggling with dealers, of driving miles to find no such advertised tub existed.

Owning the saloon meant long days and late hours. She rarely got home before three a.m. and almost never slept past nine. Unwinding happened a lot faster with the warmth of the water surrounding her, and the stars twinkling above took her mind off everything else. Tonight, however, even with the stars and the water, relaxation was proving problematic.

And her problem's name was Dax.

She was sore, *so* sore—her inner thighs from the sexual calisthenics, her nipples from his beard stubble and teeth. Her clit from his hard, grinding thrust. He'd stretched her and scraped her and left her raw. But even now, soaping her tender skin, she loved knowing it was Dax who'd done this.

What she still hadn't figured out—and probably needed to—was why she'd let him get to her in the first place all those years ago. They'd both grown up in Crow Hill, though had never run in the same circles—unless she counted attending the same schools, which didn't make sense to do. All kids living in the speck of a town went to school together. And she sure hadn't felt for Bubba Taylor the things she'd felt for Dax.

Thinking of those things . . . She closed her eyes, raised her knees, spread her legs, and let her fingers linger between them. One finger stroked one side of her clit, a second finger stroked the other. Up and down she rubbed, pulling at the sensitive flesh, pinching the hard knot of nerves. The water sloshed as she squirmed, as each deeper pass brought her closer to re-creating that first glorious breach of her body by his.

Glorious. Yes. It was the only word that fit. She'd waited her entire adult life to have Dax in her bed. Or in this case, to have him back her up against a door. Those minutes in her kitchen, though all too short, had been furious and consuming and so *so* hot. And yet . . . She hooked one foot over the tub's edge, eased her fingers between her pussy's slick, soapy lips.

Dax Campbell was one of a kind, always had been, always would be, but for some reason she'd expected more. Stupid, really, when a kitchen quickie was all lust had allowed them. More required, well . . . more. Time was the obvious. Touching, teasing. Gazes that lingered. Anticipation, arousal. Steam.

She groaned, a soft throaty sound, and slid her middle finger deep into her sex, wishing for Dax, his mouth, his hands. His impressively able cock. She pictured him with his shirt open, his fly open, his shaft thick behind the cotton of his briefs. He was beautiful. Bold and aggressive, and she increased the rhythm of her stroke and remembered his fit.

She'd had lovers. Some exquisitely experienced teachers. Others new to the game and appreciative of her tongue. She loved the physical intimacies shared between a woman and a man, but she did not mix pleasure with the business that provided her living. When struck with an itch she needed help scratching, it was easier to find a cowboy in a San Antonio honky-tonk than risk word of her sex life getting back to the likes of Bubba Taylor.

Because that's all she wanted from a man. A sex life. She had girlfriends. She had guy friends. She had her saloon and her house, and she had Crush—though the twenty-pound tabby would likely argue that if anything, he had her. What she did not have, did not want, and certainly did not need was a debilitating emotion prettied up with poems and promises and pink paper hearts.

She would never do that to herself. Never let herself be bound so inextricably to one man that losing him would be the end of her. And it would happen. She'd seen it happen. Her father had mourned her mother to the point of forgetting who he was. Half the time Arwen wasn't sure he hadn't forgotten about her. Or at least that she was his daughter, and not just a piece of the woman he'd lost.

This, right here, right now is enough, she told herself, her legs open, her nipples tight around the rings piercing them, her body hurting, soaring, looking for the relief that was just out of reach.

For the pleasure that reminded her she was very much alive—and very much worth remembering.

"I'll have what you're having."

Dax. As if she'd conjured him. As if he'd known. Instead of scaring her half to death, his voice sent ripples through the water to tickle her skin. Her pulse raced, beating at her wrists, in the hollow of her throat, deep inside her sex. She brought up her arms to rest on the tub's edge and took a calming breath. Her eyes drifted open.

Slowly, she turned her head, found him lounging against her door, one shoulder against the jamb, his hands shoved deep in his pockets. His shirt hung open as if he couldn't be bothered with the snaps when he knew it would be coming off, and that strip of shadowed skin left her unaccountably flustered.

She wanted to ask how long he'd been there, how much he'd seen, but it didn't matter. This was what she wanted. Her naked. Dax soon to be. God, he was gorgeous, and she was undone with wanting him, and already his cock bulged behind his fly.

"I'm having a warm and very relaxing bath," she said after finding the words. She stirred the water with her fingertips, creating eddies and tiny lapping waves. She clenched her sex, imagining his tongue. "You're welcome to join me."

"Thought you'd never ask," he said, his voice deep, husky, aching with more than the weary fatigue etched at the corners of his eyes.

And that was the moment she knew she was in trouble. If she didn't set boundaries before they took things further, she'd be unable later to recall the reasons for needing them. She could want to touch him. She could lust to have him touch her, pierce her, slide into her and make her come. But she could not need him. She could never need him. He was only here for her to enjoy and get out of her system for good.

She watched him strip, losing the boots and socks first, then the shirt. His buckle came next, and once he'd unhooked it from his belt, he let both ends dangle around his hands as he unbuttoned his fly. She didn't even pretend to try and hold his gaze. Hers was caught by the movement of his dexterous fingers, by the prize behind the denim as he shucked off his jeans and walked toward her in nothing but tight white briefs.

He stopped, moved his hands to his hips. "Is this tub big enough for two people?"

She pulled her knees to her chest to make room. "It's big enough for three."

That had him frowning. "Have you had three in here?"

"Not yet," she said, and laughing, wrapped her arms around her legs. He was so cute, so completely discombobulated. And who knew so easy to tease?

He looked down at the water, looked back at her, still frowning. "Are you planning to?"

"We'll see." She reached out then, hooked a finger in the leg of his briefs and tugged. "Lose 'em, cowboy."

"Yes, ma'am," he said and rolled them off.

He stepped into the tub then, and being eye level with all that male flesh had her a little giddy and breathless. And as tired as she'd been a half hour ago, now she was wide, wide awake. Awake and wishing they had more hours ahead than her insanely busy schedule for tomorrow allowed. At some point, she really did need to sleep.

Speaking of which . . . "It's the middle of the night, you know."

He leaned back beneath the high faucet, resting his head and arms on the tub's curved lip, stretching out his legs so that his feet brushed her hips. "Nope. It's the first thing in the morning."

"You look like you haven't slept." His body was a work of

art, his limbs long, leanly muscled, dusted with the same golden brown hair that grew in a wedge on his chest. His stomach was flat, his abs defined, as were his pectoral muscles.

His hands, however, were worn—bruised, scratched, a nail or two torn. And his face, his beautiful cheekbones and long lashes and lips that kissed like he could give her the world, was an exhausted mess of dark circles and lines etched deeply at his mouth and eyes.

"I slept," he finally said. "In bed at ten. Up at three. Trip to town in a record-breaking twenty minutes."

She wondered how many of the county's sheriffs would ticket the Campbell black sheep for speeding, how many had grown up with him and would look the other way. "That's not much sleep for the days you're keeping."

"Can't be helped. I promised the guys no more hanky-panky on company time."

That brought a grin. "Is that what I am? Hanky-panky?"

He opened one eye, but that was all. Not another part of his body moved. The water's surface remained still. "Not from way over there, you're not."

And that was her cue. She got to her hands and knees, straddling his legs and crawling onto his lap. Then she realized this water level would never work.

She nudged his hip. "Lift up. You're sitting on the plug."

"You have sex toys in the tub?"

"Just you, cowboy." She nudged him again. "The plug for the drain? The tub's about to overflow. And we're not even moving."

"Got it," he said, and obeyed.

She slid her hand between his thighs, her knuckles brushing against his sac where it hung heavy and warm, then against his ass where she stayed and played while the water surplus swirled around her fingers as it flowed.

Dax gave her a grunt and wiggled. "Careful with the goods there, woman."

"I'm always careful," she said, replacing the plug and lingering, pushing the tip of her finger against his tight hole, laughing and retreating when he twisted away. "And you're way too tense."

"No wonder, you knocking at locked doors down there."

Yesterday, in her kitchen, he'd briefly let her in to play, and she'd remind him of that soon enough, but first . . . "Do we need to revisit the condom issue?"

This time, both eyes opened and his frown returned. "What? It hasn't even been twenty-four hours. I'm not that big of a whore."

"Are you going to be?" she asked, settling on his lap, his cock thrusting upward and caught between them.

"A whore?" When she nodded, his face broke into a wickedly dimpled grin. "If you'll let me."

He was big beneath her, broad and strong, and she ached to learn what he liked, to have him inside of her. To feel his hands and his teeth on her skin. To touch him in ways no other woman had. For as long as it took to work him out of her system, he was hers.

And when she was done, he would never *never* forget her.

She reached up, stroked a hand down his face, feeling the scratch of the stubble he hadn't shaved. "You whore with me, you can ride bareback. You whore elsewhere—"

"Look at me, Arwen," he said, his eyes fierce as he grabbed her wrist. "I'm half dead as it is. Where am I going to find time, not to mention the energy, for anyone but you?"

A flutter of something uncomfortable spread from her chest to her core. She wasn't frightened, but suddenly well aware that she knew nothing of the past sixteen years and what they'd done to him. In her mind, he was the Dax she'd created out of the boy she'd crushed on in school, and fantasies weren't always safe.

"Fine," she said, her gaze moving from his to her wrist and back. "Just making sure we're clear."

"As clear as the rainwater that would make everything about my life as a rancher a whole lot easier," he said, letting her go, awake now and stiff with worry and distracted when she'd wanted him pliant and in this moment with her. "Sorry. I didn't mean . . . I shouldn't have . . . Shit. Coming here probably wasn't the best idea I've ever had."

And that wasn't the best apology she'd ever received, but he'd made it and without prompting. "Why did you come?"

"So I could come," he said, waggling both brows, the water sloshing as he gave a playful thrust of his hips.

All the better that they were on the same page. She wanted him for sex, that was all. Wrapping her arms around his neck, she threaded her fingers into the damp hair at his nape. "You don't need me for that."

"Yeah, but you make it a hell of a lot more fun." Then he reached for the rings in her nipples and used them to tug her against him as he opened his mouth over hers.

SHE TASTED LIKE Arwen. Funny that he knew that about her after nothing but yesterday's kiss. Knew how sweet she was. How warm and wet. How demanding. He probably liked that best of all. He got what he wanted and didn't have to sweet-talk or beg.

Cupping the back of his head with one hand, the head of his cock with the other, she moved up and down as they kissed, a fucking motion that had the rings in her nipples scraping at his. All he could do was sit back and take it. Take it and try not to die.

She pulled her mouth free, kissed his jaw, his cheekbone, his brow, his closed eyes. He allowed her that liberty, too, sitting still, at her mercy. He liked it a lot, letting her have her way. After the kitchen where he'd called the shots, she deserved it. He wasn't selfish as a rule. He'd just been starving.

"You can play along if you want," she said, her thumb stroking a particularly sensitive spot that had his balls drawing close and tight.

He cracked open one eye. "I'm playing the part of the willing victim."

She nipped his earlobe, growled. "That's got to be a new role for a Campbell. Victim."

Uh . . . wow. He'd thought himself too mellow these days to get irritated by a reminder of his roots, but damn if she hadn't just yanked a big one. "Really? We're going to bring families into this? Because I don't think there's a tub big enough—"

"Shh." She pressed an index finger to his lips. "That's all I wanted. Some sign of life."

"This doesn't do it for you?" He caught her hand still stroking his cock and pumped into their joined fists. "It sure seemed to hit all the right spots when I had you up against your kitchen door."

Her finger moved, outlined his lips, pushed between, along his tongue, then withdrew. "It's going to be hard to ever look at that door and not think about you."

He was a professional bullshitter, not easily had. His ego on the other hand . . .

He moved his hands to her ass and eased beneath her, sliding into her when she next lowered her hips. Her head fell back on her shoulders. She closed her eyes. She sat still, impaled, her pulse a rhythmic throb in her throat.

His pulse throbbed elsewhere. It pounded inside her. It pounded in his chest. It pounded in his fingertips where he gouged her skin. He swallowed, waiting, and finally she smiled, a secret sort of sexy grin she caught in the corner with her teeth. Then she looped her arms around his neck, laced her hands, and rode him.

Up, down. Up, down. Grinding in a figure eight against the base of his shaft. Easing away until she barely held him. Teasing him. Making it hard not to give up and let go. *It would be so goddamn easy to let go.*

"I was thinking of you earlier while bathing," she said. "Thinking about this." Up, down. Grinding. "And there you were. My real-life fantasy."

The woman was not playing fair. "You always leave your back door unlocked?"

"Only for you," she said, rocking, taking him deep, withdrawing. "Just for you."

A howl clawed and snarled high in his chest. He wrapped an arm around her back and brought her close, burying his face between her tits and inhaling. She smelled like the water, like fruit and herbs, and his stomach rumbled, wanting things he couldn't name.

He bit at her nipple ring, sucked flesh and silver into his mouth, winced at the metallic burn. His free hand found its way between their bodies, and he toyed with her clit, tweaking, tugging, working her as she squirmed, as tiny, breathy *oh*s and deeper, richer sounds escaped her lips.

He used his fingers, his teeth, and his cock on her, hurting her, soothing her, gauging her reaction, and giving her less or more. Her noises became commands of "Not so much," and "Harder," and "Yes, right there, please."

And this time when she tossed back her head, he knew from the fluttering contractions she was coming. She was beautiful to watch, her parted lips, the tip of her tongue, the flush coloring her skin like summer peaches.

She finished with a shudder that sucked the air from his lungs and he groaned. Only when he was able to breathe again and the vibrations had faded did he pull out of her body. Then he spanked her once. Hard. "On your knees."

She obeyed, sitting back and giving him the room he needed to get to his feet. Cock in his fist, he braced his legs against the tub's sides and nodded.

Her eyes glittered as she took him into her mouth. He looked down, watched her lips, her cheeks, her tits bouncing as she sucked him and tongued him, her fingers using him like she was a singer and he was her mic.

Lust clutched hard, and his legs began to shake. The base of his spine twitched and tingled. His gut caught fire and burned. That was when she reached a hand between his legs, pushing a finger against the ridge behind his balls before sliding it to the rim of his ass.

He slammed a palm against the wall on his left, furrowed the fingers of the other into the rows of her wet hair and grunted like a pig. He felt her smile and he closed his eyes and he didn't even stop her when she pushed deeper into his hole.

Instead, he grit his teeth and let her. Desire wrapped him up and tightened around him, squeezing as she made him forget everything but his cock. Nothing existed but the slick heat of her mouth, her finger in his ass, the fingers of her other hand ringed around his balls.

He was drowning in sex, suffocating, going down. Her lips caught at the ridge of his cock's head, and with each movement of her finger, he clenched against what felt like a threat to his rules against involvement. What was he thinking, letting her in? He did not let women in.

As if he'd voiced his thoughts, she turned her attention to the slit in his cock and the seam beneath, flicking her tongue over his skin until he rose up on his toes. She was too good, and was taking too much, and he wanted to give it to her but not like this. Not like this.

He pulled out of her mouth, twirled a finger. "Hands and knees."

She shot him a look, an arched brow, a quirk at one corner of her mouth, but did as ordered. He followed her down, palmed the flat of her back to hold her and guided his cock between her legs.

Another time he'd go slow. A time when he wasn't feeling so unhinged. Her tub, her house, her invitation but his rules. He didn't care how practiced her mouth, how quick her tongue. He was not letting her in.

He drove into her, holding on to her hips as he thrust. Around them, the water sloshed, splashing at his thighs and her elbows and onto the floor. Each time he hit bottom, she cried out, and he pounded harder, ramming into her, his balls slapping her ass.

Relief was all he wanted. From the worry and the exhaustion. From the crazy aching sense of being turned inside out when he had to keep his head on straight. From the emotions sprouting like weeds to make a mess of a really good thing.

Need built like a bomb in his gut, swelling, pressing, his cock a fuse and Arwen the match. Beneath him, she writhed and twisted, lighting him up.

He stared at the stars through the skylight and burst, spilling inside of her and thinking as he collapsed that he'd just borrowed himself a whole lot more trouble than he had ever caused in Crow Hill.

But at least he hadn't let her in.

SIX

SEVEN O'CLOCK FOUND Dax at the counter in the Blackbird Diner, coffee in hand, corner stool swiveled toward the door, bootheels hooked over the rungs, knees spread. The breakfast rush was swinging, the smells of bacon and chorizo and eggs and hash browns competing with the aroma rising from the four pots of coffee that never saw a break.

The morning chatter clacking at the booths and the tables was as loud as the orders yelled from the kitchen and the squeak of the waitresses shoes on the floor. Black-and-white tiles. Just like those in Arwen's kitchen—a thought he had to shove away or he'd find himself heading back to her house instead of returning to the ranch as promised.

He wasn't exactly proud of how he'd cut out of there, saying nothing as he'd dressed and nothing but good-bye with his exit. He owed her more than that, but first he'd have to nail down what had sent him packing, then figure out how best to apologize for packing at all.

The one thing he did know was that it had to be done—just not today. Because even though he'd dipped into his pool of sleep hours in order to spend time in her tub, he was testing the limits of his partners' patience by staying in town to catch Darcy.

By now, Casper and Boone would've put in a couple hours of hard labor each. Dax had spent those same two hours in the front seat of his truck outside the Hellcat Saloon, napping while he waited for the sun to show its face. Not exactly the legal three-way split of labor, profit, and loss he'd agreed to. And definitely not a great start to the day.

He'd fucked up with Arwen. He was in the process of fucking over his boys, and fucking himself in the process. For all he knew, Darcy would as soon tell him to fuck off as be happy to see him. But he was here, and good or bad, he'd deal with what came his way.

Chest tight, he brought his mug to his mouth and blew across the surface as he scanned the customers a second time. He didn't think he'd missed his sister, but then it had been awhile. Awhile, hell. It had been half her lifetime. He was a first-class dick. He shouldn't have waited this long to look her up.

"Dax Campbell? Is that you?"

Hearing his name, he twisted on his stool. The woman behind the counter wore a snug black polo with the diner's logo embroidered in red above an amazing rack. Her tits were familiar. And he knew her blond hair, was pretty sure he'd seen it spread across a truck seat at some point in the past.

She was about his age, meaning he'd have known her in school, and she had the cutest dimple curled into her right cheek—

"Well, hell." A big fat true-as-true-gets grin spread over his face. "Teri Stokes. How ya been, girl?"

"I've been great." She showed him her left hand. "And it's Teri Gregor now."

"Whew. That's some rock." He held her fingers, let out a whistle, very glad he'd kept his appreciation of her assets to himself. "Mr. Gregor knows how to take care of his woman."

"He most certainly does," she said, withdrawing her hand and topping off Dax's mug from the carafe she held.

Her smile had Dax thinking of Arwen. Taking care of her. Putting a look like that on her face. A ring like that on her finger. A ring on any woman's finger. Nope. Not going there. Not letting any woman in.

He added a heaping spoonful of sugar to the coffee and stirred. "So where's the lucky bastard? I'd love to say hello to the guy."

"At the moment?" Shrugging, she returned the pot to the row of burners behind her. "I'm not really sure. Shane was somewhere in the Middle East last time we talked."

The Middle East? "Shane a military man?"

"A Navy SEAL. Best of the best."

And that would explain why Teri didn't know where he was. Dax sipped, set his mug on the counter to cool. "You running the joint now?"

"I am." She stacked her hands behind her and leaned against the wall, her gaze taking in the customers, the servers, what the pass-through window allowed her to see of the short order cooks at the grill. "Dad still shows up every morning, but mostly to shoot the breeze with the same bunch who've been trying to kill it for years."

That sounded like the Gavin Stokes who Dax remembered. Knowing everything about everyone. Having an opinion about most. Never forgetting a face . . . or a crime.

Tugging down the brim of his hat, he glanced at the clock

above the door. Maybe he had it wrong and he'd have to hook up with Darcy someplace else. Someplace where he wouldn't feel like a wanted poster.

"What're you doing here, Dax?"

"For one thing, my best to lay low," he said, turning back to Teri and his coffee.

"Probably not a bad idea. Though I can't think of a worst place to avoid the gossip mill. And the hat?" She shook her head, calling him out. "Not much of a disguise."

He grinned because she was right. "Actually, I was hoping to catch my sister. Thought she might have breakfast duty seeing as how I hear she's the firm's most junior employee."

Teri huffed. "Not to mention she's the only female."

Yeah. That. "You're acquainted with my father then."

"Is there anyone in Crow Hill who isn't?"

"Dunno, but I'll bet more than a few wish they weren't." He gave a toast with his mug, brought it to his mouth. The door behind him opened to let in a blast of summer-morning furnace. And damn if he didn't find himself missing the Montana cold.

"Dax?"

At the sound of Darcy's voice, he choked, coughing and swallowing as he swiveled and jumped from his stool. He'd barely opened his arms before she was in them, a burst of energy hugging him, her fingers digging troughs in his shoulders and nearly tearing his shirt, her honey-brown hair catching in the stubble of his beard.

"Why do you smell like . . . oranges?" she asked before stepping away and looking up, her big green eyes, shaped so much like his, misty and strangely sad.

He started to ask what was wrong, but didn't get a chance because that was when she slapped him.

"Ow, Darcy." He rubbed at his jaw. "What the hell?"

"That's for not telling me you were back. I had to hear it at lunch yesterday from a friend."

"I've been meaning—"

She raised a hand and sliced him off. "You don't write letters. You don't make calls, send emails. You leave without saying good-bye. You show up without saying hello."

His sister. Arguing her case in the court of hurt and outrage. "Hello."

She punched his arm, then punched him a second time. "Not funny."

He really didn't need her to beat him up. He did a damn good job of that on his own, and Boone and Casper made sure to cover any spots he missed. "You hit me again, I'm going to start taking it personally."

"Oh, Dax," she said, her voice breaking, her frame, already petite, seeming suddenly smaller, swallowed up by a white blouse and navy blue power suit as out of place in Crow Hill as snow. "You are such an ass, letting sixteen years go by."

"I love you, too, Darcy," he said, because she was right and denying it would only make him more of an ass. Besides, his chest didn't have room for the extra pain.

Cradling his face in her palm, she rubbed a thumb over his cheekbone. "You know you look like crap. I expected older, but not . . . crap."

"Hard life out there for a single man," he said with a wink.

Her grin had the circles beneath her eyes going dark blue. "And you are still full of shit."

He didn't even bother to duck her next punch. There was a lot of hurt here needing getting over. What was one more bruise? "Let's get out of here. Do our catching up without an audience."

"Sounds like a plan," she said, nodding. "But let me grab breakfast for the office first."

He bristled. "I'm not going to the office."

"You don't have to," she said, shaking her head. "I'll drop off the food and we can go to the house."

"I'm not going to the house."

"Jesus, Dax. I get that you don't want to see the parents. Sixteen years, remember? No one's there."

"Just so we're clear—"

"Campbell!"

For fuck's sake. What now? Dax turned, saw Henry Lasko waving him down, the burly man's face a shade of red that couldn't be healthy.

"I want a word."

And people in hell want ice water. Henry Lasko, Gavin Stokes. Only two reasons of many that Dax had to stick to the ranch if he was going to make Crow Hill home—though how he was going to fit Arwen into that plan he couldn't say.

"Let's go," he said, taking hold of Darcy's arm.

She shook him off, tugged on the hem of her suit jacket, lifted her chin. "It's okay, Dax. He's talking to me."

SEVEN

MUCH AS HE'D done twenty-four hours earlier, Dax slid to a stop in the ranch yard, his tires raising a cloud of dust, chewing up and spitting out gravel, as he drifted on the hard-packed earth. He was late, again. He'd broken a promise, again. But he was pretty damn sure the news he was bringing with him would get him off with time served.

Seeing Boone at the barn fighting lug nuts on the flatbed, he headed over, frowning at the sight of the right rear tire shredded into a mess of rubber coleslaw. One more chunk of change out of their shallow pockets. Yay. "What the hell happened?"

"Diego. He hit what looked like a piece of old surveying equipment in the Braff pasture."

Huh. "Too bad we never got around to replacing the spare."

But Boone didn't respond, just kept straining against the crowbar, and before Dax could say more, Casper walked out of the barn, leading the bay named Remedy no one else had figured out how to handle. All Casper had to do was give the horse a look.

Much like the look he was giving Dax now. "Thought you said something about seeing Arwen on your own time."

"I did. I've been with Darcy." Dax looked from Casper's tilting bullshit meter to the back of Boone's head. "We, gentlemen, may well be in for more grief than a serious lack of rain."

That was enough to get Boone's attention. He tossed the crowbar toward the toolbox, where it clattered and bounced, and straightened, stretching his arms overhead and cracking his vertebrae. "How so?"

"Seems Tess was in talks with Henry Lasko about leasing him the ranch. She passed on before anything was finalized, but it was all in the works. Henry had hired an attorney to draw up the papers."

"Let me guess." Catching Remedy off guard, Casper cinched his saddle tighter. The horse swung his head around, but thought better of taking a bite of Casper's arm. "Campbell and Associates."

Dax didn't reply. He didn't have to. As often as the two butted heads, his father had been Henry Lasko's attorney—as well as his friend—for years, and Boone and Casper both knew it.

Rolling his head on his shoulders, Boone squinted against the sweat dripping into his eyes. "Guess it was pretty hard on Tess, trying to keep the place going without Dave."

"Leasing meant she could stay in the house." Dax shortcut the details Darcy'd given him during their breakfast reunion in the cab of his truck. And damn if she hadn't been a spitfire, letting Henry know the diner was not the place to talk business. "Selling didn't leave her much in the way of options. She'd have had to leave the ranch and most likely town."

"It doesn't matter what had been in the works. If the lease

papers weren't signed, the will trumps. I'm not a lawyer and I know that," Casper said, stroking Remedy's neck.

Boone leaned against the edge of the flatbed. "That doesn't mean Lasko can't make our lives hell, like cutting off what credit we have left at the feed store. His family's been in Crow Hill since the beginning. They've got a lot of weight to throw around."

"Yeah, well, we don't have to catch it," Dax said. The thought of not sticking around had been marinating since his visit to the diner.

"What's that supposed to mean?" Boone asked.

It was Darcy who'd got him thinking about it. Making a go of the ranch was already going to bust their collective ass. Having a lawyer all up in it would only make things worse—especially with that lawyer being his old man. He, for one, would've been fine never setting foot in Texas again. As long as he could've seen his boys from time to time.

He answered Boone's question with his own. "If you hadn't gotten the call about the inheritance, would you have ever come back to Crow Hill?"

"I've been back, jackass. I make the trip from New Mexico every year at Christmas to see my folks."

Huh. "You see anyone else? Tess and Dave? Josh Lasko? Teri Stokes? Who, by the way, is still hot as hell. And married."

"I come out to see Tess and Dave, but that's about it." Boone shrugged. "I pretty much stick close to the house. Mitchell family holidays mean a lot of home cooking and games of Scrabble with football blaring in the background."

Casper's turn. Dax looked over. "What about you?"

Leaning a shoulder beneath Remedy's withers, Casper nodded. "I got kicked into next year by a couple of bulls, and both times came back here to recuperate since the old place is empty now. Didn't get out much since I was too busy hurting."

Frowning, Dax glanced from one man to the other. "How come I didn't know this?"

"Because you never got in touch to ask," Boone said, fetching the crowbar.

They had him there. He'd driven out of Crow Hill with his father bellowing behind him, his mother on the porch with a highball glass in her hand, his sister away at cheerleading camp and missing all the fun. In cutting his family out of his life, he'd somehow cut out two-thirds of the Dalton Gang as well. That had been just stump-licking dumb.

"I didn't mean for that to happen." He pushed his hat back on his head, mopped his brow in the bend of his elbow, resettled his hat as his words sunk deep. Then he sidestepped the subject on the table. "And it's not like I knew where to find either one of your sorry asses anyway."

"Well, we're all here now," Boone said, slamming the ball of his foot into the stubborn wheel, then a second time for good measure. "And we've got our own legal counsel not tied to Crow Hill. Faith'll shit a brick if we have to get him involved, but we're not floating without a life raft. So thick or thin, I'm staying. I'm ready for a place of my own, even if I have to share it with you two assholes."

Casper swung into his saddle, tugging back on the reins when Remedy started thinking for himself. "Tess leasing the place says to me she wanted us to have it. She'd have sold it to Henry otherwise, taken the cash and split. Dave was gone. She didn't have any reason to stick around. It may look like she made the easy choice, but I'm not sure that's the case. I don't have family to keep me here, but I'm staying. For Tess."

That left Dax holding his third of the Dalton Gang bag. "Shit. I was hoping we could flip this bitch for a quick buck and get out of town before the mob showed up with pitchforks."

With Casper snorting like a pig, Boone said, "We're gonna have to pay for our sins, Dax. No way around it."

Dax thought of Gavin Stokes. Of Henry Lasko. Of his father and Arwen's old man. "Hell on earth?"

"It's Crow Hill. You were expecting something else?" And then Casper gave Remedy his head, the horse's hooves stirring up a choking cloud of dust so thick and brown Dax couldn't see Boone or the flatbed on the other side.

EIGHT

FAMILIES. LORD. WHAT minefields. Arwen should've known better than to bring up the Campbells while in the tub with Dax. With his history? What had she been thinking? Especially with the beginning of their affair so full of promise, Dax open to more than what she gathered he was used to from the women in his bed.

Their sex play had been arousing, the warm water around them relaxing. His taking her against the kitchen door had left her sex drunk and stumbling, but having him naked and hers to explore had introduced her to true intoxication.

Then came her offhand mention of his family and the earthquake shift in Dax's mood, like a switch thrown from make-believe to real life. And real life, when she wasn't looking and least expected it, always got in the way.

She'd been thinking about it since—his leaving the tub, dressing while half wet, saying good-bye but barely—and wondering if he'd disappeared because of her big mouth or because she'd been too bold. Wondering, too, if it had been something else entirely to cause him to withdraw in the middle of everything, as if he had places to go, people to see.

And that's what had bothered her most of all. She'd known from their kitchen encounter that he'd treat her well and be thorough. But even wanting him only for sex, she hadn't expected the sex to be so . . . impersonal. And that contradiction made her want to kick herself. She couldn't have it both ways.

No involvement meant just that, and expecting more couldn't serve any good purpose. Dax Campbell was a man like any other. That's what she had to remember. That all the hours she'd spent dreaming about him in high school would've been better spent acing small business accounting or finding a way to separate her father from his booze.

A loud Hellcat roar erupted in the far corner. The whoops and hollers that followed rose to the rafters. Conversations in the great room ground to a halt, and the background music dropped behind the din. The nightly ritual was crazy wild and not for the faint of heart, but it brought back her regulars and converted first-timers to fans.

It was also what Arwen loved best about the saloon. The uninhibited nature of her Kittens, the spontaneous explosion of energy in the room, the absolute willingness of the customers to play along, clapping their hands, stomping their feet—and for those who arrived during the bar-top routine, waiting to be seated until the dancing was done.

Off to her side, a man took the stool at the end of the bar. "Be right with you," she said, tossing the words over her shoulder as she unlocked the corner closet housing the light and sound system controls. Scanning the labels—"Cotton-Eyed Joe"? ZZ Top? Asleep at the Wheel?—she decided tonight she was in the mood for Charlie Daniels. She queued up the song and the laser show, then locked and shut the door.

As the first fiddled notes of "The Devil Went Down To Georgia" hit the speakers, the Kittens dropped what they were doing and, in a flurry of shrieks and ponytails, hopped onto the bar. Their boots on the polished wood rattled like castanets and pounded like deep bass drums. Red, green, and blue lights swept the room, lighting rapt faces.

Watching the Kittens' feet shuffle and fly, Arwen got back to her customer. "What can I get you?"

"I'll have what they're having."

She grabbed a forgotten longneck before it rolled to the floor, found both her mental and physical footing before glancing Dax's way. Then she berated herself for letting him knock her off balance in the first place. But really, with the way he looked and the intimate things she knew, who could blame her?

His skin showed a long day spent in the sun, and his eyes appeared all the brighter because of it. He was clean—she smelled his soap when she breathed in—and his hair beneath his hat was still damp. The collar of his khaki shirt showed years of washing and fit like he couldn't imagine ever giving it up.

He wasn't the Dax from high school. He was a dangerous man, arrogant and hard and with needs of his own, and that got in the way of her plans. She dug an icy bottle from the stainless steel chest behind her. "You're a sneaky bastard, you know that?"

Dax grinned, an ear-to-ear showing of big bad wolf teeth and black-sheep-don't-give-a-damn. Both courtesy of the family issues she'd brought into the tub.

"Learned to be one early on," he said, taking the beer she handed him. "Only way to avoid running into fathers. Strange, but they forget the fun of being teen boys the minute their daughters turn into teen girls."

She thought of her own father keeping her close. Thought of the times he'd forgotten she was there. "And that surprises you?"

He swallowed, lowered the bottle. "I'm not a father. I can't say."

"Is this the same reason you learned to kiss and run?" she asked, pushing aside the picture of a pink-faced bundle of joy cradled in a cowboy's arms. Pushing aside, too, the tickle in her tummy the picture wrought.

"No," he said, shaking his head. "That was about giving up hanky-panky on company time."

Her fault for thinking she could get him to change his mind. That she'd be worth it. And where in the hell was that coming from? Their relationship—and calling it that was already a stretch—wasn't about his worth or hers. It was about sex. Plain and simple.

"Has that been bothering you?" he asked, his eyes reflecting the colored light show. "Me cutting out?"

Nope. Hadn't bothered her at all. Except for the part where she was at a loss to understand the way it had played out. "Why would it? You had things to do at the ranch. Fences to ride. Shit to shovel. Whatever."

He waited, nursed his beer, his gaze sharp and never leaving hers. Not even when one of the Kittens danced close, her long bare legs and denim shorts begging for notice. Not even when Arwen, perspiration tickling a path between her breasts, reached beneath the bar for the bottle of water she kept close.

"I had to see Darcy," he said as she drank, dropping his gaze and flicking his thumb at his longneck's rim. "But I did you wrong, and it's been bothering me a lot, and I'm sorry. It won't happen again."

She was pretty sure he hadn't been seeing Darcy at five a.m. which was about the time he'd left, but he'd apologized all the same, and she had no reason not to be gracious. "I'm not looking to hog-tie you, Dax. If you don't want to see me, or you think I'm looking for more than a good time, there's no reason for us to be together. And there's never any reason to run. Contrary to what my girls say, I'm really not a witch."

He gave her a wink as he lifted his bottle but said nothing more, letting the music die down, the lights in the dining room come up, the Kittens jump from the bar and get back to their tables. Then all he said was, "This is a hell of a place. I figure you've got to be a little bit witchy to run an outfit this size."

She laughed. "Don't tell me I've managed to impress"—she stopped herself from saying *a Campbell* and quickly substituted—"you."

"Are you kidding?" He nudged his hat up an inch. "Last time I was in here, it smelled like the back end of cows and hard-broken dreams."

Broken dreams and broken hearts and broken lives. All of which she'd scoured with bleach and covered with fresh paint in colors of barn red and brick gold and green tomatoes still on the vine. Very little of the Buck Off Bar remained, and only those who knew where to look would see the past.

She saw it every day. Here and in her house. "There's always some of that in Crow Hill, but I think we smell a little better now."

"Smell better. Look better." He gave a nod and another glance around. "Both the staff and the customers, not to mention the building. But mostly the owner. Big improvement there."

That earned him a smile. "Buck Akers had seen better days before his first birthday. But I'll take it as a compliment. Thank you."

"So what's with the scaled-back *Coyote Ugly* routine?" he asked, gesturing with his longneck to incorporate the great room. "No chugging booze and setting fires?"

"We're more of a family establishment." Though the last hour before closing had been known to get out of hand—which was why seven nights a week, she was the one to lock up. Her invest-ment, her livelihood. She paid with a lack of sleep. "There's only one dance each evening, and the Kittens rotate who starts it."

"Kittens?" he asked, the corners of his eyes crinkling. "Not hellcats?"

Her gaze scanned the saloon, taking in the girls she'd hired. All were from the same small town as she was and close to her in age, but looking at them now, innocent and feisty and button-cute . . . Lord, she felt like a dinosaur. No, a dinosaur fos-sil. In fact, she couldn't remember a day in her life she'd felt like anything but.

She'd certainly never had the luxury of feeling . . . kittenish. "Sorry. I'm the only hellcat here."

"But you don't dance?"

"Are you kidding? I'd be the one to fall and break my neck, and then who'd write the checks for my insurance?"

He nursed his beer, let that settle, turned his stool so he faced her where she stood at the end of the bar. "So what triggers it? The dancing."

"Could be anything. A joke. A birthday celebration." She shrugged, toyed with a coaster. His gaze was compelling, nudging at personal boundaries, searching for more than he had any busi-ness knowing about her. "A rowdy, hands-on customer needing a time-out. Someone drinking from the top shelf."

He considered that, crossed his arms on the bar, and leaned closer still. "Tell me something."

"Okay," she said, her skin heating, the small of her back damp and tight, her nape tingling with unaccountable nerves.

"Why are you still here?"

"Because I'm the boss. And I have to close up at the end of the night."

He shook his head. "I don't mean here. I mean *here*. In Crow Hill. Why didn't you leave?"

Seriously? Did he think everyone who ran into hard times had the luxury of walking out? When he'd split, had he even known what a hard time was? "Because this is my home. Because I had responsibilities."

"That's it?"

She bit down on things she shouldn't say. Private things she told no one. "Because I had the balls to stick out the tough stuff."

His mouth grew grim, his eyes dark and hostile. "You saying I didn't?"

"Are we talking about you now?" And why were they having this conversation at all when she'd told herself who he'd been in the past didn't matter?

"I had to leave," he said, his voice flat, as if even he would no longer buy the snake oil he'd sold at eighteen. "Staying meant adios to having a life of my own. Or at least to the one I wanted."

Poor little rich boy, she thought, but remained silent. He'd been a hell-raiser, a heartbreaker, a self-centered ass, and she'd pined for him anyway, hated that she had. Hated him more for not knowing her feelings much less her name. And, wow. Wasn't she the drama queen, resurrecting crap that had been over and done with years ago?

"Fine. I stayed because leaving wasn't an option." He could interpret that anyway he wanted.

"Your situation was . . . different."

"Why? Because my father hadn't carved out my place in the family business the day I was born?" Then she bit her tongue and looked away because the truth of things stung. She'd bought the very bar where her father had spent most of his time. And Dax knew it.

At least he was kind enough not to challenge her at some Freudian level. All he said was, "I wasn't looking to start something. I was just curious. Figured you'd have wanted to hightail it outta here, leave the bad memories behind."

"Who said they were bad?"

"You grew up in a bar, Arwen," he said, his exasperation evident in the set of his jaw, his tone of voice, his distance.

"With a father who wanted to keep me close."

He bit off a laugh, lifted his beer. "You think that's why he brought you here with him?"

She reached into the bag of excuses she'd used as a child. "That, and he couldn't afford a babysitter."

"Nothing about him being unable to stay sober?"

"If rumor had it right, he had that in common with your father." And there she went again. Dragging his family into the fray.

She shoved her hands into her hair, pressed her palms to her temples. "Look. It's really simple. I stayed because this is where I wanted to be. The opportunity to buy the bar came up and I took it. Crow Hill needed someplace to eat besides the Blackbird Diner. And somewhere to drink that didn't have Buck Akers hands all over it. It's not that big of a deal."

"Are you sure?" he asked, because obviously he wasn't quite done. "I mean, you're using your dad's old booth from the Buck Off Bar for a kitchen table."

A reminder, that's all it was. Of where she'd come from. And where she would never go again. She repeated, "It's not that big of a deal."

He held up both hands. "I believe you."

"Thank you." And could they *please* not go there again? "Now, can I get you another beer? An order of nachos or wings?"

"Nah, I should get going before anybody sees me," he said, tugging down on his hat brim until she couldn't even see his eyes.

"That hat's not fooling anyone, you know."

His mouth twisted into half a grin. "Teri Stokes told me the same thing the other morning."

She stopped with her water bottle halfway to her mouth. "You saw Teri?"

"At the diner."

"What were you doing at the diner?"

"Waiting for Darcy. Thought I told you that."

"You know she's married, right? Teri?"

This time his grin dug dimples into the scruff of his cheeks. "You filling me in or warning me off?"

"Do I need to?"

"I haven't forgotten our agreement."

"Agreement?"

"About me being your whore," he said, and her belly tingled at the memories of him in her tub.

"Good, because I have plans for you."

"Glad to hear it, but they'll have to wait."

And after all that. She pouted her disappointment. The heat of their earlier back and forth had her in the mood to get laid. "You're not coming home with me?"

"No can do. I'm on probation. Can't afford to have my pay docked."

"You get paid?"

"Room and board."

"So if your pay gets docked—"

"I'll be sleeping on a straw mattress, using a saddle for a pillow, and if the horses are in a mood to share, eating oats for breakfast." He held his bottle by the neck, twirled it. "With Remedy calling the shots in the barn, I don't see that happening."

There was something about the picture of Dax Campbell relying on the kindness of horses that broke her heart. For the price of a law degree, he'd have had the world at his feet. What he had instead was a bad reputation and little to show for the past sixteen years.

"My bed's your bed for as long as you need it."

She wasn't even thinking of sex when she made the offer. But the change in their positions . . . it got to her. The nobody and the someone and the jokes life played.

He lifted his head, pushed on the brim of his hat with his longneck, giving her a better look at the weary defeat taking him on. "You're hard on a man, Arwen Poole."

Admitting a weakness—for sleep, for good food, for her—did not make him a weak man. Surely he knew that. "If you come home with me tonight, I'll see that you get a good night's sleep."

"If I come home with you tonight, there won't be any sleeping done. You and I both know that."

"I have a spare room. There's a lock on the door. Go. Now. Set the alarm. Get into bed. You need sleep more than you need . . ."

"My pipes cleaned?"

"Yeah."

He looked at her as if waiting for a punch line, but this was all she had, and so she waited. He could stay, or he could go. He could take her up on her offer and see the truth for himself, or he could leave and always wonder.

"You're sure?"

She nodded. "Door's open. Guest room's off the kitchen to the left. Full bed, navy comforter. You might have to kick Crush off the pillows."

"Crush?"

She gave a sheepish shrug. "He's orange."

"And he likes pillows."

"Pillows, feta cheese, and belly rubs." She circled the end of the bar, spun his stool so he was facing the saloon's front door, then rose up close to his ear, pressing her body to his and inhaling deeply. Her breasts grew heavy, and her nipples tightened, and the desire that spiraled white-hot to her core robbed her of the ability to breathe.

This was all she wanted from him. This feeling. Who he'd been in the past and who he was now didn't matter. And dwelling on either would only get in the way of working him out of her system for good. "This offer expires in the next fifteen seconds. If you're still here when I get back from pouring my guys another round, be prepared to take your clothes off."

NINE

LYING ON HIS back, his hands stacked beneath his head, Dax stared at the ceiling and listened to Arwen's house breathe. Water pipes clinked in the attic. The a/c kicked on and the windows rattled. Boards popped with the change in the temperature, groaning and old. A branch of the live oak throwing cover from the west gave the roof an occasional scrape.

Home noises. Comfortable noises. Noises only a guest would hear.

No strings. She'd let him into her house, trusted him not to rob her blind. Trusted him with her cat. Trusted him when few in Crow Hill ever had, and when he'd done nothing to deserve her investment.

That had kept him up for a while, trying to figure out what she was thinking, but not for long. He was as beat as he kept hearing he looked, and since he couldn't do anything about his workload or genetics, the only thing for it was sleep.

He'd set the alarm for five, and a glance at the digital display had him shutting off the clock before its scheduled buzz. He hated to move. The bed was heaven, but then he'd been sleeping on a bunk that had seen better days and the weight of too many bodies.

On the pillow beside him, Crush stretched and glared, obviously not a fan of four forty-five. Dax reached over and scratched the cat's stomach, his arm going numb from the vibrating purr turning his muscles to mush.

"Gotta go," he whispered, extricating himself slowly from the sheet and the comforter but mostly from the rumbling cat in case it decided to flex its claws. Wearing nothing but his briefs, he stepped across the hall to the bathroom, took care of business, then went back for his clothes.

He got as far as pulling on his jeans before thinking better of dressing the rest of the way. He had a few minutes to spare, and he owed his hostess a proper—though, granted, a quick—thank-you.

It was when he stopped in the open doorway of Arwen's room that he changed his mind. Not about showing his appreciation for the use of the guest quarters, but about saying it with more than his mouth.

Truth be told, her bedroom décor was pretty much a bucket of ice water poured down his pants. The pink and cream and lace made him think of his grandmother. Of pigtails and little girls.

It did not make him think about sex, though once he'd focused on what he'd come for, Arwen's ass in black boy shorts quickly took care of that. She lay on her side, a cotton-candy-colored pillow tucked to her chest.

Her back was bare, her dark hair a tumbled mess around her shoulders, her knees drawn up in the fetal position, her bottom as close to naked as it needed to be for him to forget everything else.

He could slip a finger beneath the fabric of her undies and be inside her before either of them blinked. He could turn her on her back and push into her with his tongue. He could turn her on her stomach and slide his cock deep in her ass.

And yet he found himself wanting to take her to dinner, to go dancing, drinking. To hold her in his arms, her body close to his, and sway to some classic George Strait.

Where that had come from he had no idea, and he didn't care to find out right now. Not when he was hard and thick, his tip already wet, his balls anxious and heavy.

He set the bundle of his boots and shirt on the floor, dropped his hat on top, shucked down his jeans and shorts and stepped out of them. Then he crawled onto the bed and hovered above her, a palm on the mattress at her back.

Still sleeping, she rolled into his arm, the position lifting her top leg to his liking. He pulled aside the crotch of her shorts, his knuckle grazing her heated skin, then rubbed the head of his cock through her folds, spreading both his moisture and hers.

She shuddered, moaned, and he pushed into her, filling her until his sac bumped her ass.

"Good morning," he said, and her eyes fluttered open and her tongue came out to wet her lips. "Just wanted to give you a proper thank-you for the use of the bed."

"I like your idea of proper," she said, still half asleep, the husky raw note in her voice inviting, as was the play of the moonlight through her windows on her skin.

She was curvy and lush and all kinds of ripe, and he enjoyed a whole lot the way she tightened around him, pulling on his cock, keeping him. He planted his other hand on the bed beneath her tits, trapping her as he thrust, withdrew, thrust again.

Then he stayed deep, grinding against her, losing a little of himself he didn't think he'd ever get back. "You should see my collection of improper ones."

"Show me," she said, pulling her knees to her chest, and pushing her bottom toward his groin. "Start with hard and fast."

That he could do, and he only wondered for a moment if she'd picked it because he had to go, or if she wanted to get back to sleep, or if she got off that way best of all. And then the moment was gone and she was twisting her hips—and him, too—doing a mean figure eight with his business.

A match lit deep between his legs, fire eating him up like tinder, burning as he pumped and drove himself home. She grunted each time he hit bottom, and she reached between her legs, using the vee of her fingers to catch at the ridge of his cock with each pass, using her thumb against her clit and writhing.

It was too much, all the noise and the fingering and the way her pussy sucked him in and spit him out. He slammed into her, his balls slapping her, his thighs on fire, his shoulders torched with the strain. He tossed back his head, beat himself against her, his testicles aching, his cock the only thing he knew.

He balanced himself and grabbed her leg, turning her from her side to her back, hooking her knee over his elbow to spread her wide. Then he became the rutting beast she'd asked for, giving her every bit of hard and fast he'd held back in the tub. Held back for years before that because he'd never had a woman ask for it all. And he'd never wanted to let a woman in.

She whimpered, panted, and he knew he was hurting her, but she wouldn't let him ease up or slow down, and her cries echoed in his head, as did her repeated and breathless, "Don't you dare stop."

He didn't. He fucked her until he saw stars, and somewhere in his head he knew she finished, shuddering beneath him in a violent wet rush of contractions. But he was shaking, bucking, his muscles beat all to hell by brutal twelve-hour days.

His strength sapped like a weeping willow, he collapsed on top of her, spurted inside of her, rubbed his face in the silk of her hair where it lay in ribbons on her pillow.

"I'm not usually that improper," he finally found his voice to say. "Seems kinda heathen to rush through something deserving more time."

"Go to work," she told him, rolling away. "I'm sleepy."

"Yes ma'am," he said, though it was twenty minutes before he moved, and even longer until he let himself realize he'd opened up a can of big-time trouble.

TEN

*H*ENRY LASKO'S BEEN *a client of this firm for thirty goddamn years. If he wants a meeting, he gets a meeting. I
don't give a gold-plated fig if you're in the middle of
wiping your ass. You sit down and hear what the man has to say,
or you start walking. Understood?*

It had been an hour since those words had exploded down the
Campbell and Associates hallway, thundering off the walls like a
sonic boom. An hour, and Darcy's head was still spinning. Part
of that was the ringing in her ears, and part was her lack of success at shaking The Campbell's reprimand.

He'd threatened her position. After all the years she'd spent
busting her butt to fill Dax's boots and earn her place in the family firm, The Campbell had threatened her position. And over
Henry Lasko's ridiculous claim to the lease on the Dalton ranch.

But the rest of her headache was due to the fact that she *had*
started walking, and in the last hour she'd perspired through her

panties and her bra, her slip and her hose, her blouse and her suit and her shoes. Not that her condition was much of a surprise.

When she'd passed the First National Bank twenty minutes ago, the marquee had flashed a severe temperature advisory in a big red digital ninety-nine. The longer she walked, the closer the heat would inch to the day's forecasted one hundred and five. Yet here she was, one foot after the other, unable to stomp out the anger driving her toward heatstroke.

On the morning of her Blackbird Diner altercation with Henry Lasko, The Campbell had—unbeknownst to her—been on his way out of town. He'd heard the news of their run-in, of course, having spies and suck-ups like most men of power. But it wasn't until this morning and his storming into the office that she'd been treated to the reality of his disdain. The extent of his disregard. His complete disrespect.

Imagine that—asking a client to make an appointment. Though no doubt it was the embarrassing when and where of the request that was the problem. She'd done so in front of an audience of Henry's peers. And in front of Dax. That, more than anything, had set off The Campbell.

And thanks, Dax, for screwing me over again.

Would've been nice to have the firm's third and more levelheaded—or so she'd thought—attorney stand up for her. But Greg had done nothing except observe the exchange from his office doorway, looking all *GQ*-hot with his shoulder on the jamb and his arms in designer cotton crossed over his impressive chest, his stylish glasses framing his crystal blue eyes.

No, Greg was too busy being the protégé to toss her a life preserver or something else appropriately nautical to keep her from drowning. Drowning, *pfft*. Maybe in her own perspiration. But never in such a display of contempt.

Glancing at the traffic as she approached the corner of Main and First, she moved to her right and ran smack into Josh Lasko as he exited Nathan's Food and Drug, the white pharmacy bag he held ending up crushed between their bodies.

"Oh, gosh, Darcy. I'm sorry." He was slow to set her away, holding her to keep her steady. "Are you all right?"

She was still getting over the earthy clean smell of him, the feel of him. His plaid western shirt starched to a crisp. His hand on her arm squeezing, his thigh nudging her hip. She'd never been this close to him and hadn't realized, or expected, he'd be so solid and hard. So tall with his boots and his hat.

And he'd said *gosh*.

A sweet giddy pleasure rushed over her, then disappeared when she realized how disheveled she must look. *Nice. Real nice. The icing on the cake of the day.* "My fault. I wasn't looking where I was going."

"Well, I wasn't exactly paying attention myself. Just digging for my keys like there's some big hurry in getting back to the store."

That made her smile, calmed her racing pulse. That and his saying *gosh*. "How're you doing, Josh? How's your dad? I saw him the other morning at the Blackbird." The words were out before she could kick her big mouth closed. Everyone in town knew of her altercation with Henry Lasko. "He looked like he was feeling a lot better."

"He's good. He's getting stronger every day." He showed her the bag he held. "Just picking up a refill on his meds. He mentioned that he'd seen you."

Of course he had. Darcy sighed.

Getting into this with Josh was only going to further spike her blood pressure, but . . . her bed. She'd lie in it. "Yeah, I'm sorry about that. I just thought it would be better if he and I talked privately rather than in the middle of the breakfast crowd."

Josh didn't say anything, just continued to worry the bag in his hand. "You going somewhere? Can I give you a lift?"

Bringing up a hand to shade her eyes, she looked beyond Josh and down the street before giving him a sheepish shrug. "Uh, I'm not exactly sure."

He grinned, a slow-moving pull of his mouth as if he had all sorts of time to finish. "And you're walking there?"

What was she going to say? That The Campbell had yelled at her and she'd run away from home? "Stupid, huh."

"I'd never say you were stupid, Darcy. Just that it's not a good idea for anyone to be out in this heat." He nodded toward his truck, parked at the curb. "Why don't you come back to the store, cool off, then we can get you to where you're going?"

"Thanks. That sounds like a plan." She must've been hotter than she'd realized because she didn't think twice about accepting. And she let him place his palm in the small of her back to guide her to his truck that wasn't but six steps away.

For the whole of the six-minute drive, the memory of his touch lingered, the weight of his palm, the imprint of his fingers. She propped her elbow on the door, leaned her chin into her hand, and stared out the window, pretending it wasn't Josh behind the wheel, his legs working the brake and the clutch, his shoulders flexing to shift and to steer.

It had to be the heat, the way her pulse was racing, her skin tingling, her throat tightening around her urge to swallow, her breasts growing heavy, because this wasn't her. Except the heat didn't explain her recent thoughts of Josh out of his Wranglers, and *oh, God, why had she gone there?*

She closed her eyes, a soft moan escaping before she could grab it back, another following when she gave into the remembered feel of his hand.

"You okay?" he asked.

"Fine," she lied. "Just fine."

They reached the end of the short trip, and he parked at the rear of the store, telling her, "Sit right there."

She did, watching as he walked around the cab to open her door. This time she kept a step ahead of him as he ushered her up the steps and into the office. She couldn't have him touch her again. Not today when she was so out of sorts and . . . wilted.

Once inside, she stopped and took in the cramped space and thought about the big room where she worked, the wall of walnut bookshelves, the computer screen that did double duty as a TV. Top of the line equipment. Furniture requiring no assembly. Carpet so thick she spent most of her time out of her shoes.

All that, yet she couldn't keep it together—the paperwork stacked on the floor to be filed, the tumble of books in her knee-hole needing to be shelved. On Josh's desk, there wasn't a pencil out of place or a single sticky note on the edge of his laptop screen.

Was this Henry's influence, Josh holding down his father's fort while the older man recovered? Or was this who Josh was, calm and neat and caring, and she'd just never noticed the way his hands moved, so deft, so engaged?

She sat in a folding chair, twisting her fingers together, wondering when she'd last been cared for. Wondering, as well, if it would take her tripping over a file box and breaking her neck for The Campbell to notice she needed a clerk—if she still had her job after this morning, or even still wanted her job—and that with her caseload, she was too busy to serve as his.

"Sorry about the accommodations." Josh fired up the coffee-maker on the file cabinet in the corner, poured bottled water into the reservoir and lifted two mugs and two individual pouches of ground coffee from the top drawer. "I know it's hot for coffee, but I like the order of it. Water, ground beans, mugs. Nothing I have to think about. It just gets done. And if you want it cold, I have ice."

Fancy machine for a feed store. "Is this where you bring all your dates?"

"Just my lawyers," he said without missing a beat.

Why had she said that? Dates? Seriously? "This is going to be my Waterloo as an attorney, you know."

He turned, frowned. "Why do you say that?"

"My father and your father on one side. My brother and his boys on the other. Then there's you and me, and I'm not sure if we're at odds, or if we're a team, or if we're Switzerland." She inhaled the coffee's comforting aroma. "It feels like some incestuous Hatfield and McCoy standoff."

"Or a Montague and Capulet showdown?"

Darcy's stomach tumbled. That would only work if she and Josh were star-crossed lovers. She looked from her hands in her lap to the fit of his Wranglers . . . his waist, his legs, his back end. Then she took a minute and closed her eyes because the things she was thinking were going to mess up this moment out of time. And oh but she needed this moment out of time.

"I doubt when my dad hired yours to draw up the lease papers he had any idea what was in Tess's will. No one could've anticipated that." Josh switched out cups and coffee pouches, pulled milk from a small fridge, packets of sweetener from the drawer. "Should've seen his face when he heard the ranch was going to the Dalton Gang."

Darcy could imagine. "Good thing he and The Campbell weren't in the same room. Their combined blood pressure would've blown off the roof."

"Did you think it was strange? Dax and the others inheriting?"

"Why? They were the closest thing the Daltons had to kids."

He set a coffee mug in front of her, turned for his own. Then he dropped into his chair and leaned back, propping one boot on the desk's corner, then propping the second and crossing his ankles. "Yeah, but none of the guys were around when Tess and Dave needed them most."

His legs were so, so long. His feet in his boots so big. "I'm not sure."

"How do you mean?"

"Maybe not in the couple's later years, but if I recall correctly, they came close to losing the ranch before the boys began working for them." She tore open a packet of sweetener, poured it into her mug. "The cheap teenage labor probably saved them as much heartache as hard cash, and kept them going as long as they did."

"Yeah, I guess you're right," Josh said, drinking his coffee black.

So the milk and sweetener were for her? How had he known? And why was she still so warm when the air-conditioner was blowing and she hadn't touched her drink? "I hate feeling like I have to choose a side in this war. The Campbell or my brother. I don't get why there's a war at all. The will was clear. The ranch belongs to the boys. It's up to them to revisit the lease."

"You don't have to choose a side. Just do your job. Unless you don't want to do your job."

She lifted her mug, stared into it. "You make it sound so easy."

"Life should be easy."

Was that what it was like to not be a Campbell? To not expect the worst? To not wake up and smell biscuits and dysfunction? To not skip the biscuits completely because picking up breakfast tacos for the office left no time? *Jesus*. She couldn't imagine what tomorrow morning would hold, at home, at work . . .

And whether it was Josh's influence or her own suddenly weak will, she decided she wasn't going to be there for whatever it was.

She needed time to work out what *she* wanted. And she couldn't do that while at The Campbell's beck and call.

She returned her untouched drink to the desk. "I hate to ask—"

"Ask." Josh swung his boots to the floor, sat forward, met her gaze and held it. "Anything, Darcy. Just ask."

And then it hit her. If life was easy, he'd made it so. Things with Josh were simple, clear, cut-and-dried. That left no room for the sort of theatrics her family thrived on. Involving him more than she already had wouldn't be fair. "Would you mind driving me back to the office? I can't go anywhere without my car."

He held her gaze then gave a nod as if coming to a decision. "Can you drive a manual transmission?"

"Sure, why?"

"Why don't you just take my truck? I can use the company truck for now."

"I can't ask you to do that." To be so generous, to continue their involvement.

"You didn't ask. I offered."

"I know, but—"

"I'm guessing your walking has something to do with the will and the lease and the trouble it's causing your family."

"In a nutshell."

"Well, the way I see it, there's no need to see your father again until you decide what you're going to do. And you *should* take your time. No need to rush." He let that sink in then added, "There's never any need to rush."

His gaze held hers until her eyes burned, until her throat swelled, until her chest tightened. She needed to blink, but couldn't look away, could only listen. Could only dream and imagine and wish that she wasn't a Campbell, that he wasn't a Lasko.

He went on, reaching across the desk for her hand and wrapping her fingers in his. "What's the worst he can do? Fire you?

Disown you? Dax got on with his life just fine without Wallace Campbell running it."

She hated Josh thinking she had no mind of her own. And she started to tell him she was the one running her life, *thank you very much*, but stopped because the truth struck her like a two-by-four. Yes, she'd made the decision to become an attorney, but as much as she loved the law, she'd done so because Dax hadn't.

Because her brother leaving had turned the family upside down. Because at sixteen years old, she'd wanted to right it. Giving her father what he wanted was the only way she'd known how. And here she was, thirty-two, sweating through a gorgeous suit that had cost her a fortune by running away from the man she'd worked her whole life to please.

That right there was what it was like to be a Campbell. That right there was what she had to show for her years. She pulled her hand free and pushed to her feet, swiped at her eyes and pretended the moisture was perspiration. No, that it was sweat.

Goddamn improper sweat. "I'm sorry. I probably should've had you ice my coffee. I'm feeling pretty flushed."

Josh was around the desk in seconds, lowering her into her seat as though she were a rare sort of flower. As though she, Darcy Francis Campbell, mattered even without her last name, and certainly without her degree. "Sit. Take off your jacket. I'll get you some ice water."

She shrugged out of the jacket, felt the silk of her blouse peel away from her armpits. Ugh. What she needed was her ice water served in a shower, or in the Olympic-sized pool at home. But that wasn't going to happen. Not today, and probably never again.

Since she'd just decided she didn't live there anymore.

ELEVEN

As ARWEN BRAKED to a stop in front of the Dalton ranch house, parking next to a truck with a magnetic sign for Lasko's on the door, the pans in her floorboard shifted forward and threatened to spill. She bit off a sharp, "Oh, crap," breathing easier once everything had settled.

The jostling sent the smells of barbecue sauce and smoked baby-back ribs and *borracho* beans with jalapeños to fill the cab, reminding her she hadn't eaten since breakfast. Food in front of her all day long, yet she couldn't get away from the business of her business long enough to eat.

Oh, she'd snag a strip of grilled chicken breast when walking through the kitchen, or a carrot before it found itself grated into a salad, a slice of garlic toast hot from the oven because she couldn't resist the buttery smell. But lately she'd been more distracted than usual—a condition she blamed on Dax.

Most specifically, she blamed it on his crawling into her bed the other morning and staying after she'd told him to go. She'd fallen asleep with him wrapped around her, and she'd slept so deeply, so soundly, she'd expected him to be there when her alarm went off. Expected, and been disappointed to find herself alone.

She still hadn't figured out where the disappointment had come from. He'd given her what she wanted: A good fucking. That should've been enough. And it was enough. She knew that. She didn't need to be cuddled. She didn't need his comforting weight, or to be soothed by his breathing beside her.

What she did need was to put her finger on the reason why her plan to work him out of her system wasn't the quick and easy setting one more piece of her past behind her she'd thought it would be. On the one hand, she didn't mind. Sex with Dax . . . Where to begin?

It wasn't even about his body, which he used so well, or about the orgasms he never failed to deliver. Defining what made sex with Dax seem like more than sex was beyond her. And looking too hard for an answer made too much of their physical compatibility when that was all she was interested in.

But that same compatibility had put a kink in her well-laid plans. And that was the part she *did* mind. She'd worked hard to shed where she'd come from. And she didn't want anything—or anyone—to get in the way of where she wanted to go from here.

Then again, she really should lighten up. What she had with Dax wouldn't last forever. Crow Hill was too small for them to go their separate ways, but it was her home, not his. Honestly, she didn't give him more than six months before he ditched Boone and Casper and returned to parts unknown.

Nope, she was done with insecurity and instability. And soon enough she'd be done with the black sheep who'd come back to claim a worthless piece of land—not for a woman he'd looked right through the last time he'd seen her and would forget once he was a mile down the road.

Figuring the kitchen to be at the rear of the two-story ranch house, she ignored the strange twist in her midsection and hopped onto the porch. She pulled off her sunglasses and pulled open the screen door, stopping once she'd taken a step inside. Huh. The kitchen looked abandoned, as if Tess Dalton had been the last person to use it months ago.

The room was cool, though stale and musty; obviously, the window unit rattling above the antique sideboard hadn't been on long. The floor was dull and dusty, the countertops, too. A dish drainer held a plate and a coffee mug, and a faded floral apron lay draped over the lip of the sink.

She swallowed, caught off guard and saddened by the sight, then startled at the sound of an indrawn breath. She wasn't alone. Someone sat at the head of the table, arms crossed on the covering's cracked yellow plastic, face down, hair spread around her shoulders in a honey-brown fan.

Arwen stepped closer, spoke a soft, "Hello?"

The other woman's head came up. It was Darcy Campbell. She'd been sleeping, or crying, or maybe both, and she took several seconds to focus before offering a weak smile.

Weak enough to set off an alarm and urge Arwen forward. "Darcy? Are you okay?"

"I'm fine. I guess I fell asleep." She swept her hands over a face that was pink with the sun and devoid of makeup. "What are you doing here? What time is it?"

"It's almost seven. I brought supper." Arwen gestured with her sunglasses toward the door. "But I'm thinking I'm in the wrong place."

"I know, right? I thought the same thing when I got here. I expected either a sink full of dirty dishes, or a trash can full of beer bottles and bologna rinds." She sat straighter, took in the kitchen. "It's like no one has been here in months."

Arwen's impression exactly. "Are the boys sleeping in their trucks? Or the bunkhouse? And why, when they have this house?"

"I don't know. I was going to find Dax and ask him. But after I plugged in the a/c, I waited to make sure it wasn't going to short out the whole room." She gave a small laugh. "Next thing I know, here you are, and the day's half gone."

The other woman's explanation did little to dispel Arwen's concern. Tossing her sunglasses to the table, she pulled out the chair at a right angle to Darcy and sat down. "Are you the one driving the Lasko truck?"

Darcy gathered her hair away from her face, twisted it, and held it against the back of her head. After several seconds with her eyes closed, she let it go and nodded in answer. "It's a ridiculous soap opera of a story."

No doubt it was also the reason she was alone in a deserted house, perspiration and tears dried in streaks on her face. "I've got time. If you want to tell it."

"Trust me. It's nothing."

Arwen wasn't having it. "It's not nothing if you're out here in one of the Lasko's trucks, sleeping on a kitchen table in a very nice suit that, if you don't mind me saying, has seen better days."

Smiling absently, Darcy smoothed her skirt down her thighs. "I ran into Josh while walking in town. I was going to have him take me back to the office for my car, but he convinced me there was no need to risk seeing The Campbell. That I should just use his truck."

The Campbell? Oh, yes, of course. Wallace Campbell, Esquire. Never mind that Darcy had been walking in town to avoid him. "Is this about your dad and his dad and the lease that never was? Y'all butt heads or something?"

A deep vee appeared between Darcy's eyes. "Seems everyone in town's heard about it by now."

Arwen nodded. "I pour shots for a lot of locals who can't stop talking once they're drunk. I knew weeks before she died that Tess planned to lease the place to Henry."

"Then you probably know about the incident in the Blackbird Diner the other morning."

Nope. That was a new one. "Gossip mill must be running slow, though Dax did tell me he met you there."

"You saw Dax? When?"

"He was at the feed store when I dropped off a lunch order last week. And he was in the saloon a couple of nights ago." She didn't mention that he'd also been in her tub, in her bed. In her. A flush swept through her body, and her voice caught when she asked, "Why?"

"Just a little surprised. He seems to be sticking close to the ranch. He was back almost a week before I found out. I actually heard it at your place from Luck."

Oh, right. The sneaking around. The hat pulled low. The drinking in the dark corner of the bar, ignoring the dinner crowd and the dancing Kittens. Ignoring everyone but her. Then sleeping in her guest room. Waking her up with the prodding tip of his cock before leaving.

She reached for her sunglasses, toyed with the earpieces. "You know how it is when a new guy hits town. Female antennae start twitching."

Darcy gave a soft huff. "With my workload? My antennae

don't pick up much chatter. See above re hearing about Dax from Luck. I don't even remember any buzz when Greg arrived. No one calling for details or fix ups or anything."

"I imagine the interest in the Dalton Gang boys is more about who they were in the past. The girls have definitely been speculating about the new and improved versions." Arwen wondered . . . "You know that leaves Greg wide open."

Darcy didn't even hesitate. "That's not going to happen."

"You're not interested? Really? He's amazingly hot, you know."

"Guess you have to work with him to see beyond the GQ pinup material. Not that there's anything wrong with his being a pinup. He's just not my type."

Arwen thought about Josh Lasko's truck parked outside. "Are you more into . . . Wranglers?"

A slow-to-come smile softened the stress lines on Darcy's face. "Josh is a good friend. That's all."

"Are you sure?" Arwen asked, because she didn't believe it for a second.

Darcy canted her head to the side and gave Arwen a steady look, one brow arched pointedly. "Didn't you say something about food?"

"Oh, crap." Arwen hopped up, dug her keys from her pocket. "I forgot. I brought the boys some barbecue and fixings. Kinda felt sorry for them after hearing how hard they're having it."

"Faith's budget is not making it easy on them, that's for sure. It's gotta be pretty tough finding out the place you've inherited is going to be more work than it's worth."

Arwen settled her sunglasses in place. "Hearing that, I can understand why Tess was going to lease it out. At least the boys can provide most of their own labor."

"I wonder how long they'll stay," Darcy said, echoing Arwen's earlier musings as she got to her feet. "C'mon. I'll help you with the food. Might as well bring it in here."

The screen door opened just then, and she and Darcy both looked up.

The man who stood in silhouette wasn't Dax, that much Arwen knew, and her disappointment was unaccountably heavy.

He wasn't as lean and rangy as Dax, but neither was he as big as she remembered Boone Mitchell being in high school. This one's shoulders were wide, his arms and especially his thighs powerfully muscled. A rodeo cowboy, not one who'd spent the last sixteen years working ranches, and returned to Crow Hill to do the same.

Casper Jayne.

He took off his hat, scraped his hand over the buzz cut of his dark blond hair. "Darcy."

"Hey, Casper." Darcy was the first to move, wrapping her arms around his neck and rising up on her tiptoes to kiss his cheek, smiling. "It's like Christmas came early this year, all of y'all gone so long and all back at the same time."

"Takin' some getting used to on our end, too."

She pulled back, ran her hands down his shoulders, straightening his shirt, mothering. Or sistering, Arwen supposed, watching Darcy tend to the man who was twice her size. "You're looking good. Or at least a lot better than Dax."

"Having seen more of your brother than I care to, I'm not sure that's a compliment." He lifted his gaze from Darcy's, glanced over her head at Arwen. "I'm guessing from the Hellcat Saloon truck outside that you're Arwen Poole."

Yeah, because he wouldn't have remembered her otherwise. She came forward, offered her hand. "I am. We may have passed in the hallway at school a time or two."

He nodded, resettled his hat after letting her go. "Did I hear you say something about food?"

"In the truck." She started toward the door where he was still standing. "You're welcome to help."

He took a step out onto the back porch, held open the screen door, followed her and Darcy down the steps to the truck. The wood creaked ominously beneath the fall of six hurried feet, and dust from what once was the yard rose in clouds to coat their legs.

The state of things got Arwen to wondering if the house had been left alone because the guys couldn't afford the needed repairs, or if there was a deeper sense of respect for Tess and Dave that had them bunking elsewhere—a thought she filed away as they reached the truck.

She handed off the larger, messier pans of beans and barbecue to Casper, loaded Darcy up with potato salad and loaves of Texas toast, and brought up the rear with the hot peach cobbler and wheeled five-gallon cooler of iced tea.

Weighted down with the small feast, the three returned to the kitchen where Arwen arranged the food on the table. Then she grimaced. "I meant to bring disposable plates and utensils. Are there enough dishes here to use?"

"I have no idea," Darcy said, turning to Casper and waiting.

His gaze moved between the two of them before settling on the steaming aluminum pans. "I guess Dax didn't tell you we're staying out in the bunkhouse."

Good grief. Men. "Do we need to load back up and take this over there?"

But Casper was shaking his head. "There's no table. Only a couple of chairs. We do a lot of standing up. Or eating on the porch."

And on the porch would mean in the heat. Sounded like things were worse than she'd thought. "Well, we can take things over there, or I can let down the tailgate and we can use the bed of my truck. Or we can stay here. Your call."

Blowing out a heavy sigh, he pulled off his hat again, tossed it to a counter, then scrubbed both hands down his weary face. "No. It's dumb not to use the house. It's our place, though hard to think of it that way. Or look at this kitchen and not expect to see Tess whipping a wooden spoon almost as fast as any beater I've ever seen."

Arwen stared at the sweat gathering on top of the cobbler pan. She'd only known the Daltons as the couple who'd employed the boys. But Casper's poignant memory . . . Her chest tightened with the realization of what Dax and the others were going through, coming back here when everything they'd known and loved was gone.

"I'll find the dishes," Darcy finally said. "Since they've been sitting awhile they may need to be rinsed."

Yes. Something productive. "I'll help. Casper, maybe you call the others? Tell them chow's on?"

"I can do that." He backed out the door, hat in hand.

Arwen looked over at Darcy as she counted out forks, knives, and spoons. "I'm not sure I ever knew how close the boys were to Tess and Dave."

Darcy nodded. "I think during his senior year, Dax spent more time over here than he did at home. And honestly I can't blame him. Those last few months before graduation were not happy times."

Arwen remembered. None of what went on at the mansion on the hill was happy. She wouldn't have known details, but she did recall returning to school in January after that last Christmas vacation as a senior. The rumblings had darkened the hallways even before the ringing of the first period bell.

Did you hear about Dax Campbell? He's not going to law school. Told his family at Christmas dinner. His father nearly shit a brick. First Campbell male in five generations not to join the family firm. He wants to cowboy. Man, he's cracked.

Puzzle pieces shifted and clicked, and Arwen's tummy tumbled. What a complicated man she'd taken into her bed. What a strong man, standing up to all those expectations, knowing himself and what he'd wanted at an age when it was all she could do to get herself to school for fear her father would forget about her and vanish while she was gone.

She cleared her throat, started loosening the crimped edges of the tops to the pans. "It can't be healthy for them to keep this place as a shrine, or whatever it is they're doing."

"Agreed," Darcy said, closing one drawer, opening another. "I'm going to see if they'll let me pack stuff, do some cleaning. At least get rid of the Daltons' personal things."

"You have time for that with the hours you work?" Arwen asked, knowing Darcy was right. It needed to be done. "You probably put in more time than I do."

The younger woman shrugged, laying the handful of flatware on the table, going back for plates. "My client list is pretty small. Not much going on at the moment."

That totally contradicted what Darcy had just said about her workload, but before Arwen could dig for more, footsteps pounded against the back stairs and porch, the screen door whipped open, and Dax burst into the kitchen as if expecting a fire.

Finding company instead, he looked from one woman to the other, his gaze going from fierce to fiercely protective. "Darcy? Arwen? What the hell's going on?"

"Nice to see you, too," Arwen said, ignoring the prickling sensation at her nape, the tight pull of her breasts and her belly, waving an arm to indicate the spread laid out on the table. "I brought supper."

"Sorry, sorry." He pushed his hat up on his forehead, settled his hands at his hips. "Casper said you were waiting in the kitchen. He didn't say it was about food."

Casper walked through the door then, catching the backhanded swing of Dax's arm to his midsection with a loud, "Oomph." Boone Mitchell followed on his heels, forcing his way past.

"Don't do that again," Dax said to Casper.

"Don't do what? Let you know you've got women waiting for you? Since when?"

Then Casper bullied his way by and headed for the table, leaving Dax looking at Arwen, and Arwen wondering what had gone through his mind to put that look of panic in his eyes.

Wondering, too, why the look of relief that followed felt like a shot to the heart.

TWELVE

NINETY MINUTES LATER and hating to go, Arwen scooted her chair away from the table and stood. She wasn't looking forward to wedging her full-as-a-tick stomach behind the wheel of her truck, but she needed to get back to the saloon for closing. Besides, she doubted any of her supper companions would miss her. Or even notice that she was gone.

Except for Dax. He'd had his eye on her all night.

Sure, he'd exchanged barbs with the boys, argued about grazing and hauling water and all the money they didn't have. And after making sure his sister was okay, he'd teased Darcy about looking like hell and what exactly might be behind her driving Josh Lasko's truck.

But even while gnawing on the ribs, his gaze had held Arwen's, lingering and potent and fiery enough that she couldn't blame the flush of heat raising her blood pressure on the jalapeños. And, oh boy, had body parts heated under his entirely inappropriate scrutiny.

The attention of the others, however . . .

Having shed her suit jacket, shoes, and pantyhose, Darcy stood at the sink washing dishes, muttering to herself in some sort of rejuvenated sense of purpose that Arwen was happy to see. Even lacking experience with a traditional family unit, she could empathize with Darcy's frustration at having her father dismiss her input, her feelings. Her.

Casper and Boone had the look of men in food comas, eyes closed, boots propped on empty chairs, hands laced on top of bellies filled to bursting. Arwen thought Casper might even be snoring, while Boone chewed on a piece of hay in lieu of a toothpick. No idea where he'd found it because he hadn't moved since sitting down.

The pans of food, though not emptied, had been nicely dented, and that had her smiling. She hadn't done the cooking, but she'd provided a much needed and appreciated meal, and there were enough leftovers to feed the boys a second time.

She would've provided more if she'd had any clue about the ranch's capacity for food storage. Then again, she did need to watch the bottom line, because as often as she was accused of running a charity by the girls she hired, she really wasn't. She just found it hard to say no to someone in need.

"C'mon." Dax broke into her reverie, hands on his thighs as he pushed to his feet. "I'll walk you out." Boone, Casper, and Darcy all chimed in with their waved good-byes and thank-yous.

"Bye, y'all," she said to the others, then to Dax, "You don't have to do that," though she did stop halfway to the door to wait for him, to watch the roll of his hips as his long legs covered the distance, to remember what he felt like inside her and to die a little bit with wanting him. "I think I can find where I parked."

"Funny girl," he said with a wink, his hand on the small of her back guiding her onto the porch and down the stairs and across the hard-packed yard.

She let him. Let him lead her, let him touch her, let him take charge of getting her to where she needed to be. Silly, when it was a short walk and she had plenty of steam. But something about this particular Dax Campbell made her want to lean—a something intensified by his near panic ninety minutes ago upon arriving in the kitchen to find her.

And that just wouldn't do. Leaning was only a few short steps from depending, and losing oneself wasn't far behind. She knew that. Had watched those emotions destroy her father. Even so, when they reached her truck and Dax held out his hand and said, "Keys," she handed them to him like a mindless Stepford wife.

He opened her door, but before she could do more than put a foot on the running board, he grabbed her arm and turned her to him, stepping into the vee of open space, blocking her, crowding her, moving in to breathe deeply of her hair.

"Mmm," he murmured, kissing her temple. "You always smell so good."

Suppressing a shiver, she brought up her hands between them, thinking to nudge him away and find her control, but flexing her fingers into the muscles of his chest instead. "Right now I smell like barbecue."

"And oranges. Or lemons. Something fruity and cool."

Her bath beads. "And I'll bet when you got out of my tub, you smelled the same way."

He chuckled, the thrum of the sound like the stroke of his tongue against her skin. "That's what Darcy meant when she said I smelled like oranges."

Now that was funny. "Did you tell her why?"

"I didn't know why." He stepped back, looked down at her, his gaze flaring.

She cast a glance toward the house, her heart racing, her blood rushing like lava beneath the surface of her skin. She couldn't afford the things he was making her feel. She couldn't. She just couldn't. "I imagine she's figured it out by now."

He fingered a thick, silky lock of her hair, watched it spread over his fingers, frowning as it caught on a nick of callused skin. "That was a nice thing to do. Bringing the food."

She shrugged. She had to regain her footing before falling further. "Just making sure you keep up your energy."

"Why's that?" he asked, but she could tell he was elsewhere.

She decided to bring him back, to remind herself, too, of where they stood. "Because of you being my whore."

"Oh, right." He still wasn't looking at her, was still lost in her hair.

Lord, what had she gotten herself into? "You say, 'Oh, right,' like it's no big deal."

He moved in again, nuzzled his nose to her neck, nudged up into her hairline, nipped at her earlobe, and blew over the dampness he'd left till she groaned. "Is it? A big deal?"

It was going to be if she didn't push him away because, oh, he melted her. She was weak in his presence, spineless when he was near, and she arched her neck, her sex damp and tingling, and because of all that, her voice was harsh when she found it. "Of course it's a big deal. What kind of question is that?"

He stopped, straightened, gave her the space she wanted, she didn't want, she wanted. "I don't know, Arwen. I thought we were playing here."

She held his gaze, a shift of emotions knocking at her center, and asked, "Here? As in here and now, this moment? Or here, as in you and I hooking up?"

He huffed, shook his head, looked down at the ground then looked back, his eyes darker now, the glint of flirtation pinched out. "Is this like the movie where Julia Roberts didn't want to kiss Richard Gere? You and I can do the nasty, but I can't tease you about it?"

"You've seen *Pretty Woman*?"

"Show me a guy who hasn't, and I'll show you a guy who never figured out how to use a movie to get in a girl's pants."

"No, this isn't like that." First of all, because she wasn't a hooker, but more importantly, because falling in love meant losing everything else in her life that was important.

"Then what's it like?" he asked, pulling off his hat, plowing rows through his hair with his fingers before settling his hat back in place. "And, yes, I want to know, and I'm listening, because I'm sorry. I really can't figure out what we're doing."

Simple. "We're having sex."

"That's it?"

"Do you want more?" They had to resolve this now. She couldn't deal with revisiting it every time they touched.

He rubbed at his eyes, his frustration as obvious as hers. "No, it's just—"

"Good, because I don't either." There. Black and white. As clear as it could possibly be. "I've got a business that takes up all of my time. It provides my living, so it has to be my priority."

He crossed his arms, leaned against her open door. "We can play without getting serious, you know. And I think with our schedules we could both use the distraction. At least I could."

"Then you'd better define what you mean by *play*. Just so I'm clear." And why wouldn't he drop it? Why was he making this so hard?

"Shit. I don't know. Dinner. Dancing. A movie. I can't remember the last time I saw a movie in a theater. Hell, I can't remember the last time I saw a movie on DVD. Or the last time I took a date to see one."

She held his gaze as she hopped into the truck's cab, thinking she could put an end to this by driving away, realizing too late he still had her keys. "You don't have to wine and dine me to get in my pants."

He stared at his feet, kicked the toe of his boot at the dirt, brought his head up and looked at her from beneath the brim of his hat. "What if I *want* to wine and dine you? Show you a good time?"

She took in the sun-darkened skin in the hollow of his throat, the scruff covering his chin and his cheeks, the deep-set grooves at the corners of his eyes. Then she took in his earnestness, his vulnerability.

The last thing she wanted to do was hurt him. "Trust me. You've been showing me a very good time."

"But it's not all about you," he said, still holding her gaze, his own searching, probing. Daring.

His words took her aback, sending an uncomfortable shiver down her spine. "You're not having fun?"

"Hell, yeah, I'm having fun."

But . . . He didn't elaborate, even after she waited, so she asked, "Do you want to watch a movie?"

After several tense seconds, he nodded. "I think I do. And I want popcorn."

"Popcorn. Okay." She took a deep breath, draping an arm on the steering wheel. "What kind of movies do you like?"

"Movies that don't star Julia Roberts. No chick flicks or romantic comedies or sick girls who die. What was that one? *Steel Magnolias*? I can't even tell you how many times I walked in on my mother bawling at that one."

She laughed. "She's done suspense, you know. And psychological thrillers."

"Really?"

"*Erin Brockovich? Sleeping with the Enemy?*"

Dax shook his head. "How about some Quentin Tarantino?"

"No gratuitous blood and guts."

"Fine. You pick the movie. Just make sure there's no Julia Roberts."

Oh, please. "No Julia. No blood and guts."

"Is this what they call a compromise? Because I'd heard it was a great way to deal with women," he said, and then smiled when she rolled her eyes, his expression full of good times and bad times and really bad good times.

For an extra long moment she remained speechless, her body sizzling, her sex needy. She looked up at him then, nodding, hoping she wasn't making a huge mistake by taking this leap of faith. It frightened her to think that she was. Frightened her to think she'd have to call this off if she was.

She didn't want to call this off, and that frightened her most of all. "I need to go."

"Okay."

"I'll see you soon?"

"Yeah," he said, scrubbing at his jaw. "Though we're going to have to figure out how to manage popcorn and a movie with our schedules."

Was he second-guessing this date thing already? "Sunday nights are pretty slow. I can't take off the whole night, but if you come over once you're done for the day, I can go into work for close."

"Control freak?"

"I'm my own business manager. If that makes me a control freak, I cop to it gladly."

The look he gave her was equal parts heartbreak and exhaustion. "Maybe you could come over here and manage the ranch, turn it around like you did the Buck Off Bar."

"I thought Faith was managing things for you."

"Faith is pinching our pennies. We're on our own after that."

She'd listened to their dinner conversation, heard more frustration than joy or pride. "Just the three of you? Doing it all?"

He shook his head. "We've got Diego Cruz and his brother-in-law part time. Besides Boone and I know what we're doing. We've been ranching all our lives."

"Just not in Crow Hill." Where the sun baked the land and the men who worked it, and dried up hopes and dreams along with creek beds and all things green.

As if reading her mind, Dax sighed. "Just not in Crow Hill. But we listened for years to Dave Dalton telling us how things should be done. That may not seem like much, looking at this place now, but he was a rancher to the bone."

He looked around, shaking his head as he took in the view. "I don't know what happened here, but I'm gonna blame bad luck and Mother Nature. No one can wrangle either one worth a shit, and more often than not, they plot and plan and gang up on a man." He focused his gaze on something in the distance, if not all the way in the past. "It's a tough life. But it's the only one worth living."

Unaccountably moved, she cleared her throat and lifted her hand to his cheek. "You surprise me, Dax Campbell. You're a lot deeper than you let on."

He waggled both brows. "Does that mean we can go steady?"

"It means you get your date."

"What if I want another?"

Too much, too soon. "We'll see."

"We make time for one, we can make time again."

She took a different tack. "And what are we going to do? Because I can't think of anything that won't require leaving town."

"Ah, I'm the man," he said jabbing an index finger into his chest. "You leave the date planning to me."

Oh, good Lord. "That sounds awfully male chauvinist."

"Just taking the bull by the horns, baby. Taking the bull by the horns."

THIRTEEN

"THAT DIDN'T LOOK like a host just walking a guest to her car."

Still thinking over his conversation with Arwen, Dax wasn't exactly ready to get into anything with his sister. He dropped a kiss on Darcy's head where she stood at the back door, and returned to the table to graze. "What, not only are you the lawyer I was supposed to be, you're a spy, too?"

"I'm nosy."

"Same thing."

"If I were a spy, I'd be reporting on you to the parents," she said, following him across the kitchen and wrapping her hands around the top rung of a chair.

He sat, and his jaw grew taut. "Do they want you to?"

"Mom's hinted at it but won't come right out and ask. Just wonders if there's any news from town. And The Campbell just guzzles his Glenlivet and snores."

The Campbell. That always made him laugh, Darcy taking their Scottish heritage so seriously here in the middle of the wild wild west. He was surprised she hadn't had them all wearing kilts instead of jeans and spurs.

"I'm still waiting."

"For what?" Gnawing on the end of a rib, he gave her a lazy glance.

She circled the table, turning the chair next to him sideways to sit. "What's going on with you and Arwen?"

"I don't know." He shrugged, continued to gnaw.

"But you're sleeping together."

He nodded. "Kinda came out of nowhere."

"I knew it," she said, punching his shoulder and laughing. "Bet Mom would have a coronary if she found out."

That drew a snort. There was some really bad joke here about dipping his wick in the wrong Poole, but he was too tired to make it. "No reason for her to."

"Is your affair a big secret?"

Good question. Better question. Was it an affair? Or just wick dipping?

It had been like pulling teeth to get Arwen to agree to a date. And why the hell was he insisting on buying the cow when he was getting the milk for free?

He reached for another rib, thinking not for the first time that he was off his game. He couldn't decide if it was the years away or the coming back to blame. "The boys know. Now you know. Can't think of a reason anyone else needs to."

"Do you like her?"

He gave Darcy a side-eyed frown. "What the hell's that supposed to mean? I hope I like her. I get naked with her."

His sister rolled her eyes. "Yes, she's hot. Even I can see she's hot. Every guy in town knows she's hot. I doubt many wouldn't like to get naked with her. But getting naked with someone and liking that someone are not mutually exclusive, as I'm sure you learned during the Dalton Gang's younger years."

"What do you mean, every guy in town knows she's hot?" And then he remembered Bubba Taylor and his crew eyeballing Arwen at Lasko's. A memory that had him feeling mean.

"You're not really that dense, are you? Or wait." Darcy leaned closer, her eyes wide as she studied his face. "Are you jealous?"

He shooed her away. "No, I'm not jealous. I'm in her bed. They're not. Why should I be?"

"Because they want to be there?"

"Wait," he said, changing the subject. "What did you say about our younger years?"

"That you three boinked like indiscriminate bunnies."

"Huh." And then he went silent because there wasn't much to say. She was right. He and Boone and Casper had made a lot of bets while doing a lot of drinking, and bedding the girls they put on their lists didn't have much to do with liking them.

He'd been a hell of a jerk. He hadn't been alone in it, but that didn't relieve him of the responsibility of owning up to it. Which he supposed he'd be doing on a regular basis—whether he liked it or not—if he didn't keep his hat brim pulled low.

He tossed his last rib bone back in the pan, licked his fingers, and wiped them clean on his thighs, then rubbed his gut that was overstuffed and aching. "I guess we should get this trash out of here."

But Darcy ignored him, picking at loose cotton threads puffing out of a crack in the tablecloth. "What are you going to do with the house?"

"What do you mean?"

"Casper said y'all haven't felt right being in here. That it feels too much like trespassing."

He let that settle, looking from his sister to the sideboard and Tess's collection of salt and pepper shakers covering the surface. He knew if he opened the top drawer, he'd find the expensive silverware she'd never used but polished every other Saturday.

If he opened the door on the left, he'd find clipped recipes she kept meaning to try filed in big black binders. One for cookies, one for cakes, another for pies because she knew he and Boone and Casper all had a thing for desserts. But she'd kept baking their favorites instead, and that had been just fine with them.

The door on the right was where Dave had stored the bottles of Jack Daniel's and Jose Cuervo he rarely had occasion to use, so he never noticed how watered down the booze had become over time. Dax leaned an elbow on the table, rubbed at his jaw. He wasn't sure it was trespassing keeping them out of the house as much as missing what they'd never known they had.

They certainly knew it now.

"Do you want help going through the Daltons' things?" Darcy asked, nudging him back to today. "I'm happy to do it. Nora Stokes might take some of the furniture on consignment. I'm pretty sure several pieces are antiques."

Nope. "We're not selling the furniture."

"Okay. What about their personal effects?

He sat back, scrubbed both hands through his hair. "I don't want to talk about this, Darcy. Not right now."

"I get that, Dax, but I'm in a bind."

"How so?"

"Because I really need a place to stay. I thought if it wouldn't be a problem, I could use the house for a while, maybe help y'all sort through things, make the house yours so you'd be comfortable here. The bunkhouse is a wreck."

"It's worse than that," he said, before his mind kicked back to something else. "Wait. Why do you need a place to stay? The folks boot you out for consorting with the enemy?"

"Not exactly," she said, looking away, her mouth twisting.

Now this was interesting. "You crossed the big man?"

She leaned forward, her arms on her thighs as she worried one of her nails. "Remember the other morning with Henry Lasko? When I asked him to come to the office to talk to me?" Dax nodded and Darcy went on. "The Campbell heard about it and gave me my walking papers."

What the hell? "He fired you? Over that?"

"Not really. Not yet. But he threatened to." She looked up, shrugged. "And so I walked."

"Darcy, shit."

"Yeah. Shit.

"So, what? Are you done there? What are you going to do?"

"I don't know. I'm sure I could go back. But . . ."

Ah, the elephant in the room. Or in this case, in clan Campbell. "You don't want to go back. You're there because I'm not."

"Someone in the family has to take over the family firm."

He didn't think it was possible to dislike his father more than he did, but the old man screwing over Darcy had Dax's blood pressure rising. "What about his partner? I heard he has a new hotshot in the office."

Darcy shrugged, looked down, went back to picking at the crack in the time-and-sun-dried tablecloth. "Greg's not a partner, though not for lack of putting in the hours. Odds are he'll be The Campbell's choice, even though I'm family and he's not. For one thing, I'm a woman. For another—"

"You're not me."

"Sad, but true."

"Hey, now. It's not so bad being me."

Darcy's only response to that was an arched brow.

"C'mon. Give your worn-out brother a break." When she still said nothing, he added, "I hear I look really good in jeans."

"Jesus, Dax," she said, punching him again. "Bad enough I have to hear that crap from other women."

"Yeah?" He rubbed at his shoulder. "Women talk about me?"

"You've got Arwen. What does it matter?"

"Just keeping my options open," he said, the words choking him like a big fat lie.

"You're a pig. Look what she did for you." She waved her hand over the spread of leftovers needing to be stored in the fridge. "She sure didn't bring all this out here for me or the boys."

Which reminded him. "Why are you driving Josh Lasko's truck?"

"My car's at the office. I wasn't in the mood to go back."

"Hmm. So, you're out a job, out a vehicle, and out a place to live." He reached for her hand, lifted her arm into the air. "Ding, ding. We have a winner. At least I have a piece-of-shit ranch to my name."

Growling, she jerked her arm away. "Like I said. You're a pig."

God, he had missed this girl. Missed her sassy mouth. Missed her way-too-solid punches. Missed her growing up. And that was a shame he'd be a long time getting over. "Is that any way to talk to the brother you've just asked to get you out of a jam?"

"Does that mean I can stay?"

He feigned a careless shrug. "I guess it can't hurt."

"Seriously?"

"As long as the boys don't object." He raised both palms, staving her off before she landed in his lap. "But don't touch anything. Not until I check with them."

And then he hooked a boot around the leg of the table, bracing himself as she launched into his arms.

"You're the best, Dax. The absolute best."

Yeah, the best at abandoning a sixteen-year-old girl to fend for herself in a family where selfishness seemed to be the one Campbell trait he'd embraced. "Not a pig? Not an ass?"

"Not today," she said, taking his face in one hand, squeezing as she dropped a kiss to his cheek, then exhaling and letting him bear her weight as if she'd been waiting for sixteen years for someone to lean on.

At that moment she could've called him any part of any animal's anatomy and he would've felt like a king.

FOURTEEN

ARMS CROSSED ON the corral's top rail, one boot braced on the bottom, Dax looked out at the wide-open spaces and watched the shadows shift with the setting sun. The last of the rays cut across the prairie, doing their best to convince him there were greens and yellows out there when all he saw was brown.

He wasn't that easily fooled. The light was a trick, playing with his imagination, making him remember what this place had looked like before Mother Nature had fucked the Daltons, leaving them with little more than a penny to their name. Now it was his penny, his name, Casper's, Boone's.

They were broke as old horses, poorer than dirt, strapped like beggars needing pencils. But hey, they owned a ranch. Acres and acres of fenced land, horses and cows, a flatbed truck and a tractor, a bunkhouse and a barn. Both of those could use tearing down and rebuilding. And a whole lot of the fencing wire was hanging on creosote posts approaching the end of their days. Then there was the big rambling house they'd left sitting empty since settling in.

Nothing about this homecoming was turning out like he'd expected. Not that he'd thought he'd come back to a ticker-tape parade, but neither had he expected . . . brown. From where he stood, things were looking pretty well screwed. For him, for Darcy. For the boys. Arwen was about the only one who seemed to have it together, and that in itself was fucked up.

Casper's upbringing had been a dismal mess of alcohol and abuse, but compared to Arwen's home life, it was almost as good as Dax spending his childhood in the mansion on the hill. Now here she was, a business owner like him, hers thriving in a town that wasn't, his waiting for the right time to draw its last breath.

The fact that he'd gone running like Remedy stung by Casper's spurs when he'd heard she needed him in the kitchen was still giving him hell. Running for Darcy was one thing. She was blood, true family.

Arwen wasn't. The sweetest piece of ass he'd had the pleasure to know, yeah, but that was it. Except that didn't explain his asking her for a date, if the roundabout way he'd gotten there could count as asking. And dating was just one step away from letting her in, so yeah. Whatever he was doing, he needed to stop. He could fuck her, lose his troubles while he did, but he could not lose his head.

"Nice of Arwen to bring the food," Boone said, stepping up beside him, draping his arms over the railing, a longneck dangling from one hand.

"Wouldn't happen to have an extra, would you?" The words were barely out of his mouth before Boone handed over the bottle he'd shoved into his jeans pocket, taking Dax's mind off his worries as beer usually did. "Thanks. And, yeah. She's a good one."

"You two working on getting out of the bedroom?"

Dax didn't answer. He didn't know what he and Arwen were working on, and that bothered him more than was smart. "Darcy asked if she could stay here awhile."

"Yeah?" Boone brought the beer to his mouth, drank deeply, gestured with the bottle. "She still living in the big house?"

"Still there, though not feeling the love," Dax said, twisting the cap from his. "Guess she and the old man got into it over Henry Lasko."

"He can't think his claim's got any teeth. Lasko or your old man."

Dax shrugged. "All I know is she got chewed out for blowing off Henry at the Blackbird the other morning."

"Tough break." Boone was silent for a minute. "You talk to Casper about the house? Darcy using it?"

"Not yet. Just came up after supper." And Casper had left not long after for parts unknown.

Boone looked down, kicked at the corral's bottom rung. "Where's she now?"

"Cleaning up, I think."

"Taking her time about it considering we finished eating a while ago."

A prickle of possessiveness had Dax bristling. "Like I said. She doesn't want to go home."

"What's she doing with Lasko's truck?"

"She needed a set of wheels. Josh told her to take it."

Boone nodded, didn't press. "So what did you tell her? About staying?"

"I gave her the okay, but say the word and I'll lock the place and send her back to town." He took a long pull on his brew then added, "She wants to clean up, go through Tess's and Dave's things."

"Huh. Better her than me, I guess. It needs to be done."

"I've been thinking the same. Thinking I'd really like to sleep on something that felt like a bed."

"I can't see Casper minding. Might as well let her have at it. As long as she doesn't toss anything without running it by one of us first."

"Fair enough." He drank again, got back to looking at the wide-open spaces, the shifting shadows, the setting sun. "Fair enough."

"Hard to see things this bad. Can't imagine how it must've tore at Tess to even consider leasing the place."

"I told Arwen earlier we needed some of her magic, the way she turned around Buck Akers old bar. Be nice to do the same here. Make Tess and Dave proud."

"As long as we put in the work, I don't think they'd hold it against us if things go south."

"We're almost to Mexico already. Not a lot of room left to travel."

"I hear that, man." Boone finished his beer and stepped back. "Think I'll see about that cobbler. If Darcy'll let me in the kitchen."

"Good luck with that," Dax said, picturing his sister standing up to Boone. Picturing his sister giving in to Boone. Picturing his sister alone with Boone . . . "Though cobbler does sound good. Think I'll join you."

FIFTEEN

"LET ME ASK you something." Arwen picked a grape tomato from her salad and popped it into her mouth, trying to gather the flurry of thoughts confusing her.

It was Sunday evening. Six o'clock. Four days since she'd taken the food to the ranch, and she hadn't seen Dax since. Two hours from now he'd be at her house for their movie date, and her anxiety had reached epic proportions.

Every self-preservation instinct she'd honed over the years told her she was insane for bringing him into her life. Yet her body had hummed with her need for him all day, already anticipating the movie's end and the yummy sex to follow.

Across from her, Faith Mitchell dragged a French fry wedge through a pool of ketchup, ate it, then another, before saying, "Shoot."

Taking in the amount of food on her companion's plate, Arwen asked, "How do you eat like you do and manage to look like you do?"

Faith reached for her Coke. Not Diet Coke. Not Coke Zero. Straight up Coca-Cola Coke. Bubbles fizzed around the crushed ice as she drank and returned the glass to the table. "That's what you wanted to ask me? About food?"

Everly Grant, the third of the group of girlfriends who'd managed to coordinate schedules for dinner, laughed. "It may not be what she wants to know, but I sure do. You eat more than most men I've had the dubious pleasure to dine with."

"Metabolism, and haven't we had this conversation before? I can't do anything about it, and I'd gift it to every woman if I could, but I can't. Don't hate me because of my genes." Finished with Everly, Faith gave the other woman a wink before turning back to Arwen. "Your turn. But I'll be eating while you ask."

Smiling at that, Arwen poked her fork into the bed of spring greens that she wasn't the least bit hungry for. "Why do you stay in Crow Hill?"

"Because I live here. I work here."

An echo of what she'd told Dax, so she understood the sentiment, but her situation growing up had been so disparate from Faith's it was hard to reconcile any similarity between their decisions to call the small town home. "But why did you come back after getting your degree? Why didn't you stay in Austin?"

"My family's still here. I started at the bank, and I liked the work, and I love the people. I mean, I loved Austin when I was there, but a girl can only party for so long before the need for sleep catches up with her." Another French fry. Another long swallow of Coke. "Why? Are you second-guessing making your life here? Because what you have done with the saloon is amazing. You should never second-guess this type of success."

"She's right." Everly gave a nod toward Faith, pushing away her own plate and half-eaten club sandwich. "But then she usually is, which makes it a whole lot easier for me to run instead of staying to argue the same points."

"You're leaving?" Faith asked. "What, you've got a Sunday night editing emergency?"

"Very funny." Everly got to her feet, straightened the white tuxedo shirt she wore under a man's black vest and over a pair of skinny jeans, then retrieved her bag from where it hung on the back of the chair. "Seems this week's edition can't be put to bed without a letter to the editor from Patricia Campbell. I've got an appointment at the mansion on the hill since she can't be arsed to actually write it."

At the mention of Dax's mother, Arwen felt the hair at her nape sizzle. "What's going on with her?"

"Oh, something about emphasizing abstinence in what serves as Crow Hill's school district's sex education curriculum." A roll of Everly's eyes covered her opinion on the effectiveness of that. "Anyhow, I'll see y'all next week? For lunch?"

"Sounds good," Faith said, and Arwen returned Everly's wave, watching the other woman wind her way through the saloon's great room toward the swinging front doors. When Luck Summerlin crossed Arwen's field of vision, she motioned her over.

"What's up?" Luck leaned across the table, stacking the empty plates and gathering up utensils and napkins and Everly's water glass.

"I'm getting ready to leave, but I'll be back at midnight. You've got my cell number if you need me. I can be here in two minutes if you do."

"Sure thing, but it's First Baptist's potluck night, so we'll be lucky to do half our regular late supper business."

Not that Arwen liked the loss of income, but a lighter crowd did make her feel better about leaving Luck in charge. "All right. Just give me a call if anything comes up."

"Will do, but we'll be fine. Enjoy your night." Luck hefted up the dishes, looked at Faith. "A refill on your Coke?"

Faith nodded. "That would be great."

"Okay then. Right back with it. And another iced tea for the boss."

"Thanks," Arwen said, feeling the heat of Faith's gaze but waiting until Luck was out of earshot to ask, "What?"

"You're asking me about staying in Crow Hill. You've hardly touched your food. And now you're taking off work for at least part of an evening." She paused as if waiting for Arwen to do the math then asked, "What's going on?"

Arwen weighed how much she wanted to confess to Boone Mitchell's sister. "I've got a date."

Faith blinked, and blinked again. "You? A date?"

She didn't have to make it sound like the end of the world. "Popcorn and a movie at my house. No big deal. I need to get back here to close up so can't go far."

"You're worse about work than I am, you know."

"It's possible."

"You need an assistant manager. Luck would be a good one."

"Maybe."

"No maybe. Do it. Your schedule's as bad as mine, and mine drives me insane."

"We'll see."

And then Faith finally asked the question Arwen had been waiting for. "Who's taking you out? Or I guess that would be taking you in?"

"Dax Campbell," Arwen said, stirring sweetener into the glass of iced tea Luck set in front of her.

Faith tossed her napkin from her lap to the table, collapsed against the back of her chair, and raised an artfully shaped brow. "You want to say that again?"

"Not really."

"Since when does Dax Campbell date? Since when does he do anything but love 'em and leave 'em?"

Arwen grimaced. "Thanks, Faith. I really needed to hear that."

"Obviously you do, because you don't date either, so why in *hell* would you choose Dax Campbell to start with? Is this about the legend of the Dalton Gang? Because as much as I don't want to think about my brother with his pants down, Boone would make a much better fuck buddy."

"It's a date, Faith. I didn't say anything about pants down."

"You said Dax Campbell. Same thing. You knew what he was like in high school. Do you really think he's changed?"

That brought a smile to Arwen's face. She'd seen how he'd changed, seen how he hadn't, but that wasn't for Faith to know. "I had a crush on him in high school."

Faith's eyes went wide. "Get out. You're kidding me. You're not kidding me. Why?"

She shook her head. "A mad crush. A bad crush. A soul-crushing crush. I honestly thought I would never get over his leaving town. And I'm not sure I know why."

"Wow. I don't even know what to say."

"It was a long time ago, but yeah. When I heard he was back . . ." She let the sentence trail, hating that she'd admitted as much as she had. No one had ever known that her heart had been broken just like those he'd loved and left—and he hadn't even known her name.

"When you heard he was back, you thought why not? You're not the girl you were in high school. Why not prove he wasn't worth the time you spent drawing hearts with your initials and writing *Mrs. Dax Campbell* in your diary?"

Ouch. "That's pretty close. Except I didn't have a diary."

"Doesn't matter. We're talking about Dax. He will hurt you. That's who he is. That's what he does."

Something tingled along Arwen's spine. "Did he hurt you?"

"Me? Oh, hell no. Even if I'd been interested, Boone wouldn't have let him get near me. No, my mad, bad, soul-crushing crush was on Casper Jayne."

"Oh my God. I'll bet Boone didn't like that at all."

"I'm not even sure Casper let himself believe it for fear of Boone's fists landing in his beautiful face." Faith breathed deeply. "And, God if he isn't even more gorgeous now. Those shoulders and thighs, and why am I even thinking about him? I do not need his recklessness in my life."

"They're all beautiful, you know. Their cheekbones. Their eyes. Their mouths." She shivered. Pictured Dax naked and shivered again. "I think back to high school, and wow did they ever fulfill their potential. Hard enough to resist all that oozing charm when you're sixteen years old, but now?"

"Uh-uh," Faith said, shaking her head. "Don't fall for him, Arwen. Have fun if you must, but don't let him get to you. And if he's the reason you're wondering if you did the right thing staying here—"

"He's not. I promise," she said, not quite sure she was telling the truth, but less certain if she was telling a lie. "It's just . . . the Dalton Gang coming back got me to thinking about growing up here, who left and why—"

"And who stayed and why."

She nodded. "Sometimes I wonder if I'm still here only to prove a point."

"Point being that you're not your father?"

"That's not exactly what I was thinking." And why was that the first place Faith had gone? "I'm not a drunk who lives in a bar, so not sure there's anything to prove."

"You're the daughter of the drunk and you own said bar. There had to be more to buying and remodeling the place than you just wanting to open a restaurant. You could've done that from the ground up."

"Most of this is from the ground up."

"What about the booth in your kitchen at home?"

Arwen looked down, stabbed at her salad. "I spent a lot of time in that booth."

"Exactly." Faith reached for her Coke but didn't lift the glass. "Here's a question for you. If you *had* left Crow Hill and opened a restaurant somewhere else, would you still have furniture from the Buck Off Bar in your house?"

"The booth fits the space and I like it."

"And you keeping it has nothing to do with where it came from."

"Well, sure." Arwen gestured with her fork before setting it down, her salad wasted, her appetite desiring Dax. "It reminds me of what I had to work with, what I've done with it, how far I've come."

"That's it?"

She wasn't liking the tone of this conversation. "You've obviously put a lot more thought into this than I ever did."

"If you say so."

"C'mon, Faith. It's a kitschy keepsake that just happened to have come out of Buck Akers's old bar."

"I said I believe you."

"No, you said, 'If you say so,' and those don't mean the same thing at all." Enough. This wasn't getting her anywhere. "Anyway, I need to get home and change."

"Into something more comfortable?"

"Into something that doesn't smell like a hamburger."

"All the better to keep Dax from gobbling you up?" When Arwen delivered a withering look, Faith held up both hands. "I'm sorry. Truly. I just can't help caring and not wanting to see you get hurt."

"I know. But it's not going to happen. I promise." Arwen leaned over to give her friend a hug, adding once she'd sat back, "Besides, a hundred bucks says he'll be gone in six months."

"I'll see that and raise you another hundred that it'll be sooner if it looks like they can't make a go of the ranch. Think about it. The only thing he's done long term is stay away from Crow Hill."

"Trust me. That thought is never far from my mind. He's good for the here and now, but until I meet a man who's middle name is Stable and last name is Secure, no one's getting to me."

SIXTEEN

DAX STOOD ON Arwen's front porch trying to remember the last time he'd gone on a date. He didn't want to remember the last woman he'd tumbled across his pickup's front seat, or the last one he'd taken against the wall in a bar bathroom, or who it was he'd last bent over a stack of hay bales in a barn, but his last real date.

He was having a hard time.

Even in high school he hadn't done much of what could be called dating. He'd never had a steady girlfriend, not then, not since, but like his two Dalton Gang compadres he'd been more of a mind to sample every sweet young thing he could.

Hell, he'd planned to do the same once he got back to Crow Hill. Then he'd seen Arwen at Lasko's and forgotten all about his plans.

He kept telling himself it was the ease of it all. He wanted sex.

Arwen wanted sex. They had sex. How simple and perfect was that?

Except . . . things between them had changed. Sure, their hooking up had started out all naked and nasty, but since then, she'd offered him a place to sleep, she'd brought him supper, she'd agreed to this date—a date he'd wanted, a date he'd insisted on. And he'd done what exactly?

Nothing, except bang her for all he was worth.

Hmm. So maybe things for her hadn't changed at all. Maybe this was part of her having her shit together. She was all independent and thoughtful and generous and caring, but when it came down to the nitty-gritty, she didn't need anything from him but sex.

That should make him happy, right? What guy wouldn't want to be Arwen Poole's fuck buddy? Uh, yeah. Didn't make any sense that he was questioning things, and he didn't like that he was, but here he stood, doing just that instead of getting on with ringing her bell.

Before he could question anything else, the door opened. His head came up from where he'd been staring at the porch boards, and now the only question was why he'd stood there so long without knocking.

She wore her usual jeans, but her top was some sleeveless, thigh-length gauzy number, and her hair was a wild mass of loose curls around her shoulders. He breathed her in and his stomach growled, and seeing her bare feet on her hardwood floor, her toenails painted the same pink as her bedroom, completely did him in.

She stood with one arm raised as she held on to the door. "Do you realize you're on my front porch, in plain view of anyone who might pass by?"

"I do," he said, leaving it at that rather than admitting he'd considered using her back door.

"You're not even hiding behind your hat."

He pulled it off completely to show he had it in him.

"I think we're making progress here, though we could make it a lot faster if you'd come inside." She pulled her dark fall of hair back from her face, her lashes drifting down then up again in a slow, lazy sweep.

He would've gone inside anyway, but his cock insisted he do it now, and he was pretty sure she wasn't wearing a bra. The sway of her unbound tits completely sucked away what was left of his brain. One step over the threshold, he wrapped an arm around her waist, brought her to his body, and covered her mouth with his.

He'd been waiting to kiss her properly since the other evening when he'd told her good-bye at her truck. He did so now, kicking the door closed and sliding his tongue into her mouth as he cupped her ass and squeezed. She moaned, rubbed against him like a cat, her nipples over his chest, her pussy against his thigh.

Two layers of denim, and he felt her dampness, her heat, and he dug his fingers deeper between the cheeks of her backside, then forced her across the room and down onto the couch. He covered her, held her hands above her head and humped her, grinding and sliding until he couldn't breathe and he feared his cock would snap off at the root.

Planting his palms on the cushion on either side of her head, he raised up, stared down. "If you're trying to kill me, be warned. My assets aren't worth shit."

Giggling, Arwen rolled out from beneath him, and he pushed to sit, collapsing back to relieve the pressure on his cock. But in the next instant, she was straddling his lap, leaning forward, her mouth on his neck beneath his ear.

She kissed and she licked and she bit him, and her hands were everywhere, her fingers busy little teasing things driving him mad. It took all he had in him to take her by the waist and set her away.

They'd made an agreement. He had to stick to it or she would win and he would lose what manhood he had left—if any. "Here's how this works. Date, then sex."

She pouted, dragging a middle finger up and down his throat, her nipples tight and tempting beneath the fabric of her shirt. "That makes it sound like the sex is an afterthought. A maybe. A possible outcome to the night."

"No, it's just to make sure the date happens because knowing you, you've been going crazy thinking about having me and forgot to get my popcorn."

"That's not true," she said, flouncing down to the cushion beside him. "It's microwaved, but it's hot and fresh. And buttered."

"Good to hear," he said, sniffing the air. Yep. Popcorn. "So what are we watching?"

"A western."

"My favorite. Clint Eastwood? John Wayne? Gary Cooper?"

"Nope. This one's the story of a six-shooting spaceman, a cosmic hooker, a pilot savant, a girl in a box, and a man named Jayne."

He arched a brow. Was she kidding? "I don't even know what to say to that."

"Trust me. You'll love it," she said, jumping up and heading for the kitchen and, he hoped, his popcorn.

"Maybe the hooker part," he called after her.

She was back in a flash and giving him a look. "Are you always such a man?"

"I thought that's why I was here. Because I walk tall and carry a big dick."

This time she rolled her eyes. "Tell me you didn't just say that."

"You've seen it," he said, draping his arm along the back of the couch. "You know the truth."

"What I know is that you need to shut up and watch your

movie." She dropped down beside him, set the popcorn between his legs. "Date night, remember?"

He remembered, and as the movie played his mind drifted, wandering back to high school as if that's where he'd find answers to whatever the hell was wrong with him. Because something had to be wrong. He'd said no to a woman who'd climbed into his lap and asked him with her body to fuck her. A gorgeous woman. A woman who had managed to kill his desire for any other.

In the future, sure, he'd get back to his randy Dalton Gang ways, but even as the thought crossed his mind, he didn't see it. He wanted Arwen. And it kinda made him feel all settled and shit to be thinking of sticking with her, especially when he'd intended to pick up where he'd left off sixteen years ago, sampling all the female wares Crow Hill had to offer.

He lowered his gaze from the TV screen to where she sat curled against him, her knees drawn up to rest on his thigh, her feet bare, her head in the crook of his shoulder. He toyed with a strand of her hair, watched a smile play over her face, followed the movement of her hand as she absently rubbed along his inseam before reaching into the bag of popcorn. His gut tightened, and not even from the physical contact.

He was comfortable. He couldn't remember the last time he had been, the last time he'd felt like he belonged. Maybe as a kid growing up in the mansion on the hill, but that hadn't lasted long. As soon as he'd figured out he was expected to go to law school, he'd begun to feel like a stranger in his own house, hell, in his own skin.

Even on the ranch he felt like he was just passing through. He hated that. For himself. For Boone and Casper. He wanted to call the place home. It had been more of one than his own during high school, but a lot of that had been the people who'd lived there making it so.

All these years and miles later, the Daltons' influence remained, along with Tess's aprons and Dave's spittoons, and though it felt like a violation to be boxing up their things, he appreciated Darcy taking on the chore. And, yeah, he could make a home there with Casper and Boone. There was a reason they'd stayed fast friends and become such in the first place.

But something was missing. And he was pretty sure that something was sitting next to him on a sofa long enough and wide enough for what he had in mind without having to waste time getting to her bed. He pictured her moving the popcorn, turning her gaze to his, her eyes soft like a foal's, her lips damp as they parted.

Background music would play as he held her gently and lowered himself over her, kissing her, smoothing her hair from her face. They'd breathe together, he'd slide a hand beneath her shirt, cup her breast, tease her, wait until she was ready before lifting the fabric, licking at her nipple, sucking her until she begged . . .

Except as soon as the movie was over, she sat forward, arched her back, and stretched her arms overhead. Then she shifted on one hip to face him and bumped his knee. "You got your date. Now I want my sex."

And just like that the sensation of all being right with his world got doused with a bucket of cold water. He looked at her, watched her pulse beat in the hollow of her throat, watched her chest rise and fall as she breathed. Watched her irises disappear as her pupils dilated.

Aw, hell. Who was he kidding? Watched the rest of his life fall into place.

And that had his heart racing because getting there from here was not going to come easy. Not when Arwen had set the terms of their involvement and he'd been stupid enough to agree. Fine.

She wanted sex? He'd give her sex. He'd also make sure she knew there was more to sex than his cock and her pussy and her finger in his ass.

He leaned forward, set the popcorn bag on the coffee table, and reached for the snaps of his shirt. "How do you want it?" He popped the buttons, shrugged out of the shirt, moved to his belt buckle. "Where do you want it?" He freed his fly's top button then bent to tug off his boots. "And why aren't you getting undressed?"

"Could you possibly make sex sound any less sexy?" she asked, scooting away from him to the end of the couch.

Good, he mused as she pulled her knees to her chest and tugged her shirt down over them. They were getting somewhere. "You said you wanted sex. I just want to make sure I'm giving you what you want."

"You're giving me a porn movie. From a male point of view."

"So the sex is part of the date? Like peach cobbler after baby back ribs?"

"Yes. Why would you think any differently?"

"Let's see. What exactly was it you said? That I got *my* date, and you wanted *your* sex? Not that you wanted *us* to have sex, or hell, that you might want *me*?"

"Well, of course I want you. You're here, aren't you?" And then she cocked her head to the side, considering him, the smile sliding over her face crafty and sly. "Did I hurt your feelings? Did you want me to seduce you?"

"Does it matter what I want?" *And what the hell?* He sounded like some pansy-assed teen. A teen girl at that. Shit. Fuck. Shit.

She laughed then, tossed back her head and laughed. "I did, didn't I? I hurt your feelings. I'm sorry, really. I didn't mean to. I just—"

"You just want sex. I got it." He stood, shucked off his jeans, left his briefs in place because he wasn't up to exposing more of himself.

"Oh, Dax. I am sorry. We agreed you'd get your date and I'd get my sex, and I never thought you might want more. Especially when you told me the other evening that you didn't. You remember telling me that, don't you?"

"I remember. And I don't want more," he said, dropping back to the couch and doubting there'd be any sex had here tonight.

She rolled up to her hands and knees, crawled toward him. "Good, because I can't have you here if you do."

Huh. That was interesting, and something new. But even when she worked her way into his lap and started working on him, he stared at the television and stayed quiet, ignoring her weight, her sweet scent. Ignoring the twitch in his balls, the rise of his cock.

His not wanting more and her not wanting more should've made for a perfect connection. The only thing he could think that might be hosing him up was Arwen running the show. And really, he'd have to be a bigger dick now than he'd been in high school to let that get in the way of the sex she delivered, as abundant and welcome as rain.

She pushed the heels of her palms together beneath his ribs and leaned in, her tits flat to his chest, the metal loops in the centers like tiny brands, burning him. Her mouth at his jaw trailed kisses as she made her way to his ear.

She breathed there, softly, in and out, then said, "You know that I want you here, don't you? I really, really do."

He grunted. He really, really didn't want to be anyplace else, and he moved his hands to her hips, then wriggled his fingers beneath her shirt to her skin, skating his palms up her sides until the weight of her breasts rested on his thumbs. Then he turned his head into hers and kissed her, his fingers gouging the flesh covering her ribs.

She slid her tongue against his, her hands down his belly and beneath the elastic straining to hold his briefs flat. Then she backed her way off his lap to the floor, kneeling between his thighs and urging him to lift his hips. He did, and she got rid of his shorts, leaving him with his socks and a good ten inches of greedy anticipation.

Licking her lips, she took him in her hand, then took him in her mouth, then took him to the back of her throat. He curled his fingers into the fabric of the couch and clenched every muscle he had, his neck straining as he dropped his head against the cushion and closed his eyes.

Fuck. She was good. So goddamn good. She knew when to use her tongue, how to use her teeth, where to use her fingers and her way-too-inquisitive thumb.

His balls were aching when she ringed them and tugged them down, and his cock jumped, the tip brushing the top of her mouth. She pulled her lips along his shaft, holding the head by its thick ridge, lapping at the bead of fluid warning her. Warning him that if he stayed where he was, she wouldn't be getting the sex she wanted for at least a little while.

He looked down, met her wicked gaze, started to say *To hell with it* but knew he wasn't that guy. So he threaded his fingers into her hair, pulled his cock from her mouth, and told her, "My turn," as he urged her to her feet. Scooting to the edge of the cushion, he tapped the back of her knees to bring her closer, and went to work on her jeans.

The button slipped free easily, and the zipper didn't give him a bit of trouble, and he opened the denim to find her sweet skin and a strip of pink lace above the cotton that covered the part of her he'd come to see. He leaned forward, pulled at the elastic with his teeth, let it snap back against her skin, and inhaled.

Holding her shirt to her waist, she squirmed, shivered, and he tugged her jeans down her thighs, leaving her panties in place because he loved how she looked, smooth and soft and not the least bit naughty when she was the naughtiest girl he'd ever known.

He loved that she was. *Loved it.* He ran the backs of his fingers over her mound, feeling the pillows of her lips and her hardened clit and the slit that his nose told him was ready for his meat. What the hell made him think he needed a date when he had this?

Exhaustion had to be turning him mad. His cock, her cunt, and his world was complete. And if he kept telling himself that, if he kept the distance between them she said she wanted, he might just convince himself it was true.

He slipped his index fingers beneath the leg of her panties and tested his theory, finding the seam of her bare pussy slick with her lube. Smiling, he leaned forward and opened his mouth, breathing hot air against her. She moaned, whipped off her shirt, and speared her fingers into his hair. Then she spread her legs.

Oh, yeah. She smelled good. Hot and sea-salty and horny, just the way he liked her. His cock jumped, brushing her inner knee and causing them both to pull in a sharp breath. He'd had enough with waiting.

He stood up, slowly sliding his body along hers, the head of his cock leaving a trail of pre-cum from her panties over her belly where he nestled himself against her. Then he grabbed her to him, pivoted, and tumbled them both to the couch. He landed on his back, then rolled over, putting her beneath him.

Eyes closed, at Dax's urging Arwen lifted her hips. He pulled down her panties and tossed them to the floor. She was naked but he still wore his socks, and that had her grinning. It was silly and she didn't know why, really, except that it made him real and human, and she needed that right now.

Needed to know she wasn't the only one capable of falling.

Neck arched, she reached behind her, holding on to the arm of the couch as he hooked her legs over his shoulders, bent, and settled his lips between her belly button and the strip of her pubic hair. He hummed against her, kissed, bit, licked, worked his way lower and finally, *finally*, sucked her clit into his mouth.

Lord, his tongue. He used the tip like a finger, circling the bud of nerves. He used it like a cock, sliding along the sides and beneath, pushing up until she whimpered and squirmed. He moved down, licking his way through her folds, teasing the rim of her entrance, turning his face to kiss the crevice between her pussy and her thigh.

That wasn't where she wanted him, and she used her knee to urge his head back.

He laughed against her, his breath tickling. "Is this the sex you were talking about?"

"It's a start." Already, she wanted to come. But even more than that, she wanted the build-up, the pleasure that came frighteningly close to pain. "You're just drifting a bit off course."

"Not drifting. Searching," he said, using that tongue to draw a line along the seam of her pussy's lips, flicking at her clit, piercing her before withdrawing with a hard downward stroke.

She gasped, aching, opened her eyes. "Searching for what?"

"Hot spots. Sweet spots."

"I'm happy to point them out."

"Hell, where's the fun in that?" He slid her legs from his shoulders and planted his hands on her thighs. He spread her wide, took her in with a hungry, "Mmm-mmm-mmm."

The grin on his face, all devouring, dominant male, sent a shot of heat to her core, and reckless need consumed her. She was his, completely, and helpless to understand why.

What she did know was that this was not, *not*, how to go about getting him out of her system for good.

Strange she had to remind herself of that. "You'll never find them if you're only using your eyes."

"My eyes are having a very good time here."

"My pussy would like some of that, please."

"Yes, ma'am," he said, and this time he pushed his tongue deep inside her, used it like a cock to fuck her, in and out, in and out, barely giving her a chance to lose herself in the sensation before abandoning her again.

But even as she growled, he returned his mouth to her clit, inserting a finger into her cunt, adding a second, stroking her inner walls while tonguing her to madness. He sucked at her plump flesh. He caught her clit with his teeth and tugged. He crooked his finger and found the spot she'd been waiting for him to hit.

She arched into his touch, wanting more of it, wanting it harder, wanting . . . She didn't know what, but he seemed to be holding something back.

Did he not want this? Was he not having fun? "Dax?"

He removed his fingers, kissed his way from her clit to her ass, from thigh to thigh, from her belly to the hollow of her throat. Then he rose up over her, his hands on either side of her head, and stared down. "Arwen?"

She looped her legs around him, hooked her heels in the small of his back. "Where are you?"

He prodded her with his cock. "Right here."

"Your body, yeah, but where's your head?"

"A second ago it was between your legs."

"You know what I mean," she said, holding his gaze.

Why was she letting his distance be an issue when his distance fit perfectly into her plans? Except she hadn't anticipated the worry tangling her up at seeing his smile stop short of his eyes. She wanted him with her every moment, not halfheartedly fulfilling his side of this ridiculous bargain they'd made.

Though when his prodding became more insistent, and he realigned his hips and wet himself with her moisture, her worry vanished. How could she think of anything but his body driving into hers, filling hers, lifting hers off the cushions with the force of his thrusts? This was all she wanted.

Wasn't it?

Burying her face in the crook of his neck, she dug her fingers into the balls of his shoulders and held on as he rode her, bucking against him and using her heels on his ass to urge him deeper. He growled at her ear, dropped to his elbows, and threaded his fingers into her hair.

And he talked to her, words that made no sense, dirty words, words that were more noise than anything, that rolled up from his gut with a stirring, stunning vibration. She listened, unable to say anything, barely able to breathe, yet so hindered by her own silence she had to let go.

Panting, whimpering, she twisted beneath him, finding the hard base of his cock and grinding her clit against him, listening all the while and overwhelmed—by the sounds, the sensations, what she knew were going to be huge sweeping complications making a mess of her life.

He pushed his thighs higher, climbed up her body. She kissed his chest, nuzzling his pectorals and searching out his nipple with her teeth. She latched on but didn't bite, sucking and tonguing instead, and drawing a visceral grunt from his throat.

"You keep that up and I'm going to be done here."

And suddenly she wanted to make that happen, to give him whatever he needed to lose control. To show him his dating was nothing compared to her sex, that no one could do for him what she could. To make sure he would remember her and think about her the way she'd never forgotten him.

Rocking her hips upward, she drew her knees along his sides, reaching one hand between their bodies. She lingered at her clit, shuddering at the strum of nerves, then slipped lower, fingering herself while he fucked her.

He laughed, a wicked, taunting burst, and then he stopped, biting off a sharp *fuck* because she'd caught the base of his shaft in the ring of her fingers and squeezed. She held him, released him, slid to his head as he pulled out of her cunt and thumbed the underside seam. This time his *fuck* came out on a growl, and that's when she went after his balls.

She cupped and released, rolled his nuts in her palm, then rubbed the extension of his erection that ran to his anus. At that, he leaned to the side to dislodge her, grasping her hand with his. But she knew what she was doing and she guided their fingers to the place where their bodies were joined.

She looked at him, watching the shift in his expression as she touched him, as he touched her, as their hands became as much a part of the act as her pussy and his cock.

Moisture slicked the way for their play. She laced her fingers with his, held his shaft, released it, ran his knuckles through her folds as he slowly moved his hips. Up and down, his cock entering her, pulling out, the ridge of the head caught by their hands, two of their fingers slipping inside to stroke and stir her arousal further.

Through it all she held his gaze, watched sweat pop on his brow, saw the muscles in his jaw jump as he ground down. His nostrils flared. His lashes swept like brushes as he blinked in slow motion.

And finally he asked her, his voice a deep rutting groan, "Is this the sex you wanted?"

She didn't answer right away. She couldn't. Her body burned and ached, and she didn't want to lose this spot when she was so *so* close to coming. But neither did she want to see that look come back to his eyes, the one he'd finally let go of. The one that frightened her with its distance, when distance was the goal.

So she told him the truth. "I wanted you."

He barked out a laugh, gave a shake of his head. "If you only knew."

But that was all he said. He broke their gaze, broke her hold on his hand, tucked his face next to hers and picked up speed, pounding her as if exorcising demons.

She held on because it was all she could do. He drove her up the couch until her head bounced off the arm, and she moved one hand to the floor to brace herself. The other she hooked around his neck, and this time she was the one whispering to him.

She doubted he was listening, or that he processed the words if he heard them. And that was okay. The words were as much for herself. *It's going to be okay. Everything's fine. This is good. We're good. We're so, so good.*

Then she stopped, gasped, held her breath and let her orgasm build in a crushing mindless rush. She knew he came with her. He lifted his head, straining, and the hot sticky spill of his semen sent her over the edge. Her head spun endlessly. Darkness rose up to devour her.

No man had ever given her this. No man had ever come close. She feared looking too closely at why Dax Campbell was able to take her this high, but she feared even more discovering why he'd willingly made the journey with her.

SEVENTEEN

DARCY WAS STANDING on her tiptoes on the kitchen counter, reaching into the back corner of one of the overstuffed cupboards' top shelves, when a knock sounded on the back door. Since when did anyone paying a visit to the ranch knock without sticking their head in the door and hollering?

She wasn't about to get down and answer it, and risk knocking the stacks of china at her feet to the floor. She was fairly sure she had a complete—and unused—place setting for eight, and from the look of the pattern and the stamp on the bottom, one that might fetch a pretty penny from a collector.

"Come in," she called over her shoulder, looking for chips or cracks or scraped paint on the sugar bowl she held and finding none. Nice. Real nice.

The door opened, the creaking screen followed. "It's me, Josh."

Aw, hell. Not now. She caught the cupboard's door to keep

from tumbling, her heart pounding as she glanced to the maze she'd created with the dishes—and which she now had to step out of without looking like a lumbering cow.

"You need some help?"

Yes, please sweep me up in your arms and carry me away. Snort.

"No, I'm fine." She backed up on the balls of her feet to the counter's edge, held the cupboard's center brace for balance, and moved first one foot then the other to the chair she'd used as a stool. Only after she was safely in the seat did she turn to face him, brushing her hair from her eyes and wishing she'd put on more makeup than lip balm and a quick swipe of mascara.

He looked good. He always looked good. Tall and rangy and comfortable in his skin, his jeans laundered and creased, his boots shined, his yoked shirt—this one long-sleeved and khaki—starched to a crisp. She wondered what he'd look like dirty, all messed up and sweaty and wrinkled after a day on horseback riding herd.

Then she wondered what he'd look like naked. "See? No broken bones, no broken dishes."

He gave a single nod. "You haven't made it to the floor yet."

Ah, that. She hopped down, saying a tiny prayer of thanks when she landed gracefully, and adding a flair of a curtsy for fun. "Better?"

He took off his hat, hooked it on the back of a chair. "I can breathe now, yeah."

Something wild and inappropriate fluttered at the base of her throat, and she told herself it meant nothing, the flutter, his words, but couldn't shake the lie. "What are you doing here?"

He held up her key ring, the one she'd last seen on her desk at work before The Campbell's words had sent her walking. "I brought your car."

Of course, she thought, and swallowed. It had been five days since she'd last seen him. Could she be anymore ridiculously self-centered, taking advantage of his generosity *and* losing track of time? "I'm sorry. I can't believe you had to come after your truck."

"I didn't come after my truck."

"Oh?"

"I came to see you."

Oh. Well. She wasn't sure what to think about that. Josh Lasko had never sought her out before. And though he'd caused her a lot of breathing trouble, she wondered if this was a first for him. If slamming into him in front of Nathan's had set something in motion, like atoms colliding, or dominoes falling.

Silly thoughts. Silly woman. "Would you like something to drink? Iced tea? Coffee?"

"You don't have to wait on me, Darcy," he said, his hands at his hips. "I don't mean to interrupt."

"I'm not waiting on you, and you're not interrupting." She'd lived with Patricia Campbell too long not to play the hostess, even in a house that wasn't her own. And it gave her something to do besides avoid his too-sharp gaze. "I've been at this awhile and could use a break myself."

"I'd take a cup of joe, then, if it's not any trouble."

If she had to fly to Indonesia and pick the beans herself, it wouldn't be any trouble at all. She gestured for him to sit. "Not a bit. I'll put on a pot. Won't be but a few."

The chair scraped over the dried-out linoleum when he pulled it from beneath the table, creaked when he settled into it, creaked again when he leaned forward, his elbows on his knees.

He squeezed the knuckle of his pinky with the thumb and index finger of his other hand. "How're you liking ranch life? Gotta be a big adjustment after living up on the hill all these years."

Where to begin? She'd had to sweep spiderwebs from the corners of the bedroom she'd claimed before she could use it. She'd had to mop the hardwood floor, soap the iron bed frame, wash the linens, and air the quilt on the backyard clothesline. She'd had to pull down the curtains, clean those as well as the window behind, and get Dax to install a ceiling fan.

And that was just to have a place to sleep, forget dealing with the scary dark depths of the closet for the clothes she'd had Marta, the Campbell family housekeeper, bring her. Or the bureau she'd emptied of old newspapers and tools that belonged in the barn and enough single socks to make fifty-plus mismatched pairs. Then the bathroom, ugh; it had taken twice as long. So, yeah. The adjustment had been huge.

"Honestly? I'm loving it," she said, rinsing the leftover coffee from the morning's pot and pouring fresh water into the machine. "I haven't been still for a minute, and I ache from all the bending and lifting. But I can lie in bed at night and see the stars through glass I polished with a whole lot of my own elbow grease."

She glanced at him then, almost wished she hadn't. He was still, leaning forward the way he'd been when she'd last looked, but unmoving now, his hands, his eyes, even his chest all still as he waited to breathe. She didn't know what he was waiting for, what he was thinking, what he saw when he looked at her, but dear *God*, the way he looked at her.

Her hands shook, and a flush blossomed between her breasts, tightening her nipples and rising up her neck to her face. She knew she looked like disheveled crap—which would thankfully explain away her blush—but his eyes told another story. And every fantasy she'd ever had of him ran on a movie reel loop through her mind.

Oh, boy. *Oh, boy.* Probably not the best idea to talk to Josh about lying in bed, about seeing stars. At least not to this Josh who seemed so full of purpose, so single-minded and focused.

Finally, he dropped his head, then straightened, sitting back in the chair and stretching out his long legs. He crossed them at the ankle, crossed his arms over his chest. "Not a lot of call for physical activity as an attorney, I reckon."

Coffee. Filter. Mugs. Those were the things she needed to concentrate on. Not his eyes. Not his body. Not his big brass belt buckle that lay flat against his stomach. About the not-so-flat zippered fly beneath.

She measured the ground beans, spilling less than a quarter teaspoon on the counter, which she counted a success. "As sore as I am, it's obvious I could've used a lot more. Maybe if I'd filed my own paperwork and shelved my own books, instead of waiting for The Campbell to realize I needed a clerk."

"You been in touch with him?"

She shook her head, punched the button to start the pot brewing then reached into the cupboard for mugs. "He hasn't been in touch with me either. I guess one of us will give in sooner or later."

"Hardheaded bunch?"

A smile pulled at her mouth, and she turned, leaning against the counter as the coffeemaker gurgled and steamed. "The Campbell is. I suppose Dax and I inherited some of that. Or had it nurtured into us, as I'm not sure that's a trait instilled by nature."

"Is he handling your cases? Your father?"

"I dropped an email to Greg and asked him to take care of things for now. He hasn't been back in touch except to say he'd let me know if he had any questions."

"That's good, yes?"

"Yeah. It's good." Or not. It could mean she was easily expendable, which she'd already decided was the case. She'd just yet to put it into words. It was hard enough thinking it after spending the last decade of her life trying to be the son her father had always wanted.

She looked out the window over the sink, watching a cloud of dust rise in the distance from the direction Dax and the others had headed this morning, three cowboys on horseback looking like this was the only place they'd ever truly belonged. She was thrilled her brother was back, thrilled he'd done what he'd wanted with his life and was happy.

But it would be a whole lot easier to celebrate if his getting his way hadn't ruined things for her. Except that wasn't what had happened, and it was time she acknowledged that fact. The truth was she hadn't been strong enough not to ruin them for herself.

Forgiving the girl she'd been at sixteen wasn't hard. She'd been too young to understand what she was doing, but by twenty-five, walking across the UT stage to accept her law school diploma, she'd been all too aware.

Now here she was, six years later, hating that she'd spent a decade of her life working to take her rightful place in the family, when it had never been hers to claim.

Swallowing the lump of emotion sitting in her throat like dry bread, she poured coffee into both mugs then carried them to the table, setting Josh's—black, because she remembered—in front of him.

"Thank you," he said, reaching forward and pulling the mug closer, his hand skimming over hers as she let go to fetch the carton of milk from the fridge, sweetener packets from the pantry.

She joined him at the table, though she sat on the other side, her fingers trembling from his touch, his warmth, his calluses and rough skin, imagining it touching more than her hand. She poured her milk, stirred sweetener into her drink, then waited until his mug was at his mouth, and asked, "So who's minding the store?"

"Dad," he said after swallowing. "Made it clear he doesn't care about doctor's orders. He can sit behind the counter at the store just as easily as he can sit in the recliner in front of the TV. And he's damn tired of TV." He looked down, staring into the mug he held between his hands. A lazy grin lifted the edges of his mouth, cut dimples into his cheeks, crow's feet at the corners of his eyes. "'Course, he didn't use those exact words."

"I can imagine," she said, lifting her coffee to sip. She was, unfortunately, well acquainted with Henry Lasko's vocabulary. But knowing the father didn't for a moment diminish what she felt for the son—though what she felt was too complicated to explore when he had come to see her and she was still hung up on that.

At the sound of another vehicle arriving, she frowned, canting her head. Another car, the low thrumming engine sporty and foreign and not belonging to anyone on the ranch. Ah, the dust cloud she'd seen earlier.

Her stomach clenched. Unless someone had lost their way or the boys had a visitor, she could hazard a guess as to who was behind the wheel. And if she was right, well, Josh was wrong. This wasn't a good thing at all.

"Excuse me a sec." She went to the window over the sink, took a deep breath, watched the black Audi skid to a stop next to her car. Nope. Not a good thing at all.

Deciding to get the bad news over with, she headed for the back door. Shading her eyes with one hand, the nails of the other biting into her palm, she stood on the porch and watched her second guest of the day exit his car and approach. "Greg? What are you doing here?"

Her coworker wore dark sunglasses, dark suit pants, a dark tie flung over the shoulder of his crisp white shirt. His shoes, once dark, were now covered with the dry dirt that served as the ranch house yard.

"Darcy." He glanced over her shoulder. "Josh."

"Greg," Josh said from behind her. Strange how having him there made what was to come easier to face.

Greg shoved his hands in his pockets, looked off toward the corral. Even from this distance, Darcy could see the tic in his jaw as he obviously chewed on the words he'd come to say. Something made her want to let him off the hook. This wasn't his battle, and he didn't deserve the shitty end of the deal.

"It's okay, Greg. Just say it."

He turned back, left his sunglasses on. "I cleaned out your desk. I've got a box in the car with your personal things. Wasn't sure what you wanted me to do with it."

So simple. A decade of her life reduced to a box that fit in a sports car's front seat.

She glanced at Josh. "Is my car unlocked?" He nodded, and she looked at Greg again. "Just put it in my car."

He slung his key ring around on one finger and palmed the keys as he circled his car to the passenger side. She watched the transfer of the box, hugging herself tightly, seeing a nearly laughable symbolism in the opening and closing of the doors.

That done, Greg returned to his car, hesitating before climbing inside, finally removing his sunglasses and looking up, his eyes a brighter blue than Dax's. "I'm really sorry this happened."

"Me, too." It was an automatic response. She wasn't even sure if she meant it. She was pretty sure she didn't feel it, or anything else for that matter.

He gave a single nod then slid behind the wheel, waiting until he was a hundred yards from the house before punching the accelerator and stirring up another wall of dust and dry dirt.

Josh cleared his throat. "Looks like you got your answer."

She stood where she was until Greg's car disappeared, then turned and walked into Josh, purposefully this time, wrapping her arms around him and hoping he didn't care that her tears were ruining his perfectly laundered khaki shirt.

He was solid. A rock. He didn't move except to place his hands on her shoulders and squeeze.

"I never wanted to be an attorney, you know," she told him, her fingers making a wrinkled mess of the fabric at his back where the shirt hung loose above his tightly cinched belt.

"What did you want?"

"For my mother to pay as much attention to our family as to the ones she did for show. For my father to stop drinking long enough to remember he had a daughter." She closed her eyes, squeezed them tight, took a deep shuddering breath. "For my brother to come home."

Josh stepped back, claimed her chin with one hand and waited for her to look up. She did, her vision blurry but clear enough to see there was no question in his eyes, no request for permission, nothing but the certainty he wanted her to see.

Her heart fluttered and anticipation rose the hair at her nape and—*oh, God*—his head came down, his mouth opening before he pressed it to hers, and she thought she might very well die.

He kissed her softly, held her face with his hands, used his tongue against hers, used his lips, too, and his teeth, nibbling and nipping, leaving her mouth to explore her jaw, her neck, coming back and threading his fingers into her hair to keep her still.

She couldn't have moved if she'd wanted to. He was gentle, caring, and kind, and she held on for dear life, scared by the idea of letting him go. And because of that she had to. She could lean on him, but she had to stand on her own two feet or she'd never find her way.

Knowing that, she allowed herself one more minute to indulge, to step into him, to press her body against his and feel his thighs along her thighs and his belt buckle against her belly, and the lines of his ribs hard on her breasts.

She rubbed his back—his spine, his shoulder blades, his waist—slipping just the tips of her fingers between his shirt and his jeans, and only for a moment, then she brought her hands to his face, smoothing her thumbs over his cheeks before breaking the kiss.

"Thank you," she whispered, still tasting him . . . coffee and warmth and Josh. "For being here. For coming to see me. For picking up my car. For lending—"

"Enough," he said, his eyes glittering, his lashes, pale and thick, sweeping down. A vein pulsed at his temple. His jaw clicked as he ground it. But finally he let her go, her hair sifting slowly through his fingers, his fingers lingering on her shoulder, then her arm, until he found hers and laced their hands and squeezed. "I want to see you."

She didn't insult him by pretending not to know what he meant. She just nodded, smiled, and told him, "Okay."

EIGHTEEN

DAX REINED HIS horse to the far left, Boone rode the middle, and Casper, on Remedy, held to the right. Along with Bing and Bob, the Daltons' aging border collies, the three men brought up the rear as they moved the small band of cow-calf pairs from the pasture they'd grazed the last few weeks to the next in the rotation.

The early morning sun was blinding, the temperature already on its way to triple digits. But the view, as brown as it was, left Dax totally blissed, and for not the first time wondering why he'd felt the need to cowboy anywhere else.

There was nothing like the dome of sky blue that covered Texas, high and wide and endless. Or the mountains of white clouds suspended there, still as their rocky counterparts, puffed like kids' cheeks in a spitting contest.

Hell, what he'd give for their big daddies to roll in, monsters in gray and black, vomiting thunder and lightning and gallons of lifesaving rain. He wanted to stand in the wide-open spaces when it finally happened, head back and arms spread and open mouth catching the downpour until he drowned.

In the meantime, he'd sweat and bake and turn as crisp as everything around him, and do a whole lot of praying. Moving the pairs as often as they were going to need to wasn't the most efficient way to run an operation. Dave Dalton and sixteen years had taught him that. But Mother Nature hadn't left them much choice.

If this was a good year, a wet year, grass growing and creeks running high, their acreage could easily support the cattle Tess had left them—as well as the head she'd had little choice but to sell at the beginning of this six-month drought.

This wasn't a good year. Wells were near to dry. Grass wasn't growing as much as dying. The state of things made it easy to understand Henry Lasko being hell-bent on getting his hands on their land, but it wasn't going to happen.

Overall the animals looked healthy, maybe a bit on the thin side, but the hay Tess had lined up weeks before he and the boys took over made up for the shortage of grass, and kept them from having to sell off any more of the herd.

Good thing, too, because Faith was none too happy they were having to float that bill along with a lot of others. Selling underfed beef at a loss was just one more hit they didn't need, yet it was hard to ask for extensions from folks in just as tight binds.

"Hee-ya! Hee-ya! Hee-ya, motherfuckers!"

At Casper's yell, Dax glanced over to see him running down two mommas and babies who'd cut away from the rest and gone renegade. He laughed so hard he snorted. Casper had been the only one of the three to rodeo, meaning he could rope and ride like a son of a bitch, but he'd forgotten a whole lot of what he'd learned about herding.

Boone reined Sunshine closer to Dax, gave a jerk of his head in Casper's direction. "Guess he'll remember what he's doing sooner or later."

Dax watched the two mommas drop down the other side of a rise and cut through a stand of mesquite, Bing hot on their heels. "Even if he doesn't, Bing'll have to be the one to give him a hand. I've got heifers coming out of my ears over here."

"Huh. How's Darcy doing with the housecleaning?"

Frowning, Dax looked over. "Speaking of heifers, you mean?"

"No, asshole," Boone said, frowning back. "It was just a question. Kinda looking forward to moving in when she's done and bulldozing the bunkhouse to the ground."

"Darcy's doing fine, as far as I know. She hasn't talked much about it." Then he registered the rest of what Boone had said. "You think we should doze the bunkhouse?"

"Diego's got a pop-up on his truck. Fully loaded and enough room for his nephew." He stood in his stirrups to get a better view of Casper and Bing, and then settled back in his seat. "Unless Casper can't get his shit together, we won't need to hire on anyone who might use it. No reason I can see not to clear it out of there. Maybe use the space for a new barn. Down the road. Put it up as we can, tear down the other once it's done. No rush on any of it, a' course."

"Guess you're right." Though it was obvious they were all still reluctant to move in to the house. They could do so now and let Darcy work around them, but they hadn't. Wrecking the bunkhouse would take the decision out of their hands. Made sense, he supposed.

They rode in silence for several minutes, listening to Casper in the near distance. Boone finally said, "Gotta admit, it's nice having supper waiting at the end of the day."

Dax's frown deepened. "As long as you don't get used to it. Darcy won't be living with us long term."

Boone gave a shrug. "If you say so."

What the hell was that? "Uh-uh. We don't do sisters. Never have. You know that better than me, but you know it."

"That sister rule was awhile ago."

Boone had put his foot down in high school. But this wasn't high school, and Dax wasn't liking the sound of things, and so he countered. "You clearing the way for me to go after Faith?"

"Hell no. You've got Arwen. You don't need Faith."

His having Arwen was giving Dax hell, especially after their movie date and the things they'd done on her couch. "Casper, then. If I recall correctly, he's the one the rule was written for in the first place."

"Shit. Casper can't even manage two skinny cows and their runt calves. You think he's going to handle Faith?"

Point made. Still . . . "I'm pretty sure there's a reason Josh Lasko's truck's been sitting in front of the house the last few days."

This time Boone was the one who frowned. "Darcy and Lasko? You think?"

"I dunno. Just putting it out there." Mostly because he didn't want to think about his sister with Boone. Not that he wanted to think about her with Josh Lasko either. In fact, he pretty much preferred not thinking about his sister that way at all.

"Speaking of Lasko," Boone said, adjusting the brim of his hat against the sun before going on, "I've been thinking some more about Tess and the lease."

"Yeah? How so?"

"We could use the money."

They could, but they needed the land as much as Henry. "And these cows are going to graze where?"

"Say we lease him fifteen hundred acres. He can run two hundred head or so and we can use the cash to supplement our feed."

"You been reading a stupid guide to ranching?"

"No. I've been looking at the books with Faith."

Oh. That. Still . . . "Calves get sold next month. We'll need those fifteen hundred acres once we start breeding again."

Boone gave a loud huff. "And if it doesn't rain soon? What good will those fifteen hundred acres be then?"

"Making it Lasko's problem, you're saying?"

"Something like that."

"You run this by Faith?" Because as much as he liked the idea of the income, such a deal had mega potential to bite them on the ass. It could too easily look like they were unloading worthless acreage. Then again . . . "I mean, Henry obviously knew the risks or he wouldn't have had the papers drawn up for Tess to sign."

"Yeah, but I dunno. Might be worth it. Might not," Boone said. "I was mostly thinking out loud. Wondering if we could figure out something that would benefit both outfits and make Faith happy."

From the far side of the rise they heard another loud, and this time angry, "Hee-ya! Hee-ya! Hee-ya, motherfuckers!"

Dax fought to keep a straight face, nudging Flash's flanks before saying, "You know, I'll bet Casper could make Faith happy."

Boone let loose a long string of expletives and gave Sunshine her head.

But Dax was way ahead of him, reins in one hand, hat jammed in place with the other, laughing like an asylum inmate as the quarter horse lived up to her name.

NINETEEN

"I'M NOT SURE what happened exactly. All I know is that he's at Coleman Medical and his wife is nowhere to be found, which is the weirdest part of it all."

Two days after her date with Dax, Arwen was having hell concentrating on work. She was bound in raw emotion, struggling to break the intimate, visceral ties that had been too much a part of the sex to separate from the physical act. That bothered her. A lot. It meant she wasn't working Dax out of her system but opening up, taking him deeper. They were mating in ways having nothing to do with their bodies.

If she wasn't careful, she'd never be able to get rid of him, she mused, and groaned.

With her discipline shot, the hallway gossip had no trouble snagging her attention, even though her focus should've been on the campaign her advertising firm had put together for the Hellcat Saloon. And this was why she had to rein in her relationship with

Dax, back to the sex it was supposed to be. She had a business to run, a business that was her life. He and his amazing cock had to go. Soon.

Curious and totally distracted and desperately in need of a break, she glanced from her monitor to the two girls still whispering outside her office door. She saw Callie's black hair netted at her nape, and Luck's blond ponytail swinging between her shoulder blades. Then, swearing she heard the name Wallace Campbell, she left her chair, circled her desk, and eavesdropped in plain sight.

"He collapsed at the office this morning," Callie was saying, glancing from Arwen to Luck and back. "Stacy was on her way in on her bike and had to stop for the ambulance. Greg Barrett was the only one there. She heard him talking to the paramedics."

Unless a Campbell and Associates client had gone down, they *were* talking about Wallace Campbell. No one else worked with Greg now that Darcy was gone. At least not that Arwen had heard, and with the way gossip flowed in the saloon . . .

She stepped out into the hallway. "Wallace Campbell? He's in the hospital?"

Callie nodded, her blue eyes dramatically wide. "My sister called. She's a nurse in the ER. He had a heart attack. It's bad."

"Oh, God." Arwen's hands flew up to cover her mouth. Her heart pounded, lodged at the base of her throat and choked her. "Has anyone told Darcy? Or Dax?"

"I don't know." Luck shrugged helplessly. "No one has seen Darcy in days. She's not picking up her cell. Her office and home lines go to a machine. I don't think anyone has Dax's cell number. And no one ever answers the phone at the ranch."

Arwen ran her hands into her hair and held it away from her face, thinking. Dax would be riding herd. Darcy would be at the house. "I know how to reach him. And I know where Darcy is. I'll go see them. I'll tell them. I'll let them know."

Luck and Callie exchanged looks, and Luck was the one to ask, "Arwen? Are you all right?"

She had to get to Dax. She didn't know why. He hadn't spoken to his father in sixteen years. She couldn't imagine that he'd want to speak to him now, but him knowing about his father's condition was all that mattered. He had to know. He had to.

"I'm all right. I'm fine." She let her hair fall, grabbed Luck's arm. "I know it's lunch rush and I know we're slammed and I'm sorry, but I've got to go. Can you keep it together?"

"Yes. Of course. Go do what you need to do."

"Thanks." She patted her pockets, looked around wildly. "Okay. I need my keys. My phone. My wallet's got my license and my proof of insurance. Is that all? Is that it?"

This time it was Luck who reached for Arwen, taking her by both hands and squeezing hard. "Arwen, stop, breathe. You can't do anything if you don't breathe."

She stopped. She breathed. This was stupid. She wasn't going to be of any help to anyone if she didn't get it together. "Thanks. I'm sorry. I'll try not to be long. And I wouldn't go—"

"It's an emergency." Luck turned her toward her desk. "I know. Get your stuff and go. Go."

Arwen's hands were shaking when she grabbed her phone from the top of her desk, her wallet from the center drawer, the keys to the saloon's truck from the pegboard inside the kitchen door. She gave Luck a quick hug and another, "Thank you," then fairly flew out the back, sprinting across the patio and yard and through the gate.

She had the truck started and in gear before she ever thought to close the door, doing so as she whipped backwards out of the lot. She slammed to a stop, gravel crunching and spinning beneath her tires, then shifted into first and shot forward, leaving long strips of rubber on the pavement in her wake.

She sped down Willowbrook Avenue, turned onto Main Street, punched the accelerator and gunned the big truck's engine, crossing her fingers the lunch hour meant Sheriff Orleans had abandoned his speed trap for one of Lizzy Nathan's famous soft tacos and wouldn't get in her way.

When she blew by Lasko's, she grabbed her phone from the seat and dialed Josh.

He picked up on the third ring. "Hello?"

"Josh. It's Arwen Poole."

"Arwen. How's it going?"

"Have you heard about Wallace Campbell?"

"Nothing new, no. Why?" he asked, his voice hardening on the question.

"He's had a heart attack. He's at Coleman Medical. I'm going to the ranch," she said, aware of what she'd just revealed, more aware that it didn't matter, mostly aware she'd been insane to think she could so easily get rid of Dax. "I thought you might want to do the same."

"On my way," he said and disconnected, leaving Arwen alone with her worry and a drive that went on forever. Under normal conditions the trip took at least half an hour, and though she was able, at her speed, to cut a chunk out of that time, she didn't think she'd ever get there.

She saw nothing along the way but the long strip of asphalt, the white dashes of the center line whipping by in a blur, her mind whirring so wildly she nearly missed her turn, her truck taking it in a long drifting fishtail that sent her heart careening.

Halfway up the ranch's long private road, she met Diego Cruz coming toward her. She slowed, flagged him down. He pulled up beside her and smiled.

"*Buenos dias*, Señorita Poole."

"Diego. Can you tell me where to find Dax?"

"*Sì*. He's in the west pasture with Señor Mitchell and Señor Jayne."

The west pasture. That meant nothing to her. "Is there an easy way to get there?"

"The gate you just passed? That will take you there. Just follow the tire tracks and the trail of flat grass."

Sounded easy enough. "Can I make it out there in my truck?"

"That truck?" Diego nodded. "If you back up down the road, I will open the gate for you."

"Thank you, Diego," she said, shifting into reverse and stopping on the far side of the gate to give him room. He hopped down from his truck's cab, freed the chain, and pushed the gate open. Arwen drove through, waving as she bounced over the cattle guard, hoping she could find her way back.

The grooves he'd called tracks were deep in some spots, invisible in others, and the grass nearly dead as far as she could see. Lovely. She gripped the wheel tightly, grimacing when she bounced through a particularly iffy stretch of ruts, but determined to ignore the sharp clutch of her nerves and tense muscles.

Scanning the horizon, she saw the small herd of cattle before she saw the three men on horseback, but not before they saw her. Dax was the first to rein his horse around and start toward her. Boone and Casper followed, and by the time she'd stopped, Dax had dismounted and the other two were only a few yards behind.

"Arwen? What's going on?" Dax asked, his hat brim pulled low as he walked toward her, just not low enough to hide the measure of fear painted like a warrior's mask on his face.

"It's not good," she said, her heart pounding like a fist in her chest.

The volcano she'd seen hovering beneath his calm surface before gave a warning rumble. "You're here. The boys are here. Is it Darcy? Is she okay?"

"She's at the house. With Josh. She's fine."

"Josh is with Darcy." He wasn't stupid. He could put two and two together. "It's one of the parents. Something happened. What?"

"Your father's at Coleman Medical," she said, watching his sunbaked face blanch. "He's had a heart attack."

Dax pressed his lips together, shoved his hands to his hips, glanced across her head to where Boone and Casper sat on their horses, waiting. "And I'm supposed to do what, exactly?"

He swung his gaze back to her then, his eyes cold and dark, sweat pooling hotly in the hollow of his throat, the sun kissing him with bright bursts of light.

"Don't shoot the messenger, okay?" She took a deep breath, settling her own nerves because his were popping like glass breaking. "I just thought you should know."

He looked away again, bit off a raw, "Fuck," then yanked his hat from his head and dried his brow in the crease of his elbow. "Shit. Fuck. Just fuck."

She looked toward the other two Dalton Gang members, gave a shrug in lieu of a plea for help. Should she go? Leave him here? Let him stew in the company he trusted?

Or should she wait, give him the time he needed to make the decision he had to make. Because she knew he would. His reputation aside, he wasn't a bad man.

"Go on," Boone finally said. "We'll finish up here."

"Flash—"

It was all he got out before Casper cut in, riding forward to take Flash's reins. He nodded toward Arwen's truck. "Get outta here. Let us know what you find out. All things considered, I hope the news isn't bad."

Dax was nodding when he turned for her truck, his long legs powering over the ground, his boots sending dirt clods and the grass rooted in them flying. She hurried behind him, circled the cab as he climbed into the passenger seat, jumped behind the wheel and started the engine.

She didn't say anything else. She didn't offer words of comfort or platitudes or ask him about his day, what he was thinking, what he was feeling. All she did was drive, telling herself she'd done the right thing, even if right now it didn't seem right at all.

Her hands tightened on the wheel, Dax's on the denim of his jeans. The truck bumped and jolted as she steered down the rutted trail, her shoulders aching with the effort until finally she had to let up on the gas or risk losing an axle.

Dax swore under his breath. "Stop. Just stop. Let me drive."

"I've got it." She knew he was nervous, but she'd made it this far, she could make it out.

"Arwen. Stop the fucking truck now."

"Fine," she bit off, clamping down on the single word as she braked.

Dax shoved open his door, tumbled out, but instead of coming around to hers, he walked into the pasture. She watched him through the windshield, her hands shaking even as she held on to the wheel to steady them. But as much as she wanted to go to him, she stayed where she was. Until she knew what he was going through . . .

God, but this was *so* unfairly complicated. Throwing this at him when he'd only just returned to the place he'd had to leave to get the life he wanted. And of course life wasn't fair. She knew life wasn't fair. But it killed her to see him so lost.

He turned in a circle as if he didn't know where he was or what to do or how he was going to get out of there. He turned again, stumbling, pulling off his hat and lifting his face to the sun. Then he leaned forward, his hands on his thighs, his whole body heaving as he breathed.

He was breaking her heart, and she pressed her fingers to her mouth, blinking rapidly to clear the tears threatening to fall. She couldn't imagine the damage the past he carried with him had done, the toll the last sixteen years had taken. The pain he would never admit to, would see as a weakness when he wasn't weak at all.

Finally he straightened, coming around to her open door. But he didn't get in. Instead, he paced back and forth, muttering, eventually shouting, "I hate him. Goddamn but I hate him."

"I know," she whispered, but more to herself than to him.

He stopped, looked up, and came for her then, grabbing her wrist as if to pull her out of the seat. She jerked at his hold, unable to break it, though the pain that lanced through her ankle as she stumbled to the ground had her wondering if she'd broken that instead.

"Great. Thanks. I needed that," she said, hobbling. "I told you you could drive."

He didn't say anything, just stared at her feet, still holding her wrist, his whole body shaking.

"Never mind. I'll be fine. Let's just go." But even then he didn't move, just raised his gaze to hers, his eyes frightened. So, so frightened.

"I don't know what to do," he said, his throat collapsing around the words.

She couldn't breathe. God, she couldn't breathe. "I know. Oh, honey, I know. I'm sorry."

"I've been rid of him for years. Or I thought I was rid of him. That he was gone, but he's not. He never will be. He's always going to be there."

"No." She shook her head, thought of the mother she'd never really known, thought of the father who she'd had to let go. "He won't always be there."

That was what he had to realize. What was going to drive the decision he made next. Wallace Campbell could very well die. For all Arwen knew, he'd done so while his son battled the demons that came with the family name.

He looked down at her, his eyes unfocused, his mind going places she couldn't but that scared her all the same. She didn't know his past. He'd been her one-sided crush in high school, the hot guy she'd taken to bed in her dreams, imagining his hands when touching herself in the dark of the night where no one could see.

But now . . .

She knew enough of who he was to understand this was going to turn his life upside down. He didn't have to see his father. He didn't have to go to him. He could saddle his horse and ride herd every day, keeping his ranch alive. But the things about his father that he'd stored in the attic of his mind had just tumbled down the stairs. And that changed everything.

He closed his eyes, his throat working as he swallowed, his jaw clicking as he ground it tight. Then he looked at her, reached for her, slammed her against the side of the truck, speared his fingers into her hair, and brought his mouth down on hers with such force she tasted blood. His, hers, she wasn't sure, though her bottom lip stung from the pressure.

She wedged her hands between their bodies to push him away, but the dampness on her cheeks stopped her. Tears, and she knew she wasn't the one letting them go, so she wound her fingers into the heated fabric of his shirt and kept him close, giving him her mouth that he seemed to desperately need.

And then her mouth wasn't enough, and his hands left her hair and found the button at her waistband. He freed it, unzipped her, tugged her jeans down to her knees, then went to work shoving down his own.

She wanted to stop him. She didn't want to stop him. He was out of his mind and it frightened her to see him like this. To know he was stronger than she was, and that he wasn't thinking, but only feeling, and looking for relief the only way he knew how.

This wasn't about her. It wasn't about their affair or their bargain or anything but Dax being ripped apart. Trying to rein him in, to soften the act, to calm him would be akin to telling him this was wrong.

If this was what he needed to remind him of who he was, there was nothing wrong about it. So she didn't argue when he stepped on the bunched-up fabric at her knees and pushed her jeans and her panties to her boots.

She was ready when he lifted her against the truck's rear quarter panel. The metal was hot against her bare backside, but not blistering. She looped her arms around his neck, opened her knees and made the most room she could with her ankles bound.

He flattened his palms on the truck bed beneath her arms, tilted his hips, and drove home. She gasped at the intrusion, wiggled to adjust, dropped her head back and stared at the sky as he fucked her.

He grunted and he cursed, words she couldn't make out and didn't need to. All she could do was hold on for the ride, give him this and hope it was enough to soothe the demon that gripped him.

His cock filled her, stretched her, beat at her with such force she felt the rips and tears as they happened. Her flesh burned, but the hard grinding base of his shaft had her clit on fire. And the angle of his stroke hit everything just right.

She came in crazy wild waves, her legs shaking, her sex gripping his cock and milking it until he followed, spilling, spewing, semen and words and unimaginable pain and helpless anger and raw primal fear. She took it all, held him, stroked him, coaxed him to mourn, but he pulled away, walked away, faced away and just stood there.

She leaned against the truck, her pants around her ankles, cum dripping down her thighs, her lower body fully exposed to any passing cow or cowboy, and she couldn't even move. She was spent, emotionally, physically—even mentally if her inability to think about what to do next was any indication.

Eventually she pulled herself together, dressed, wincing at the skin too tender for the soft cotton of her panties. He'd used her. He'd abused her. But more than that, he'd needed her, and she'd been there for him, and was glad.

Wiping her eyes, then her nose, she looked up and watched him pull up his pants. "Do you still want to drive?"

"No. You go on. I'm gonna . . . stay out here awhile."

Here? In the middle of a pasture? With the temperature already a hundred plus? "You don't have to go to the hospital. But let me drive you to the house."

He shook his head, looking down as he buckled his belt.

He'd just fucked her senseless, yet seeing his hands adjusting his pants had her aching all over again. "Dax—"

"No." His gaze whipped up to hers. "And don't wait for me at the house. Go home or back to work or wherever."

She couldn't just leave him out here. "Dax—"

"Fuck, Arwen. Just do what I say, okay?"

She said nothing, just stared at him, anger rising and tugging at her tongue and urging her to fight back. She knew better than to let anyone talk to her that way. But Dax wasn't anyone, and this wasn't a situation that fell into normal. And so she shifted into gear and drove away, leaving him lonely, leaving him as he'd asked.

The picture in her rearview mirror nearly killed her. His long legs ambling slowly, his hands stuffed in his pockets and his shoulders hunched as he stared at the ruts in the road. She thought her chest might explode. It hurt. Her lungs. Her throat. Her heart.

She kept one hand on the wheel, but brought up the other to cover her mouth, trying to hold back her sobs. That didn't work, so she used it to wipe away the tears streaming from her eyes until finally she gave up, driving blindly, the tiny figure walking behind her disappearing into the distance as she watched.

TWENTY

Darcy stood in the Coleman Medical emergency waiting room, arms wrapped around her midsection to keep the shivers coursing through her at bay. She wasn't really cold. She wasn't really feeling anything. She'd gone almost completely numb, an unblinking statue, an unmovable roadblock. But she couldn't stop shaking.

She stared at the swinging silver doors that led into the ER, the tiny reinforced windows too high for her to see anything happening down the corridor beyond. Once in awhile a staff member pushed through, but even then all she could see was the long tiled floor, the white walls, the curtained partitions.

She couldn't see The Campbell at all, and he was the reason she was here. No one knew anything, or if they did they weren't telling her, and until someone came out to give her news, good or bad, or to let her know there was no change in his condition, she was staying put. She was done walking away.

She had no idea where her mother was. The staff at home hadn't seen her since this morning. She wasn't answering her cell. Greg, who'd been with The Campbell at the office when he'd collapsed, was clueless. Who knew where the hell Dax was, though he was useless; he hadn't been in touch with their mother since his return. And Josh was out of suggestions.

Josh . . .

He sat behind her in one of the plastic chairs not meant for anyone's comfort. Last she'd looked, he was hunched forward, his elbows on his knees, one hand worrying the knuckle of the other's pinky. His hat kept her from seeing his face, only the line of his jaw and his neck before his shirt collar got in the way.

Eyes closed, she remembered him coming to tell her what had happened. She'd been in the back of Tess Dalton's closet when he'd arrived, folding clothes, smoothing out the wrinkles, trying—and failing—to do so dispassionately. Instead, a nearly overwhelming sense of responsibility had her taking care with every single piece.

At the sound of Josh's boots on the stairs, she'd called out, expecting Dax. When Josh had appeared in the bedroom, she'd known he wasn't there to kiss her again, and everything inside of her had gone cold and black.

He'd pulled off his hat, held the brim with both hands and stared at the floor gathering words. Blood had rushed to her head as she'd waited for him to speak. And for the first time she'd noticed he had a cowlick on the right of his forehead. Hair that should've been mashed flat by his hat stood up and waved.

In the end, all he'd said was, "Your father's in the hospital," and she'd tumbled out of the closet, searching for the shoes she'd kicked off before going in.

Halfway down the stairs she'd remembered her keys were in

her purse in the bedroom she was using. Josh had stepped aside for her to burst past, then on her return trip blocked the staircase and demanded she let him drive.

Since she remembered nothing of the trip to the hospital, his insistence on chauffeuring her had turned out to be a very good thing. The only thing about the past few hours that was.

"Darcy?" He spoke from directly behind her, the heat of his body tempting her to lean into him. But she couldn't lean. Not yet. She couldn't lean.

She shook her head. She didn't want to talk. She wanted Dax. "Have you heard anything from my brother?"

"No, but—"

"Arwen found him, right?"

"I'm supposing she did, but—"

"If you want to help me, find my brother." The words sounded harsh to her ears and she wanted to suck them back in and swallow them down and start over. Start the whole day over, the week, the month. She wanted to be living at home again, to be working with Greg and The Campbell.

Except she didn't want any of that. She just wanted Dax. "I'm sorry—"

At that, Josh moved in front of her, used the length of an index finger beneath her chin to force her to meet his gaze. "If you don't come and sit down, I'm going to pick you up and carry you out of here. I'm going to take you to the Blackbird and feed you. I'm going to sit in the cab of my truck while you lie down in the seat and nap. I'm not going to lose you when I've just found you. Now what's it going to be?"

His eyes never wavered. Neither did his voice or his resolve. She couldn't imagine that he'd manhandle her, but the threat rang with enough conviction that she found herself nodding. She was tired, and she was hungry, and she was not wearing the last few hours gracefully. Leaving didn't sit well, but her staying wasn't doing anyone any good.

"He's right," said a voice behind them.

Darcy spun to see the Campbell family physician running a hand through his hair and looking as tired as she felt. "Dr. Kirkland? You're here. Have you seen him? No one will tell me anything."

"I have, and no one has told you anything because there's been no change since he first arrived." He shoved his hands to his hips, his tie askew, his dress shirt wrinkled.

He'd been in Austin at a conference luncheon when The Campbell had collapsed, but had come when the hospital called. "So, what? We just wait?"

"I wait. You go home," he said, raising his hand when she opened her mouth to tell him she wasn't going anywhere. "He's being monitored, and you have my word I'll let you know the minute there's an update."

"I'd rather stay here. So you won't have trouble reaching me."

"Darcy—"

"No," she said, before the doctor could say more. "I want to be here."

The moment the words left her mouth, Josh placed his hand on her shoulder. "C'mon. At least to get something to eat. If you want to come back after that, I'll bring you. I promise."

She kept one arm crossed tightly over her middle, rubbed at her forehead with her other hand. What she wanted was for everyone to leave her alone, but since her wants didn't seem to be in the cards, she nodded, and let Josh guide her through the ER doors to the parking lot and his truck.

They made the ride to the diner without speaking, a Blake

Shelton playlist at low volume keeping the silence from growing awkward and nearly lulling her to sleep. She knew her exhaustion was fueled more by worry than needing to rest; it was only eight o'clock. But knowing didn't change the urge she had to close her eyes, just for a minute or two.

When she finally stirred, they were parked in front of the diner, Blake Shelton was still singing about a red roadside wildflower, and Josh was reading a book on his BlackBerry. Reading, as if they'd been here long enough for him to need something to do.

She pushed her hair from her face, glanced at the clock's dashboard display. Then she bolted upright. "Josh?"

He hit a couple of buttons on his phone, tucked it into his shirt pocket. "Ready to eat?"

"You let me sleep. We've been here half an hour."

"More like forty-five minutes, but yeah. You were tired enough to doze off. I didn't want to wake you when you obviously needed the nap."

She wanted to argue that his letting her sleep wasn't part of their deal, but found she had no ground to stand on. He'd brought her to eat, fulfilling his part of their bargain. "Did the doctor call?"

"He didn't call me, and I didn't hear your phone go off." He pulled the keys from the ignition, opened his door, and got out, rounding the cab to open hers. "Let's grab a bite before they close."

It was just getting dark, the only lights those from the parking lot and the diner's big front windows. She slid to her feet and looked up at Josh, his face a mosaic of shadows. "I really hate that you keep seeing me at my worst. I don't want you to be here because you think I need to be rescued."

He reached for both of her hands, pinned them to her sides and stepped closer, backing her into the truck's rear quarter panel and blocking her body with his. "Tell me you didn't just say that."

She swallowed, a tingle of apprehension tripping down the fuse of her spine. "What? That you're here because I need rescuing?"

"I doubt you've ever needed to be rescued in your life."

She smiled at that. "I fell in the pool at home when I was five. It caught me off guard and I panicked. My nanny jumped in to save me, dress shoes and all."

He shook his head, his eyes dark as he held her gaze. "That's not what I meant and you know it."

"You rescued me the day I stupidly walked away from the office," she told him, and wondered now if the stupid part had been walking in a near triple-digit temperature or leaving the office instead of standing her ground.

"I gave you a ride. Got you out of the heat." He squeezed her hands, let them go, slid his palms to her wrists then her elbows. "You would've done the same for yourself sooner or later."

His hands were on her shoulders now, and the firecracker in the small of her back was burning. She raised her arms, settled her hands at his waist. "I was so mad that day. I wasn't thinking straight. If not for you, I might've fainted dead away in the middle of Main Street."

"Are you thinking straight now?"

How was she supposed to answer that when her mind was torn between being here with him and what was happening at the hospital? "I'm worried about The Campbell. And I don't know if I'm more afraid that the doctor will call or that he won't. I know that's not what you want to hear, but that's where my head is."

"Sounds like pretty straight thinking to me. If you'd had anything else on your mind, then I'd have been worried."

She gave him a grin, cocked her head to the side. "I do have one other thing going on up there."

"Yeah?"

"Food," she said, digging her fingers into the trim muscles above the waistband of his jeans. "I'm hungrier than I'd thought."

"Then let's go," he said, but he didn't move away.

And since he didn't, she did. Away from the truck and into him. Against him. Moving her hands to his back and pulling him to her. Slowly, she rose up on her tiptoes, her breasts flat to his chest, her hips cradling his as he pushed back toward her.

"Dessert first," she whispered against the corner of his mouth before she caught at his lips with hers, nipping with her teeth, nudging with the tip of her tongue.

Still, he didn't move, and she worried she'd been too bold, that she'd read him wrong, heard him wrong. That his wanting to see her wasn't about . . . this. Except what else could it be?

And then she felt him growing stiff, thickening against her belly, and she kissed him harder, and his hands at her shoulders slid into her hair. He held her, stepped her backward into the truck, pushed his body to hers and finally kissed her back.

His tongue found hers unerringly, and was slick and hot and sure. He took her with purpose as much as passion, leaving his mark, claiming her. She melted into him, lost her breath, lost her head.

Her breasts grew heavy, her nipples as hard as his cock behind his fly. He tasted like goodness, and he made her want more, want everything, want all of him because he also made her forget.

She wanted to stay here, to live here, to wake up and have this be her world. Josh and his mouth and his hands that made everything better. Even at the end of the day he smelled like sunshine and fresh air and he centered her, kept her from coming undone.

When he pulled free, she closed her eyes because he had the

strength she needed, the control she lacked. Not always, but to-night. Tonight she was a mess of emotion and knew better than to trust any of what she was feeling.

He walked to the back of the truck. She stayed where she was, giving him the time and space he needed. Time and space she used to steady herself, too. To gather her thoughts for when he returned.

Moments later, she heard the scrape of his boots over the parking lot's loose gravel. He stopped in front of her, nodded in the direction of the diner's door.

She held up a staying hand. "Just so you know, that wasn't about me needing to be rescued."

"I never thought it was."

"And it wasn't about tonight, the hospital, any of that."

"Okay," he said, moonlight catching on his dimple as he smiled.

"Just so you know."

"I know." And he left it at that, taking her hand and not letting go until he'd tucked her away in the back corner booth and settled in the seat across from her.

The wink he gave her said he knew as well as she that they'd stopped more than a few conversations. And the wink she gave him in return said she wouldn't have had it any other way.

TWENTY-ONE

AX SAT IN his truck in front of Arwen's cottage looking for a reason not to shift into gear, not to drive away and return to his vagabond life. It was tempting, that existence, no expectations save for those of any rancher he'd hired on with. No family wanting him to step into shoes that didn't fit. No debt dragging him down and taking the fun out of what he loved doing.

No woman making him comfortable enough to want to hang around.

Yeah. That.

Three days ago, Arwen had come to the ranch and delivered the news of his father's condition. He hadn't seen her since. He hadn't talked to her since. He hadn't talked to Darcy. He hadn't been to the hospital. All he'd done was work, laboring dawn to dusk until he couldn't move his arm to lift a longneck, his feet to step into the tub at the end of the day.

He'd eaten only because he had to, and not much at that since it had been Boone doing the cooking recently and the boy had a heavy hand with the salt. Sleep had been a matter of his exhausted body demanding he stop running on empty, and turning off his mind when he couldn't find the key. What was left of his common sense knew he couldn't keep going like this and live to tell the tale.

All these years later, he'd thought his past settled, yet his father, even in a coma, was still running his life. And for some bizarre reason he was letting him.

More than once while lying in bed and staring at the roof in the bunkhouse, he'd thought about packing up, signing away his share of the ranch to Casper and Boone, telling Darcy good-bye, promising to keep in touch. Then he'd thought about making those calls from down the road, once Crow Hill was nothing but a speck on the map of his memory and he didn't have to look anyone in the eye.

But he couldn't do that to his sister, or the boys. He couldn't do it to Arwen. Most of all, he couldn't do it to himself. If he was going to go, he had to do it right—the right way and for the right reasons. He wasn't going to be a hotheaded dick about it the way he'd been at eighteen, even if not sticking around was still a dick move. At least he'd come far enough to be able to admit that.

In the meantime, he was damn sick of his own company, and he knew Arwen, who'd been clear about wanting him only for sex, wouldn't ask questions—though she might want the answer to the one he was mulling over: *Why was he still sitting here when she was inside?* That was assuming she wanted to see him at all after the really shitty way he'd treated her when she'd come to deliver the news of his father.

It was nearly four a.m., and the lights in her bedroom and bath were both on. He thought about her in her tub, thought about joining her there. Thought about leaving for the ranch an hour from now smelling like a citrus grove and having to put up with shit about it from the boys.

Best he could figure, he hadn't yet moved because a part of him was still stuck on her rushing to tell him about his old man when she knew they weren't close, they didn't speak, hell, they hadn't seen each other for sixteen years. And yet it had meant something to her for him to know his father had come up against something out of his control and been cut down. Maybe for good.

Darcy knowing, he got. Darcy had devoted a lot of blood, sweat, and tears establishing her position as a Campbell, which was a totally fucked up thing to have to do. But Arwen, more than anyone, had to know bloodlines didn't make family.

Respect took care of that, as did discipline handed down from a place of caring, not power, instruction offered as guidance, not grudging obligation. Expectations driven by investment, not some bullshit tradition that was more for show than anything.

Tess and Dave Dalton had been his family. Boone and Casper were his family. Darcy, too. And watching Arwen's truck bounce across the pasture to find him, he'd been hit again with a powerful sense of everything in his world coming together, a close-knit bunch of misfits, the Dalton Gang, extended.

Even after hearing what she had to say, that sense had stuck, and he couldn't deny that feeling of rightness, completeness, as much as his desire to lose himself in her body, was the reason he was here.

His hand was on the door handle to make the body-losing thing happen when the interior of his truck's cab lit up like the fourth of July. Squinting, he looked out his side mirror at the red, white, and blue cherry top spinning on the sheriff's cruiser behind him.

Great. Just great. News of his affair with Arwen was about to become grist for the ridiculously efficient Crow Hill gossip mill, his efforts at lying low slapped useless.

He cracked open his door, only to be greeted with Sheriff Orleans loudly belted, "Hands where I can see 'em, bub. Step out of the truck slowly. I want you on your belly, now."

Well, that shit wasn't going to happen. The belly part anyway. He ached and creaked and didn't want to chance getting stuck on the ground. With his arms extended through the window, he used a boot to shove open the door and climbed down.

Standing there, he leaned forward, forearms on the frame, and turned his head, grinning into the beam of the sheriff's flashlight. Then—not that it would do a damn bit of good—he poured on the Dax Campbell charm. "Hey, Sheriff. Long time no see."

Switching off the light, Ned Orleans gave a loud guffaw then holstered the big Colt revolver he'd drawn, keeping his hand on the butt as he came closer. "Dax Campbell. Should've known I'd find one of the Dalton Gang skulking around one of Crow Hill's prettiest ladies."

"The more things change, the more they don't. Or something like that, eh, Ned?"

The sheriff stopped, braced his free hand on the top of Dax's door. "Does that mean you're sitting out here because you drank a little too much while watching the saloon's Kittens dance? Cuz I've got a cell where you can sleep it off if so."

"Nope. Sober as a judge," he said before he could think better of it. Judge brought to mind courtroom, which brought to mind attorney, which brought to mind Crow Hill's one and only law firm.

"Listen," Ned began, hanging his head, rubbing at his jowl with his gun hand. "Sorry to hear about your father. I know you two aren't exactly close, but it's a shame to see a good man struck down."

A good man? Really? When had that happened? But Dax wasn't interested in the sheriff's cell, so he checked his sarcasm before saying, "Thanks. It's appreciated."

"Wallace has had a hard last few years, you know, ever since—"

"Sheriff?"

At the sound of Arwen's voice, Dax and Ned both turned. She stood at the end of her walkway where it met the street. Neither of the men had heard her come out, and even though Dax pulled in a deep, searching breath, he didn't smell her.

She was barefoot, rubbing the sole of one foot on the top of the other, her arms crossed to hold her bathrobe in place. It looked like silk, the light of the moon and that from the street lamp on the corner of Willowbrook shining off the pink polka dots scattered on the background of white.

Pink. He should've known.

Her hair tumbled around her face and shoulders, all rumpled and messy like she'd just left her bed. That reminded him that it had been way too long since he'd joined her there. Then he remembered the last time he'd seen her, what he'd done, the way he'd treated her.

He swallowed, a fist of remorse slamming into his gut and robbing him of air. Fucking her against the side of her truck had been a pretty shitty way to treat her when all she'd done was bring him news she thought important for him to hear.

He needed to make up for that. He owed her a better time. He owed her an apology, a big one, and realized that could be a problem. After his behavior, he wouldn't blame her for not wanting to hear anything he had to say.

"Sorry for the disturbance, Ms. Poole." Sheriff Orleans hitched up his belt, circling the bed of Dax's truck. "Looked like this one might've been sleeping off a drunk, and I didn't want him doing it on the street when the jail's not but six blocks away."

She mashed her hair to her cheek, sleepily tucked it behind her ear. "Your lights have my living room looking like a carnival ride."

Dax wasn't sure if she was pissed, telling off the sheriff in a way that wouldn't get her arrested, or if she'd really had her sleep interrupted. He'd have to move closer to get at the truth, but until the lawman gave the word, Dax was married to his window for better or worse.

"Ah, let me get those turned off. Then as soon as Mr. Campbell here's on his way, I'll make a loop through the neighborhood and be on mine." His good ol' boy laughter bellowed into the quiet night and caused Dax to wince. "Gotta have the constituents feeling safe and sound in their beds."

Right. Especially with elections coming up, because judging by the signs scattered along Main Street's sidewalks, Ned had young blood looking to oust him from the cushy job he'd held for twenty plus years.

From where he stood, Dax heard Arwen's sigh. She hadn't been expecting him, and he wanted to tell her not to give up her privacy for his sake. He was happy to take the fall for loitering. But it was too late.

"It's okay, Sheriff." She motioned Dax forward with a wave. "He's here to see me."

Sheriff Orleans looked from Arwen to Dax and back a couple of times, then blurted out the obvious. "At four o'clock in the morning?"

She shrugged, wrapping her arms tighter. "It's the only time our schedules don't conflict."

"So you two . . ." He waggled a finger from one to the other, and Dax finally straightened with as sheepish a grin as he could manage.

After that, the sheriff ambled toward his car, shaking his head and muttering under his breath. The only words Dax—passing the other man as he crossed the street—was able to make out were, "Goddamn Dalton Gang."

Kinda funny, that. Or it would've been if the look on Arwen's face hadn't been quite so ominous.

"Were you asleep?" he asked.

"Almost."

"I thought you'd be in the tub."

She shook her head, shoved her hair from her face with both hands. "I got home extra late. Was too tired. Got undressed and crashed on the couch."

He took a long step in reverse. "I can go."

"You're already here," she said, and he counted that as a good sign and moved toward her again, going so far as to join her on the sidewalk.

But he kept his hands to himself, not knowing how welcome he really was and not wanting to cross any newly drawn lines. "You know our secret's out."

"And thanks for that."

"Sorry. It wasn't intentional."

She gave a shrug as she turned and walked off. He waited because she hadn't invited him in, and only followed because she left the door open. Once inside, he shut it, and hearing her in the kitchen headed that way. "Thought you were tired."

"Now I'm hungry," she said, yanking open the refrigerator door.

"It's four thirty."

"And you came here in the middle of the night just to give me a hard time?"

Of a sort, he mused privately, but then he frowned, leaning a shoulder on the doorjamb and stuffing his hands in his pockets. "The sheriff said something about my old man having a hard last few years. Any idea what he was talking about?"

"Do you care?"

"No, but I'm curious."

She tore the top from a container of yogurt, stuck a spoon inside and stirred. "I assume it's about you leaving and not letting anyone know where you've been all this time."

"I don't know. It sounded like something more."

"Guess you'll have to make a visit to the hospital and find out, won't you?" she asked before sticking a spoonful of the yogurt into her mouth.

That got his goat. "When's the last time you made a visit to see Hoyt, huh? Where is he these days?"

"I didn't know Ned had mentioned my father. Or," she added, lifting a brow, "that you'd come here to compare our paternal dysfunctions."

"I came here to see you."

"Then don't dig for what I might know or might've heard."

That made him want to pin her down until she cracked and told him. Until he stopped and realized what he was thinking.

What the holy *hell* was wrong with him?

He shook his head. "Sorry. No digging. I swear."

"And no asking about my father."

"If you say so."

"But"—she gestured with the spoon—"I get to ask about yours."

"How is that any kind of fair?"

"You're what? Thirty-four? And you're still looking for life to be fair?"

He bit down, ground his jaw, said nothing.

She arched a brow. "Why you haven't gone to see him?"

Two could play at this game. "Why are you using your father's old booth from the Buck Off Bar as a kitchen table?"

She slammed the half-eaten carton of yogurt on the table and flounced by. "I'm going to bed."

"Is that an invitation?" He should go, hit the road. He didn't need this shit in his life.

And then he changed his mind as she said from halfway down the hall, "Think about the last time you saw me and see if you can figure that out for yourself."

TWENTY-TWO

JUST INSIDE HER bedroom door, Arwen closed her eyes and shuddered. Her body ached for her to call back that, yes, he was invited to join her. Her body, however, wasn't in charge. Her body didn't understand that she'd spent the last three days pissed off and worried and hurting and angry because he hadn't been in touch.

And that was just stupid because now that he was in touch, she was blowing him off. She wanted to blame her reaction on being tired, but knew it was more about the tangle of emotions wrapped around her like a web of silk, strong and seductive and dangerous. Dax's web. Dax's silk.

She was the fly to his spider and no matter how relentlessly she struggled to escape his trap, she didn't have strong enough wings.

At the side of her bed, she dropped her robe and stood naked, anticipating. She could hear his boots on the floor as he left the kitchen and entered the hallway. She counted—one, two, three, four, five—until his steps stopped, and she knew he was at the door to her room. She breathed deeply, turned, waited.

He came in, holding her gaze as he unsnapped his one cuff then the other before moving to his throat and tugging at the snaps down the front of his shirt. He popped them slowly. One at a time. Each sound causing her to jump, to tremble.

With his shirt hanging open, he took another step, then balanced from foot to foot as he tugged off his boots. His next step brought him almost close enough to touch. But she didn't. She stayed as she was, her nipples tight, her pussy wet, and watched him free his belt from its buckle then work on his fly.

He took his time. The first brass button. The second. The third. Inch by inch, his briefs came into view. His briefs and the heavy load they held to his belly. His erection was thick, straining against the fabric, the head of his cock a bulbous tease. And then he was done, his clothes open, his body ready, yet still he didn't move.

She couldn't stand it, seeing him there, the skin of his torso shadowed, his legs covered, his cock so close, so big where it filled the open vee of his fly. She wanted him. Desperately. But she kept her arms at her sides, kept her hands loose. She didn't reach for him. She didn't twist her fingers together to keep the nerves eating at her skin from burrowing deeper.

This was sex. Nothing else. Yet the look in his eyes told the truth of the tale. He'd come here looking for something he needed. Something he couldn't find anywhere else, get from anyone else, and that responsibility weighed on her too heavily.

She was supposed to be working him out of her system. She was supposed to be putting every bit of her past behind her. Dax was making it impossible for her to do either. He was in her house, and in her head, and she feared he was in her heart.

Not just knocking at it, or playing with it, but worming his way to a spot she wouldn't be able to reach to remove him. Because she knew it would happen.

They would finish whatever this was between them and he would leave Crow Hill, and after he was gone she would not—*would not*—keep any part of him alive the way she had the first time.

He came closer, one step, then another, stopping in front of her, close enough to touch but doing so only with his eyes. They held hers as he shrugged out of his shirt, and she breathed deeply, scenting him, the hint of sun and heat that stayed with him.

The skin of his hands, his wrists, that of his face and neck was baked to a darker bronze than that covering the rest of his torso. A cowboy's tan. A working man's tan. His pectoral muscles and his shoulders and his neck telling the story of the manual labor he required of his upper body.

She couldn't help herself, and she reached out, sliding her fingertips along his collarbone, the skin beneath resilient and firm. He kept his hands at his hips, but pulled in a sharp breath, and her stomach clenched in response. This thing between them . . .

"Hurry," she whispered. It was all she could say, her chest rising and falling as she watched him shed his jeans and his briefs.

Then he was naked in front of her, his forehead against hers, his toes on hers, his hands holding hers at her sides, his cock between them insistent. They stood together, breathed together, let the room disappear as together they became one.

She closed her eyes and felt the sting of tears, but left them to well behind her lids. Wiping them away would mean taking her hands from Dax's and she couldn't bring herself to do that.

He lifted his chin, brushed his lips along her hairline, whispered, "Do you know how beautiful you are?"

A shiver ran like a river down her spine, pooled at the base, spread lower and worked its way between her legs to ready her.

"You're the one who's beautiful. Your mouth. Your hands. The way you touch me. The way you look at me."

"Just not the way *I* look, eh?" he asked with a laugh.

She opened her eyes, lifted her hands, and threaded her fingers into his hair, holding him. "I didn't know what to expect. When I heard you were back. I'd pictured you all this time as I knew you in high school. Cocky and brash and always with the sort of grin that turned girls to puddles at your feet. But now . . ."

"I hear I look really good in jeans."

"In them, but even more so out of them."

"Guess it's a good thing you're the only one who gets to see me this way. All those puddles might start a flood—hey, that might be the solution to our drought. I strut around naked, and the water flows."

She shook her head, her lips drawn into a grin she couldn't help. "And here I was trying to be serious."

"Life's too hard to take seriously."

A dozen responses rose but she squashed them all.

"On the other hand," he said, grinding his hips and rubbing his hard cock against her.

She stepped away, gripped both of his biceps and shoved him onto the bed. He bounced once, braced himself on his elbows and arched one brow, looking from his cock standing at attention to her then back again and again until all she could do was laugh and climb on top.

"Much better," he said, his hands on her thighs. "I thought I was going to have to take care of this on my own."

She thought of his hands stroking his cock. "Do it."

"What?" He frowned, then his expression took on that look she loved, big bad wolf and black sheep all rolled up in one, and when she lifted his hands from her thighs, and moved them to the plane of his belly above his jutting cock, he didn't argue.

Instead, he said, "I'm sorry. About the other day. About the way I treated you."

Not this. Not now. "You made me come."

"You know what I mean. I was thoughtless and selfish and my head was all fucked up. I took it out on you. I was an ass."

She didn't want to talk about the other day. She didn't want him to be human and kind. She didn't want to need him for anything but this. "Make me come now."

She raised up onto her knees, lifted one thigh to accommodate his reach, and found the head of his cock with her pussy, sliding down until he filled her, leaning forward, her hands on his shoulders, until she couldn't move.

All she could do was feel, holding him, squeezing him, riding him. Hurting herself because she couldn't imagine ever giving him up.

He held her hips, met her downward motion with upward thrusts, lifting the both of them from the mattress again and again. His strokes soothed and startled and she cried out as the pressure built. He scraped her clit, the hard base of his cock, the plump head when he withdrew, the cushion of hair darker than the rest on his body when she ground against him.

After the truck and the pasture, she needed this. To be on top. To be in charge. Getting what she wanted. Getting off the way she wanted. Using Dax the way he'd used her. Except this wasn't the same. She wasn't fucking him to forget an external blow.

He was the source of her upheaval, and she wasn't punishing him but herself, pulling his web tighter, binding them with each stroke when what she wanted was for them both to get off then go their separate ways.

Didn't she? *Didn't she?*

She slowed to allow the awareness of his body in hers to heighten, to feel, to really feel, to let go. She paused, moved again, overwhelmed with the emotion sweeping her away, and when she stopped and shook her head, he brought her down and held her close, rolling them over and covering her, protecting her, burying his face in the crook of her neck and rocking her.

He was gentle, taking his time, tuned into every move she made. Her vulnerability frightened her. She was his and she was open and each stroke of his cock drew a gasp or a moan because she needed this, needed *him*, and that need confused and confounded.

And so she gave up, became nothing but her body, rising with him as desire pulled her toward the brink. His legs bracketed her legs, and his hips cradled her hips, and they were wet together and hot together and it was all too much. She cried out, shuddered, collapsed as the storm swept through her. The same spinning wind took him higher, and he strained as he reared up and spilled his seed.

They lay quietly for a while after that, Dax on his side, spooned around her, their feet braided together, his penis soft against her back, then he finally spoke. "About the booth in your kitchen."

First Faith. Now Dax. The booth was her business, but at least this subject put her back on solid ground. "Yes?"

"It's okay that you've kept that piece of your past."

"Thanks for your permission."

"Shit, Arwen." He rolled away, flung his arm over his eyes. "Do you have to twist everything I say? Or turn it into a big joke to make me look stupid?"

Did she do that? Were her defenses so ingrained she didn't stop to consider what he was saying and why, but reacted instead? "I don't mean to do that. It's just . . ."

"It's just what?" he asked, and when she remained silent, he shifted toward her, braced on an elbow, his head in his hand, his free arm along his side and his hand at his hip instead of on her.

She wanted his hand on her. "I'm not trying to make you look stupid. It's just . . ." *What was she supposed to say? She didn't know what to say.*

"I get it. It's how you deal. A defense mechanism. You don't want to talk, you snipe or you shut down or you change the subject. I don't want to talk . . ."

"You leave."

"I guess I do," he admitted, and then moved his hand to her stomach, above her pussy, below her breasts, as if sex was the last thing on his mind. "Or at least I take myself out of the way."

"Like you did when you got out of my truck the other day?"

He nodded, began to rub circles on her skin with one fingertip. "I don't even remember getting back to the house. It was close to dark. Casper and Boone were waiting on the back porch."

"They were worried."

He snorted. "Yeah, that they were going to have to pick up my third of the workload."

"I hardly think that's what was going through their minds."

"Oh, who the hell knows what they were thinking? That I was insane, most likely."

"At least a little bit crazy."

"Or a whole lot of crazy." He dropped back against his pillow then, tucked his crossed arms beneath his head. "I just couldn't deal. Not with the news coming out of nowhere like that. If he'd been sick, I'm pretty sure Darcy would've mentioned it."

"Unless he didn't tell her."

"Which wouldn't surprise me. She's like an afterthought to him. Always has been."

"And yet she's the one at the hospital standing vigil."

He took his time, finally responded with, "I'm going to have to go see him, aren't I?"

"I think you knew that a couple of days ago."

"It's just . . . I say he means nothing to me, but know that's not true. It's what he means that I'm having trouble with."

"He's your father. He'll always mean something."

"What does Hoyt mean to you?"

She pictured her father the last time she'd seen him. He hadn't even acknowledged her presence. In his condition, sober by then but still mourning the loss of her mother, that was hardly surprising. What was surprising was how much it had hurt. She'd cared for him for so long. She'd done her best to be there, and it had meant nothing to him.

"I don't know. I want to think he did all he knew how to do. He kept me with him. I was never shunted off to a foster home, though I know some people thought that was where I belonged."

"My mother."

"Yeah, I never got that."

"She couldn't control what was going on at home. She needed something to dig into."

"Someone else's life."

He nodded. "It's how she survived her own. The one I'm pretty sure she would've done anything to get out of as long as no one had to know."

"She didn't love your father?"

"She put up with him and all his screwing around. That's all I know."

"That says a lot more about her than it does him."

"What? That she wasn't putting out and he had to go elsewhere?"

"No, jackass. That she could overlook infidelity to keep her family together."

"Ah, but that's where you're wrong. It wasn't about keeping her family together. She put up with him so no one would know the truth."

TWENTY-THREE

THE DAY'S SWEAT running in a river down his spine, Dax stared into the refrigerator in the ranch house kitchen, hoping dinner would jump out at him and he wouldn't have to cook. Since the day of their father's heart attack, Darcy'd been AWOL, leaving him, Boone, and Casper to feed themselves.

They were perfectly capable, but they weren't Darcy, or Tess, with her tables full of meat and potatoes and pie for dessert. Or Arwen, with her aluminum pans of beans and barbecue and cobbler. His stomach rumbled, but the fridge wasn't giving up anything but five pounds of hamburger wrapped in white butcher paper, and it was too late to see what the back porch freezer held.

A quick check of the pantry yielded spaghetti and jarred sauce. Even he could manage a pot of pasta. Not that a rib eye didn't sound a whole lot better, but the Dalton Gang wasn't living on a rib-eye budget. And he was beginning to think that was going to be the lay of the land until Faith let up on the purse strings.

Not that he'd ordered supper from a country club menu while cowboying in Montana, but hell. There was something wrong when a cowman couldn't enjoy the fruit of his own damn labors once in awhile. And he didn't mean enjoying it all ground up, a pound mixed with noodles and sauce and spread between three grown men.

No, he wanted meat, a big juicy marbled steak from a gorgeous grass-fed bovine, meaning he'd have to go elsewhere since *gorgeous* didn't describe the beef cattle calling the Dalton Ranch home. At least not this year, this season; maybe next, if he was still around.

He slammed a cast-iron skillet on the stove top, tore open the hamburger and eyed it for a few before digging in his hand and halving it. Two and a half pounds. Fuck the budget. He wrapped up the rest, returned it to the fridge, lit the burner beneath the skillet, and went looking for a pot for boiling water.

He was bent in half with his head in the cabinet when the screen door squeaked open and bounced shut in its frame behind him. "Hey, don't we have a big pot here somewhere? For the spaghetti?"

"Top shelf. Back on the right," Darcy replied.

Dax raised up, banged his head on the edge of the counter. "Shit, Darcy. Give a warning next time. I thought you were one of the boys."

She held out her arms, looked back at him without smiling. "Nope. It's just me. Your sister. The only one of our father's children who seems to care if he lives or dies."

Rubbing the back of his head, he looked at her for a long

moment, then filled the pot with water and set it to boil before using a fork to break up the meat. "You been there all this time? At the hospital?"

When she didn't answer, he glanced back. She was standing in the same place, wearing the same blank expression, her arms now crossed defensively over her chest. Her eyes were tired, the circles beneath like dark horseshoes against skin that was more ghostly than pale and free of makeup.

But he'd asked her once. He wasn't going to ask again. It was obvious she'd come here with something on her mind. And as much as he probably didn't want to hear it, he'd give her the floor for as long as it took her to unload. Her ball. Her court. He was only here for the show.

"You need salt in the water. For the pasta," she finally said.

"Thanks." He set aside the fork and found the saltshaker, then found himself asking. "What are you doing here?"

"Coming to find out what you're doing here."

"I live here. Last I looked, so did you. Since you hadn't been around, I figured you'd moved back to the house."

"Why would I do that?"

Because it was closer to the hospital? Because almost everything she owned was in the bedroom suite she'd lived in her whole life?

Because she was eaten up with guilt for abandoning the father who'd abandoned her first and thought being there would turn back the clock?

He stirred the browning meat, shrugged. "I don't know, Darcy. You weren't here. I assumed you'd gone home. Unless you've shacked up with Josh Lasko."

He turned as he said it, and he hadn't heard her cross the floor, so he wasn't prepared for her open palm connecting with his face so hard that he jerked backward, stumbled a step, and took the skillet of ground beef with him.

He looked down, watched the grease pool on the floor, the skillet wobble, the crumbles of meat scatter like feed from a trough. Then he looked up. Darcy's pale face was red, her eyes dry, fury rolling off her in waves.

He curled his hands over the counter's edge and leaned back. He had a feeling she was mad at the world as much as him; he just happened to be the closest punching bag. But he asked anyway, "I guess you're mad at me?"

She snorted at the obvious. "Why haven't you been to the hospital?"

He swallowed, his chest and throat tight. "No real reason for me to go, is there?"

"Goddammit, Dax." Her voice rose with each syllable. "Our father is there."

"Like I said." He left it at that, stayed where he was, continued to hold her gaze.

She blinked rapidly, as if fighting tears, trembled repeatedly, as if suffering hypothermia. "Do you hate him that much? That you can't make amends before he dies?"

"Is he going to die?" Dax asked, more worried at the moment about Darcy than their old man.

"The doctors aren't saying much. He's still in a coma"

Dax sighed. "Then how do you suggest I make amends?"

"I don't know. I don't know." And then exhaustion claimed her. She backed up, reached for a chair, pulled it from under the table and sat. "I don't know anything."

What he knew was that his sister was not in a good way. "When's the last time you slept?"

Darcy shrugged.

"And food? Have you been eating?

"I don't remember." She fluttered a hand, used it to push her hair out of her face then propped her elbow on the table and leaned into it. "Josh brings me things."

So his wondering about Josh and his sister hadn't been that far off the mark. "You've been there all this time? And he's been with you?"

"Yes and yes," she said, and then huffed, turning her head enough to glare at him. "Unlike my brother."

Dax let that pass. "What about Mom?"

Another shrug. "It's been just me and Josh and Greg."

"Who the hell is Greg?"

"Greg Barrett. From the law office."

Oh. That Greg. "What's he doing there?"

"I don't know, Dax," she said with a fling of her arm. "He was there when The Campbell collapsed. I guess he cares what happens to him."

Right. Anything to assure his place in the firm. Dax reached over and turned off the gas flame beneath the pot of water. A waste of fuel when he'd lost his appetite. "You're going to end up in an adjoining room if you don't take care of yourself."

"I don't care—"

"I do. Darcy. Shit. That's enough." He took a deep breath, scratched the scruff on his cheek, the skin still stinging from her slap. He was no good at this family crap. "If he's in a coma, he won't know you're there—"

"He might. And anyway. I'll know it."

"So his *might* makes it worth being there and you getting sick in the process?"

"I'm not sick."

"You're not well."

Her tears broke loose then, her chest heaving, her sobs loud and snotty like those of a scrawny bawling calf. "What do you expect? I'm doing this all on my own. You're not there. Mom's fallen off the face of the earth. Josh and Greg are trying, but they're not family. You are. You're all I have."

His gut clenched, his heart, his lungs, his throat. He couldn't swallow or breathe, and he closed his eyes against the pain. If she was counting on him for anything, she was going to be sorely, *sorely,* let down.

He didn't feel like family. He didn't even feel like a hired hand. He felt like a stranger, one who knew nothing about what she might need from him.

Except he did know. He'd known all his life.

He'd given it to her when she'd come home from winning a cheer competition that he'd been the only Campbell to attend. When she'd received her nearly perfect SAT scores and no one else had been around to pop the cork on a bottle of champagne.

When she'd finally passed her driving test, only to broadside one of Brad Coleman's loose cows on her drive home, planting their mother's Cadillac face down in a ditch. Dax had been the one to rescue her, winching her out of the ditch and the dead cow into the bed of his truck because their father couldn't be pulled away from his Glenlivet.

Sidestepping the grease and the meat, Dax made his way to where Darcy sat hunched over, making herself small and unimportant. He squatted down, wrapped his arms around her. She didn't even hesitate, but looped hers around his neck and buried her face in his shoulder.

They stayed like that until his shirt was soaked and she was all cried out, until his thighs burned from the strain of not moving and being there for her. Until loud boot steps clomped across the porch and the screen door opened again and Dax looked up.

Boone came in first, Casper right behind, both frowning at

finding their supper on the floor. "What the hell, Campbell?" Casper circled the table. "This a joke? Or you trying to get out of KP duty?"

Dax waved toward the door. "Holler for Bing and Bob. They can eat it. I'll start over."

"Jesus, Dax. You can't let the dogs clean the floor." Darcy straightened, wiped her hands down her face, and got to her feet.

Shaking his head, he stood and pushed her back down. "They can have the meat because the floor hasn't been swept, much less mopped, since you did it last. I may be a heathen, but we're way past the five-second rule here, and I'm not about to risk whatever's been living in the filth moving in and calling me home."

She gave a careless shrug, knuckled away the dampness that had her eyes red and bleary. "You're disgusting."

"Thank you."

"I should probably go."

This time when she got up he let her, but told her, "You should probably stay."

"I can't," she said, her smile small and weak. "You know where I'll be if you need me."

He pressed his lips tight, ground his jaw, keeping in the words pushing against his tongue. This wasn't the time or the place, and his sister was in no condition to hear that she was wasting her time. That their father, if he didn't die, would never change.

He walked her to the door, tugging her out of the way as the border collies raced in to feast, then followed her onto the porch. "And you know where I'll be if you need me."

"Yeah. That's the part that makes me sad," she said, turning and leaving him there to soak up the guilt that rained down while wishing for water to wash it away.

TWENTY-FOUR

HALFWAY TO TOWN, Darcy pulled off the county highway onto the road's rocky shoulder and shifted into park. She had no idea where she was going. She didn't know what to do. She was running on empty, numb, frozen. Paralyzed with indecision.

Since The Campbell's collapse, the hospital had been her entire world, but she couldn't face the beeps and chirps and squeaks of rubber-soled shoes on the tile floor when the sound she most wanted to hear, The Campbell's voice, had been silenced.

Being stuck with the smells when she breathed in was bad enough. Her clothes, her skin. Her hair. She reeked of harsh antiseptic, of waxy pine. Of the soap dispensed in the ER restrooms and of the building's stale air.

Her hands were dry, her nails ragged, her cuticles in desperate need of her manicurist's attention. Or they would've been if she could've made herself care about anything but The Campbell's condition.

Stupidly, she'd expected Dax to jump behind the wheel, drive her back to the hospital, and stay at her side, making everything better just by being there. And the reason that was stupid was because Dax hadn't been there for her in years.

Sure, he'd let her cry on his shoulder, even after she'd left a big red palm print on his face, but she was on her own. Grown-up Dax wasn't the brother she'd counted on to pick up the pieces every time she shattered.

And why was it taking her until now to realize she was as dysfunctional as the rest of her family by putting herself in that position again and again? She was worth more. She deserved better. And yet her behavior was ingrained.

She didn't know how to stop trying to build the family she wanted out of the one she had.

She picked up her phone from the seat beside her, pulled up the contact list, and stared at the only other number she could think of to dial. It rang twice, and when her call was answered, she said, "I just saw Dax."

"And?" Josh asked.

She swallowed, humiliated. "I don't know where to go."

"You okay to drive? Do I need to come get you?"

"No, I'm fine."

"Meet me at the store."

"Okay." She disconnected, put the car back in gear, ignored the stabbing guilt that insisted she go to the hospital instead.

The trip took another twenty-five minutes, and she didn't think of anything but seeing Josh, her touchstone, her anchor, her port in this storm nothing in her experience had prepared her for. Josh, who'd kept vigil with her. Josh, who'd told her he wanted to see her. Josh, who'd become so much more to her than a pair of long legs in Wrangler jeans.

And what was she to him except a woman who couldn't find her footing? She hated the thought of being a burden, yet here she was again, turning to him when she couldn't find her way. How sad was it that this was her life?

The back door was open when she arrived at the Laskos' store, Josh propping a shoulder against the frame, his hands in his pockets, his ankles crossed, one boot toe down on the flashing. She met his gaze, held it as she turned off the car, as she got out and climbed the steps, brushing past him on her way through.

She carried his warmth with her as, stomach tumbling, she walked into the office where he'd brewed her a cup of coffee and dispelled every misconception she'd had about who he was. He came in behind her, let the back door slam and latch, the space growing tiny and close. Intimate.

Without a word, he placed his hand in the small of her back, guiding her out of the office and into the rear of the store. She kept her head down, a hand raised to hide her face. It was a weak attempt at keeping from being recognized. She wasn't up for small talk, not even to answer questions about The Campbell's condition. Not today.

As if sensing her unease, Josh blocked her body with his, ushering her through a second door. This one led into a warehouse running the length of the structure and housing the store's bulk supplies. A staircase in the front corner took her into the building's attic, and she was all too aware of Josh behind her as she climbed.

Except it wasn't an attic. At least not one similar to the unfinished space above the ranch house, where Tess and Dave Dalton had stored a lifetime of memories in boxes and trunks and crates.

Or of the sort at the mansion on the hill, where her parents put extra furnishings they couldn't be bothered to get rid of.

No, this attic was a loft apartment and had Josh's stamp all over it. Open ductwork and support beams ran the length of the gabled ceiling. The floor was hardwood, the walls barn red with tongue-and-groove slats.

A freestanding divider, no more than six feet high, separated the largest part of the living space from what she assumed were the sleeping quarters and the bath. And since it backed up to the kitchen, she imagined it housed the room's plumbing and wiring and cable.

It was cozy, the furniture outfitted in weathered blues and grays with accents of red and gold. The sofa and recliner were leather, the tables oak, the throw rugs knotted from rags and handmade. She breathed in and smelled what she swore was Murphy Oil Soap, and then she turned and looked at Josh.

"Is this where you live?" Even expecting him to say yes, she had to be certain.

He nodded, pulled his hat from his head, tossed it to the seat of the recliner, and raked his fingers through his flat hair. "Jane got the house when we split. I spend most all my time at the store and didn't want to rent a place. Seemed like a waste of money. Simpler just to get rid of the garbage up here and build it out."

His living here would explain why he'd been able to spare his truck for so long. No commute and he could walk anywhere in town. She stepped further into the room, the quiet seducing her, the calm, the shadows. She could curl up in the recliner and sleep for a week. Or she could once she had a shower.

"You can stay here as long as you need to."

She closed her eyes, wrapped her arms tightly across her middle. "With you?"

"I'll be here, but I won't be in your way. You'll have all the privacy you need."

And if she didn't want him to give her privacy? "This is your home. I would be in your way, not the other way around."

He came closer. She heard his steps, their echo, the brush of denim, and then his hands were on her shoulders, his thumbs clearing her hair from her collar. "You can have the bed. It's a king. I'll sleep out here."

Out here where he wouldn't fit. "Josh—"

"Darcy, you're about to go under. If you're not going to take care of yourself, I'm going to do it for you."

She wanted to argue. She wanted to stand strong. But more than either of those, she wanted to collapse and let him do exactly what he was threatening to do. "A couple of days. That's it. And I'll sleep on the couch."

He pulled her against him. Or he stepped into her. She wasn't sure which. All she knew was that he'd lowered his head and his lips were against her neck and her whole body shivered and tightened and came alive.

He slid his hands from her shoulders down her arms, to her elbows, to her wrists, holding her there, immobile, his mouth at her jaw, at her ear, her hairline. He was warm at her back, solid and strong, his erection thick against her hip.

She wanted to turn into him, to touch him, to learn his jaw and his ear, the scruff of his beard, the scent of him in the hollow of his throat, but he wouldn't let her go. He kept her there, made her wait, made her want, her skin electric, her blood hot. Desire pooled deep in her belly, dripped lower, her panties growing damp.

"Josh," she whispered, the single word, his name encompassing all the things she didn't know how to say.

"I know," he said, his voice low and close to her ear and rattling her further. "But this doesn't change anything. You sleep in the bed. I sleep on the couch."

"Are you sure?" she asked, looking over her shoulder and into his eyes. She wanted him here and now and thought she just might break.

He reached up, brushed tangled strands of windblown hair from her face, and his voice when he spoke was as thick with longing as his words were bold. "I'm not going to rush the very sweet pleasure of loving you."

ARWEN WAS SITTING in a back corner booth near the bar when Dax found her, sliding onto the bench opposite and looking like hell. It was late, coming up on closing. She had all but the last hour of the day's receipts in front of her, and her laptop networked to her office accounting files, but something in his expression—impatience or annoyance or a guilty hurt—told her she was done for the night.

He said nothing, just dropped his head against the banquette and stared at her, waiting. It was obvious he had something on his mind. Equally obvious, she was going to have to worm it out of him. She stacked the few slips of paper still needing her attention on the keyboard and closed them inside of the laptop. The rest she paper-clipped together and set on top.

Signaling Luck Summerlin at the bar for two draft beers, she pushed aside the computer then crossed her arms over her chest to wait for Dax to give her an opening. Until his drink arrived, however, he did nothing but pull off his hat, drop it to the seat beside him, and shove his hands through his hair. Then he lifted the frosted mug and downed half of the contents, returning it to the table and spreading his arms along the back of the banquette.

"Thought you had an office," he said, his jaw tight, his mouth in a strange sarcastic twist.

Her first instinct was to call him on it. Her second was to pay no attention because that's what he wanted her to do. He was itching for a confrontation, a way to blow off steam since they were in public, in *her* public, and sex was out of the question.

"I do," she said, tamping down her curiosity. "But I'm in there a lot, so when things are winding down and it's quiet enough, I like to work out here. Different sounds. Different scenery."

He glanced around, rolled his head on his shoulders and cracked his neck, then returned his attention to her when it seemed what he wanted to do was climb the walls. "I remember Buck Akers doing the same thing. The boys and I would play pool and make as much noise as we could, trying to distract him."

Not surprising. "Did it work?"

"Who knows? We were drunk."

"You weren't of legal drinking age when you lived here."

"And that was going to stop us?"

She cocked her head. "Why do you refer to everything in your past in the plural?"

He came back to her immediately, as if the answer was so easy it required no thought. "Because my life was a plural. Me and Casper and Boone. All for one, one for all."

Except it wasn't. Not exactly. "But you left on your own. And they left on theirs. Best I recall, you three didn't even hook up until freshman year when the Jaynes moved to town."

He shrugged away her observation. "Boone and I were friends before that."

"So Casper's to blame for all the trouble the Dalton Gang caused?"

He pushed the coaster beneath his mug forward, pulled it back. "He is a reckless son of a bitch."

"Still?"

"Well, he's not riding bulls any longer, but he has no fear."

"Faith said the same thing."

Dax snorted. "Better not let Boone know his sister's got the boy on her mind."

"Why's that?"

"We don't do sisters. It's part of the code."

That had her biting down on a laugh. "The Dalton Gang has a code?"

"Just like any notorious brotherhood."

She stopped herself from rolling her eyes, but only just. "Speaking of sisters, how's Darcy doing? With your dad and all?"

His pulse at his temple jumping, Dax reached for his beer, and his mask that had only begun to crack fused. Ah, yes. The reason he was here, the one he needed to talk about but didn't want to talk about and wouldn't talk about until she forced the issue as he knew she would do.

That's how close they'd become. She knew he carried a heavy weight. He knew she offered a safe place to put it. But still they danced, coaxing and circling and making the other work for it instead of stepping into trust.

Scary place, trust. Open and rife with vulnerability and no way out.

"Dax?"

"Can I get another beer?"

She thought about leaving him there to draw it herself. Then she thought better and called the request to Luck, keeping her eye on him as she did. "Tell me about Darcy."

Shaking his head, he turned his empty mug in a circle on the table. "She's pretty much a mess. Came by earlier. Slapped the shit outta me."

"What?" Arwen's pulse jumped. "Why?"

"For not going to the hospital."

"Wait. You still haven't been to the hospital?"

Luck arrived with the beer then, setting it down and walking away while Arwen's blood pressure rose. She'd raced to him. The minute she'd heard Wallace Campbell had been struck down, she'd raced to him.

She'd driven into the pasture where he was working cattle. She'd driven away with him beside her, stopped when he'd told her to, let him fuck her against the side of the truck when the physical release was the only way he knew to grieve. Or at least she'd thought he'd been grieving.

She'd seen him double over as she'd left him there. Watched him until her own tears forced her to concentrate on the ruts that served as a road. He'd come to her later, he'd apologized, they'd spent as much time talking as having sex. About his father, about hers, about his mother—things with their families neither had ever told anyone else.

And he still hadn't gone to the hospital?

Her own mug was waiting and she lifted it, his gaze snagging hers before she got it to her mouth.

"I know what you're thinking."

"Oh," she said. "I seriously doubt that."

"You're thinking I'm a dick."

She drank, saying nothing. His admission was totally unsatisfying. She wanted to be the one calling him names. "Good for Darcy. Slapping you."

He worked his jaw as if it were still sore. "Spilled spaghetti meat everywhere. Bing and Bob enjoyed it."

He wasn't going to get to her. He wasn't. She didn't feel sorry for him. She didn't ache for him. He was not going to turn her life upside down. "So when are you going to go see him?"

"Change that to an *if* and maybe I can give you an answer."

"When, Dax?"

"Hey, boss?"

At Luck's interruption, Arwen turned. "What's up?"

The younger woman stood at the end of the bar, and gestured over her shoulder where Callie and Amy both waited. "We're done here. You need anyone to hang around?"

"Y'all go on." Dax drawled out the words before Arwen had a chance to respond. "She's safe with me."

Luck didn't move. Neither did Callie or Amy. Arwen couldn't help but smile. "I'm fine. Be sure and lock the back door."

She turned back to Dax, held his gaze as the girls left, listened to their chatter fade down the hall, to the door slamming, the locks clicking into place.

He lifted his mug in a toast. "All locked in and no place to go."

"I have a place. Right next door. I plan to go there as soon as I'm done here," she said, her hand on her laptop and the night's unfinished work. "And since we've already had this conversation, I don't know why you stopped by."

"I wanted a couple of beers. I wanted to see you."

"Even knowing what I was going to say?" Unless he'd needed to hear her say it again. Needed another dose of convincing because the first hadn't stuck. "Just go. Get it over with. Do it for Darcy."

"If I go, she's the only reason. And you."

"Oh, Dax," she said, sitting back. Why had she ever thought she'd be able to get him out of her system, even for as much as a day?

He reached across the table for her hand, ran his thumb over her knuckles for a long quiet moment. The saloon creaked and popped around them, settling in for the night. They were the only noises until he spoke.

"I never stopped thinking about them, you know. The family.

After I left. I thought about Mom. Thought a lot about Darcy, wondered if she hated me for leaving her to deal with the mess. Mostly I thought about him. Did he wish he'd done things differently? Did he care that I was gone—"

"Of course he cared—"

"No," he said, his head down and only his gaze coming up. "He didn't care. He never cared. He doesn't have it in him to care. I'd say I can't fault him for it. It's just who he is. But I do. Because who in the hell doesn't care about their own kids?"

She knew he wasn't that naive, that he was simply looking at his life through lenses colored with his past. Just as she looked at hers through the ones she'd painted with the crayons she'd used to pass time in the bar. "Parents who've been hurt, who're so lost in their own misery they don't have any caring to give."

She wasn't looking at him, was focused on their joined hands, but she felt his gaze searching, studying, lingering, and learning, seeing her maybe for the first time. Or at least in a way he hadn't before, a way she hadn't wanted him to. Arwen, the girl he'd gone to school with, invisible, wallpaper. Alone.

"Your father."

She shrugged. "Like you said. It's just who he is. Who he was."

"He kept you with him."

"He kept me in a bar, Dax. A bar. He didn't even know I was there half the time. Buck checked on me, made sure I had food, that I wasn't too hot or too cold. That I had shoes. Shoes." She closed her eyes and cleared her throat of the hurt before looking at him again. "You want to compare caring, what parent doesn't put shoes on their own kid?"

"I'm so sorry," he said, his voice low, angry, lost. "I didn't know. I mean, I knew it wasn't good because of my mother, but I didn't know. About the shoes."

She blew off his sympathy. She didn't need sympathy. "It was a long time ago. I got over it. And I've got a fucking closet full of shoes."

"Plus the booth from the Buck Off Bar in your kitchen."

She glared, and he laughed. She pulled her hands from his, which only served to make him laugh harder and make her glare until she couldn't glare anymore.

"You know I'm right. You're not over it anymore than I am. Our fathers were, our fathers *are* drunks. We may not have been abused or abandoned, but we sure as hell weren't brought up believing in Santa Claus and Disneyland."

Santa Claus. Lord. Had she ever for a minute believed? Nostalgia—the good parts, not the bitterness, the sadness, the hate and regrets—drew her mouth into a soft smile. "I hung my stocking on Buck's fireplace."

"The one in the bar?"

She nodded. "We didn't have one in our house and Buck wanted to make sure I didn't miss out on Christmas morning."

Dax picked up his hat, tipped it. "Hell of a guy, Buck Akers."

They fell silent after that, finishing off their beers, fingers touching, playing, teasing without words but connecting them in ways Arwen had never connected with another soul. It thrilled her and frightened her and left her wishing she could see even six months down the road. Was she wasting her time here? Was she risking too much?

Would he eventually leave?

She sat back, moved her hands to her lap then crossed her arms over her chest. "So, you're going to go see your father?"

"Are you going to go see yours?"

She needed to. "If I can arrange to get off."

"I can get you off now."

Jesus. "You know what I mean. Time off. Not . . . that other thing."

"Tell me you've never had it better."

"The sex?"

He gave a single nod, his gaze hooded, his pupils enlarged, his pulse pounding like hoofbeats in the hollow of his throat.

She swallowed, her chest tight as she thought of his hands, his mouth, the length and thickness of his cock, the way it tasted, the heat of his balls against her face. "Never."

"But we're not going to have it tonight, are we?"

She shook her head, thankful he'd been the one to say it. "I've got work to do. And you . . ."

"I know. I'll go. And . . . I'll go."

"Tomorrow?"

"Yeah," he said. Then he stood, came around to her side of the booth, and planted one hand on the table, one on the banquette above her head. Looming over her, he dropped his gaze to her chest, to her lap, raised it to her mouth then to her eyes.

She breathed him in, the sun and the soap and the sweat that always lingered. And she waited, wetting her lips, but she waited in vain because he was gone, walking toward the door she would need to lock behind him. But she couldn't move to do it.

She could only watch his long rolling stride carry him across the great room, and know he was taking way too much of her with him.

TWENTY-FIVE

THE ECHO OF Dax's boots as he strode down the Coleman Medical Center hallway brought him more than a few curious glances and a couple of annoyed frowns. He figured folks thought him determined, worried, and in a hurry, when he wasn't anything more than pissed off. He didn't want to be here. His coming here wasn't going to do anyone any good.

But here he was, and there was the door to his father's room just ahead, and with the audience he'd picked up along the way, there was no backing out of this promise he'd made to Arwen. He needed to stop doing that. Agreeing to things she asked of him when she obviously had an agenda and all he had was a hard dick.

The words *pussy* and *whipped* circled in his mind, and he pushed his hat lower on his head, squeezing them into submission. Getting this one-sided visit over with and getting back to the ranch and the work waiting there couldn't happen fast enough.

What was the protocol for visiting a coma patient anyway?

He had nothing to say to his old man, and even if his father had had one of his canned lectures ready, delivering it without some sort of mind-meld would be an issue. Sticking his head in the door and waving the flag should fulfill his familial duty and get Arwen and Darcy both off his back.

Except people were whispering. They knew who he was, that he had finally left the ranch to show his face in public. The gossip mill would be churning. Dalton Gang stories from the past brought out and examined in a new light. Holing up until shift change might be the way to go. Or it would be, except he was here, and turning around now would mean more curious glances, more annoyed frowns.

He pushed into the room, his hate for his father rising in a mad choking, strangling rush of sixteen years worth of unspoken words. The door whooshed closed behind him, trapping him, imprisoning him, and he walked to the bed, his steps quieter now that he'd run out of hall stomping room. He crossed his arms over his chest, balanced on the balls then the heels of his feet, and stared down.

If not for the tubes and wires taped and draped over the old man's body, Wallace Campbell would've looked pretty much the way he had for most of Dax's life. His jowls were saggier, sure, his hair thinner, his forehead sporting more lines. His cheeks were pale rather than ruddy with drink. His nose, too, though it was as bulbous as ever and mapped with new veins.

Dax waited for whatever feeling was supposed to take him over at seeing his father so helpless, and seeing him for the first time in years. But nothing happened. Not a blip. No regrets, no sadness. No wishing he could go back in time and make different choices. He knew who his old man was, what he was. Knew the life he'd lived had brought him to this. Knew if he died, few would mourn his loss.

Oh, many would make noise, lots of weeping and gnashing of teeth, but that wasn't the same, was it? He wondered if Darcy would be the only one to shed tears of true sadness. He couldn't imagine his mother crying without an audience to see the show. Always, *always*, she'd been about the show, who was watching, who could she impress. She'd time her sobs accordingly.

Fucked up family, the Campbells.

"Strange seeing him so quiet."

At the voice behind him, Dax turned, expecting to see Dr. Kirkland, but seeing someone he didn't know instead. The man leaning into the corner behind him was younger than Dax by a couple of years, and dressed like no one in Crow Hill ever dressed—tailored suit pants, a crisp white shirt that had to have cost a fortune, as had the tasseled loafers and the neatly knotted silk tie thrown over his shoulder, as if he didn't want it dragging in his stew.

"And you are?"

"Greg Barrett." He pushed away from the wall, a fluid motion, and came forward, offering his hand. "I work with Wallace."

"Right. The son I should've been," Dax said, shaking hands with his old man's protégé because he wasn't completely without manners.

"Yeah. About that." Greg moved to stand at the foot of the bed, crossing his arms in a mirror of Dax's earlier posture.

"Don't worry." Dax went on the offensive. He didn't want to hear a lot of jibber jabber about rightful positions in the family business. Quite frankly, he didn't give a shit about what happened to the firm except where it concerned Darcy. "I'm too old and worn out to start law school."

Greg gave a snort that had Dax frowning. "He's not dead yet."

Might as well be. Though Dax kept that thought to himself.

"He's been dead to me for years. You have a problem handling the workload, take it up with Darcy."

"He fired Darcy."

Ah, the final cut. He wondered if his sister had planned to tell him. "Guess that leaves you to run the show."

"That," Greg said, the word hanging as he counted beats—one, two—finally adding, "And the fact that he's my father, too."

The air in the room stilled until the only sounds were those of the machines monitoring what life still flowed in Wallace Campbell's veins. Dax's ears rang with the beeps, the chirps, the incessant mosquito-like buzz, and he knew all that noise had him hearing things wrong.

He raised his gaze from the man tethered to the bed to the man standing at the foot of it. He studied Greg's face, not liking what he saw. His eyes, though Greg's were bluer. Darker hair, but hair meant nothing. Neither did the height the two men shared. The build. The wide hands and long fingers. He shared the same with Casper and Boone.

And yet Dax couldn't let it go. Greg looked too much like him for him to let it go. His chest heaving, his voice low, he asked, "What did you say?"

Greg nodded, arrogant, sure, moving his hands from his chest to his pockets. "Thirty years ago. A conference in Houston. My mother was a legal secretary attending with her employer. From what I've been told, it was a whirlwind, and nine months later, there I was."

"And he knows this?"

Another nod.

"Does Darcy know, or only The Campbell?"

"The Campbell?" Greg arched a brow. "I thought that was just what Darcy called him."

It was. He didn't know why the words had slipped out, but he repeated, "Does Darcy know?"

"No."

"He hired you knowing this?"

Finally, Greg moved, turning only his head, his gaze holding Dax's and daring him. "He's known it since I was born."

Dax's eyes went wide, disbelieving. "What?"

"Does that surprise you?"

"That my father is a cheating son of a bitch? No."

"How about *our* father being there for one of his kids from day one?"

The only thing that surprised him was the fact that he was still standing here. And that he hadn't let loose the gripping anger tightening his muscles to strike out. Problem was, the person he wanted to hit couldn't hit back.

That thought had him going after the next best thing. He took two long forward steps, and swung, his fist connecting with Greg's jaw and sending him sprawling across the sterile white floor.

And then he walked out of the room, down the hallway past whispers and curious eyes, his steps louder than when he'd arrived, his anger like jet fuel, propelling him.

TWENTY-SIX

DAX BALANCED ANOTHER short log from a felled mesquite on the wide oak stump Dave Dalton had used to split wood for his barbecue pit. He eyed the circular target, hefted the ax over his shoulder, and bounced up, swung down, the blade finding its sweet spot, the log cracking.

The fact that he's my father, too.

Another short log, another bouncing swing, another resounding crack. Sharing a father with that prick made them half brothers. Half brothers. He didn't want a half brother, and he sure as hell didn't need one. He had Boone Mitchell. He had Casper Jayne. He had Darcy. And he had Arwen. Half of anything more was half too much.

The fact that he's my father, too.

Again with the log, the swinging, the cracking. Greg Barrett. Greg Campbell. Dax wondered if while his sister was working with the bastard, Darcy had considered the possibility they shared

Wallace Campbell's genes. If they did. Which only their old man or a DNA test could verify.

Even if there'd been nothing to tip her off, she had to have wondered what an urban pretty boy was doing practicing law in Crow Hill. Dax hadn't been curious enough to ask, but it had struck him as strange. People were born here. People moved away or they died here. No one purposefully chose Crow Hill as a place to live.

The fact that he's my father, too.

Log. Swing. Crack. And what about their mother? Did she know? Had she kept their father's secret? Was that why she'd put herself in the middle of other families' dysfunctions? Trying to fix them and forget what was happening with her own? Convincing herself her husband spawning a son with another woman wasn't such a big deal?

Knowing his mother, that didn't make sense. He couldn't imagine her hanging around all these years if she'd known. About the affairs, sure. Those were well enough hidden and no surprise. She was married to a powerful man who couldn't keep his pants zipped, her own Clinton or Spitzer or Edwards. But not the kid.

His mother would never put up with another woman's kid reaching for a slice of the Campbell pie. Image meant everything to Patricia Campbell, but since she wasn't around now, and none of Darcy's questions had produced answers as to their mother's whereabouts . . . Could she have found out? And how, if only the two men at the center of the deception knew?

He had to decide what to do with the information—though he couldn't do anything without confirmation from his father that Greg Barrett had sprung from his loins. And since a DNA test was out of the question—even if he'd had the money, no way was he asking for Greg's toothbrush or hair—that wasn't going to happen until the old man came out of his coma. Until then, Dax would be carrying Greg Barrett's words alone.

Before he could grab another log from the dwindling pile, two long shadows fell over him. Casper and Boone, Casper saying, "It's the dead hell of summer, dude. Drought. Wildfires. What's with the wood?"

"I'm thinking it's about the ax, not the wood," Boone said, and Casper snorted.

"If he's in the mood to go medieval, I've got a post hole digger with his name all over it. Diego just got done clearing the space for the new holding pen to go in behind the bunkhouse. Seems that would be a more productive way to expend all that energy."

Then Boone again. "Though I thought Arwen was taking care of that energy expending thing."

Muscles burning, sweat rolling into his eyes, Dax straightened and said nothing, jamming the ax head into the stump and reaching for his shirt. He dried his face, his neck, his pits, then shrugged it on, wincing. The skin on his back was burned to a crisp. He'd lost track of time, lost his head, been out here too long looking for lost answers.

Breathing hard, he shunted off Boone's dig about his sex life along with the crap he wasn't ready to deal with, much less share, even with the men he held closer than brothers, half or not. "July Fourth's coming up. The barbecue cook-off. Are we not keeping up tradition and entering?"

"Hell, Dax. Which one of us knows how to barbecue at a competitive level?" Boone bent, picked up a stick of mesquite and brought it to his nose. "But damn if that stuff doesn't have my stomach rumbling."

Casper raised his gaze from the chips and chunks and sticks of mesquite scattered in a circle around the oak stump. "We don't, but I hear the cook-off's going to be held on the back lawn of the Hellcat Saloon this year."

"Arwen's hosting," Dax said. "And she's got a team entering. She's not judging, and wouldn't do us any favors even if she could."

"Huh." Boone tossed the stick back to the ground. "Wonder who they're going to get to judge if your old man isn't up and around by then."

Casper put in, "I heard the committee was thinking of asking Darcy and that Greg guy from the office to wave the Campbell and Associates flag."

"Fuck that." Dax spat wood dust and frustration and anger to the ground.

Boone, his frown darkening, circled Dax, working the ax head from the stump and carrying it out of his reach. "Thought you and Darcy were getting along."

"We are."

"Well then." He pondered that, checking the cutting edge of the ax with his thumb. "Didn't know you knew Barrett."

Dax mopped his forearm over his brow, clearing the sweat he'd missed, then pulled down on the brim of his hat, weighing how much to say. "Met him at the hospital earlier."

The men both went silent, both went still. Dax looked from one to the other, hoping to leave things at that. He didn't want to talk about the visit until he'd tamped down enough of the initial shock to better handle the things he was feeling.

Finally, Casper spoke. "You went to the hospital?"

A nod. "Arwen made me promise."

Casper considered what he'd said, looking to Boone who only shrugged, then back. "So that's the way of it, then? You're doing what the little woman tells you to do?"

"Fuck you, asshole. I promised Arwen, but I did it for Darcy."

"Uh-huh."

"You saw her the other day. The shape she was in. I was a shit not to go when Arwen first told me. Darcy shouldn't have had to deal alone." The way she'd been dealing alone since she was sixteen years old.

He'd left her. He'd thought only of himself and he'd split. Yeah, he'd been eighteen and stupid, but he was older now, and his sister deserved better than that same sort of selfish douche-baggery.

He looked at Casper. "You got the holding pen marked, or you want me to just start digging?"

"Hey, you still got demons to work out of your system, I'm happy to get out there and be the brain to your brawn."

Boone snorted. "You've had to resort to thinking because the ladies aren't digging your wrangling moves?"

Casper gave Dax a wink. "Figured I'd give it a shot. I hear Faith likes her men hung upstairs as well as down."

"You son of a bitch," Boone said, advancing with the ax in his hand. "We don't do sisters. You'd better not be laying a hand on Faith."

Dax grabbed the ax as Boone walked past, a grin taking over his face. "I'm thinking it's not his hands you need to be worrying about. Or even his well-hung brain."

"Hey now." Casper began backing away, enough steam coming out of Boone's ears to power a locomotive. "I can't help it if Faith's of a mind to compare the head I've got on my shoulders with my big one."

And then he took off for the barn, Boone after him, leaving Dax shaking his head. He settled the ax in the stump again and took in the mess of mesquite. At least it would be easier to clean up than the mess of his life—and he'd get some good barbecue out of it.

TWENTY-SEVEN

THE SIGHT THAT greeted Arwen as she stopped behind the Dalton's ranch house had her pondering the size of her mistake. Really? She'd thought she'd be able to get Dax Campbell out of her system for good? Was she out of her mind?

How could she when just looking at him left her unable to draw a normal breath? When watching his body brought to mind his moving inside of hers? When seeing his hands at work reminded her of his calluses scraping over her skin, the reach of his fingers, their deft and nimble strength?

She shivered, clenched the muscles of her sex, blew out a long, steadying breath. He was tossing sticks of split wood into a wheelbarrow; mesquite, she thought, most likely for smoking meat. The blade of his ax was embedded in a stump, and she wished she'd arrived earlier to watch him at work.

She imagined the force behind his swing, his muscles as they bunched and released, sweat glistening on his skin. And then she stopped imagining because she'd come here to talk to him, not for more of what she couldn't get enough of—a truth that dug its powerful claws deeper every time he came to her bed.

She was certain he'd seen her arrive, though he'd yet to acknowledge her presence. Her truck was big and red and hardly inconspicuous, and driving across the property to park had raised a monster cloud of dust. She was letting it settle before leaving the cab, and the wait allowed her to pull herself together.

More than any other time in his company, her trip to tell him about his father's heart attack proved she couldn't talk to him if she was scattered. Emotions—and, yes, lust was a potent emotion—got in the way and turned the rational side of her brain to mush. Today wasn't about sex. Today was about his promise.

It was time to see if he'd kept it. If he was the man she knew he could be.

She jumped from the cab, walked toward him, breathing in the heat of the day and the dry, brown dirt and the richly pungent spice of the wood. She wondered how much mesquite grew on the Dalton Ranch. Then wondered if buying several cords for the saloon would help them financially, or if Dax would balk at any hint of charity—especially coming from her.

She walked all the way to the stump before stopping, her thigh bumping the ax's haft. Shoving her hands in her pockets, she gave him another ten seconds to break the silence, but he chose to continue punishing her for forcing his hand.

And so she asked, "Did you go?"

He was bent forward, grabbing all the wood he could hold, kicking sticks closer to the wheelbarrow as he cleared a small circle. "You come all the way out here to check up on me?"

"Yep."

He snorted, shook his head, did some more kicking, some more tossing, this time with more vigor than before.

"That looks like a lot of anger."

"That's barbecue."

"Are y'all entering the cook-off?"

He shrugged, straightened, twisted, and popped his back. "We're talking about it."

"It's safe, you know."

"Safe how?"

"Your father won't be there to judge."

He went back to his task.

"Any change in his condition?" she asked, because it was obvious he'd done his duty as Wallace Campbell's son but wasn't dealing with it well.

"You mean is he still a son of a bitch? Does he still guzzle Glenlivet like water?" He kicked at the wheelbarrow. Kicked it again. "Will he ever give a shit about anyone but himself? Or stop fucking with other people's lives?"

"Then he's awake?" Because now she was confused.

"No, he's not awake. He's the same self-centered ass he's always been. He's going to lay there until the daughter he doesn't even acknowledge wears herself out waiting."

She got his concern for Darcy, but . . . "I don't think he's in a coma on purpose."

"Knowing him, I wouldn't doubt it. Anything to inconvenience everyone else."

"Was Darcy there?"

"Not when I went by, no."

Okay. "Have you talked to her since?"

"I don't know where she is. Thought about calling Josh, but figured that's not my business."

"You could make it your business."

He slammed more sticks into the wheelbarrow, biting off a

string of sharp curses when most of them bounced out. "Or I could stay out of it and let her live her life the way she wants."

"Without you in it, you mean?"

"That's not what I said." He took a break, wiped his sweat with his sleeve. "But she'd probably be better off."

"She'd be alone, Dax." Time to press the point. "But then she's been alone all this time, so I guess you're off the hook."

He jammed his hands to his hips and faced her, squinting from beneath the brim of the hat he wore pulled as low as she'd ever seen. "What're you doing here, Arwen? Trying to make me feel guilty over my sister now?"

"I came to see how it went. The visit with your father."

"For one thing, you were wrong."

About which, of many, things? "I've been known to be on occasion."

"Well you were this time for sure."

"How's that?"

"Seeing him didn't make me feel better at all. In fact, it made me feel goddamn worse, if you want the truth of it. I hate him more now than I did two days ago, so thank you for that."

Lord, he was totally overreacting. "Uh, maybe you could wait until he's awake before deciding that. You know, have a conversation? See where things stand?"

"I don't need him to be awake. I don't need to talk to him. And I know exactly where things stand." He slammed the sole of his boot against the side of the wheelbarrow, knocking the load of wood back to the ground. "What I need is for you to butt out of my business."

"Fine," she said, turning away.

"On second thought, you butting in settled things a whole lot faster than if I'd trusted my instincts, so thank you for that."

"You're an ass," she tossed over her shoulder. "You know that?"

"Like father, like son."

She kept going, then she stopped, spun, came back, and jabbed a finger in the center of his chest. "And that right there is where you're wrong."

His eyes glittered from the shadow of his hat. "How do you figure?"

"If you were like your father, or at least like you claim him to be, you wouldn't have gone to see him. You wouldn't have done it to settle things between the two of you, and you wouldn't have done it for Darcy so she wouldn't feel abandoned by everyone in her family. And you certainly wouldn't have done it for me." She poked him again, poked him harder. "You may think you're some badass black sheep come home to raise hell, but that's not who you are at all."

For a long moment, he said nothing, his gaze moving from her finger to her face and back. And then he cracked, the corners of his mouth turning up, his dimples like crescent moons in the stubble he hadn't bothered to shave. "You're pretty sexy when you get all worked up, steam coming out of your ears, lighting up your eyes."

"Steam is not coming out of my ears, and my eyes are no more lit up now than they ever are, and I am not going to have sex with you." She had to say it, even though her heart was pounding and the truth of the matter was something else entirely.

"Sure you are," he said, advancing, one step, another, then a third that had her turning and sprinting for her truck.

She was fast but he was faster and she heard his thudding steps behind her, gaining, and because she had no desire to be hit from behind and tackled, she skidded to a stop and let him catch her.

He grabbed her, lifted her, and spun her around, then very awkwardly walked the two of them across the yard.

He used one hand to lower her truck's tailgate, then lifted her to sit and hopped up beside her. But that's all he did, swinging his legs, hanging his head, touching the length of her thigh with his. "Lucky for you hefting that ax all afternoon has me beat. I doubt I could get it up even if you begged."

That had her wanting to put his words to the test. But she didn't. "What happened to you being mad at the world?"

"I'm still mad. Just not at you."

Funny, but she wasn't really mad at him either. "I'm sorry for pushing you to do something you didn't want to do."

"No you're not. You're just sorry it didn't go the way you'd hoped."

Was that true? "Why do you say that?"

"I know living with Hoyt couldn't have been easy, all that stuff about Santa Claus and shoes. But that doesn't mean what worked for you in settling things with him is going to work for me."

She wondered how much to tell him. If he'd hold the truth over her, use it against her. "I never settled things with my father, Dax. I should have, but all I did was help him pack up the house and load the U-Haul. I didn't even make the trip to Austin with him. I didn't even wave when he drove away."

"That's pretty harsh."

"He was a drunk. He spent twenty years not remembering he had a daughter. I grew up without a parent. I grew up with an adult living in the same house. I took money from his wallet to buy food and clothes and supplies for school. I ate nothing but sandwiches and cereal for years until I could cook."

"I didn't know," he said, reaching for her hand and holding it.

"No one knew. Well, Buck knew."

"That's why you have the booth, isn't it? More for Buck than anything else."

She shrugged. "I don't know why I have it. I tell myself it's so I won't forget. So I won't make the mistakes he did."

"You won't make them." He squeezed her fingers. "You won't ever forget. And even I know you don't need the booth for that."

"You're probably right."

He waited a minute, still swinging his legs, bouncing their joined hands on his thigh. "Are you going to have sex with me now?"

Eyes rolling, she tugged at her hand but he wouldn't let her go. "What happened to you being too tired?"

"I'm all rested up."

"Is there a minute of the day you're not horny?"

"That's your fault, woman. I'd been doing the monk thing just fine before you made me walk you to your truck that day at Lasko's."

"Made you walk me to my truck?" She laughed. "That is not how it happened, and you know it."

"Close enough."

She let him have that one. "How long had you been doing the monk thing?"

"Hmm. Three years? Maybe four?"

"You? Dax Campbell? Hadn't had sex for three or four years? No wonder I can't get you out of my bed."

"Do you want me out of your bed?"

She shook her head. "I thought I did. That's why I came looking for you."

"What? When?"

"That day at Lasko's. I was hoping you might be there. I wanted to get you out of my system."

"I didn't know you came looking for me. Or that I was in your system."

"Since high school."

"Huh. Why didn't we hook up then?"

"Because you didn't know I existed."

"I knew you existed."

"No, you knew Hoyt Poole had a daughter who practically lived with him in the Buck Off Bar."

"You're right."

"Of course I am."

"Are you going to have sex with me now?"

One. Track. Mind. She shook her head. "I've got to get back to the saloon."

"Why?"

"Because it's what I do."

"I really think you should do me instead. Look." He moved her fingers to his fly and held her there, filling her hand, so thick and ready, and she squeezed because she couldn't not.

"We're in the bed of my truck," she told him, as if it wasn't obvious, as if it would make any difference.

"Then it counts as a bed."

"It's metal and it's hot, not to mention uncomfortable."

"You get on top."

"Sacrificing for the cause?"

"It's my cause."

She glanced around the ranch yard, her pulse racing, her head spinning. "Where're Boone and Casper?"

"Boone chased Casper into the barn awhile ago. I grabbed the ax as he went by."

"What?" she asked, unable to stop the gasp or the laughter that followed.

"They're fine. I'm not." He laid back, unbuckled his belt, unbuttoned his fly, tugged his jeans and his briefs to his knees. Then he grabbed his cock and stroked. "Look at all this meat. Yours for the taking. Just come to papa."

Oh, she was tempted, her mouth going dry as she watched him fist the juicy ripe head of his cock. She licked her lips, cast a glance toward the barn. The thought of getting caught had her heart beating faster. And she wouldn't have to get completely naked . . .

Damn him for being impossible to resist. She pulled up one foot, tugged off one boot, undid her jeans and slid one leg free. Then she crawled toward him, her bare ass in the air, and kissed his cock the way she'd been dying to.

He was sweaty and hot and tasted like salt when she sucked him into her mouth. His skin was tight and slick, the slit in the head open and wet. She tongued him, caught the ridge of his glans with her lips and held tight before lifting up to release him.

His groan nearly rattled the truck on its wheels. "Do that again."

She did, then once more before dragging her tongue down the underside of his shaft and between his balls. He sucked in a breath and bucked upwards and she added one hand to the mix, ringing his shaft, hefting his sac, slipping lower and teasing his ass.

"You keep that up, you're going to get in trouble one of these days," he said, grinding against her fingers.

"Or one of these days you're going to admit you enjoy it."

"I wouldn't be giving you access if I didn't enjoy it."

That had her grinning, and crawling up his body.

"Wait," he said, pushing to sit and scooting to lean against the wheel well. Then he patted his lap, clenching muscles so that his cock waggled.

She rolled her eyes, making her way over to straddle him, her knees at his knees, then his thighs, then his hips. He held her and brought her forward. She settled her hands on his shoulders and waited for the prodding head of his cock.

He guided himself into place, and still she waited. Anticipation— along with the fact that they were in her truck in the middle of the yard—had her blood running hot beneath her skin.

She was electric and on fire and he slid his cock's head through her folds, spreading her moisture, opening her. Once in position, he set his hands on her hips at the crease of her thigh and pushed her down. He kept pushing until she was completely impaled and she held all of him inside and neither one of them could move.

He held her gaze, his jaw tight as he gave her a big bad wolf grin. "Now, isn't this nice? Fresh air and sunshine and a big ol' cock buried to the hilt inside of you?"

It was, but he didn't have to know that. She rose up on her knees, lowered her hips slowly, watched the tic in his jaw pop. "Or maybe it's nice to have that big ol' cock buried to the hilt in something as juicy and hot as I am?"

"That's not even a question." He gave a little grunt and a little upward thrust of his hips. "You gotta know I've never had it this good."

Something close to her heart flipped and landed hard, jolting her. "That's your overlong experiment with celibacy talking."

"It wasn't an experiment." He placed his palms on the truck bed, used them to brace himself as he fucked her. Then he stopped, closing his eyes and dropping his head back. "It was a case of not giving a shit."

"About sex? You?"

"Hard to imagine, I know. But there ya have it."

He thrust again and she rode him, grinding her clit against the base of his shaft in a smooth figure eight.

"I love the way you do that."

She was still stuck on his not giving a shit about sex. "Were you working someplace where it wasn't easy to get away?"

"When?"

"When you weren't having sex."

"There was some of that. At the end of a hard day, that hour drive to town could be put to better use sleeping. And it's not like I'd lost the use of my right hand."

"As much as you love sex, it's hard to imagine you going without."

"I love sex because I'm having it with you."

"So if it had been Amy or Callie or Luck who'd delivered Bubba Taylor's lunch to Lasko's that day?"

"I might've given each of them a go, but I would've always been waiting for you."

She couldn't take it anymore. The things he was saying . . . The words cut into her, split her open, poured themselves into the gash and spread. He took her over. He became part of her, his hands, his cock. His heart.

She opened her mouth over his and loved him, breathing against him, into him, as she caught him tight, pulling up, pushing down, gripping and milking.

He tongued her, bit her, groaned into her mouth until neither of them had words or knew anything but the hot hard slide of his cock and her cunt. He slipped his hands beneath her shirt and up her back. She used her hands looped around his neck to pull his head to her chest. He buried his face between her breasts, nuzzling, the grunts and groans coming out of his mouth muffled by the fabric.

She was going to come, and she wanted him to see, and she threaded her fingers into his hair and pulled his head away, holding his gaze, catching at her bottom lip with her teeth as light fired in his eyes.

The up and down motion took her closer, the friction heated her flesh. The moisture slick between them was warm and felt so damn good. She blew out quick sharp breaths. Dax did the same. And never once did they break eye contact, even when the waves of orgasm left them shaking.

Minutes later, Dax was the first to smile, his chest heaving as a grin broke wickedly across his face. "So you really thought you'd be able to get me out of your system, did you?"

Boy, if that wasn't the question of the day.

TWENTY-EIGHT

NEVER IN HER life had Darcy had trouble falling asleep until the last few nights in Josh's bed. It was a big bed, a roomy king with a high ceiling above and a fan lazily stirring the air. The sheets were soft, the pillows abundant, and everything was neat and earthy and warm.

She was safe, cared for, provided for—and all of it on Josh's dime. He cooked and cleaned. He refused to take money for groceries or rent. He insisted she sleep in his bed while he bunked on the couch. All of that, and he hadn't asked her for as much as a kiss, leaving her to remember the feel of his body, the touch of his mouth and his hands.

The words he'd spoken. Over and over, his words.

I'm not going to rush the very sweet pleasure of loving you.

With all he'd done for her, she wasn't going to press the point. And maybe he was right. She hadn't exactly been at her best since him telling her he wanted to see her. The last thing she wanted was to make a mistake she would never be able to fix. He was a good friend. She didn't want to lose that.

That didn't mean she had to be patient while waiting. Or that she wouldn't push when the time felt right to her.

She didn't know how to be a bystander, how to be passive when there was work to be done. She was antsy with all this being at loose ends since The Campbell had sent her walking, but tomorrow that would change. His condition hadn't worsened or improved. There was still no word from her mother. And Dax's idea of being supportive was a joke.

She hadn't yet gone by the office to see how Greg was faring, but that was on the morning's agenda. Campbell and Associates had been at the center of her life for as long as she could remember. She couldn't bear to think of the firm struggling, or going under simply because The Campbell wasn't there to throw his weight around.

But first she needed to sleep, at least for a few hours, and a glass of milk seemed just the thing. Wearing yoga pants and a tank top for pajamas, she slid from between the sheets and crossed her fingers she could get to the kitchen and back without waking Josh.

She could tell a lamp was burning in the living area, but it wasn't until she came around the dividing wall that she saw Josh wasn't asleep at all but using the lamp to read. He was sitting in the recliner, his socked feet crossed on the coffee table. He wore a pair of gray sweatpants and a faded orange T-shirt with a chipped white UT longhorn logo on the front.

When she stopped, he raised his eyes from the page to her, but didn't speak or move. He was like that in everything, so watchful, so discerning, observant, still. She hated disturbing the peace he'd found, but it was too late to back out of the room unseen. And so she came closer, gesturing over her shoulder toward the kitchen. "I couldn't sleep. Thought I'd get some milk."

"There's a new gallon. Help yourself."

"Do you want anything?"

He inclined his head toward the lamp table beside him and the highball glass with nothing left but ice. "I'm set."

She circled the sofa, leaned her elbows on the back. "I may not be around tomorrow."

"Okay."

"I'm going to go into the office in the morning," she said, not sure why telling him of her plans caused the butterflies in her stomach to jolt.

"That so?" Simple. No judgment.

She judged herself instead. "I guess it sounds crazy, huh?"

"Since you were fired, yeah. A bit."

"I just want to make sure Greg's doing okay." And why did she feel this need to explain herself to Josh? This was her life, her business. Not his—though she was the one making it so.

He turned down the corner of the page he was reading, closed the book, and moved it from his lap to the table. Then he asked her, "Why?"

"He's had the firm's entire caseload dumped on him," she said, circling the couch and curling into the far corner. "That's a hell of a lot of work."

"He gets paid to handle it, doesn't he?"

More than she ever did, no doubt. "I suppose, but—"

"Darcy, you're going to have to let it go."

"Let what go?" Was he talking about the firm? And was he kidding?

"You walked out. I'm not even talking about you being fired. You walked out."

"I know that."

And then, as if it was the most obvious thing in the world, he asked, "Why would you go back?"

"Why wouldn't I?"

"Because nothing about why you walked has changed."

That stopped her cold. She wanted to argue that he couldn't know that because she didn't know that. She hadn't visited the office since her firing, or even been back to the mansion on the hill. For all she knew, The Campbell, until stopped in his tracks by his illness, had been waiting to toast her return to the fold with open arms and a bottle of Glenlivet.

Except that would never happen. Any of it. Even if The Campbell recovered. And the knowledge gave credence to Josh's words. "It's not going to change, is it? If I hadn't walked then, I would've walked later."

Josh moved his feet to the floor and sat forward. "This isn't about you, Darcy. This is on your father and his views, his opinions."

"He doesn't have a very high one of me," she said with a snort.

"I don't think he has an opinion of anyone but himself. His needs and his wants are the only things that matter to him. He's a narcissist. Trying to make him happy won't do anything but make you miserable."

"So far that's exactly how it's been."

"Then do for yourself, whatever you want to do. Take the time to figure it out. You've got it."

She plucked at the fringe edging the throw she'd pulled over her lap. "Growing up, I wanted more than anything to be a social worker. I saw how involved my mother was in helping children who didn't have any of the advantages Dax and I did. But now I wonder if any of that was real either. If I wasn't trying to please her the same way I tried to please The Campbell by becoming a lawyer."

He didn't say anything, just looked at her, and she felt embarrassingly exposed. "I'm sorry. I'm usually not this pathetic."

"You're not pathetic at all, sweetheart. You're human and you're hurt."

She looked up, unable to stop the overwhelming sadness from welling in her eyes. She gave a small laugh, not wanting the emotion to ruin the rest of the night. "So what's it like to grow up in a normal family?"

His mouth twisted, and he shook his head. "What makes you think any family is normal?"

He made it easy to smile. "I guess you're right. We deal with what we have."

"Or we make our own."

"Our own families?"

He got up then, came to where she was sitting, cocking one leg beneath him and facing her. "Sure. Folks re-create what they've known because it's the best support system they've ever had. Or they dump what they have and replace it with what they know works."

"You're talking about relationships." She heard what she'd said and heat rushed her skin. God, could she have made this any more awkward? "I don't mean us, or you and Jane, I mean . . . like Dax turning to Boone and Casper instead of coming home."

He braced an elbow on the sofa's back, reached for a lock of her hair. "Friendship makes the best basis for a relationship of any kind."

Now he *was* talking about them. She was certain of it. And since she was already embarrassed and the lights were low and he'd told her to figure out what she wanted from life . . .

"Why did you tell me that you wanted to see me?"

His hand stroking her hair stopped, started again. "Because I do."

"But why me? We hardly knew each other before . . . this. We never talked. I only saw you at the office with your dad."

"That's your version of things, and that's okay."

Her version? "I don't get it."

"We've both lived in Crow Hill all our lives."

"Okay . . ."

"When you were in kindergarten. I was in third grade. Our classes had the same hour for recess. One day on the playground, you were upside down, hanging by your knees on the monkey bars—"

"And I fell!" God, she hadn't thought about that day in ages. "Flat on my back. I had the wind knocked out of me and scraped the crap out of my bottom."

"I don't know about your bottom, but I do know you were wearing a red plaid skirt and white panties, and I ran as fast as I could to the nurse's office." He was looking at her hair now, wrapping the strand he held around his finger.

"I can't believe you know what I was wearing. Or that you ran for the nurse."

He gave a nod, lost in the memory, a smile softening the corners of his mouth. "Principal Cayman tried to grab me as I came through the door but I twisted away. Then I dodged Coach Cuellar and Miss Lark."

"Really?" she asked, her heart hammering. Why was he telling her this? Why had he even remembered?

"Yep," he said, his smile going wide. "All three of them were on my heels when I slammed into Nurse Beeman. She'd heard the racket and was coming out into the hall. I just kept saying your name and pointing out the doors. By that time, one of the recess monitors had made it inside. They paid attention to her. I got two days of detention."

Oh, my God! "Because of me?"

"Because I didn't know what else to do. You weren't breathing. I was scared out of my shorts." He pulled his gaze from her hair, moved his focus to her face. His mouth grew harder, a tight line holding in things she was certain he wasn't ready to say. "I didn't know what else to do."

She reached up, pressed her thumb to his lips. "I was scared, too. And I can't believe you did that for me. That you were there."

He kissed her thumb, moved her hand to his chest and held it over his heart. "I've been here all this time."

But he hadn't been. "You married Jane."

"You were in law school. I didn't think you'd come back. And I thought I could find with her what I wanted to make with you."

If she'd known . . . "But she left you. She cheated on you."

"I wasn't the husband I should've been."

"Oh, Josh," she said, and then she climbed up to straddle his lap, taking his face in her hands as he settled her on his hips. She knew he would tell her the time wasn't right to take their relationship forward, even though his body beneath her was saying otherwise, but he had to know what his caring meant to her. "I wish I'd known . . . all of it. Everything. Our lives could've been so much different."

"We're only here because of what we've been through. The choices we've made. Those had to happen to make this, you and me, now, worth something."

She understood what he was saying, but it didn't make the truth settle any easier. "I don't know whether that makes me happy or sad."

"Be happy, Darcy. Don't ever, ever be sad." And then he cupped the back of her head in one of his very large hands and brought her mouth to his, coaxing her lips to part and using his tongue to love her.

TWENTY-NINE

ARWEN WAS GOING over the month's payables coming up on their net thirty date, when a knock sounded on her open door. Pencil in hand, she looked up from her desk in the saloon's small office and waved Luck Summerlin inside.

Hesitating, Luck shook her head, gestured over her shoulder with one thumb. "Someone needs you outside. In the parking lot."

Oh, yay. An interruption. Her favorite thing. "Does this someone have a name?"

"Well, yeah, but I was just asked to come get you."

"You were asked to come get me by someone who doesn't want me to know their name." Arwen wasn't stupid and this smelled so much like a trap she expected to see bear.

Luck rolled her eyes and motioned for Arwen to come. "I'm sworn to secrecy and I'm a terrible liar, so . . ."

"Fine," she said, though she was never going to get any work done at this rate. She was having enough trouble keeping her head in the game and off Dax Campbell. His mouth and his hands and the look in his eyes when he'd called her on her plan to get him out of her system.

Why in the world had she told him that? He'd be pulling it out and using it against her for the rest of his time in town.

She headed down the hall, out the back door, and across the patio per Luck's pointed instructions, kind of hoping this *was* a trap and not a delivery from some pain in the ass vendor screwing up her day. She'd skipped breakfast and was ready for lunch—not for aggravation.

The gate in the saloon's back privacy fence stood open, and just outside she saw the front bumper of a big black truck. A truck that looked an awful lot like Dax's. But it was the middle of the day, and while Dax might've shirked his duties a time or two after returning to Crow Hill, he was now a company man.

And yet, there he was, coming around the cab to meet her, his jeans pressed, his boots clean save for the dirt he'd kicked up in the parking lot, his blue plaid shirt looking sun-dried fresh. Even his battered straw hat appeared to have had some life slapped back into it, and it sat back, not forward, on his head.

Behind her, the gate closed and the lock clicked, but before she could turn and have Luck let her back in, Dax had taken hold of her hand.

"What are you doing here?" she asked as he dragged her behind him to the truck's driver's side door. "What's going on?"

"I'm picking you up."

"Why? It's the middle of the day. I have work. *You* have work."

"It's lunchtime," he said, winking down at her, his dimples flashing. "We're going on a lunch date."

"A lunch date? Are you kidding?"

"Nope," he said, and when she made no move, he grabbed her by the waist and lifted her into the truck. Then he climbed up behind her, forcing her into the center because a big box sat in the passenger seat.

"I'm pretty sure this is kidnapping," she said as his hand found its way between her legs where she straddled the gear stick.

He shifted and put the truck in motion. "Only if you call Ned and report me."

She wondered if, in true Dalton Gang fashion, he had Sheriff Orleans in his pocket by now. He certainly had a lawyer on his side. Or he did if he and his sister were speaking again.

She countered with her only ammunition. "If this is a date, then you owe me sex."

"I'm well aware of that," he said, draping his arm along the back of the seat after reaching fourth gear.

Hmm. No teasing her about working him out of her system. No double entendres. Nothing but his fingers tickling her shoulder and toying with the curled end of her ponytail. Nothing but his thigh against hers, moving as he accelerated or slowed. Nothing but the smell of . . . fried chicken?

She looked to her right, lifted a flap on the box. "You picked up lunch from the Blackbird?"

He gave a nod and another smile, his dimples like sickles in his cheeks. "Fried chicken, potato salad, corn on the cob, homemade rolls, and iced tea."

Arwen's stomach rumbled as she inhaled deeply. "God, I am *starving*."

"Good, because there's enough food for four, and we're only two."

She had to stop herself from digging in now, but if she was going to have to wait long . . . "Where are we going?"

"I thought I'd show you one of my favorite spots on the ranch."

"Is this going to take more than the hour you and I as working people get for lunch?" A stupid question since the drive out and back would take that long. And why was he suddenly wanting to show her the ranch?

"I hope so. If you want sex for dessert, that is. Besides," he told her, moving his arm from behind her to downshift for an upcoming turn, "we're self-employed."

"That just means our bosses are more demanding than most."

"Ah, but they're also more forgiving, more understanding, and downright flexible about things like lunch."

After that, they rode for a while in silence, Arwen enjoying Dax's nearness and nearly absentminded touch, the smells coming from the basket setting her stomach on edge. On top of the work her business required, she'd been so busy preparing to host the cook-off that food had become an afterthought.

She wondered if Dax had realized that, or if something else had prompted this spur of the moment date. "How're things going? With your dad and your sister?"

He stiffened a bit, dropping the lock of her hair he'd been toying with and wrapping his hand around a hook of the rear window's gun rack. "I haven't seen Darcy so I don't know how the old man is doing."

"You haven't called the hospital?"

"Didn't we wear out this subject the other day?"

Not to her satisfaction. "Is it okay to ask if you've heard from your mom?"

"I haven't. No idea if Darcy has."

"Did you ever talk to Josh?"

"You keep this up, no picnic for you."

Okay then. Easy stuff. "How're Casper and Boone?"

"Good. Working. Pissing me off." He hesitated then chuckled and added, "They enjoyed the show, by the way."

"The show . . ." She waved her fingers at her cheeks that were burning. "Oh, my God! They did not see us. Tell me they did not see us."

"They saw enough to stay in the barn until they heard you drive off."

Groaning, she buried her face in her hands. "I'm never going to be able to look at either one of them again."

"Sucks for you since they'll be at your place all day for the cook-off."

Ugh. "What are y'all cooking?"

"You're the competition. You think I'm going to tell you?"

"It won't be much of a competition if y'all got hold of Tess's sauce and rub recipes," she said, toying absently with the flap of the box.

"Tess had recipes?"

"Well, crap."

He laughed, a loud, whooping sound that faded, and then he fell silent. She leaned against his side and watched the landscape roll by. As long as she kept the conversation off his family, things were okay. And why did she keep digging in that well anyway? She certainly didn't want him asking anymore about Hoyt.

When he finally parked, she didn't have to be coaxed out of the cab the way she'd had to be coaxed in. She jumped to the ground and stretched, lifting her arms high overhead and raising her face to the sun. It was hot, but clouds had popped up to tease with a chance of afternoon rain, and the temperature had backed off for a break. It made sitting and eating on the truck's lowered tailgate less of a challenge. And the iced tea went a long way to help.

"It's so gorgeous out here," Arwen said, too full to move a muscle.

Dax tossed a drumstick bone into the box and wiped the grease from his hands. "You should see this place when it's green and the creek is running high. Pretty sure the cattle think it's heaven."

And she was pretty sure there was a Blue Bell Ice Cream commercial in there somewhere. "I would. If I were a cow."

He laughed, his hands curled over the tailgate edge as he leaned forward. "Dave showed me this place. He was good about knowing when something was wrong, then getting me to talk about it when talking was the last thing I wanted to do."

"Ah, so you've been the strong silent type all your life."

He gave her a lopsided grin. "I like to leave the talking to folks who have something to say."

"You have plenty to say. Are you kidding me?"

"To you, maybe." He waggled both brows. "And I don't even need my mouth to say it."

"I'm not talking about sex, but now that you mention it—"

"You changed your mind about dessert?"

"Only because of the time, and because I'm about to burst," she said, puffing up her cheeks. "You can have this date as a freebie."

"Can't say that doesn't leave me sorely disappointed. And sorely aching, thinking I'll be having to take care of things myself."

"Oh, stop it," she said, slapping his shoulder. "You get more sex than most guys in relationships."

"Guess it's a good thing we're not in one." He gave her a sideways glance that for the life of her she couldn't read.

It was as good a time as any . . . "What do you think you'll be doing five years from now?"

"I guess that depends on what happens with the ranch, whether or not me and the boys can ride out this drought and not lose everything Tess and Dave spent their lives on."

Not exactly what she was going for. "Say you do ride out the drought, and you come to this spot in five years and it's emerald green with water in the creek flowing clear and cold."

"Water in this creek is never going to be cold."

Fine. She'd spit it out. "Do you want what Tess and Dave had? A love to last a lifetime?"

He shrugged, looked out across the bone-dry pasture. "Sometimes I do, other times I realize I'm an ass and it's not going to happen. I'll do something stupid, pull some stunt, and then you'll realize I'm not worth all the time and effort you're investing in straightening me out."

"Is that what you think I'm doing?" But not only that . . . "And when did I say anything about being the love of your life?"

"You're the closest I'm ever going to come," he said, pulling his gaze from far away to her. "You're the closest I've ever wanted to come."

His admission had her swallowing hard, and for so many, many reasons. "What happened to dating for sex?"

"I was fine with that. At first."

"But you're not anymore?"

"I don't know, Arwen. I like it when you're here. I don't like it when you're not," he said and he reached for her hand. "And that has nothing to do with sex."

So where did they go from here, she wondered, singing the words in her head to a David Essex beat. "I should probably get back to work. And I imagine you need to, too."

But he shook his head, pushing the picnic box into the truck bed behind them. "C'mere."

"Dax—"

"No dessert. I got it. Just come over here."

When she hesitated, he slid toward her, one arm going behind her, the other hand toying with the charm on the necklace she wore. "It's been a long time since I've felt like sticking in one place.

You may not want to hear it, seeing as how you only want me for the prize between my legs, but you're the reason, and I wanted you to know. I thought this would be a good place to tell you that."

She didn't know whether to be flattered or scared out of her mind. She was here with Dax Campbell and he wanted her. Not just to fuck, but to be with, to enjoy. She couldn't say her feelings hadn't changed. She knew they had, but feelings got hurt, got in the way, turned good things into bad ones.

Turned loving fathers into heartless jerks.

Why did this have to be so hard? "Dax—"

"Let me finish. I don't know if it's the crap that's been going on, and thinking about Dave Dalton being the father I should've had, but I know things have changed. At least for me. And I can't promise to keep whatever we have to sex the way we agreed. I'm not asking you to marry me or anything wild like that, but I like you. I like you a lot. And I need to know you're okay with that."

With his liking her? What was she supposed to say? Yes? No? She didn't know? "Can we just take things a day at a time? See what happens? I don't want to make any promises—"

"Promises you can't keep?"

"I'm sorry. I don't want to say it's too soon, but—"

"It's too soon."

"Or maybe just too much for now."

"Right," he said, biting off the word. "I'll bare my soul later. When would be a good time? Can you maybe schedule that in?"

"Dax, don't do this. Lunch has been wonderful. I love that you brought me out here. Let's not start something we don't have time to finish."

"Got it. No talk that's not about sex," he said and moved to jump down from the truck.

Panicked, she grabbed his arm before he could. "I'm okay with it."

"What?"

"I'm okay with things changing. But I'm also scared." She dropped her head back, looked at the sky and laughed. "God, am I scared. A sexual relationship I can deal with. But I saw what my father's obsession with my mother did to him. He was nothing without her. Half the time he didn't remember that I existed."

"Arwen?"

She closed her eyes, took a breath, opened them, and looked over.

"I'm never going to forget about you." And then he kissed her.

It wasn't a kiss about sex. It was him telling her not to be scared, not to worry, that he would, as he'd said, never forget. But it didn't say he wouldn't leave, that he wouldn't change his mind and walk out on Boone and Casper. That he wouldn't walk out on her and go back to Montana or someplace else.

And she tried to kiss him back, but her heart wasn't in it, and he knew and he let her go, packing up what food they hadn't eaten, pouring the leftover tea on the ground. She watched the dirt lap up the moisture, wondered if it was enough to green a single blade of grass, thinking of the water she'd wasted on her yard at home when Dax had so little and needed so much.

They drove back to the saloon in silence, and with the picnic box in the bed of the truck, she sat in the passenger seat, not next to him, and she opened her own door when they arrived, and before she closed it, she asked him, "I'll see you later?"

He nodded.

"Oh, and if you want to talk to her, I saw Darcy's car parked at the feed store. Josh lives in an apartment upstairs. I imagine she's staying there with him."

"Thanks," he said. And then he drove away, and she stood there and watched him go.

THIRTY

DAX LEANED AGAINST the grille of his truck, hat pulled low, one ankle crossed over the other, hands stuffed carelessly in the pockets of his jeans. He'd left the ranch before the boys had made it out of bed and to breakfast, and headed to Lasko's alone. He was hoping with Arwen seeing Darcy's car at the feed store, he might catch his sister—or at least catch Josh—before he had to get to work.

But the sun had already broken the horizon, meaning he was late for the start of the day. This ridiculous Campbell family drama was taking up time he couldn't spare. He had a list of chores a mile long and Boone and Casper counting on him to shoulder his share of the workload. Theirs was a delicate balance, and he'd already done his time tipping the scale. If Josh or Darcy didn't show in the next five—

And there she was, walking down the ramp of the loading dock, digging in her purse for her sunglasses and keys, wearing boots and jeans and a ponytail and looking nothing like the attorney he'd seen that first morning, spruced up in the suit and heels of her trade. He pushed off the truck and started for her car, not yet sure how he was going to approach the subject of Greg.

She saw him coming her way and slowed her steps, her sunglasses hiding her eyes, but he didn't need to see them to tell she wasn't particularly glad to find him waiting. That much he could get from the set of her mouth, her hesitation, the flip of her bangs from her forehead. But then she picked up the pace as if deciding, in true attorney fashion, to get this meeting over with.

"I've been needing to talk to you," she said before he could get a word out.

First strike. Good for her. "About what?"

"Nora Stokes wants to look at some of the Daltons' furniture."

"Thought we had an agreement," he said, his jaw tight.

"I didn't sell it to her, Dax. Lighten up."

"But you talked to her about it?"

"We talked, yes. I ate lunch at the diner yesterday. She was there and asked me what y'all were doing with things. Specifically, the sideboard in the kitchen. She tried to get Tess to sell it to her years ago. That, and the highboy in the bedroom I was using."

"I told you. I'll have to talk to the boys about getting rid of anything."

"Do it, because I imagine a few thousand dollars might come in handy."

"Thousand, did you say?" He was never touching the sideboard again.

"Yes, thousand. Several of them."

That kind of cash would come in more than handy, but still. Selling Tess and Dave's things . . . "I'll talk to the boys."

"Regular little family the three of you've got there."

He shrugged. He wasn't here to argue with Darcy about the past. "You're my family first. You."

She had no comeback but said, "Something else."

"Shoot."

"Did Dave or Tess ever say anything to you about having surveys done on the ranch?"

"Surveys?"

"Geological surveys."

"For oil?" When she nodded, he shook his head. "Why do you ask?"

"I found some paperwork. I'm going to have Greg look at it."

Fuck that. One thing he did not need was Greg Barrett in his face. "He's a petroleum geologist now?"

"No, but he's got the Trinity Springs Oil account so he knows where to find a few."

And there was his opening. "What do you know about him anyway? Barrett?"

"What do I know about him? Do you mean how competent an attorney is he?" She frowned. "Do you need an attorney?"

"Why would you think that?"

"Because you're Dax Campbell."

"No, I don't need an attorney. I have one in Dallas, anyway."

"You do?"

"I didn't want our father in my business, so yeah. I took it out of town." Her wounded look had him adding, "I figured if I came to you, the old man would somehow get his hands in the pie."

"You don't have to make excuses, Dax. It's more than clear you don't want anything to do with anyone named Campbell."

"With our father. That's it. I wouldn't be here if I didn't want to make up for lost time with you."

"Sounded to me like you were here to ask about Greg."

"I'm just curious about him, what he's doing in Crow Hill."

"Why?"

"He was at the hospital when I went by."

That stopped her. "You went to the hospital? When?"

"A couple of days ago."

"Why didn't you tell me?"

"I just did, and I might have sooner if I'd known where you were."

She took a couple of steps closer to where she'd parked. "How did you find me?"

"Arwen saw your car. Is that where you're going now? To the hospital?"

She nodded. "Then out to the hill to pack up more of my things. I need some clothes. Other stuff."

"How long you gonna stay with Lasko?"

"I don't know. I haven't decided what I'm going to do next."

She had no job, no place of her own. And after all the time she'd put in at the firm. Dax hadn't been sure he could hate his father more—until now. "You're welcome at the house. I mean it. And you don't have to cook and clean."

Her mouth twisted, and she allowed a small laugh. "I've seen your idea of clean. Dog mops. Lord, Dax."

"I mopped after you left. Soap and water and everything." He paused. "Unless you're staying with Josh for another reason."

She looked down, jangled her keys as she searched for the one she wanted. "He's a good friend. That's all."

"Better than Boone and Casper? Better than your only brother?" he asked, waiting to see if she disputed his claim.

But all she said was, "I'll think about it."

And so after a minute he dug again. "Greg. What do you know?"

She shrugged. "He went to Texas Tech and got his degree a couple of years before I got mine. His mother was a legal secretary. I don't remember him mentioning other family. The Campbell worships the ground he walks on. Especially with his landing the Trinity Springs Oil account."

The mother thing jibed with Greg's story. And not mentioning his father made sense. Dax wondered if the old man had a gag order or whatever keeping his bastard from telling the truth. "Trinity Springs Oil. That's a big one."

"Big enough that pretty soon the firm's going to need another attorney or two. And that's assuming The Campbell's able to work."

"But Barrett's handling everything for now?"

She nodded. "I've thought about seeing if he needs any help. He did seem truly sorry when he delivered the news."

"What news?"

"That I'd been fired."

"Wait, what? Are you telling me the old man didn't have the balls to tell you himself?"

"I walked out. I deserve it."

"No, you didn't." That much he knew. "No one deserves that kind of disrespect."

She shrugged. "Was there something else?"

He tugged off his hat, ran his hand through his hair, settled it back in place. "I've been a shit of a brother, Darcy. I really am sorry. I should've come home or at least called to check on you. Especially with knowing how our parents are. I left you to deal with all of that and I have no excuse."

"Sure you do. You were looking out for yourself. And I honestly can't say that I blame you. I, on the other hand, took the other fork in the road and tried to mold my life to what they wanted instead of figuring out what I really wanted to do."

And how much of that was his fault? "If I hadn't bolted, you might've had time to do that. You were sixteen. No one knows squat at sixteen."

"You knew."

"I guess, though mostly I knew I didn't want to turn into our father. Seemed law school would be the first step toward making that happen, and I was not going down that road."

"How *did* you know? That you wanted to cowboy?"

"Working four years with Dave Dalton." He looked down, scuffed at the parking lot gravel. "He really was the father we both should've had."

She reached out, held his arm long enough to squeeze. "I'm sorry you lost him."

"And I didn't know it until Tess was gone, too. That was a tough bit of news to hear."

"Where were you? When you found out?"

"In Montana. I'd been there three or four years. Great place. Great boss. Reminded me a lot of Dave. I'd've stuck around had it not been for the inheritance. Turned into one of those crusty old cowboys who knows every bend in every creek and can tell you what years had the worst snowfalls and which well's going to dry up next."

"You can't do all that now?"

"Nah. Not crusty enough."

"You're on your way, letting dogs mop your floor."

That had him smiling. "So you'll think about coming back to the house? It's got to be more comfortable than a feed store."

"Are you kidding? Have you seen Josh's loft? It's as nice as my suite at home."

"People might talk."

"I hope that's a joke because you are the last person I can imagine caring about gossip."

"I care about you."

"I know," she said softly.

"I've been lousy about showing it."

"I know that, too." This time, not so soft.

"I did go to the hospital. That's got to count for something."

"Depends on why you went."

The right answer would be to say it was his duty as a son, as a brother. Instead, he said, "Arwen made me."

Darcy laughed. "At least you're honest."

"She told me it would make me feel better about him. About the way we'd left things when I'd split."

"And? Did it?"

"Nope. Of course I couldn't say all the things that need to be said since he's in no shape to listen."

"I talk to him when I'm there. He might be able to hear even if he can't acknowledge it."

"You think talking to him's going to bring him out of it?"

"I don't know, but it's what I have to do for me."

"Even though he fired you."

"He's still my father."

He had no argument for that. "I've gotta get to work before the boys skin me."

"So that was it? You hunted me down to ask about Greg?"

"He was at the hospital when I went. Made me curious about him, his attachment to the old man. Why he's in Crow Hill at all." He sharpened his aim. "Why his being here doesn't bother you."

"Why would it? There's been enough work to keep four or five bodies busy, yet we ran on two for the last several years. Greg's competent. More than competent. Why would it bother me?"

The last several years. The hard ones Ned Orleans had mentioned? "Because he doesn't belong here."

"And you're in charge of who gets to call Crow Hill home?"

He'd said too much already. "You're always welcome at the house. Even if you just want to stop by and mop. You don't have to move in."

"I'll think about it. I didn't mean to leave things in such a mess. And it's not like my calendar is filled these days."

"Any time and for as long as you want. I'd love to have you there. Maybe we could, you know, catch up."

"I'd love to hear more about Montana. Hell, I'd love to hear more about the Daltons. Not the couple I knew, but the Tess and Dave that took you away from us."

"That's not what happened, Darcy. What they did was show me how to be myself. I'm the one who messed up thinking that meant shutting out everyone else. I was eighteen. I was stupid. I hope I know better now."

"Does that mean you're not going to leave again?"

"Pretty sure Boone and Casper won't let that happen. The three of us making a go of the ranch is one thing. Two will never cut it. And speaking of which . . ."

"You need to go. You told me."

"But now that I know where you're hanging, I'll see you soon."

"Let me know about the furniture. For Nora."

"Will do," he said and turned to go before remembering what Arwen had said. "Hey, did you happen to run across a recipe for Tess's barbecue sauce?"

THIRTY-ONE

THE MUSIC BLARED from the patio's speakers. The commercial fans blowing from the corners of the backyard roared. The smoke from the pits of the teams competing in the July 4th cook-off rose thick enough to choke a team of Clydesdales. But boy, did the air smell good, and that from Arwen's Hellcat Saloon station especially so. Okay, so maybe she was prejudiced.

But while the Dalton Gang had Tess Dalton's sauce and rub, Arwen had her own secret weapon in Myna Goss. The older woman had been a staple in one of Houston's most popular barbecue restaurants for years. She'd moved to Crow Hill with her husband when he'd switched careers at fifty, leaving behind the USPS to become a guide on a nearby exotic game ranch.

The day Myna stopped by at lunch for a beer and a burger and admitted she wasn't a fan of retirement, Arwen hired her for the saloon's kitchen, doing the both of them a big favor. Myna brought experience as well as tips and tricks and ways to man a grill and a pit that had turned the Hellcat's menu into a goldmine.

Today, Myna stood at the helm of the saloon's big barbecue drum, smoking chicken, baby back ribs, and a brisket. Myna wasn't a fan of sausage, and since the Blackbird Diner stuffed their own casings with the Stokes' family recipe of freshly ground and spiced meat, Arwen was fine bowing to Myna's quirks.

Though Luck competed as part of the Summerlin family's team, the rest of Arwen's waitstaff pitched in at the saloon's station. And with Callie, Stacy, and Amy at Myna's beck and call, Arwen was free to play cook-off hostess. But mostly she was free to see how the Dalton Gang was faring in their first official appearance as a group.

The gossip had started as the trucks started showing up not long after dawn. Casper had arrived with Boone in his big black dualie, and Arwen had been surprised to see Darcy exit the cab as well. She'd been less surprised not to see Dax anywhere. With Wallace Campbell unable to judge this year, the committee had handed the reins to Greg Barrett as the only Campbell and Associates representative

Arwen wondered how Dax's sister was dealing with the loss of her job, and glanced over, caught by the sight of Josh Lasko with his head close to Darcy's. It brought to mind Arwen's picnic with Dax, the tenderness of his kiss, his desperate sort of sorrow, as if his telling her of the change in his feelings was something to mourn, even while he struggled to hold on to what they'd found.

She didn't want to let it go either. She just didn't know how to make it work. He wasn't wired to stay, and even if he didn't forget her, his remembering her wasn't enough. She'd thought it would be when the truth was she wanted him with her. She needed him to make her laugh and make her think and make her come. She needed him to love her—because she loved him. She loved him.

Oh, *God*. She loved him.

This was so not the day to come to that realization, and she did her best to blink it away. She needed to be at the top of her game, undistracted. At least Dax wasn't here . . .

Except he was, she realized, looking back at the Dalton Gang's station. He stood there with a longneck in one hand, leaning an elbow on Casper's shoulder, laughing with the other man at Boone's attempt to flip ribs.

Giving a thumbs-up to Myna, Arwen moved away, hoping to look like a good hostess making the rounds. In reality, she couldn't think of anything but Dax. She stared at him where he huddled with Boone and Casper, her heart aching, her head aching twice as bad—badly enough that it took her several seconds to tune into the whispered conversation at her side.

"Look at him, Nan. He's there next to the Campbell girl. Look at the two of them together and tell me you don't see a resemblance. A family resemblance."

"Roma! Do you really think so? I mean, there's never been a hint of rumor that Wallace fathered a child. Cheating yes. Everyone knows the man can't keep his pants up, but do you really think—"

"Are you kidding me? How many trips out of town does he take a year? How long is he gone each time? I can't imagine he hasn't left, uh, a little something of himself behind. Maybe more than one something, if you get my drift."

Her head spinning, Arwen pretended to watch Myna stir brown sugar into her barbecue sauce but stared past the other woman at Greg and Darcy instead. Both shared Dax's coloring, though his hair was lighter from the time he spent in the sun. And though she knew Darcy's eyes were green instead of blue like her brother's, she'd never paid attention to Greg's.

Their bone structure, however, their cheeks and their jaws. It really was uncanny, but could it be true? And Greg's hands when he gestured. She swallowed, told herself she was imagining things, but those hands looked so much like Dax's she could almost imagine them sliding over her skin.

She was shaking, literally shaking. But was she also taking ridiculous gossip and running with it? Was she believing the worst of Wallace Campbell because of how close she was to Dax, taking his side, supporting him?

Surely she wasn't letting herself be swayed by what she shared with Dax.

"I'm pretty sure your cook's sauce needs more beer."

Arwen jumped at the voice in her ear, slapping Dax away, grabbing the empty longneck he held from his hand. "And I'm pretty sure you are sauced and have had plenty."

He pulled another bottle from his pocket and twisted off the cap. "What's a July fourth without getting sauced on sauce made of sauce?"

He'd been drunk long before he'd arrived at the cook-off; he hadn't been here long enough to drink as much as he obviously had. Not that she was particularly surprised, but then she looked from him to the empty bottle she held to his sister and the hot young attorney who didn't fit in Crow Hill. Who didn't have any reason to be here unless . . .

"Didn't you tell me Greg Barrett was at the hospital when you visited?"

"He's a dick. Thinks he's got some claim on the firm. Bullshit. That firm is Darcy's."

"Why would he think he has a claim on the firm?"

"He's the only one left working there. He's the only one the old man gives a shit about."

The only child? Is that what Dax was saying? Was he drunk enough that she could get her answers? "Did you and Greg talk? At the hospital? Did he tell you anything about where he came from? Why he moved to Crow Hill?"

"I need another beer."

"No. You don't. You need to eat."

"I've been trying. Food's not done anywhere."

She'd seen him pestering Teri Gregor at the Blackbird Diner's pit, and was pretty sure it was a good thing her husband Shane was currently deployed. "Then you need to sleep it off. C'mon. You can use my couch."

"I'd rather use your bed. And use you in it."

Yeah, that wasn't going to happen. She hooked her arm through his and guided him across the yard, ducking through the temporary fencing she'd set up between the saloon and her cottage. His hat got caught on the way through, and she reached back and grabbed it, pushing him up the walkway toward her kitchen door.

She managed to turn the knob, and with her hands between his shoulder blades, to force him inside. He stumbled across the floor, giving her enough room to close the door behind them. She leaned against it to catch her breath, done with coddling him, done with playing peacemaker.

Done with doing all the things she'd sworn never to do for a man. He was a man. Old enough to stand on his own two feet. Whether or not he was strong enough . . . If he wasn't, she didn't want him here. Loving him made no difference if he couldn't be the man she needed him to be. The man who would help her be strong, too.

"I know about Greg," she said, rushing out with the words before she changed her mind and went soft. No coddling. No peace-making. He needed to face the past he'd run from at eighteen.

He said nothing as he spun where he stood, wobbled and righted, brought his beer bottle to his mouth and downed half of it. Then he frowned, staring into it as he asked, "What do you know? That the man can't tell good barbecue from bad? That he doesn't know shit about wearing boots? That he doesn't belong here?"

"That he's your brother."

Dax stilled, sharp and suddenly sober, his head coming up slowly, his gaze mean. "Who told you that?"

She pushed off the door, crossed her arms, gave him a shrug that said it didn't matter.

"Who told you that?" His voice was low, the words evenly spaced and powerful.

She swallowed and held her ground. "No one told me. I heard talk is all."

"Who was talking?"

"Does it matter?"

"Goddamn it, Arwen." He slammed the bottle across the room, his gaze holding hers as the glass shattered, tinkling against the tile like a sad country song. "Who the fuck was it?"

The room tightened around her, and she moved to keep it at bay, crossing to the table that had been in the Buck Off Bar, to the booth where she'd sat as a girl and dressed her Barbie in the tiny plastic heels that reminded her of her mother's shoes.

Shoes that didn't belong in Crow Hill. That were meant for a life in the city. She looked out the window, watched Crush cross the lawn, orange on green, downy white feathers floating in his wake. The circle of life.

But they were talking about Dax's life. "Is it true? Is Greg Barrett your brother?"

Blood hammered through the veins at his temples. His eyes narrowed in the shadow cast by the brim of his hat. "You gonna answer my question, or what?"

Really? That's what he wanted to know? "I'm not even sure. I think it was Roma Orleans. Maybe Nan Waters. Why does it matter?"

"Because I want to know who's telling lies."

Except it wasn't a lie. She knew that. His insistence otherwise was one thing, but the women speculating were right. Greg shared the same traits with Darcy as Dax. His coloring was darker, but all three had Wallace Campbell's eyes, though the colors varied from bright blue to green, and the shape of their smiles was identical.

"How long have you known?"

Finally, he faltered, nudging up the brim of his hat and scrubbing both hands down his face. "A few days."

She took a deep breath, blew out all of her tension when letting it go. "He told you?"

A nod. "At the hospital."

"What did you do?"

"Told him he was full of shit and decked him."

Arwen winced. "Did you tell Darcy?"

"Hell, no. I haven't told anyone, and I won't. Not until I know for sure."

And only one person could verify that. "What did he say?"

He snorted. "Besides owing his education to the old man? An education that should've been mine?"

An education he'd turned his back on. "Who's his mother?"

"Some legal secretary The Campbell met at a conference."

The Campbell. She didn't think she'd ever heard anyone but Darcy use the term to refer to their father. "What are you going to do?"

"About what?"

"Finding out if he is who he says he is."

"Nothing."

"You don't think you owe it to Darcy to tell her?"

"Nope."

"What if she hears the rumors?"

"She's a big girl."

"That's harsh."

"It is what it is."

"What if your father never wakes up?"

"Then he never wakes up."

"And if he dies? Is Greg named in his will?"

"How the hell should I know?" he fairly shouted.

Arwen waited, a clock in her head ticking as she watched Dax's anger abate. "You seriously don't want to know the truth?"

He took a deep sighing breath. "Am I going to steal his toothbrush and pay for a DNA test? I barely have enough money to feed the livestock left to my care, not to mention feeding myself, so no. I don't want to know the truth."

She didn't know what to say. How could he live like this, turning his back, not knowing, never wondering, drifting still? She shook her head, hugged herself tighter, glancing out the window to see Crush curled in a ball at the base of her yard's huge spreading oak.

And yet . . . She *had* turned her back on her father, rarely wondering, not knowing, staying selfishly involved in her life in Crow Hill without a word to the man who had suffered an unimaginable loss and yet still done his best by her.

What right did she have to criticize Dax when she was no better a daughter than he was a son?

She was fighting back tears when Dax came up behind her, wrapped his arms around her, lowered his head to nuzzle his cheek to hers. He smelled like beer and wood smoke, like sweat and the sun. Like the Dax that she loved, though right now he was making it hard to remember why.

Right now, she wanted to walk away. She wanted him sober. She wanted to have this conversation from a place where he would remember. She didn't want the distraction of his body and his hands and his warm breath on her neck.

She wanted him to face this thing that, if true, would change his life forever. She didn't want him to look for an escape, because that's what he was doing. Running. Away from the truth, away from the pain. Running to her, this time, instead of leaving Crow Hill. And if she welcomed him, accepted him . . .

He was kissing her neck and she couldn't breathe and she didn't want to enable his avoidance by giving in. God, she was torn. Was this what it meant to love someone? Offering unconditional support while they found their way?

"Dax—"

He spun her, shook his head, lifted her to sit on the table's edge. "Don't talk."

"We need to talk."

"I'm done talking. No more. Not today."

She pressed her lips together. If he wasn't going to listen, there was nothing for her to say. She needed to get back to the festivities anyway. But he was in her way, his eyes fiery, his mouth grim, his nostrils flaring, his pulse a visible beat in the hollow of his throat.

Her pulse answered, and she fought it back. She didn't want this. Not here. Not now. If he couldn't be honest with her, if he couldn't open up to her, if all he could do was rage against life being something other than what he wanted it to be . . .

He reached for her foot then, held her gaze as he worked off her boot. He dropped it to the floor, tugged off the other, making it easy to strip her of her jeans. She gave him a look. "I didn't come in here for this."

"Doesn't matter," he said, hopping on one foot then the other to get rid of his boots, too. "I need to fuck you."

His words were cold and crass and didn't consider her at all. It was his need that kept her there. Dax Campbell needed her, and an ache rose from her core to frighten her with its strength.

She was going to get hurt. He didn't love her. He needed her to give him relief. He was drunk and angry and driven by his cock. He was going to hurt her, and she couldn't tell him no because she needed him for the same wrong reasons as well as for the ones that were right.

His fly was open, the denim vee spread wide by the thrusting bulge of his cock in his briefs. The shaft was thick, the head engorged, the tip weeping already and making her wet. She lifted her gaze, taking in the strip of golden hair rising above the elastic band to bisect his well-defined abs.

She loved his body hair, coarse on his legs, kissed by the sun on his arms, the silky wedge in the center of his chest, the nest that cushioned his penis and balls and created a wonderfully sticky wet friction when he slid into her and out.

He shrugged off his shirt, tossing it into the booth as he helped her off the table, reaching for her, burying his face in her hair, his fingers nimble at the buttons of her fly, opening her jeans, tugging them down, taking down her panties, too. She wore only her socks, her bra, and her Hellcat Saloon T-shirt, and he stripped the last two away, returned her to the table.

Naked and wet, she waited, hungry, hot, watching his erection spring from his pants as he shed them. Then he moved in, one hand fisting his shaft, the other in the small of her back. She widened the spread of her legs and he dipped his hips, aligning their bodies before driving his cock so deeply inside her he hit bottom.

She leaned back on her hands, dropped her head on her shoulders, and closed her eyes, hurting where his fingers dug into her skin. She didn't care. She was naked in her kitchen, and he was thick and long and full inside of her, and her nipples were so tightly drawn, the touch of the air made her flinch.

Impaled, she couldn't move as Dax leaned in, the base of his cock stretching her to the point of pain. She gasped, gasped again as he fingered her clit, pulling up on the hood to expose her, taking a nipple in his mouth and biting down. This time she yelped, her cry echoing in the kitchen and followed by Dax's very dirty and very earthy laugh.

She hadn't locked the door, and dozens of people milled in the yard between the saloon and the house, and at any moment someone could walk inside. The thought terrified her, and yet she pulled her heels to her hips on the table and grabbed her ankles, giving Dax better access along with her trust.

He took both, holding her shoulders as he loomed above, his abs contracted, his cock deep, his balls slapping her ass as he thrust. His mouth twisted, pained. His jaw clicked. His temple throbbed. Sweat beaded on his brow and fell to her chest, burning her skin as he pounded and grunted and scraped her raw.

She loved it, the violence, the intensity, the brutal power. Loved knowing how much he held in check. She bucked up against him, the table shaking as they fucked. He laughed again, and she bit off a sharply ordered, "More," and his laugh grew wicked and low, vibrating through to her core where he stroked.

"More," she said again and he leaned over her, licking at the tip of one breast then the other, sucking at her flesh, holding her nipple with the edges of his teeth. She squirmed, and he moved his hands to her knees, pushing her wide and holding her there while he drove deep.

It still wasn't enough. She didn't know what she wanted, what she was looking for, reaching for, what was missing. He was taking her apart and she ached from the assault, craving the pain that kept her from saying words he wasn't ready for. Words she wasn't sure she trusted to be the truth.

The only one she trusted was, "More."

Dax groaned. "You're killing me here, baby. Killing me."

"Can you think of a better way to go?"

He made a sound, half groan, half laugh, and it rumbled through her limbs. "Not even for enough money to save my fucking ranch."

He pulled his cock from her pussy then, worked their shared moisture lower and found the bud of her ass, piercing the tight hole and slowly sliding deep. She kept her knees raised, moved her hands to her clit, holding Dax's eyes as he gripped the edge of the table at her sides.

Her body shivered, invaded as it was, pinned as she was, and then Dax touched her, splaying one hand on her belly to anchor her, his thumb pressing into her clit and sending her flying. She stiffened, shuddered, collapsed, her eyes rolling toward unconsciousness, tremors rocking her, sweeping through her, and all the while Dax fucking her and fingering her and finishing her off.

And then he was gone, pulling away before lifting her from the table to the floor, flipping her over, pushing her down, entering her ass from behind. He stroked slowly, his rhythm steady, the pressure of his cock no more than she could bear, though all too quickly it wasn't enough and she wiggled to let him know.

He delivered, holding her hips as he pumped. She reached for her clit, working it as sensation built again, and crying out as she came. The sound sent Dax over and he pulled his cock from her ass, shooting pulses of hot semen along her spine, spilling words that were just as sizzling as his body heat.

It was when he grabbed his shirt from the booth and leaned

forward to clean her off that she heard the first crack. She stilled, waited, heard another, and tried to push up. But Dax wasn't paying attention. He was muttering to himself, wiping her down, and when the third crack came, it was too late.

The table shook beneath them and Dax pulled her back as it shattered, the particleboard top aged and dry and no match for their weight or destructive actions. It was broken, and it could never be put back together, and all she could do was stand there with her ears ringing.

"Wow," he said, his breath hot against her ear, his heart pounding against her back, and then he added a loud *"Shit"* and grabbed her by the waist—just as the First Baptist Church's Dr. Britton crossed in front of her window and kneeled in front of her oak to pet Crush.

She huddled atop Dax's prone body, staring at the detritus of her childhood, while the man she loved lay snoring and passed out on the floor.

THIRTY-TWO

Dax thought he might have to shoot himself. Why the hell he'd thought it a good idea to take Arwen to the Crow Hill Country Club would be a mystery he couldn't see himself solving before the end of his days. But here they were, and he wasn't about to back out now, and after the way he'd treated her at the barbecue cook-off, he was damn lucky she'd agreed to go out with him at all.

She looked amazing. A-maz-ing. When she'd met him at her door earlier, he'd forgotten his own name, and couldn't for the life of him remember hers. He'd smelled oranges and herbs and her skin, been blown away by the way she'd made up her eyes, her lashes thick and dark, some glittery shadow catching the light from her porch, her mouth a deep dark pink he wanted to kiss.

He had no idea what she was doing with him, a cowboy, a bad seed, a black sheep, a dick. Yeah, he knew what folks thought of him, the way he'd run out on his kin and the hell he'd raised without making amends. But Arwen saw beneath that, saw the same truth his boys had known all along. He worked hard and he played hard and loved harder than them all. Where was the crime in that?

Opening his door while a white-coated valet opened Arwen's, he climbed down and walked to where she waited, stopping to look at her as another valet took off in his truck to park it. Her dress was strapless, a tight-fitting number that hugged her breasts and her waist, then flared into a skirt that made him think of Marilyn Monroe. He wanted to see her walk over a subway air vent, wanted to watch the material billow, see her fight it, get a peek at what she was wearing beneath.

And her hair . . . God, her hair. Shining like strong coffee in the sun. She'd curled it, swept it back on one side with a flowered clip thing the same color pink as her dress. And her shoes, her legs. They were bare, smooth, gorgeous, her heels as high as railroad spikes, though so narrow he had no idea how she balanced. But balance she did, and walk she did, her ass swinging, her skirt swinging, too, as she came to where he was standing like he'd been rooted to the ground.

"Are you sure about this?" she asked, frowning.

He shifted a bit to adjust his own erect root. "Why do you ask?"

"You're sweating," she said, leaning forward to lick his throat in the open collar of his dress shirt.

God-*damn*. "It's hot out."

"Not that kind of sweat, silly."

Silly, yeah. That was what he was. "I didn't know there was more than one kind."

"Sure there is," she said, hooking her arm through his and turning him toward the door. "There's baling hay in the sun sweat—"

"We don't bale our own hay. Hell, we don't *have* any hay *to* bale."

"Whatever," she said with a wave of her hand. "There's slick, sliding sex sweat—"

"Now that sweat I know about," he said and stopped walking. "I'm all for heading back to your place and working up a good lather."

"Hey. One-track mind guy. It's date night, remember?" she asked, and nudged him forward.

"Yeah, but since I'm the one who picks the dates, I don't see why I can't change my mind. We can watch *Serenity* again. I like Captain Mal."

This time she stopped, forced him to turn and face her, then let go of his arm and took a step away. "Look at me."

He looked. Head to toe, he looked. His cock looked, too, that one big eye open wide. "Okay."

She made a sweeping gesture with both hands. "This is for you. I spent hours making this happen."

He waggled both brows. "Bet I can undo it all in a minute ten."

Her eyes narrowed into threatening slits. "You won't be undoing it *ever* if you don't feed me Chef Alman's wasabi ginger rib eye."

He canted his head to the side, twisted his mouth. "We can probably get it to go."

"Dax Campbell, I swear." She charged, heels tapping, skirt whipping, finger coming for his chest. "If you don't take me inside right now, you will never get to taste my tits again."

He shoved his hands in his pockets, swung out his elbow. "Let's do this."

Once inside, they were tended to immediately, the maitre d' seating Arwen then turning to Dax. "Good evening, Mr. Campbell. My sympathies in regards to your father. And nice to have you with us Ms. Poole. Can I have our sommelier make a suggestion from our wine list?"

"No need," Dax said, holding Arwen's gaze. "A bottle of Prairie Rotie, please.

"The 2009?"

Uh, good question. "That would be the one."

"Perfect. I'll have it sent right over."

Waiting until they were alone, Arwen gave him a smile. "A wine man. I'm impressed."

"No reason to be. Darcy told me it's what the old man drinks when he's not guzzling Glenlivet."

She crossed her legs, swung her foot back and forth against his calf. "I would think you'd order something else."

"And reveal my total ignorance? Not a chance," he said, glancing around and wondering how fast they could order, how fast they could eat. "This was such a bad idea."

"Why? Because this is your father's social club?"

In a nut sac. "I want my hat."

She reached over, patted his cheek. "Feed me, and then I'll feed you."

He groaned. "Takeout. Next time you're hungry, it's takeout all the way."

"You know the best place for takeout in town is the saloon."

"I'm a big fan of burgers. I can afford burgers."

She looked at him for a long moment then dropped her gaze to her lap, twisting her hands there as if too nervous to speak. "I have money, Dax."

Sweet. God, this woman was sweet. "I have money, too. I wouldn't have brought you here if I didn't have money. I also have the family tab and a whole lot of sympathy to play on."

Her eyes widened. "You wouldn't dare."

"Probably not. I'm tempted, but that's more about giving the old man a big fuck-you rather than being broke."

"How broke are you?"

"Broke enough."

"Then we should go," she said, uncrossing her legs.

"Not a chance. I want to sit here, drink my Prairie Rotie, eat Chef Arman's wasabi ginger rib eye, and think how I'm going to go about getting you out of that dress."

"It's easier than you think. And I'm not wearing anything beneath it."

He choked on the water he'd just swallowed. "Nothing?"

"Nothing," she mouthed, licking her lips.

"I'm pretty sure the country club has a dress code."

"What the country club doesn't know . . ." she said, letting the sentence trail.

"So." He sat forward, thought better about it when his cock complained, and sat back. "About this nothing that you're wearing. Tell me more."

"Well," she said, toying with a curled strand of her hair. "Obviously I'm not wearing a bra."

"Not even one without straps?"

She shook her head, a slow back and forth. Then she asked, "Do you think I need one?"

"Hell no. But if you want to let that top slip a little lower, I wouldn't mind."

She crossed her arms and tugged on the fabric until the barest edges of her areolas blended with the pink of her dress. "Does that work for you?"

"You have no idea," he said, and then he felt the sole of her foot on his thigh.

"Oh, I have an idea," she said, her foot sliding higher, her arch settling over his cock that had grown as stiff as a cattle prod.

"You're playing with fire, woman."

"Fire? And here I thought we were just having sex in the middle of our date."

He reached across the table for her wrist, a move that pushed his cock against her foot, and squeezed, gave her a warning look before letting her go. "What about the rest?"

"The rest?" She moved her foot, crossed her legs and leaned just enough to the side to show a long length of bare thigh. "If you move your chair a little bit closer you can find out for yourself."

He cleared his throat. "Shit, Arwen. Don't do that to me here."

"Why not?" she said, her voice low, raw. "You don't want to feel how wet I am?"

He squeezed his eyes shut, shook himself, then lifted his chair and moved it to bump against hers. When he did, she draped her skirt and the extra length of the tablecloth over her lap.

He leaned closer, his hand on her chair's cushion, then beneath her leg until his fingers dipped into the folds of her pussy. He pushed one inside and she caught her breath, her chest rising and falling so quickly the crescents of exposed areola pebbled.

"Can we go now?" They only needed to make it as far as his truck. *He* wasn't going to make it any farther than his truck.

"I'm not ready," she said, shifting sideways in her chair and moving her hand to his thigh. "Do you trust me?"

"To do what?"

"To make staying worth your while."

He didn't know about that, but he was interested to see what else she might have up her skirt. "Give it your best shot."

"Sit back. Relax. And don't make those noises you do when you come."

Shit. "When I come—"

"Shh," was all she said before her hand found his fly and deftly worked it open.

"Arwen—"

"I think the server is on his way."

"Shit." His cock was stiff and her fingers were slipping beneath the elastic of his briefs, smearing the bead of moisture he'd already released around the tip of his head.

"I love it when you're wet," she said, letting him go and sitting back and bringing her hand to her mouth to lick the damp pad of her finger.

"Here you go, sir, ma'am," the server said and Dax tried not to die.

He screwed his eyes shut, huffed out a sharp breath, grabbing for control and instead grabbing the server's attention. When the other man stopped pouring the wine, Dax motioned him to continue.

He did, explaining the evening's specials while Arwen listened, and Dax tried not to jerk himself off. Once the meals had been laid out, Arwen placed their order, and Dax nodded when the server looked at him to double check.

"Very good. I'll have your salads out to you shortly."

As the other man walked away, Dax whispered, "Can we leave now?"

"What did I tell you?" Arwen asked, sliding her hand along his thigh again and picking up where she'd left off with his cock. "Sit back and enjoy. And none of those sounds."

"I'd say fuck you—"

She laughed, a sexy throaty burst that had heads turning their way while she stroked him and while he nearly strangled.

"I'm going to get you back for this."

"I'd say I certainly hope so, except I owe you for Boone and Casper seeing us in the back of your truck."

She thumbed the slit in the head of his cock, used the moisture to wet her palm. Then she rubbed him, around and around and around, and he heard the sounds building and reached for his wine, with a growled, "Fuck you."

"Have I ever told you how much I love the way you fuck me?"

"Jesus Christ, Arwen—"

"Or how very very much I love your cock?" She leaned closer, licked her bottom lip, held it with her tongue and breathed so hard her tits strained against her top. "I love it on my tongue. I love it in my pussy. I love it in my ass. Almost as much as I love fucking yours with my finger."

He jerked in her hand, squeezed his eyes shut, rolled them open, his balls pulling into his body, his anus clenching tight. "I goddamn swear . . ."

But he couldn't say anything else. She was stroking him, up and down his shaft, a sweep of her palm over his head, back to his shaft, to his head, yanking, spanking, pulling while she held his gaze, her eyes wide and wild, her lips parted. She was just as turned on as he was, and that was going to do him in.

"I want to eat your pussy," he said. "I want to smell you. I want to taste you."

"I'm on your finger," she told him, and he remembered and brought his hand to his nose, breathing in and sucking at the juice she'd left on him.

"Right now," she whispered, crossing her legs and leaning in close. "If you could have me. Tell me how you'd want me."

He'd been picturing it all night. He didn't even have to think. "In this chair. In my lap. Your skirt to your waist so I could see my cock in your cunt. Your top down and your tits in my hands. I want to come all over your belly. I want to come in your mouth."

"I want you to come. I want you to come now. Help me," she said.

He wrapped his hand around hers and pulled in the rhythm he knew well until the blood pounding in his head took over. He grabbed the tablecloth and groaned, slumping into the chair and holding her gaze as she finished him, pulling until he had nothing left and couldn't even move to fasten his pants.

She sat back, a look of cat-licking-cream pleasure on her face, and reached for her wineglass, draining it as dry as she'd drained him, excitement lighting her eyes when the salads arrived.

"I'm starving," she said, then looked over and asked, "You?"

"Hungry? Yeah. Able to lift my own fork?" He shook his head, unable to find the strength to give her the evil eye when she laughed.

THIRTY-THREE

"YOU ASKED ME once about taking over the ranch and turning it around like I had the Buck Off Bar."

They were in bed, naked, exhausted, sated with good food and good wine and excellent service and sex, and Arwen didn't know about Dax, but she was sore and raw and aching. All in all it seemed the perfect time to plant the seed she'd had growing since he'd mentioned being broke at dinner.

"Yeah, so?"

He asked the question sharply, but she didn't take offense. He was half asleep. She and her nefarious purposes were keeping him awake, and he knew exactly what she was doing. He just didn't know why. "You do remember?"

"Yes, Arwen. I remember."

"Okay, then," she said, glancing down to where he lay, eyes closed and curled around her. "Keep that in mind and don't immediately reject what I'm about to say."

"You're making me not like it already," he said, his tongue coming out and finding her nipple.

She lifted her breast out of his way. "You listen, or I'm walking out of here."

"I'm listening. I'm listening. Shit, woman."

"I was thinking about what you said. About your money situation. I know things are bad—"

"And I hope you have a point because I'm fading here."

Her point. Yes. *Out with it, Arwen. Spill it and take the hit.* "You lease what acreage you can afford to Henry Lasko."

He waited, one heartbeat, two, a third, and then a disbelieving and sarcastic, "What the hell did you say?"

She laid out her argument. "Tess had already planned to. Henry needs the grazing land. And you need the money."

"Fuck that. Fuck the money. We need the grazing land just as much as Henry, if not more."

And now for the next part. "Not if you sell off part of your herd. For now," she hurried to add. "Build it up again once this drought breaks."

He snorted, rolled to his back and crossed an arm beneath his head. "If that's your idea of management, I'm surprised your *saloon* didn't go under the first month."

Her idea of management was not holding on to the past for sentimental reasons, not being stupid just because smart hurt a lot more. She was also a big proponent of the long term. "But it didn't, did it? In fact, my *saloon* is the number one go-to place in Crow Hill."

"That's not saying much."

Right. She'd put the idea out there. She knew he'd mull it over, and that was pretty much all she could ask. He'd have to be the one to add the fertilizer and see what he could grow.

Still, she couldn't let his slam go unanswered. "It's saying plenty."

"Says you."

"Do you want to fight?"

"No, I want to fuck."

"We can do that." She took a deep breath, and an even bigger leap of faith. "Or we can make love."

It took a long moment for what she'd said to settle, and for him to look over, lying as he was on his back, one arm beneath his head on the pillow. The shadows in the room made it hard to see his face, harder to see his eyes and his expression.

But it wasn't hard at all to understand that he wanted her when he reached across her body to roll her on top of his. When he threaded his hands into her hair. When he pulled her head down and kissed her.

His tongue was sure in its possession, bold and strong in its claiming. He stroked it along hers, mating, playing. She pushed into his mouth and did the same, stretching her legs out atop his, settling her pussy over his balls, his cock warm and insistent where it snuggled between their bellies.

He felt so good, head-to-toe hard and so wonderfully hot. She scooted lower, kissing his jaw, his neck, and farther down, finding a nipple and teething it until he sucked back a curse and groaned. Then he laughed, a deep throaty sound that had her biting harder, had him growing harder, stiff and thick and damp.

"Be careful with those teeth, Ms. Poole. Damage any of the goods and it'll be your loss."

Cocky beast, she mused, pushing her chin into his pectoral muscle until he gave up and groaned, and then sliding one hand between their bodies to capture the head of his cock and squeeze.

"Jesus Christ," was all he managed to say, and even those words had trouble clawing their way free.

She liked this Dax. Helpless Dax. Dax surrendered. Dax unable to fight her or the demons possessing him. She wanted more of this Dax. She loved this Dax, and he would know exactly how much before leaving her bed. He needed to know. His knowing gave her the power to convince him this was where he belonged. With her. To her. Without her he would never be who he was meant to be.

The responsibility thrilled her, challenged her, and she dragged her tongue down the center of his torso, wetting the strip of silky hair bisecting him. He was salty, always salty, so much time in the sun left him baked and brown and the sheen of sweat refused to be scrubbed away. She loved that about him, loved that his body belonged to the life he loved as much as his mind and his heart.

His cock came next, her tasting of him, skin stretched to near splitting over the head, the tip that was open and salty, too, the seam beneath, the ridge of the mushroomed cap that fit her mouth and filled it. She ministered to all of it, sucking and lapping and loving, her hand ringed around his shaft just beneath, squeezing and letting go, squeezing and letting go.

"Goddamn," was all he got out this time, his hands at his hips digging into her sheets and bunching the fabric into balls in his fists.

Scooting lower, she blew a stream of warm air over his balls, licked the center of his sac, separated his testicles with her tongue. She pulled first one then the other into her mouth, rolling them gently before spitting them into her palm and slipping a finger into his ass. Kissing her way up his shaft, she held him, pumping and sucking and sliding her lips to the base of his cock and back.

He groaned, bucked upward, his cock bouncing against the top of her mouth, and he tried to tell her, but she knew. She felt it in his balls, in his ass, in the tension like rigor stiffening him. He came in bursts, long liquid pulses of semen that she swallowed and cleaned from his cock, easing him back in time and space to where she waited.

He looked at her, dazed and amazed and not far from stupid. "What do you want?"

I want you to love me. I want you to need me. I want you to stay here and be with me for the rest of our days. But she didn't say that or say anything. She just smiled, telling him with her eyes that she had everything if she had him.

"Anything, baby," he said. "Anything. Tell me. I'm yours."

That was what she needed to hear. What she'd wanted for days now to have him say. Yes, this was sex and he was drunk on it, and she could've asked him for the world and he would've given her the last penny in his pocket. She knew that, and yet she was filled to bursting with loving him and having him, and his need to give back to her was the pin that was going to pop her.

She crawled to the head of the bed, wrapped her hands around the headboard's railing, and caught her lower lip with her teeth. She rolled her hips, side to side, a figure eight above his face, his gaze slipping from hers to her breasts to her cunt inches from his mouth. And the look in his eyes nearly did her in, fierce and full of knowing and ready.

Closing her eyes, she waited, dipping down when he tapped her thighs, feeling the tip of his tongue splitting the seam of her pussy's lips, circling her clit, sliding back to push inside of her, moving in and out until he replaced his tongue with a finger, two fingers, and she rode them, a slow up and down.

He blew against her, his breath warm and raising gooseflesh, his other hand finding the bud of her ass. She pushed against him, reached for one of the rings in her nipples and tugged, the tips of her breasts drawn tight, her heart racing, blood rushing beneath the surface of her skin.

And then he bit her, her inner thigh, her labia, and sucked the whole of her clit into his mouth, holding it with his lips while he used his teeth to scrape her, his tongue to soothe the tiny wounds, the fingers of one hand in her pussy, the thumb of the other up to the knuckle in her ass.

She was on fire, burning with need, her arousal consuming, tearing her apart. The butterfly touches of his tongue had her wanting to climb the walls, to claw her way through the barriers keeping them from having this together for the rest of their lives. She wanted him. She loved him. And then she came, a rush of sensation that left her unable to breathe or to think or to do anything but succumb.

Dax caught her when she fell and pulled her to him, pulled her to her feet. Pulled her with him to the shower and then inside once he'd turned the hot water on high. She hadn't known she was shaking until the water rushed over her, until Dax held her from behind and stilled her.

"I'll think about it," he said against her ear, and it took her a minute to recall what she'd said to him about the business before he'd taken her apart.

She nodded. It was enough to know he hadn't blown her off. That he hadn't forgotten. That he'd remembered.

THIRTY-FOUR

F OR THE SECOND and what he hoped was the last time in his life, Dax found himself walking the main corridor of Crow Hill's Coleman Medical Center, and this time because it had to be done. Not because guilt over his sister standing vigil was driving him or because Arwen was making him. His father was finally awake, and though he wanted nothing less in the world than to talk to the man, a whole lot of things needed to be settled.

He kept his gaze trained ahead, his hat brim pulled low, his focus on the door at the end of the hall. He didn't want to be distracted or to hear good wishes for his old man's continued recovery. He wanted to have his say and get out, to never have to see Wallace Campbell again in this lifetime. Seeing him in hell would be punishment enough.

He didn't bother knocking when he reached the door, but pushed in before he could talk himself out of it and headed straight for the bed. The young Hispanic nurse tending to his father put herself between them and reached for the call button. He crossed his arms and waited, not saying a word.

"It's okay, Marisol," Wallace Campbell boomed hoarsely, taking the controls from the nurse's hands. "This is my boy, Dax. Been a long time since the two of us have seen one another. I think maybe we should do our catching up one on one."

"As long as you're sure, Mr. Campbell." Dismissing Dax, she looked back at the chart she held and finished whatever she'd been writing. It took her way longer than Dax thought it should have, but finally she closed the folder.

Holding it to her chest, she looked down and patted his father's shoulder. "You call if you need anything, and that includes privacy or security."

Dax's father reached for her wrist and squeezed it. "You keep taking such good care of me, Miss Mari, I may never want to leave. But I'll be fine. What man wouldn't be with his son come to visit?"

She glared at Dax as she walked past, leaving them alone. Leaving Dax to fight the sting of the pins and needles firing in his legs and pushing him to flee.

Wallace Campbell waited for the door to close, sitting straight up in the bed, and smoothing the stiff white sheet over the bulk of his lap. Once he had everything to his satisfaction, he lifted his gaze and arched a thick bushy brow. "Hello, Dax."

When Dax said nothing, he went on.

"You look . . . well, not quite as I'd pictured my son at thirty-four, but healthy at least. Maybe a little on the thin side, and you may want to have a doctor check the sun damage to your skin, but for sixteen years away, you look good."

What a crock. "You say that like you care."

The older man shrugged. "It's what fathers do."

Dax started to ask "Since when?" but that wasn't the conversation he'd come to have. "I'm only here to get an answer to one question."

His father reached for the pitcher of water on his bedside table, poured himself a glass and downed it. Then he poured another, returned the pitcher to the table, and held the plastic cup on the rail at his side—biding his time, making his opponent sweat.

A lawyer through and through. "If that's the way you want to play this. Ask me anything."

"Is Greg Barrett your son?"

After a slow lift of his brow, Dax's father asked, "Did he tell you that he was?"

"He did. In this very room. Not more than a week ago."

"Greg's a man of his word."

Unbelievable. Dax watched his father sip from his cup, staring into the water as if any second now it would turn a deep rich amber and burn its way down what was left of his gullet. "Can't come straight out with it, can you? Can't admit you're an adulterous son of a bitch."

"I've done a lot of things in my life I never plan to admit to." The older Campbell's gaze came up, held Dax's as if it would take no effort at all to throw the connection away. "Greg's not one of them."

A piercing burn struck the center of Dax's chest and bored its way to his spine. "Then it's the truth."

His father gave a single nod.

"A truth you've known from the beginning."

Another nod.

"And you brought him into the firm because of it. He didn't just show up and apply for the job."

"Unlike . . . ranchers, attorneys don't just apply for jobs."

"Whatever."

"Yes, Dax. I paid for my son to attend law school. I needed to have someone there with the firm's best interests at heart. Someone to take over after I'm gone. To carry on the tradition you weren't interested in."

"You have Darcy," Dax bit off, clenching his hands into fists.

"Darcy won't always be a Campbell."

Dax advanced, reaching the foot of the bed and slamming his palms against the mattress. He leaned forward, his chest heaving. "Darcy will always be a Campbell. Even if she marries and changes her name, she'll be more of a Campbell than Barrett can dream of being."

One heartbeat, two, then the older man asked, "And more of a Campbell than you?"

That one was easy. "Nope. She doesn't have it in her to be that big of a dick."

A grin stole over Wallace Campbell's face, and he began to nod, a bobbing sort of knowing motion that Dax didn't find funny at all. "A chip off the old block after all, are you? Good to know. I'd been wondering."

"You never wondered. You probably haven't thought about me since flipping me off when I drove away."

"If telling yourself that makes you feel better . . ."

Dax shoved away from the bed, paced the length of the room and back, stopping in the corner where he shoved his hands in his pockets. "Did Mom find out about Greg? Is that why she left?"

His father looked down, swirling the water in his cup. "We had a fight. She wasn't happy about it and decided she needed some time. A spa, I think she said."

Goddamn pulling teeth. "A fight about Greg?"

"No. About your sister."

Dax felt his hackles rise. "What about her?"

"Oh, the usual. Women. Your mother wanted me to give Darcy the partnership. I said no."

Well, at least he knew his daughter's name. "Why? She's devoted herself to the firm since law school."

"She runs on hormones. Look what happened over Henry Lasko," he said with an expansive sweep of one hand. "She couldn't even give the man the time of day."

Someone somewhere was doing a whole lot of spin. "That's not what happened at all."

"According to you."

"I was there. In the Blackbird Diner. I heard every word."

"And I'm supposed to believe you? Over Henry? A friend who's stood at my side all the years I've known him?

"Just like Darcy has, you mean?"

The other man snorted, looked away.

"Is this about the ranch? And the lease? You're taking Henry's side when Darcy knows he doesn't have a leg to stand on."

"I'm not about to break client confidence to discuss a case with you."

"Even when I own the ranch?"

"You own debt. You own nothing."

"I own a piece of something valuable enough to cause your client to run to you with his tail between his legs."

"Henry Lasko is a good man. A man of his word."

"Like Greg? You know Darcy's been here every day. Can you say that about your model son?"

His father said nothing.

"Was it worth losing your wife over? Because I have to guess that's where the fight ended up. She wanted you to give the partnership to Darcy, while you had your bastard in mind. Left that part out, didn't you?"

"Don't talk about your brother like that."

Dax snorted, shook his head, jammed his hands to his hips.

"You really are a piece of work. That man is not my brother any more than you're my father."

"Then you won't mind that I've written him into my will and you out."

As if he gave a shit. "As long as Darcy's still there. Nothing else matters."

"She is. She may have walked out on the firm, but she didn't walk out on her family."

He had Dax there. "Then I guess we're done here."

"Are you going to tell your sister?"

"About Barrett?" Dax shook his head. "No, I'll let you be the one to disappoint her. And while you're at it, go ahead and tell her that you ran off your wife, and caused your own heart attack in the process. That is what happened, isn't it? The shock of her leaving you was too much for the old ticker to take?"

The other man shrugged. "Doctors are still doing tests."

"Waste of time, don't you think? Shit you've pulled in your life? Are you really worth saving?"

"Guess we all have our youthful mistakes. How we live up to them makes us men."

"If you're what it means to be a man, count me out. My only mistake was coming here today." And it only took a half dozen steps to correct it by walking out the door.

THIRTY-FIVE

D ARCY WAS SITTING in the middle of the ranch house living room, stacks of oil field surveys and handwritten correspondence, of nuts and nails and small tools, of half-empty pouches of tobacco and unfinished needlepoint projects on the floor around her, when the kitchen door slammed hard enough to rattle the walls.

Since she'd been listening to the rumble of Casper's and Boone's voices as they pan-fried steaks and potatoes, the culprit had to be Dax. And in typical Dax fashion—which, she supposed, was typical male fashion—he had to blow off steam physically instead of voicing whatever emotion had him running so hot.

"What the hell is wrong with you?" This from Casper along with a string of more colorful words that had Darcy cringing. What was it with men? And was she ever glad she'd given up the idea of living in this house of testosterone, though if it weren't for Josh rescuing her unemployed ass, she might not have had any choice.

She really did need to stop with the dawdling and figure out what to do with her life. Going through the Daltons' things wasn't going to keep her busy forever, and it certainly wasn't bringing in a paycheck. Her savings would hold her for a while, but staying in Crow Hill meant giving up the attorney gig, since Campbell and Associates was the only game in town.

She supposed she could move, join a firm in San Antonio or Austin, though that would mean leaving Josh. Or she could stay and learn the Hellcat Saloon's bar-top dance routine. Or she could open her own firm . . .

"Campbell? You gonna say your piece, or you gonna stand there all night taking up space?"

At Casper's prodding of her brother, she grew still, leaning forward and cocking her head to hear. She could picture him with his hands on his hips, his hat brim pulled low, breathing like a bull about to charge, and her own heart began to pound because the silence in the kitchen told her this wasn't typical Dax at all. Maybe with her, sure, but not when it came to being goaded by his boys.

"I just came from the hospital," he finally said.

"That's right. I heard your old man had returned to the world of the living."

At Boone's eye-rolling comment, Darcy got to her feet, brushing the house's ever-present dust from the seat of her jeans.

"He won't be there long," Dax offered in response. "Not if I have anything to say about it."

Boone gave a snort. "You going to start pulling plugs?"

"Too late for that, though he does still have an IV." Dax bit off more words Darcy couldn't hear, then said, "Antifreeze should do the job."

"Yeah, yeah. Tough talk. Now what's going on?"

She crept closer to the kitchen door, waiting for Dax to answer Casper's question.

"When I went to see him . . ." A pause. "Back when he was in a coma . . ." Another longer pause. "Greg Barrett was there."

"Doing what?" Boone asked. "Waiting for ol' Wallace to flat-line and the firm to fall into his lap?"

"That's not as far off the mark as you might think."

"What do you mean?" Casper was the one to voice Darcy's question, but Dax didn't answer right away.

He stayed quiet, and the house grew still, tension twanging like a high wire in the air. She heard the scrape of chair legs, the bang of an iron skillet on the stove, smelled the seared beef and hot oil and potatoes. She was a half second from walking into the fray when Dax spoke.

"Greg Barrett is my brother. Half brother, anyway. My father's true bastard son."

Boone said nothing. Casper went back to cursing. Darcy didn't move. Blood rushed to her head, pounding there, and she reached for the back of Dave Dalton's worn recliner to keep from falling. Greg? Her brother? She couldn't believe The Campbell would've kept such a secret . . . except she could.

As Casper and Boone started lobbing questions at Dax, the conversations she'd had with Arwen and Luck and other friends rushed back in a nauseating wave. *Greg Barrett's the hottest thing to hit Crow Hill since the Dalton Gang left. Agreed, but what the hell is he doing here? He's as out of place as tits on a boar hog. Or as out of place as the Buck Off Bar would've been in New York.*

It all made sense. Every bit of it. Just like that, a switch flipped and the light came shining down. Greg getting the juiciest cases while she busted her ass on the most mundane. The Campbell's refusal to hire a clerk to handle the office's overflow and using her instead. Her eating salad for lunch at the Hellcat Saloon while the men lived it up at the country club. Her firing.

Most of all, her firing.

She'd joined the family firm expecting the impossible. No matter how many big dollar clients she landed, she would never, *ever,* have made partner. With Dax out of the picture, The Campbell had brought in his other son for that. His bastard son.

His only spawn with a dick and a set of balls, because God forbid a woman's name sat beneath his on the Campbell and Associates letterhead. Not as long as he still had breath in his body. Oh, no.

She had been so stupid. *So* stupid. Believing she mattered to The Campbell. That she could win his approval with the hours she put in, by bringing him kolaches for breakfast and seeing to his stock of Glenlivet. No, she hadn't been the one to land the Trinity Springs Oil account, but she'd brought in five new clients to Greg's one.

Oh, my God. Seriously? Oh. My. God. She couldn't decide between laughing and crying, and ended up hiccupping, the sound so loud that all the deep-voiced chatter in the other room stopped. Busted, she turned the corner and took in the scene in the kitchen from the entrance.

Dax looked exactly as she'd expected, hands at his hips, hat pulled low. When he saw her, his face went red. He yanked off his hat, tossed it to the table. "Darcy. Shit. I didn't know you were here."

Yeah, she'd figured that. "My car's outside."

He crossed his arms, shook his head, held her gaze. "I didn't see it. Sorry. Really, I'm sorry. Shit."

He looked pitiful, his face drawn, his eyes sad, though underneath was an anger he didn't have to explain. She didn't know how much of the rest was his fear of having hurt her, but that was the last thing on her mind. "Don't worry about it. I needed to know, and this was as good a way as any to find out."

"I guess but . . . Shit. I'm so so sorry," he said, scrubbing both hands down his face.

Casper reached out to slap Boone on the shoulder. "Let's go."

"Yeah." Boone turned off the burners on the stove and followed.

She watched as they walked out the back door, listened to their boots on the porch steps, then turned back to Dax. He really did look terrible, older and more worn than she'd seen him. "Are you okay?"

"Me? Why wouldn't I be?"

"You just found out you have a half brother."

"I have a sister. I have the boys. That's it."

He could tell himself that all he wanted, but the truth would always be there. And now, of course, she couldn't help but wonder if Greg was the only one. If their father had spread his seed far and wide and populated the state with little Campbells.

"Does Mom know?" she asked, crossing to the stove to salvage the food rather than letting it go to waste.

"I'm pretty sure her finding out was how this whole thing started."

Whole thing? Her hands stilled, one holding a meat fork, the other wrapped around the iron skillet's handle as she glanced back over her shoulder. "You mean The Campbell's heart attack?"

Dax finally headed for the table, scraping back a chair and dropping into it. He leaned forward, elbows on his knees, and stared at his hands. "He's such a dick. I can't believe he'd do this to Mom. To you."

"He did it to you, too, Dax."

"It's not the same."

"Why? Because you've been gone half your life? How does that change anything? Greg is our age. That means The Campbell was screwing his mother at the same time he was with Mom."

Emotion rose to choke her, and she returned to the food, flipping the steaks then doing the same with the potatoes and onions she guessed were supposed to be hash browns. "Now I want to know where Mom is. If she's okay."

"Have you talked to Aunt Marie?"

"She said she hadn't heard from her."

"Could she be lying? Covering?"

"It's possible. Though I don't know why she wouldn't want us to know where she is. Especially you."

"Why would that make any difference?"

"She sees me every day. She hasn't seen you in years."

"Darcy—"

"No, Dax," she said, though she couldn't yet face him. "I may be slow, but I've figured things out. You're the only one either of our parents ever cared about."

"Fuck that. Neither one of them ever cared about anyone but themselves."

That's where he was wrong. "You were the firstborn. The son who was supposed to take over the business. Carry on the family tradition. They got what they needed first time out."

She flipped the potatoes again, shoving the skillet off the burner with the spatula then dragging it back. "If I wasn't an accident, I'd be surprised."

"Darcy, shit. Don't say that."

"It's okay. Really. It's not like I haven't thought it more than once, what with the way The Campbell has made it clear I mean nothing to him. Easy enough to put two and two together." She slapped the steaks onto three plates, added the hash browns, waited for Dax to respond, to dispute her observations, but he said nothing, and finally she turned around.

He was still leaning forward, still looking down, his fingers laced, his thumbs tapping rapidly together. His answer was in his silence, and the sadness that rushed her was nearly debilitating. She caught back a sob, and Dax raised his head, and though his eyes were sober, they broadcast his struggle to keep all emotion stripped from his face.

"I'm right, aren't I?"

"He didn't say anything like that."

"What did he say?"

"He said he's writing me out of his will, writing Greg in. And you're safe."

"Safe?"

"My words, not his. I just didn't want you to worry about your inheritance."

"Does it matter? Does any of it matter anymore?"

"You matter. He's not worth the efforts it took to save him. But you . . ." He got to his feet, came closer, his hands stuffed in his pockets as he leaned against the refrigerator door. "You matter to me, Darcy. You matter to Boone and to Casper. You matter to Josh. Look at the way he's cared for you. The boy has made sure you've had a place to stay, that you weren't at the hospital alone, and yes, I should've been there with you. But I wasn't. And he was, so don't ever ask if it matters."

He was trying. Not making a lot of sense, but trying. She had to give him that. "What are we going to do? About Greg?"

"What do you mean, what are we going to do?" he asked with a huff. "Like invite him for Thanksgiving or something? I'm not gonna do shit."

Hardly a surprise. "Do you think The Campbell would have told us? If Greg hadn't? Or do you think it would've stayed their secret if not for the heart attack?"

"Who the fuck cares?"

Frowning, she crossed her arms and took him in, his stance,

his expression. How could he be so indifferent? "You really don't, do you? You walked away and you really let it go."

"I let it go a long time before that," he said, grabbing one of the plates from the counter and heading back to the table. "I let it go when Dave and Tess showed me the truth of family."

"Is it hard? Being here without them?"

He nodded, sawing with a knife at the steak. "I've got the boys. But yeah. It's not the same."

She thought back to what Josh had said to her. "You could take what you got from the Daltons. Make your own family. Maybe start with Arwen."

He snorted at that. "Can you really see Arwen living on a ranch?"

Men. Lord. "You don't have to be so literal, Dax."

"Is that what you're doing with Lasko?" Fork in his hand, he glanced over. "Making your own family?"

"I think so," she said, thoughts of Josh filling her where she felt empty. "I hope so."

"Good," he said, turning back to his food. "I want to know you're being taken care of."

She could take care of herself, but that wasn't what was going on here. "You're leaving, aren't you?"

He shrugged, chewed. "More like trying to decide if staying is worth it. The ranch is a piece of shit, but I don't want to bail on the boys, or dump on Tess's and Dave's trust."

"Would it be so hard? To stay? It's not like you're under pressure to go to law school this time. And you don't run in the same circles as The Campbell. You wouldn't have to see him *or* Mom."

A smile appeared out of nowhere, and he looked over. "I took Arwen to the country club the other night. For dinner."

"Why?" she asked, smiling, too.

"We were doing this dating thing. Not a lot of places to take a date."

"You could stay for her," Darcy told him. "You could stay for me."

"Well, I'm sure as hell not staying for Greg," he said digging into his supper again, and she knew when he did he wasn't staying at all.

THIRTY-SIX

ARWEN WOKE AT five a.m. to Dax sliding into her bed. He'd called the saloon earlier in the day to let her know he'd be coming, and she'd tried to wait up, but exhaustion had taken her down. That, and worry. Especially after Callie mentioned her sister had seen him at the hospital, and that his father was awake.

Dax never called. He showed up. He vanished. He appeared. He walked away. Their schedules made anything else impossible, and she'd grown used to looking up and seeing him looking down. This, however, was different. This was important. She'd been bracing herself for this moment ever since she'd hung up the phone.

But when she turned toward him, she found him naked, and his mouth on hers before she could speak. With the first stroke of his tongue, she knew she was going to lose him. After all this time, after all they'd shared and all she'd given him, he was going to go. He didn't think she was enough. He didn't believe in the two of them.

Or maybe that wasn't it at all. Maybe his father had confirmed what he'd already heard from Greg. Maybe he just couldn't deal, or needed time to deal. Maybe it wasn't about Greg, but about the Daltons not being in Crow Hill anymore. Then again, maybe he just didn't know how to stay. He couldn't possibly think he had no reason to.

She held his face, his cheeks scruffy as if he'd wanted to get to her and didn't take the time to shave. He was clean, his skin warm, smooth, his mouth tasting like coffee and Dax and desperation.

He rolled on top of her, his cock hard and insistent, and he didn't ask permission but reached between her legs, holding his shaft, swiping the plump cap through her folds to spread her moisture. And then he pushed in, a slow, filling, sliding invasion that sent her eyes rolling back in her head.

"You amaze me," he said, his mouth at her ear, the words deep and drawn out. "You're always wet. Always ready."

"I always want you," she told him, because it was a very simple truth, and he laughed and said, "I don't know why."

The ridge of his cock caught at her opening, and she sucked in a breath, hooking her leg higher around his hip. "Because I like being with you, and I like what you do to me, and I like you."

"You're one of very few," he said, grinding down and groaning, and she shivered and knew the many were stupid.

"What isn't there to like?"

He raised up, and she could see the light from the moon shining in through her window reflected in his eyes. Eyes that were sad, despondent. "I have a nasty temper."

She'd seen it, but she'd seen worse, and she wasn't much of an example in that regard. She used her tongue on his shoulder, used her teeth until he dipped for her nipple and tugged hard on her ring.

She tweaked one of his nipples before he grabbed her hand and pinned her. "I don't put up with bullshit."

"Most people need to be called on it more often."

"Are you agreeing so I won't stop fucking you?"

"I'm saying it because it's the truth. And so you won't stop fucking me."

"I've never had as much fun as I've had fucking you."

"Another reason I like you," she said, the words strangled because his sounded so final, so . . . gone.

He buried his face against her neck then, breathing deeply, shuddering, his hips grinding until she shuddered, too. Then he moved his mouth back to hers, touching more than kissing, his lower body pulsing in that way he had that did her in.

Long strokes, slow strokes, drawing her pussy along his shaft as he nearly withdrew, pushing her back to stroke hard, stroke fast. She was wet and aching, her clit tight and throbbing, and she wrapped him up in her arms and her legs and held on, keeping him close where she needed him.

He ground hard, pulled out, and asked, "Turn over?"

Anything, she wanted to say, but all she did was roll to her side, reaching into her bedside table for a vibrator before stretching out on her stomach and pulling a knee to her chest. Dax slipped in behind her, his thigh pushing against her as he found her ass, and as his cock penetrated slowly, she slid her vibrator into her pussy and turned it on.

He groaned, fucked into her and withdrew, groaned again and bit off a laughing, "Are you kidding me?"

"Do you like it?"

"I like you. I like that you can get off. I like that you don't tell me no."

She pushed down to let the vibrator thrum through his balls. "Goddamn. Yes. I like it."

"I knew you would."

He pulled out, pushed in, groaned again, and shuddered. "Got me all figured out, do you?"

If only she did. "This part anyway."

"This part's good," he said, shifting his hips.

She worked her toy and her hand, pleasuring them both, and the darkness became the heat and sounds of their bodies, the moisture, their gasps and their breathing and the slap of skin on skin. Her vibrator hummed, and Dax's moans rattled, and she felt it in her fingers and her nipples and the center of her body where his cock throbbed.

He slipped a hand between her legs, took the vibrator from her hand, and fucked her to the rhythm of his cock in her ass. She gripped the edges of her pillow, buried her face, rocking back and forth until she couldn't rock anymore.

She cried out, his name, maybe, or other words, or noises that came from a place she didn't know. He filled her, and carried her higher, holding her until he knew she was done, then following her, one long slow stroke then a shudder that bounced the bed off the wall before he collapsed on top of her.

They came back after showering, curling into intimacy, drifting just this side of sleep. She wanted to stay there, awake, touching him, listening to him, learning and imprinting him. She wanted to remember that his right dimple was higher than his left, that his beard grew thickest just beneath his chin.

She wanted to hear the noises he made when he came, when he laughed, *oh, God*, he had the best laugh. She didn't want to forget for a minute his wit, how sharp he was, how smart. Or how gentle he could be, how considerate. How alive.

"Stay with me," she heard herself saying when she ran out of shelves for the memories.

"For a while? Sure." But his answer wasn't enough.

"Not just this morning. Stay. With me."

And this time his answer was a silence so loud it echoed in the hollow of her heart.

THIRTY-SEVEN

"REALLY SORRY TO see things come to this," Boone said. "I get that it's hard to come back and find your family fucked into some seventh hell of dysfunction, but Darcy's a good girl. Tough that you'll be leaving her here all alone."

"Go on," Dax said with a snort, slinging one of his two duffels into the bed of his truck. "Ignore the code. Touch my sister. Just don't come crying to me when Josh Lasko takes off your face."

"Huh." Boone leaned a shoulder against the truck's cab. "So that's the way of things then. Guess I should've moved a little faster."

Dax thought back to some of what Darcy had told him when they'd talked into the middle of the night. "Sorry, dude. I don't think Flash would've been fast enough to catch that train."

"You should take the horse," Boone said. "Flash is going to miss you."

That was highly unlikely, and besides, Flash belonged here just like Remedy and Sunshine. Just like Boone and Casper. Just like Bing and Bob. "If I hadn't sold my trailer for gas money to get here from Montana, I'd be doing just that."

Casper stepped closer to Dax's truck, elbows braced on the bed railing. "This time you're going to stay in touch. You don't, we'll hunt your ass down and shove every single one of next spring's calf nuts down your throat."

If Dax hadn't already been choked up over leaving, that would've done it. "Soon as I hit a city worth a salt lick, I'll get a cell phone. I'll call the house. Leave the number on the machine. Ball'll be in your court after that."

"Uh-oh," Boone said, pushing straight and taking a step away. "Something tells me you making a run for the border isn't going to come without a price."

Dax looked up in time to see Arwen's truck come into view. "Shit. I was pretty damn sure we'd finished this up last night."

Not with words because he hadn't said a thing, but Arwen had known. He could tell. He'd learned her too well not to be able to tell, and goddamn what the hell was he thinking, leaving all of what she gave him behind?

He climbed into the bed of his truck to figure the best way to pack in his gear. "You're welcome to stick around. Imagine she's just come to say good-bye."

Casper snorted loud enough to wake a dead pig. "No thanks. I like having my scrotum just where it is."

"What he said," Boone added, hoisting up the new set of post hole diggers Faith had grudgingly approved and walking off.

Dax didn't blame them. Arwen wasn't coming to tell him good-bye. The way she'd been driving told him that, and if he'd had any question after the dust storm she'd stirred up on the road, the way she parked in the yard answered it. Girl would be doing good to ever get that truck in gear again.

She hopped down from the cab, her hair flying, long legs eating up the ground. "Going somewhere?"

And here we go. "Montana, I imagine, though I might make a stop in Utah. Nice place. Ever been there?"

"Sorry, no. I haven't had a lot of opportunities to travel."

"You should make them. A lot more out there than Crow Hill."

"You don't say," she said, glaring from behind a pair of sunglasses that hid most of her face.

He straightened, jammed his hat tight, and looked down at her. "What do you want, Arwen?"

"I don't know," she said, shaking her head, her words tight and sharp and huffy. "I don't know. To talk some sense into you? To talk some sense into myself?"

"How's that working out?" he asked as he hopped to the ground because this confrontation wasn't helping either of them.

She kicked at the dirt, shook her head. "You know, I told Faith not two weeks after we got together that I'd bet a hundred bucks you wouldn't stick around six months."

He tossed his saddle in the back of his truck. "Look at you, the fortune teller. You could open a side business, tell clients how fucked up their lives are long before they've got a clue."

"I never said your life is fucked up."

"You said it. You just didn't use words."

She reached for him then, catching the fabric of his shirt when he jerked his arm away. "Goddammit, Dax. Listen to me."

He spun on her, feeling his eyes go wild, the heat of the air he pulled in singeing his nostrils. "I've been listening to you, Arwen. I've been listening to you for weeks. You've turned my fucking head inside out. Turned my fucking dick into a porn star. Turned my fucking heart into this ache that won't quit. I can't think around you. I can't breathe. I can't do this. I cannot do this."

"What can't you do?"

"I can't . . . be me. I can't be me when I'm with you."

"How have I stopped you from being who you are?"

"Because you want me to be someone else. Someone who doesn't hate his father or who can hang on and make a go of a piece of shit ranch. Someone you made up in high school to go with whatever fantasy you had. But I'm an ass. I always have been. I always will be. You and me dating, or whatever the hell we've been doing, isn't going to make that go away."

"So this is my fault, then, that you're leaving."

"No. It's my fault. The ass thing, remember?"

"I'm not about to forget," she said, her hair whipping around her shoulders as she turned and strode away.

"Arwen," he called as he locked down the bed cover protecting his things.

"What?"

"I'm sorry about breaking your table."

"Right," she tossed back.

"And one more thing."

"What?"

He wanted to turn and look at her. He didn't. "Go see your father."

"What?"

"You heard me. He did his best for you. It might not have seemed like it at the time, but he did. And you don't want a passel of regrets down the road."

THIRTY-EIGHT

THE STRAP OF her tiny purse held tight to her shoulder, Arwen walked down the pebbled sidewalk shaded by a canopy of thickly laced oaks. The grounds were immaculate, the brick of the apartment houses free of water stains and made brighter by the dark green ivy climbing the walls.

It had been a long time since she'd made this trip. Shame gripped and squeezed when she allowed herself to count the months that had turned into a decade. For years she'd feared her father would leave her, would walk out one day, forget her and never come back. And yet when he'd finally driven away, the relief that he was out of her life had staggered her.

Dax was right. She had no room to talk—especially since her father wasn't anything like Wallace Campbell. Hoyt Poole had loved her, no doubt loved her still. She was the one who hadn't been able to deal with the man he had turned into after her mother's death, but that was on her, not on him.

When she'd called him to tell him she was coming, she'd reached his machine and left a message. She hadn't given him her number. She didn't want him to call her back. She'd told him where she'd be and when, and left it at that.

She had a lot to say, and it had to happen face to face. She wasn't brave enough to make her amends any other way. And again, Dax was right. She didn't want any additional regrets.

She found a bench in the courtyard of the building, not far from the enclosed patio blocking her view of the entrance to her father's home. She sat at one end, smiled at the woman sitting at the other. She didn't want to sit where she could see his door, growing nervous as she waited, making him wonder why she was early, should he come out, or meet her at the time she'd told him to. They would both be wrecks as it was.

"I doubt you'll recognize him."

Her purse strap twisted around her fingers, Arwen glanced at the woman sharing her bench. "Pardon me?"

"Your father," she said, inclining her head toward Hoyt's apartment. "He's changed a lot. You may not recognize him."

"You know who I am?" she asked, because it just seemed rude to tell a stranger she didn't know what she was talking about.

The older woman nodded. "He talks about you all the time. But obviously you haven't read his letters to know about me."

Letters? "He's never written me."

"Oh, sweetie, he writes to you all the time. But now I'm wondering if he's never mailed them." The woman turned on the bench, held out her hand. "I'm Andrea Staples. Hoyt calls me Andi."

"I'm sorry. I'm really confused."

"Of course you are," Andrea said, withdrawing her hand, which Arwen hadn't meant to ignore. "I've just been so anxious to meet you that I didn't stop to think you'd have no idea who I was. And Hoyt's been a basket case of nerves today, and I didn't want you out here alone in case he's late."

"You and my father are . . ."

Andi cocked her head, her blue eyes bright and young, her hair a sleek bob of white. "Boyfriend and girlfriend? Or is that too strange to say at our age?"

Strange, unexpected . . . She'd been prepared for changes, but not for this. "I don't know what to say."

"That surprises you, doesn't it? Because of your mother. You thought she was the love of his life, which she very well may have been. But I had my first love, too, and yet here we are, growing old together."

Arwen reached up and rubbed the pounding ache from her temple. "You know about my mother."

"I know about Beverly, yes," Andi said, crossing her legs and tucking close the fabric of her skirt. "And about you. And about all the time you spent with Hoyt in the Buck Off Bar."

This woman might be her father's . . . girlfriend, but Arwen didn't know her, and was not going to talk about the bar. Except her father had talked about the bar. "You said he'd changed. How has he changed?"

Andi crossed her arms. "Well, he's sober, for one. He hasn't had a drink in the seven years I've known him."

Seven years. She'd been seven years old when her mother had died. She'd been stealing money from her father's wallet seven years later. And seven years after that she'd told him she didn't want to see him anymore.

All this time she'd pictured him alone, drunk and in mourning, forgetting, ignoring. And yet here he was, living a normal life, sober, in love. It surprised her, but it lifted a heavy weight. As hurt as she'd been, she'd never wished ill on her father.

"I'm glad," she said, and meant it. "When he left Crow Hill, he promised he'd stop drinking. I didn't think he had it in him."

"I think it took getting out of Crow Hill for him to realize he did."

"It's where he lived with my mother. It's where he lost her."

"Sometimes we need that distance to see things clearly," Andi said, holding Arwen's gaze as thoughts flitted through her mind. Was that what Dax was doing now? Seeing things clearly? Or would that not happen until he reached Montana?

"Hello, Arwen."

At the sound of her father's voice, she sucked in a sharp breath, and her heart broke, and she was sobbing even before she lifted her gaze to his. Even then she only made it to his shoulders. Seeing that much of him had her hunched forward, pain piercing her midsection until she thought her back would break.

Hoyt Poole dropped to a squat in front of her, wrapped his arms around her, patted and rubbed and did what he could to comfort her. But Arwen was beyond comfort. Why had she let so much time go by? Why hadn't she forgiven him?

Why had it taken losing Dax for her to understand?

"Oh, Daddy. I've missed you so much."

"I've missed you, too, sweetie." His voice was husky but clear and confident, and his arms felt strong, his shoulders, too. And he smelled like her father, the wonderfully comforting woodsy scent she'd always searched out beneath the booze.

He wasn't weak anymore. "I'm so sorry. I'm so, so sorry. I should've come to see you long before now. I was stupid to wait. I was afraid you wouldn't want to see me, or talk to me. That you'd walk away. I made up all sorts of reasons I shouldn't come—"

"Arwen, look at me." She did, and he stared into her eyes, his bright and focused and so wonderful to see. "You are beautiful. I knew you were, but you're so much more now. Andi, isn't she just gorgeous?"

"She's perfect. Here. Let me take a picture of you two." Andi hopped up from the bench, pulling an iPhone from the pocket of her skirt. "Hoyt, sit beside Arwen. There. Just like that."

And just like that, her father's arm around her, their heads pressed close, Arwen let go of her past.

THIRTY-NINE

AFTER LEARNING THE truth from Dax about Greg, Darcy had spent the night at the ranch house instead of driving back to Crow Hill. She and Dax had stayed up late and talked. He'd told her about Montana. She'd told him about high school, about law school, about throwing her cap in the air at graduation and looking up to see The Campbell leaving the auditorium as it came down.

Dax had admitted to her that he loved Arwen, but he'd never in his life loved anyone, and he didn't know what to do with that love. She'd told him that she loved Josh, and laughed when he frowned, the big brother she remembered and adored looking after her. Then they talked about Greg, what to do about Greg, whether they wanted to do anything at all, and realizing they had to. He was kin. And he needed to know the other side of Wallace Campbell. The man who wanted a successor, not a son.

She'd stayed the next two days, too, and watched from her

second-floor bedroom window as he'd come back from a trip to Arwen's and packed. When Arwen had arrived later, she'd heard the two of them argue, not the details of their fight, but the tone. She ached for her brother, for the woman he loved, the woman she was pretty sure loved him, too, and it had her comparing their explosive relationship to what she had with Josh. He was just as intense, just as passionate, but he was the definition of still waters.

This morning she'd gone back to work organizing and cleaning and looking at the Daltons' furnishings with more than decorating in mind. Even though he'd packed, Dax still hadn't left, and she wasn't going to leave the ranch until he did. Or so had been the plan. Until Josh had called. She'd told him everything. About Greg. About Dax leaving. About realizing she was free from her ties to The Campbell.

He'd said four words. "I want you. Tonight."

The rest of the day had been a blur.

Now she sat cross-legged in the middle of his bed, the pillows jumbled comfortably behind her, the sheet and blanket tangled around her feet. She didn't know what to say, and words were impossible and unneeded and would do nothing but float in the air between them. She'd wanted this and waited for it, and her senses were like a sponge, absorbing everything about the man in front of her taking off his clothes, baring his body to complete what the baring of their souls had begun.

He'd removed his boots earlier. They sat by the front door with three other pairs, beneath the rack where he hung all his hats. Both were the first thing he shed at the end of the day, and the last thing he put on before leaving. She liked knowing that about his schedule, about him, how orderly he was, how set in his bachelor ways. And yet he'd adjusted for her without a single complaint, making room, cooking for two, sharing his shower, giving up his bed.

She hadn't wanted him to give up his bed. She'd wanted him to join her, to hold her, to fall asleep against her back, his breath stirring her hair. She'd wanted to feel his warmth and his weight, to push her sole against the top of his foot, to feel his knees spooned into hers. She'd wanted to look into his eyes as he moved above her, into her, sinking deep inside her body, his shoulders straining, his neck taut. And finally, *finally*, all of that was going to be hers.

He was beautiful. So very very beautiful. And she was certain if she told him that, used those words, he would tell her he wasn't beautiful at all. Oh, but he would be wrong. He was tall, his limbs long, the proportions perfect. His shoulders weren't too broad, but built exactly as wide as they needed to be. And they were strong. She knew that from touching him. He might work behind the store's register, but he had no trouble hefting huge bags of feed or seed or soil.

And she loved loved *loved* his hands. So capable and so big, and the way he'd touched her before now, gently, reverently, with purpose every time, she loved that, too. She couldn't wait to see the rest of him, to learn the rest of him, and he was taking way too much time undressing, and she couldn't stand it anymore.

"Hurry," she told him, balling the sheets in her hands because he'd told her not to take off a thing.

When he came to her he was naked and aroused and not the least bit shy or put off by her audible gasp. He climbed onto the bed, crawled over her, not stopping until he'd covered her with his body and pushed her down, pinning her with his weight.

He aligned his hips with hers, pushed his penis between her thighs, and settled his forearms above her shoulders as he stared down into her eyes. "Do you know how long I've waited for you?"

As long as she'd waited for him. She just hadn't known she'd been waiting. "You don't have to wait any longer. I'm here. I'll be here as long as you want me."

He brushed her hair from her face, used his knuckles to caress her ear, her neck, her cheek. "I want you for the rest of my days. I want to go to sleep wrapped around you. I want to wake up the same. I want to talk about what's for supper over breakfast, and talk about our days curled up on the couch. I love you, Darcy Campbell. I want you to be my wife. But right now what I want is to get you out of your clothes."

Because she had no voice, she nodded. Because she wanted everything he did, she lifted her arms when he nudged her to let him take off her top. Because she couldn't deny him anything, she lifted her hips when he rolled away to strip her free of panties.

When he reached for a condom, she took it from him and sat up to sheath him, her throat tightening further when she touched him, when he jumped in her hand, when he groaned. She lay back then, looping her arms around his neck and bringing him with her, opening her legs for him, opening her heart for him.

He pushed into her slowly, taking his time as he did with everything, holding her gaze as he filled her, emotion like water in his eyes. His tenderness was going to make her cry, that and the way she knew he loved her, would always be there for her, would never let her wonder where she fit in his life.

"Are you okay?" he asked once he'd gone as far as he could go. "Am I hurting you?"

"I'm fine. I'm wonderful." She found herself laughing. "I'm so good you wouldn't believe."

"Would you like me to make that good better?"

Could it get any better than this? "Oh, yes, please."

"My pleasure," he said, and brought his lips down to hers, his tongue sliding between them as he rocked his hips against hers. She gasped into his mouth, breathed into his mouth, hooked her heels in the small of his back and held him tight. The base of his cock rubbed her, and each stroke of his body deep into hers brought her up off the bed. When he slowed, she wanted to hit him to get him started again, but then he moved his mouth down her neck to her breast and slipped a hand between her legs to play.

"You taste so good," he said, the words breathed against her damp skin. "And you smell so good," he added, and she closed her eyes. "And you feel so goddamn good," he finished with, and that made her smile because she didn't think she'd ever heard him curse.

And then she chuckled and he raised his head, smiling down. "Having fun at my expense?"

"Having a very, very good time at your expense. You make me happy. You make me . . . happy," she said again, though it seemed so insufficient a word for the joy sweeping through her.

She wanted him to know her joy, to share her joy, and she reached for his hands, lacing their fingers against the mattress, shoulder high. He pushed down, holding her, and she looked into his eyes and said, "Love me."

"For the rest of my life," he said, and she knew then she'd found the rest of hers.

FORTY

"THANKS, DAD. I love you, too. Tell Andi hello for me."

Arwen hung up the phone, her hand resting on the receiver, holding on to the tender connection. She pictured her father with Andi, laughing, teasing, then pictured him as she'd seen him for most of her life, looking older than his years, depressed and dejected, his smiles few and far between and forced just for her because she was a little girl and needed her daddy to smile.

It was hard to reconcile the Hoyt Poole she'd grown up with in the Buck Off Bar with the man she'd seen two days ago in Austin. She was happy for him, that he'd turned his life around, that he'd found a good woman to share it with him. That he'd moved on and was looking forward.

She was more happy about that than anything else because it gave her hope. Her short-lived romance with Dax hadn't ended in tragedy, and her mourning was nothing compared to her father's.

If he could keep thoughts of her mother tucked away to remember fondly, she could do the same with her memories of Dax, the man she loved, happy and healthy and raising Dalton Gang hell.

Or she could one day. Just not yet.

Who knew the past she'd been trying to put behind her would plant itself so completely in her present—and that she would be happy to have it there? She had Dax to thank for forcing her to see her father, even if the choice to do so was hers.

Too bad her forcing him to see his had produced an opposite result. She couldn't regret that she'd done so, even if they'd both paid a terrible price. At least Dax knew where he stood, and that his decision to leave at eighteen had been the right one.

God, she was going to miss him. From a distance of two days, she couldn't imagine getting over him for a very long time. Hearing her father talk about the steps he'd taken to get sober, she knew change of any kind would require patience, and the strength not to give up.

She knew it to be the truth and it seemed so obvious when encouraging someone else. Hard to remember when she was the one needing to be encouraged.

The irony in that had her smiling, and doing so at her own expense. The one thing she'd been most afraid of as a child had never happened, and yet she'd lived all her young years with the fear her father would forget her.

"Arwen?" Callie called, interrupting her musings. "There's something outside you need to see."

Good Lord, again? She sighed. At least this time she knew it wouldn't be Dax surprising her with a picnic. "Don't you mean someone who wants to see me?"

Callie shook her head. Amy and Stacy and Luck moved to hover behind her, their eyes wide as they waited. "No. You need to come and see this for yourself."

This. Not her. Not him. She pushed back from her desk, putting weights on top of her paperwork so she didn't return to receipts and invoices caught in the ceiling fan blades, and when she stood and moved away from the hum of her computer and the streamed music, she heard it.

Heard more than the thunder that had been teasing Crow Hill all day. "Is it raining?"

"It is," Luck said, moving out of the doorway. "Buckets and gallons. The patio's almost deep enough for ducks."

They wanted her to see the rain? Oh, hell. Why not? It had been so long since they'd had more than a spit, it was like Christmas coming down, Santa pouring presents from the sky. She could use a gift or two, she thought, especially after the week she'd had, and she followed the trio down the hallway to the door.

"There," one of the girls said, pointing across the saloon's backyard toward Arwen's cottage. She brought up a hand to shade her eyes from the glare and squinted into the rain.

The first thing she saw was the truck. Big and black. Dax's truck. Then she saw him. Dax. Sitting on the steps in front of her cottage. Not on the porch or the porch swing but sitting on the steps in the rain.

She started across the patio, not even stopping when Luck called, "Do you want an umbrella?" She just kept going, desperate, splashing through the puddles as she wound her way around the picnic tables, stepping into pools overwhelming the parched ground in the yard.

Her boots kept her feet dry, but when she reached the sidewalk that would lead her to Dax the rest of her was soaked. She didn't care. She didn't care. He was here, not on the road, not halfway out of town.

Once in front of her house she slowed, gathering the thoughts bouncing off the trampoline of her pounding heart. What should she say? What should she ask? Should she wait for him to speak first? She didn't want to do anything that would drive him away, and yet she didn't want her words to be the reason he stayed.

That decision had to be his. It had to come from his heart.

"I thought you were gone," she said, approaching him slowly.

He looked up at her, the brim of his hat keeping the rain off his face, and he smiled. "I got held up. Casper needed help with the fencing for the new holding pen we're putting in behind the bunkhouse."

We're putting in. Not *they're* putting in. "Nice of you to help him out. I'm sure he appreciated it."

"What he appreciated is not having to pay me," he said, but he laughed about it, and without any bitterness at all. "And then Boone wanted to settle on a contractor to take down the bunkhouse. We had several bids and I told him to handle it, but he wanted to nail it down before I left."

We had several bids. Not *they* had several bids. "Did you?"

"Yeah. We're going to use John Massey's company. Or they are anyway. The boys."

Oh. There was the *they* she'd been dreading. She'd been reading too much into his words. Putting too much hope into a pronoun when she should've remembered he always talked about the Dalton Gang in the plural. His leaving Crow Hill would never change that. She came closer to better hear and sat beside him, wrapping her arms around her middle and hunching forward over her knees. "Callie will be happy. I know she's been worried about the slowdown in his work."

"Huh. Didn't know they were together."

"About three months now." She was wet and strangely cold and it was really hard to have a conversation with rain beating her in the face. But she wasn't about to suggest they move. Dax didn't seem bothered at all.

"Thanks to Faith's finagling, looks like we're not going to have to lease any of the acreage to Henry."

"That's good news, yes?"

"Really good. We won't have to sell off any of the herd either."

"I'm glad it worked out. I really didn't want you to have to. It just seemed like a temporary solution."

"It was a good suggestion. Just hard to hear."

Hard to hear? She could tell him a thing or two about hard to hear, sitting here listening to him talk about the ranch like he still lived there, like they were a couple discussing this thing he did for a living that he loved.

"I wanted to tell you, too . . ."

"What?" she prompted when he let the sentence trail.

"Darcy talked to Nora Stokes and she wants to buy some of Tess's antiques. Thinks she can get several thousand bucks for a couple of the pieces."

"That's great. That'll help y'all a lot."

"That's not all. Darcy found some old oil surveys. She gave them to Greg and he had the Trinity Springs Oil folks look at them. Seems the Dalton Ranch is sitting on a very promising sweet spot."

"Oil? Seriously?"

He nodded, slinging water from the brim of his hat. "Boone and Casper are meeting with them next week."

"But not you?"

"I wasn't going to be here so they made the plans."

Wasn't. He wasn't. Not that he wouldn't, but that he hadn't planned to be. God. Oh, God. "But now? Are you going to be here? For the meeting? Since you haven't left yet?"

"I did leave. Earlier. This morning. Took off before daybreak."

She could hardly breathe. "Is this as far as you got?"

"No. I got to the edge of town. Saw the sign. Crow Hill, Texas.

Population 2,875. How long ago do you think that was? Twenty ten? Was that the last census?"

He wanted to know about the census? Her heart was pounding like the Kittens' boot heels on the bar, and he was asking about the census? "I don't know. I think so. I remember filling out the form."

"Huh. I think it said twenty-two hundred when I left after high school."

"No reason to live here unless you're born here. No reason to come back if you leave."

"You're wrong about that," he said, and finally, finally turned toward her. "I saw that sign and I pulled to the shoulder and I just looked at it. And I thought what the hell am I doing leaving when the only thing I've ever wanted is here?"

"The ranch?"

"No, Arwen," he said, and she swore the water in his eyes wasn't rain at all. "You."

"Okay," she said, choking because she knew there was more. That his wanting her wasn't going to be easy. The fight between his head and his heart had been going on as long as she'd known him.

He reached for her hand, and she gave him both, and he squeezed them tight. "Tell me we can do this. I need you to tell me. I need to hear you say it."

"It doesn't work like that, Dax."

"Then how does it work. I don't know shit about making anything work."

"Of course you do." She bounced their hands on his thigh. "You've worked the ranch. You've kept your friendship with the boys. You and Darcy did a good job making up for lost time. You and I worked beautifully."

"We did, didn't we?"

"Do you trust me?"

"I do."

She closed her eyes, let that settle, opened them, dripping, and asked, "Do you love me?"

The grin that broke over his face was all teeth and dimples and happy happy joy. "Yeah. Oh yeah. Hell yeah. Shit yeah."

She was nodding like a maniac and sobbing. "Then we can make this work."

"Not yet."

"Why not?" she nearly screamed.

"You have to love me, too."

Her chest burned, constricted, her love for him drowning her. "I never wanted to love you. It scared me, the idea of loving any-one, but especially you."

"Why?"

"You . . . consume me. You make me look twice to see if I'm doing the right thing. You make me feel things I don't know how to balance with the rest of my life. I thought I had everything figured out. I thought if I stopped wondering about you, that would be it. But thinking I could ever work you out of my system has to be the biggest mistake I've made in my life."

"I like that I upset you. You needed to be shaken up."

She held out a trembling hand. "Like this?"

"So? Do you love me?"

"With all my heart."

"That makes staying worthwhile."

"You are? Going to stay?"

"Believe I will. But the pink bedroom's going to have to go. No pink, and no goddamn brown."

She leaned close, took his face in her hands, and nuzzled her nose to his as water sluiced between them. Then she kissed him, his lips warming her and his tongue arousing her and his hands holding her reaching all the way to her heart.

"I can't believe you're here," she said, her mouth at the corner of his. "I am so, so happy you came back," she added, dropping a dozen tiny kisses across his brow. "And you can paint the bedroom any color you want," she finished with, her arms around his neck so tightly she heard him gag.

"So, maybe I can go tell the boys now? Let 'em know they can stop bitching about having to hire on a couple of new hands?"

"Two?"

"Casper wanted three. Boone said Faith was too tight. Then Casper said . . . Never mind what Casper said." He got to his feet then, shook the water from the brim of his hat like a dog shaking its bath. "Let's go."

She was drenched. She was freezing. She was so in love she could hardly stand still. "You want me to come with you?"

"Arwen Poole," he said, hooking an arm around her waist and pulling her to him. "I want you with me every day of my life. For better or for worse. In sickness and in health. For poorer or for even poorer than that."

"Oh, Dax," she said, sniffling, brilliantly happy. "I love you."

"I love you, too, baby. I love you, too."

KEEP READING FOR AN EXCERPT FROM
ALISON KENT'S NEXT DALTON GANG NOVEL

UNBREAKABLE

AVAILABLE FEBRUARY 2013 FROM HEAT BOOKS

WITH HIS BACK against the side of his truck, Casper Jayne braced for the bad news his gut said was coming. The same gut that had kept him in his bedroom when his old man had stumbled wasted through the door. That had sent him to the ground from his third-story window when his old lady had waved guns and threats. That had told him nearly two decades ago to get the hell out of that house if he wanted to live.

The very house he was now standing in front of.

The one-page, handwritten letter folded to fit in his back pocket felt bulky and heavy and made it hard to get comfortable as he watched the inspector circle the house he'd lived in before leaving Crow Hill at eighteen. The house was now his, as useless as tits on a boar hog, and would be hell to dump *or* to keep.

It had been a pit as far back as he remembered. His old lady hadn't done a damn thing to make it livable the years they'd called the rambling monstrosity home, or even later, when his life was rodeo, his old man in the wind, and she'd been the only one keeping the fires burning.

Gutting the interior and starting from scratch might be his only option, but first he needed to know if the structure itself was sound. Check that: He needed to know what it was going to cost him to make it so. Especially since he was cash poor and getting his hands on the money he did have meant barreling his way through the woman who held his purse strings.

A woman tighter than a ten-day drunk.

He suspected he'd have an easier time getting her to give up what she hid beneath the suits she wore than the funds he needed. And he wasn't sure he wouldn't rather have the first than the second. But since both options hung off the edge of possibility's realm, what he wanted didn't matter a lick.

He took off his hat, ran a hand across the bristled buzz of his hair, resettled the beat-to-hell straw Resistol, and pulled the brim low. But he didn't push away from his truck. He stayed where he was, crossing his arms as the man with the electronic gadget in his hand and acorns popping beneath his feet kicked at the sidewalk, the cement buckled by the roots of the yard's hundred-year-old live oaks.

The inspector pecked out another note on the screen before walking through the thigh-high gate missing two pickets and hinged at a cockeyed angle. He stopped, swung it back and forth, then screwed his mouth to the side before looking at Casper from behind sunglasses that hid his eyes but not his expression. They both knew there was more wrong with this house than was right, but Casper didn't care what the other man was thinking.

He needed an official report to back up his request for the cash to do what was needed. Even shouldering the bulk of the labor himself, the supplies would set him back the cost of a herd of good horses. He doubted the house had been worth that much when he'd spent his nights staring at the holes in the ceiling and hoping the balls of newspaper he'd used to plug them would keep out the biggest of the spiders at least.

"Sure you don't want me to take a look inside?" This was the third time the inspector had pushed to get through the doors. "Let you know what you're looking at with your heating and cooling systems? Your plumbing fixtures? Your outlets?"

Casper shook his head. He wasn't ready for that. Besides, there was no cooling system. Never had been, unless he counted opening the windows and praying for a breeze. The space heaters he and his mother had used had been no match for the lack of insulation or the gaps in the siding—and the two of them hadn't done more than try to control the temperature in the four of the two dozen rooms they'd used.

Summers and winters. Both had been hell. "Just give me the external damage. What am I looking at?"

The other man glanced at the house again—the wraparound front porch and badly canted columns, the Victorian gables over windows made of cardboard instead of glass, the oaks spreading from either side to meet in the middle, branches laced as if praying for the house to be put out of its misery—before turning to Casper with a shrug. "You could raze the whole thing and come out ahead."

Easiest solution, but it wasn't going to happen. "I know it needs a new roof—"

"A new roof's the least of it." Frustrated, the inspector made an encompassing gesture that took in the house and the tree and the entire half acre that resembled a landfill more than a yard. "Your fascia board's rotted through most of the way around. Eaves and gables both. Same with the soffit. Kid hits a baseball against the house, the vents are gonna fall plumb out. Your gutters are hanging on by a thread, and you don't have a single attached downspout. Both of the chimney masonry caps, the support beams on all the porches, the grade of your lot . . ."

"Yeah, yeah. It's a piece of shit. I got it."

A shrug, and, "This house is not where I'd be pouring my investment money. Like I said, razing's your best bet."

And, again, that wasn't going to happen. As long as Casper got his hands on the money, the risk of making over the house was his. What he did with it after that . . . He nodded toward the tablet the inspector held. "Can you print out a report on that thing? Give me a list or whatever?"

"I've got a printer in the truck, sure," the man said, making his way to where he'd parked his mobile office behind Casper's big black dualie.

"What about a fax machine?"

"Yep. I can send it wherever you want it to go." He opened the passenger door, glanced over as Casper approached. "I can send the bill, too. All I need is a name and a number."

For the first time since the letter from his old lady had arrived, Casper felt the hard tug of a smile. What he wouldn't give to be a fly on the wall of the office when this particular paperwork arrived.

"Send it over to the First National Bank."

"Attention of?"

His smiled tugged harder, and grew just a little bit mean. "Faith Mitchell."

ONE MORE THING. That was all Faith Mitchell needed to go wrong. One more thing and she wouldn't have any trouble telling the higher-ups to take this job and shove it. She got that the bank was not a charity, that good business didn't allow for extending a loan indefinitely, or offering additional credit to account holders already unable to pay what they owed.

But after the chewing out she'd just received for daring, *daring*, to suggest the bank give the Harts another month before foreclosing on property that had been in the family over a hundred years, she was beginning to think it took a special kind of heartlessness to turn one's back on the honest-to-God need created by the nation's depressed economy and the state's ongoing drought.

The Harts were good people, struggling to make their living off the land the same way Henry Lasko, Nina Summerlin, and so many others were doing. The same way Tess and Dave Dalton had done for years, before passing on and leaving their ranch to Crow Hill's notorious Dalton Gang.

As teens instructed to give the elderly couple a hand, the three had earned the Daltons' love and trust while raising hell with the rest of the town. As grown men who'd returned to work the spread they'd inherited from Tess and Dave, the three were now fighting to get ahead like all of the area's ranchers.

Since Faith's brother, Boone, was one of the trio, she got to see his side of the picture as well as where the money men were coming from. That probably had a lot to do with the sympathy she felt for the Harts. Yes, they'd put up their land as collateral, but no one could've seen the drought coming—and staying—or anticipated the depth of the economy's downward spiral.

Turning one's back on the sort of ridiculous request outlined in the fax she'd received earlier was a different thing entirely. Casper Jayne knew exactly how tight the ranch's finances were. His own were no better, and he wanted to pour tens of thousands into a house that would be better served by going up in smoke? Please.

Her position as loan officer aside, the risks involved in his request were innumerable. The wiring in the house would have to be brought up to code before he could even think about powering the tools to do the job. Unless he *wanted* to start a fire as a way to get out from under this newest burden.

Hmm. The camel, the straw. Did he even have a homeowner's policy? If he did, and if she approved just enough—

"Faith?"

"Not now, Meg," Faith said, dismissing the tempting thought of arson and waving one hand toward her assistant while reaching for the phone with the other. Might as well give the Harts the bad news.

But Meg insisted. "You've got a visitor."

"Okay. I'll be done here in—"

"How 'bout you're done now," said Casper Jayne, pushing past Meg before she could stop him.

Not that anyone had ever been able to stop him.

Abandoning the phone, Faith sat back and laced her hands in her lap to keep from jumping up and choking him. One more thing. Hadn't the thought just gone through her mind? And he qualified in ways nothing else did, all long and tight and wiry, with thighs he'd used for years to grip the backs of bulls. Thick thighs. Purposeful thighs. Thighs she wanted to ride and had her close to moaning.

Her reaction was just stupid. She'd known him since he was sixteen and she was fourteen and he'd become best friends with her brother Boone and Dax Campbell, the group's hell-raising third. Playing his big brother role to the hilt, Boone had made sure she and Casper seldom crossed paths, and Casper hadn't pressed the point.

So what if she'd been brokenhearted? She'd been a girl, and that had been forever ago. She should be immune to him now.

For some reason, she wasn't. For some reason, as soon as he'd returned to Crow Hill, her teenage crush had become a very adult fascination. And the way he wore his jeans didn't help.

But he was crazy reckless, a lesson in insane abandon, wild and out of control. She didn't need that in her life now any more than she had in the past. If nothing else, that much was a given.

He was standing, staring. Waiting. Taking up too much room in her office, breathing too much of her air. And God help her if she wasn't undressing him, peeling those jeans away, wrapping her legs around those thighs, grinding against him.

Could this day possibly go any further downhill? "What are you doing here?"

He walked closer, taking slow steps, lazy steps, his hips at her eye level and causing her so very much grief. *Please, please go away.*

But he and his thighs and his championship belt buckle stopped in front of her desk to tease her. "I came to see you."

"If it's about the fax, you're wasting your time and mine."

"I wanted to explain things in person before you had a chance to say no."

"No."

"C'mon, Faith—"

"No," she said again, watching his nostrils flare, his bright hazel eyes flash. Watching the tic pop in his strong square jaw. A bead of sweat crawled over his Adam's apple to the hollow of his throat.

She swallowed hard, but she held his gaze. She knew him, and she would not be tempted. She would not. *She would not.*

"You enjoy this, don't you?" he asked, planting his hands on her desk blotter, leaning forward, bringing with him the scent of horses and hay. "Making it hard on a man."

She took a deep breath and a long pause, then said, "No, I don't. But you know as well as I do that you don't have the money for the extreme makeover that house will need before you can even think about putting it on the market."

He frowned, hovered a couple more seconds, then straightened, crossed his arms, and raised one slashed brow. "Who said I'm going to put it on the market?"

"You're going to live there? And still work the ranch?" She gave him a *whatever* shrug, because he needed to know he didn't bother her at all. "What else would you do with it?"

"Dax lives in town with Arwen, and he still works the ranch."

"Dax lives in Arwen's house. He didn't rob Peter to pay Paul for a place to stay."

"It's my money. I'll be using it for me. No Peter. No Paul."

"It's the ranch's money first, and only a third of that is yours. And not even that, really, because of the debt y'all are dealing with."

"I added my rodeo winnings to the coffers, remember?"

She did, but he'd obviously forgotten the rest. "And you signed paperwork turning it over to the partnership. It's not yours anymore."

"Not any of it?"

She thought of old dowries and entailed estates. "Not enough for what you need."

He paced the width of her office, his thighs, his jeans, his stride, and the roll of his hips bringing the word *yes* to the tip of her tongue. Bringing a sheen of sweat to her chest and her nape. Bringing one hand to her blouse's collar where she pulled the two sides close. This ridiculous—God, what was it? Lust? Longing?—had to stop.

Across the room, he curled his fingers over the windowsill and parked his backside against it, his eyes downcast as if a solution lay woven into the carpet's pattern. "What about the oil money?"

She tried to contain her sigh. "You want a loan against your mineral rights when you don't even know what's down there?"

"The well's due to spud next month. Sooner if the rig can get there. Everyone's saying the prospect looks good."

"Until the well's producing, *good* doesn't mean anything."

"Well, fuck me."

She didn't get it. Why in the world would he want to put money into a second losing proposition? Why didn't he sell the lot and the house *as is* and be done with it? She didn't get it, but she wasn't going to ask because asking meant personal involvement, and even though her brother was a partner in the ranch, she had to separate her business from her personal life.

That's what he needed to understand. She wasn't singling him out or punishing him. As much as this was about his request, it wasn't. "Casper. If I approved this expenditure, I'd lose my job."

He brought up both hands, scrubbed them down his face, looking as exhausted as he was resigned. "Guess I'll have to get one that pays then."

Or he could start acting like he had some sense and let this go. "A job? Doing what? You already work dawn to dusk."

"That leaves me about ten hours," he said, walking back to her desk. He stopped between the two visitor chairs, gripped the back of both with strong, capable hands . . . hands with short clean nails, golden hair trailing along the edges from his wrists. "That should be enough."

"To do what?" she asked, imagining the thick slide of his fingers and squirming in her seat. "And when are you going to sleep?"

"I don't sleep much as it is." He rocked against the chairs, back and forth. "I hear Royce Summerlin's looking for someone to break a few horses."

"You. Breaking horses." She gave a scoffing laugh because he was too close, the seams of his jeans worn and nearly white and messing with her head.

"Why not?" he asked, his hat brim casting a shadow across his eyes.

She sat forward and picked up a pen, looking at the Hart's paperwork on her desk instead of giving Casper any more of her time. She had work to do, and he was bothering her. Making her itch. Making her damp. Making her heart race and her blood run hot.

Making her foolhardy. "Because you're a bull rider."

"I've ridden a lot more than bulls." He pushed up to stand straight. "And I've broken more than a few of my rides."

She brushed him off without looking up. "Don't be sex-talking me. It's not going to get you anywhere. The answer's still no."

He came closer, until his thighs in her peripheral vision were the only thing she could see. "Sex talk? Really?"

Heat bloomed beneath her white blouse and blue blazer. What in the world was wrong with her? It was his fault. All of it. She wasn't herself when he was around. She wasn't anyone she recognized. She was imprudent, allowing in thoughts she had no business thinking, saying things that came with trouble attached.

"Sorry," she said, returning her pen to her desk and meeting his gaze. "It's just . . . I know you. Everything out of your mouth is a double entendre, and that's only when you're not being outright provocative or crass."

"Crass? Are you kidding me?" He narrowed his eyes. The corner of his mouth lifted dangerously.

Her laugh was more nervous than she liked. She knew she didn't have him wrong. "More like you're kidding yourself."

"You, Faith Mitchell, have wounded me."

"And you, Casper Jayne, are a scoundrel and you know it."

He took a minute to respond, as if first running his life through the filter of her words. He looked confused, and suddenly not quite sure of where they stood, or where to go next. "Is that why you wouldn't have anything to do with me in high school?"

Now who was kidding whom? "*You* didn't want anything to do with *me*. I got that message loud and clear."

"Oh no, sugar." His voice was deep, hungry, his gaze sharp and to the point. "The message you got was your brother's."

"Whatever," she said, because this conversation was one step away from precarious, and she could *so* easily fall.

"And anyway, you know the gang's got a hands-off policy about sisters."

That sounded as much like a coward's way out as a challenge. She couldn't stop herself. "You'll climb on the back of a two-thousand-pound bull, but you won't stand up to Boone?"

A vein throbbed in his temple. Heat rolled off his body to wrap her up, tangling her in his scent and the strength of his thighs. "You want me to stand up to Boone? Is that what you're saying here, Faith? Because all I need is a sign and I'll make it happen."

She'd been giving him signs for years. He needed to figure this out for himself. And she needed to figure out if this was really what she wanted—and why his company had her flirting with a trip off the path of straight and narrow and onto the road less traveled where so many things could go wrong.

Why it always had. "Look. Can we talk about this later? I've actually got work to do here."

She wasn't any more keen on calling the Harts now than she'd been before Casper barged in. In fact, having to turn down his money request made her feel even worse about giving the family their bad news.

But she was too close to making a mistake here. She knew that. She couldn't think when he was around. She knew that, too. And so she waited for him to go.

A wait made in vain.

He hadn't moved, hadn't turned so much as his gaze away—as if he were looking for, waiting for that sign. "Later when?"

His voice, when it came, was gruff and demanding, and it was all she could do to breathe. *Be careful what you ask for, Faith Mitchell.* "I'm coming out to the ranch tonight to go over our parents' anniversary party plans with Boone. Will that work for your very busy schedule?"

"I'll be there," he said, and then he strode out of her office, and it took her a very long time to get back to work and stop thinking about his thighs.

ABOUT THE AUTHOR

A native Texan, **Alison Kent** loves her cowboys and is thrilled to be writing about them for Berkley Heat. She is also the author of more than forty contemporary and action adventure romances, and *The Complete Idiot's Guide to Writing Erotic Romance*.

If there's a better career to be had, she doesn't want to know about it, as writing from her backyard is the best way she's found to convince her pack of rescue dogs they have her full attention. Alison lives near Houston with her petroleum geologist husband, where every year she fights the heat to grow tomatoes, and spends way too much time managing a feral cat colony.

You can find her online at alisonkent.com, on Twitter at twitter.com/alisonkent, and on Facebook at facebook.com/author.alisonkent.